A SAPPHIRE FALLS NOVEL

ERIN NICHOLAS

ISBN: 978-0-9988947-0-6

Editor: Kelli Collins
Line Editor: Nanette Sipe
Cover artist: Dana Leah, *Designs by Dana*
Print formatting: Kim Brooks

Dedication

To Kelli who takes my craziness seriously, but doesn't let
me take it too seriously.

After You

Chapter One

Only one thing had not gone according to plan in Kyle Ames's entire life.

Her name was Hannah McIntire.

And she was currently sitting at a back table in the bar in his tiny hometown of Sapphire Falls.

Even from across the room, with the inside-a-bar-at-night lighting, he could tell she looked exactly the same. Her long brown hair, streaked with red and gold highlights, was perfectly styled. Her long legs were crossed under the skirt of a pretty flowered sundress, paired with a sweater and sandals that matched exactly. He couldn't see her hands or face from here, but he knew that her nails would be manicured and her makeup would be flawless. He also knew that the glass in front of her was filled with iced tea and flavored with one packet of calorie-free sugar substitute, and that the only thing on the menu she would be interested in was the grilled chicken sandwich. And she would scrape the cheese off that as soon as she saw it.

Hannah McIntire was the most put together, predictable, organized, goal-oriented person he'd ever met. She was his soul mate in every way.

Or, at least she had been, before she'd become the most unpredictable thing to ever happen in his life.

Kyle's chest tightened and he took a step in her direction. It was time for some answers.

But he was brought up short after step two by his best friend. Derek stepped in front of him, putting a hand on Kyle's shoulder. "Whoa, what are you doing here, man?"

Kyle scowled and tried to move around him. "I'm here to welcome Hannah back to town."

Derek moved with him, cutting him off. "Well that's a

horrible idea."

"Knock it off," Kyle said, stepping the other way. "*You* texted me to tell me she was here."

Derek took a wide-legged stance in front of Kyle, blocking his view of the room. "That's bro code. I can't see my best friend's ex back in town after three years and not tell him. But I was really hoping you wouldn't come down here."

Kyle gritted his teeth. "Why were you hoping that?"

"Because I was kind of hoping that you wouldn't care."

Yeah, well, Kyle had kind of hoped that he wouldn't really care too. He'd assumed that at some point before he died, Hannah would show up back in their hometown. And he'd really fucking hoped that by then, he wouldn't care. But he'd also hoped he'd have another couple of years before that happened. Or ten. Or that he'd be old and senile and not remember her.

That hope had been dashed the second he'd read *Hannah's here.*

Because he cared. He definitely cared.

He just wasn't sure if he cared because he'd never been so pissed at someone in his entire life as he was, still, at Hannah McIntire.

Or because he'd never loved someone as much as he'd loved Hannah McIntire.

"So all your bullshit about being over her was actually bullshit," Derek said, giving Kyle a look that said *I know you.*

Kyle glared at him. "I *am* over her."

"Then why did you come running the second you knew she was here?"

Because he hadn't really thought it through. He'd just reacted. It had been instinct. Is that what Derek wanted to hear? That Kyle had seen the words *Hannah's here* come across his phone screen, and he'd gotten in his truck and driven straight over? "Maybe I came to yell at her."

"Yeah, you can't do that either." Derek wrapped a huge paw around Kyle's upper arm and nudged him, not so gently, toward the kitchen.

Derek was taller than Kyle by about three inches, but built more like an All State wide-receiver than the All State running back Kyle was. Kyle took three steps with him, only because he realized that it was possible Derek had a point, but as soon as they were behind the bar, with a solid piece of wood between him and Hannah, Kyle yanked his arm out of his friend's grip.

Unfazed, Derek pushed open the swinging door that led to the kitchen area. "In here."

Kyle sighed and stepped through the door. Derek followed, letting it swing shut behind him.

"So I can't talk to her at all?" Kyle asked.

"Not in this mood," Derek said. "Whatever this mood is. You need to calm the hell down."

"I'm calm." He was *always* calm. He was driven. He was confident. He was determined. But he was always calm and cool.

"You're not calm. You look like you want to shake her, or throw her over your shoulder. And really, neither is a good choice."

Kyle felt Derek's observation and the truth of the situation hit him directly in the chest.

Hannah was here. *Here*. At home. In Sapphire Falls. For the first time in three years. For the first time since they'd broken up. And yeah, there had definitely been a moment of *mine* that had ripped through him at seeing the words *Hannah's here.*

"I just want to *talk* to her," he said, trying like hell to *sound* calm and cool.

"Not tonight. Not first thing like this," Derek said. "You knew you were going to see her in a couple of weeks. Just stick with the plan."

The plan. Two of Kyle's favorite words. He loved

plans. He lived by plans. A plan implied preparation and control. Two of his other favorite words.

He shoved a hand through his hair. He had not been prepared for Hannah being back in Sapphire Falls.

No, that wasn't true. He'd known for almost a month that Hannah was going to be back in town. And even if he hadn't been certain to run into her because of Alice's medical care, he would have seen her anyway. It was Sapphire Falls. You couldn't order extra bacon on your cheeseburger around here without people knowing and having an opinion about it.

But what the hell was she doing here *now*? Alice's surgery was still two weeks away.

He'd known that she would be accompanying Alice to her appointments with him, but he'd thought he had time to get ready for that. Damn, he'd had no idea he would react like this to the news she was officially back in town. In the flesh. Within driving distance.

He'd *thought* he was prepared. But seeing *Hannah* and *here* in the same sentence had sent a need coursing through him that he never could have prepared for. He was definitely not in control of his emotions right now. And that was absolutely not okay.

It shouldn't surprise him, he supposed, that Hannah was the one thing, the one person, who could really shake him up. But it did. Because for ten years, Hannah had been the most stable, reliable thing in his life. It was one of the things he'd loved best about her.

"You have to pull yourself together," Derek said, obviously reading Kyle's agitation.

It had to be surprising to the other man. Kyle simply did not get agitated. But Derek must have sensed that it was a big deal, because he rarely passed up a chance to give a friend a hard time.

"And you have to keep yourself pulled together. If you look like *this*, you're going to upset Alice," Derek said.

Kyle blew out a breath. "I didn't realize how I would feel knowing she was home. I thought I could handle it."

Derek nodded. "You *will* handle it. You know she's here now. You can get your shit together before you see her."

Fuck, he hoped so. He felt like he'd just downed a couple of energy drinks, just knowing she was in the next room. He just wasn't sure if it was good energy or bad.

He scrubbed a hand over his face. "Yeah. Okay, you're right. I'll pull it together for Alice. But no promises that I won't get Hannah alone for a few minutes at some point," he said.

Derek cocked an eyebrow. "And what would you be doing for those few minutes alone with Hannah?"

Kyle frowned at him. "*Not* whatever you're thinking." He couldn't touch her. Couldn't kiss her. The fact he even *thought* those things was annoying. "Yelling. Chewing her out. Probably some swearing."

Derek nodded. "Fair enough. But watch it. Alice is thrilled Hannah's back, and you better not do anything that might upset Hannah to the point that Alice might notice."

Alice McIntire was five feet two inches, one hundred and five pounds of pure sweetness, topped with bright white hair. She never forgot a name, had never met a person she couldn't charm within five minutes, had an uncanny ability to know what people needed—a hug, a scolding, advice, a nonjudgmental ear…or a cookie. She also had a laugh that could make anyone smile. Getting on her good side was as easy as saying "good morning". And getting on her bad side was extremely difficult. But possible. And involved messing with her family. Particularly her one and only granddaughter.

Alice had everyone in the town of Sapphire Falls wrapped around her little finger, and while she didn't abuse the power, she was able to get pretty much anyone to do pretty much anything she wanted.

"*Hannah* was the one who upset *me*," Kyle pointed out. "She was the one who broke things off. Not me."

"Right, but Alice doesn't know that. Because *you* have been protecting Hannah."

"No," Kyle said, stubbornly shaking his head. "I've been protecting the town and her parents and *Alice*. She was upset enough by Hannah's decision to stay in Seattle."

Hannah had broken promises to everyone, and while her staying on the West Coast instead of coming home had messed up a lot of things, Kyle had known that if *he* was upset, it would have made it worse for everyone else. So he'd powered through his own heartbreak, put on a smile, and assured everyone that it was a great decision, and he was behind Hannah and her "amazing professional opportunity" all the way.

"Alice doesn't need to know all the details."

No one needed to know the details. He had come out of Hannah's betrayal looking like a freaking liberated, real-life hero. Everyone thought they were still the best of friends. In fact, the whole town—minus his two best friends, Derek and Scott—thought that Kyle was amazing for loving Hannah enough to let her go after her professional dream.

Yeah, her fucking *dream* had been to come home to Sapphire Falls, marry him, practice next door to him, and grow old surrounded by the eight children, three dogs, four cats, and town full of people who loved them. Or so she'd said. For ten years. He didn't know what the fuck she was doing in Seattle.

But no one here knew that. No one here knew that he could barely say her name without his chest tightening and gut churning.

He'd done it because he couldn't stand to see her family and friends—who were also *his* family and friends—hurt. And because Kyle Ames always had control. He didn't get surprised. He didn't get shaken up. And certainly not by a woman he'd known all his life and had loved for ten years.

The town counted on him to be steady and sure. It wouldn't have done anyone any good to know that their rock-solid town physician had had his entire plan turned inside out, his heart trampled, and that he'd started questioning everything he thought he'd always known. They needed to trust that he always knew what was going on and, more, that he was orchestrating everything.

And then there was Alice. He'd seen how heartbroken Alice had been by Hannah's decision not to move home. He had refused to pile onto that by letting on he was also heartbroken. No one was as important as Hannah to Alice, but he was a close second. The grandson of Alice's best friend since kindergarten, he was more of another grandson than anything, and he knew she loved him dearly. She'd been upset about Hannah not returning to live and work in Sapphire Falls as planned, but if she'd thought Hannah had hurt Kyle in the process, Alice would have been devastated.

He didn't give a shit how Hannah felt. He wasn't protecting her for her sake. But he'd be damned if he'd let her hurt Alice more than she already had.

"You know that everything Hannah did, or didn't do, is not on you, right?" Derek asked.

"Yeah, well I'm the one who's here and has to make it work. It's better for everyone to think that I've got it all covered."

"You don't have to always have it all covered, Doc," Derek said.

For all of his laid-back, fourteen-year-old-boy-in-a-twenty-nine-year-old-body tendencies, Derek was a great man and a great friend. Kyle knew that Derek was actually concerned about him. "Actually," Kyle said. "I do."

It was what he did. He had it all covered. And he liked it that way.

Not that he was the only one in town who *did* things. He was looking at one of the men who kept the town going.

Derek was everyone's go-to guy for everything from maintenance and repairs to rallying the troops. But Kyle was the planner. The guy who saw a problem and knew how to solve it. Derek, Scott, and any number of other people in town were more than willing to jump in and make the plan happen, but Kyle was the problem solver. And he loved that. It was where he was comfortable and where he felt he contributed most.

Derek shook his head. "Man, I think you love Alice more than your own grandmother."

Kyle cracked a smile at that. "She's sweeter than my grandmother. My grandma cheats at pitch, can't bake a cookie to save her life—and doesn't care—and still threatens to swat me with a wooden spoon."

"I love your grandma," Derek said with a grin.

Alice, Kyle's grandmother Ruby, and Derek's grandmother Susan, had been friends since they'd been little girls. And they routinely got together and beat Kyle and Derek in card games. Pretty much any card game.

Kyle loved his grandmother too. Ruby was awesome. She was the sassy one. She was incredibly loyal and generous with her friends, and she was happy having just two friends she could completely trust and count on. She said what she thought and tended toward grumpy more than congenial. Alice was the one who was sweet, outgoing, and friends with everyone. And Susan was the shy, quiet observer. Which was hilarious once you got to know her grandson. Though Kyle had to admit that Derek had inherited some of his grandmother's observant and insightful genes.

"Okay, so, you can go out the back," Derek said.

Kyle glanced toward the window in the swinging door.

"Kyle," Derek said warningly, moving between Kyle and the door. "Out the back. You can deal with all of this, with her, tomorrow."

God, he really wanted to go out there. But *why*? Did he

want to yell? That would make sense. He certainly had plenty of bottled-up bitterness and anger. But that didn't feel like the main reason. He just wanted to…see her. In person. Up close. To make sure she really was okay.

Dammit.

She'd stood him up. They were supposed to meet at the gazebo at midnight two years, eleven months, and one week ago. She'd known he was going to propose. That had been the plan. He would propose when she finished PT school and came back to start her practice in Sapphire Falls. They would be engaged and plan the wedding during his last year of residency. Then when he was done and came home to start his practice right beside hers, they'd get married.

Sure, it had been cheesy and unnecessary to make it all *An Affair to Remember* and to choose the gazebo as their Empire State Building. But it had also felt right in so many ways. He'd wanted it to be a grand gesture, meaningful and memorable. So he'd chosen the heart of the town they both loved and the gazebo where he'd first kissed her. The moment he'd known she was The One.

Burning the thing to the ground had crossed his mind only about a dozen times since then.

And that wasn't totally off the table, now that she was back.

"Fine. But," Kyle added as he headed for the back door, "Hannah McIntire *is* going to hear the things I have to say."

"Fair enough."

"And don't fucking text me about where she is anymore." The last thing he needed was someone keeping tabs on her for him and distracting him all damned day.

As it was, he was sure he was going to be all too aware of Hannah and what she was doing and where she was and who she was with.

It was going to be a long six weeks.

"You can't write this," Hannah said, looking up at Kade and trying, still, to ignore the fact that they were sitting at a table at the Come Again in Sapphire Falls.

It was common for them to sit across the table from one another at a café or coffee shop and talk about Kade's writing. So this should be like every other time.

Except that it was nothing like every other time.

Other than the fact that he'd written something that made her roll her eyes. *New York Times* bestselling author. Whatever.

"What do you mean?"

"You can't make everyone say 'y'all'."

"It adds local flavor."

"Except that we don't say 'y'all' here."

Kade scratched his neck. "You sure?"

Hannah rolled her eyes so he could see it this time. "I lived in Sapphire Falls, Nebraska, for twenty-two years of my life. Yeah, I'm sure. And we're farmers. Not cowboys."

"I like 'y'all'."

"Then set your stupid book in Texas."

Kade lifted an eyebrow. "It's going to be a long six weeks."

Hannah sat back in her chair. "You're telling me."

She was grateful that her best friend had agreed to accompany her to Sapphire Falls. Okay, "agreed" was pushing it. She'd had to do the "you owe me" thing. Twice. But he was here and she was glad. She could not face all of this alone. And thankfully, their relationship was based on three things they could both get behind every time: sarcasm, no bullshit, and coffee. Lots of all three.

"And it has to be *six* weeks?" Kade asked. Again.

"Yes. At least." She kept adding the "at least" but he seemed to miss it each time. She was actually hoping it would be more like four weeks. Her grandma was tough, and if anyone could breeze through rehab after a hip replacement, it was Alice McIntire. But Hannah had promised up to six, so that was a possibility.

"And I have to be here the whole time?" Kade asked. Also again.

"Yes. Unless you want to spend even longer dealing with *me* after I get home and go through rehab again."

He seemed to be thinking about that.

"Remember the whining? The hot yoga?" she asked.

"Jesus, I'll never forget hot yoga," Kade groaned.

"And remember how you hated it all? Especially the weight gain?"

"That's because I gained weight too."

"I was talking about you."

He sighed. "Fine. I'll stay. But someone in this town is going to die."

Hannah shook her head. "Why can't you write happy books?"

"My therapist says it's because my ability to see the goodness in life is tarnished."

"No, your ex-girlfriend said that. She just happened to be a therapist. She was not *your* therapist."

"She certainly psychoanalyzed me a lot," Kade said, turning his attention back to the screen in front of him, clearly disinterested in the topic of his ex.

"Well, the psycho part of that is true," Hannah agreed. She studied her best friend as he clicked away on the keyboard, writing his next bestseller. That just happened to be set in a small Nebraska town named Aquamarine Ridge. He thought that was hilarious. Hannah did not. Nor would the rest of Sapphire Falls. He'd promised to change it before the book went to his publisher, but Hannah knew she was going to have to read it before then because she didn't trust him a bit not to leave that in there.

He was a little grumpy about coming to Sapphire Falls with her. For six weeks. That could be a very long time.

But she had to do this. She hadn't been home in three years. And this wasn't just a visit. This wasn't just coming home because she'd been gone so long. This had nothing to do with her family's aversion to flying and visiting the big city. This was the only way for her grandma to avoid a long and potentially costly stay at a nursing home for her rehab.

The guilt was already weighing on Hannah. Alice had put the surgery off for several months because she'd been waiting for her superstar physical therapist granddaughter to come home. For good.

Too bad Hannah had screwed everything up, from the superstar part to the physical therapist part to the coming home part. And hadn't been able to face her family.

Yeah, six weeks was going to be a really long time.

"How's everything over here?"

Hannah looked up to find Derek Wright standing next to the table. She smiled. "Good. The food was great."

He gave her a smile but it didn't quite reach his eyes, and Hannah felt a twinge in her heart. It wasn't like she would have picked the Come Again for dinner, given a choice. But they hadn't gotten to town until after ten, and she wasn't going to show up on her family's doorstep expecting to be fed at that time of night, and nothing else in Sapphire Falls was open. So, the one and only bar in town was it. But it also happened to be the place that Derek Wright now managed. She and Derek had been friends. Good friends. She'd spent a lot of time with him. They had a lot of private jokes and great memories. Of course, pretty much every one of those also involved Kyle.

The twinge in her chest turned into an outright stabbing, and Hannah fought to not visibly grimace. Yeah, she and Derek were not friends anymore. Of that she was certain. Because of Kyle.

Kyle Ames. Her first…everything. Her ex. The man she'd practically left at the altar. Okay, she'd left him at the gazebo, but it was kind of the same thing. She'd known he'd been planning to propose. She'd been very aware of every step of his life plan, in fact.

And now the man who would, very likely and quite understandably, never want to speak to her again was her grandmother's physician and, as such, would have to talk to Hannah as Alice's primary post-op caregiver.

Yeah, that was going to be awkward.

Actually, she'd love it if it was only awkward.

She was sure it would be downright painful.

"Can I get you anything else?" Derek asked.

Hannah looked at Kade. "You good?"

"Fine," he said with a nod, not looking up from his screen.

That was pretty standard Michael Kade stuff, and Hannah kicked him under the table for it. Most of the time she told him after the fact that he'd been rude. But she'd instructed him very carefully in how things went around Sapphire Falls, and that he had to not act like the big-time, too-busy, head-in-his-story bestselling author that he was, and had to be tuned-in, polite and charming.

She was also paying for his room and all the coffee he could drink while in Sapphire Falls in exchange for his good behavior.

He frowned at her, then lifted his gaze to Derek. "I'm fine, thank you."

Derek nodded. "Okay then. Last call."

Hannah glanced at the clock on the corner of her screen. It was ten to eleven. "You close at eleven?" she asked.

Kade was a night owl, typically writing from about ten p.m. until four or five in the morning. It allowed him to avoid, well, all other people. Even virtual ones. He got no phone calls, texts, or emails during that time. Exactly as he preferred it.

Hannah, on the other hand, was definitely not a night owl. She went to yoga at six every morning and was in her clinic by seven-thirty many mornings.

Kade had chosen the Come Again as his new office within five minutes of walking inside. The bar was the only place in town open past six p.m., it had tables and outlets and, unlike at the house where they were renting the only open room, it was socially acceptable to ignore the other people in the building.

"Yep," Derek said simply about closing time.

"I thought bars in Nebraska stayed open until one or two a.m.," Kade said.

Derek nodded. "We can stay open 'til then. But we can also choose to shut down early."

Hannah looked around the room. It seemed that everyone else had cleared out except for the table where Peyton Wells was still on her laptop.

Derek caught her glance at Peyton. "We can also choose who gets to stay after hours."

Ouch. Yeah, she hadn't asked. But Derek had taken the opportunity to point out her demotion in his life anyway. "Got it." And she did. She was his best friend's ex. That was easy enough to understand. She closed out of the file for chapter one of Kade's new book. "We'll just get out of here."

Derek gave her a single nod and headed back to the bar.

She watched him go, feeling a funny sense of loss. She hadn't talked to Derek in three years. Maybe even longer than that. While she'd been in college, she and Kyle had made trips home and hung out with friends and family, but once she'd been accepted to PT school in Washington and he'd started med school, getting home had been more sporadic. Still, she suddenly missed Derek, and the way he used to tease her and flirt with her to piss Kyle off, and his always inappropriate but hilarious comments and jokes. *Shit*. This trip was going to be hard. If Derek being indifferent made her miss things, she was going to have a hell of a time resisting all the charm and good things in

Sapphire Falls.

She and Kade packed their stuff and headed out into the warm May night. They started across the grass between the jail and City Hall that would lead them to Main Street and the town square. One of those charming, good things that she'd definitely missed.

Kade didn't say anything until they were at the gazebo.

"You sure you really want to do this?"

She knew exactly what "this" was.

"This" was all of it. Coming back here, getting involved with her family again, seeing Kyle. And she didn't want to talk about it. Again. Unfortunately, they were still a good six blocks from where they were staying.

Hannah took a deep breath. "We're not going over this every day for the next six weeks. My grandma needs me. I'm here. I'll get her through the hard part and then you and I will go back to Seattle and everything will be fine. I can do anything for six weeks. And so can you," she said, shooting him a look. "Besides, you're behind on your deadline. This is the perfect place to hole up and write a book."

He'd joked to his editor, Sonya, while Hannah had been in the room that maybe what he needed to get back on track with his writing was a new series. And that maybe he'd set it in the tiny little town in the middle of America that Hannah was dragging him to for six weeks.

Hannah had given him the finger.

His agent, Mark, had given him two six-figure offers from two different publishing houses the next day.

So, he was now writing a book set in Aquamarine Ridge—though Hannah was absolutely going to make him change that name before it went to Sonya.

"Yeah." Kade looked around the town square.

The gazebo was the heart of the town, set right in the middle of the square that was bordered by the main highway on the south side, Main Street on the north, City

Hall on the east, and other businesses, including the post office, on the west. From here they could see all of the main businesses in town—Dottie's Diner, Anderson's Hardware, the grocery store, the clothing shop—and the backside of the bakery that sat along the highway beside a furniture shop and other specialty businesses.

"I think I've seen all the sights already," Kade said. "Not many distractions."

Hannah laughed and grabbed his sleeve, pulling him with her as she continued across the square. "Stop it. It's small. But there's a lot here."

"Well, there *is* a lot of land where a body could be hidden."

She looped her arm through his as they walked. She knew he was talking about his book, but she said, "There is that. So watch yourself. Sonya's the only one who knows you're here, and she gets frustrated enough with you to understand if someone who's been cooped up with you on airplanes and in a rental car suddenly snapped."

He chuckled and she relaxed. This was not an ideal situation. For either of them. She got that. But she needed Kade here with her. They'd been through much worse than her facing her family and hometown again. They'd been through rehab together. And she'd literally saved his life. Just as a for instance.

And because of that life-saving moment, he couldn't be apart from her for six weeks anyway. He would have been on his way to Nebraska after two weeks away from her. He believed she was his muse and that he'd never have another bestseller without her.

It was true that his writing career had taken off after Hannah had restarted his heart on the floor of his apartment two years and two months ago. But it had a lot more to do with him kicking his opioid addiction and his renewed sense of purpose and passion than it did with her. Still, his superstition was part of why he was here. Not the free room or the copious amounts of coffee. He cared about her and knew this would be tough for her. And he didn't believe he could write a good book without her.

He was full of crap, but whatever. As long as he was here, whatever the reason, she wouldn't end up opening a pill bottle. Or begging Kyle to take her back.

"So, I'm going to need some local flavor," Kade said. "I might head out on the town tomorrow while you're with your grandma."

"No way. Sapphire Falls isn't ready for you."

"Oh, it's not the other way around?"

She nodded. "Totally the other way around too. But without a stern pep talk before you step out the door, you'll end up making one of the Blue Brigade ladies cry or saying something horrible about Dottie's potpies or admitting that you know nothing about football and you'll end up with a fork in your forehead."

He grinned. Hannah shrugged. She hadn't been kidding.

"The Blue Brigade?" he asked. "Oh, please tell me about that."

"No."

He pulled his phone from his pocket, swiped his thumb over the screen, and began typing. It was how he took notes when he was away from paper and pen.

"What's that?" she asked, not wanting to know.

"My first question to the good people at Dottie's over potpies," he said. "The Blue Brigade is totally going in my book."

If Hannah had anything to say about it, the entire book wouldn't be going *anywhere*. Kade might enjoy messing around, teasing her about writing a book set in Sapphire Falls, but he couldn't write one of his typical thrillers based on her hometown. She had a hard time sleeping after reading his stuff anyway, and if he conjured images of her favorite place in the world as she read—and then ruined it with a bloodbath—she was going to have to find a new best friend.

"It's very difficult being best friends with someone whose books I hate," she told him. Not for the first time.

"It's harder for me," he said with a little frown.

"I'm doing you a favor," she told him. Also not for the first time. "If I wasn't around to keep your ego in check, you would be completely insufferable."

"As opposed to just mildly insufferable like now."

She lifted a shoulder. "Moderately insufferable. But yes."

They crossed Main Street two blocks down from the square and then headed the final blocks to Ty's place.

Ty's place was what everyone called the huge, old two-story house on Crimson Street that had been turned into what was essentially a boarding house. It didn't have an official name. It was really just a house. The house Ty Bennett had bought when he'd moved home to be close to the woman he was wooing—the woman who was now his wife. There was one kitchen, one living room, and two bathrooms that all of the guests shared. Then there were four bedrooms upstairs and two down, so only six people could stay at any one time—unless they doubled up. She was going to be at her grandmother's for the rest of her stay, but since they'd gotten in late, she and Kade were sharing the room tonight.

"So, I guess, if I'm not allowed out of my room alone..." Kade began.

Hannah gave him a look that said, "No you're definitely not."

"Then maybe I should come to your grandma's with you tomorrow."

Hannah frowned. "No."

"I don't know if you should go alone the first time."

She didn't know either. After the surgery, when Alice was out of the hospital and home and needing some help getting out of chairs and bed, and had some heavy equipment to move around, Hannah would need Kade there. She couldn't do that lifting with her neck issues, so Kade had to be her muscles.

But this first visit was to take Alice for her pre-op appointment with Kyle. While Hannah would love the moral support, she was afraid that both her grandmother and Kyle would be too polite if Kade was there. If there were things that needed airing out, Hannah wanted to get it over with so they could get on to the business of Alice's surgery and recovery.

Because the faster and smoother that went, the sooner Hannah could be back in Seattle. Where she was safe. Where no one expected her to hold things together and fix everything. Where there was no specific plan laid out for years in the future. Where she wasn't responsible for anyone's happiness but her own. And maybe Kade's, when he was stuck on a plot point or behind on a deadline.

"The first time will be the worst. I'll get through it. I'll just focus on Grandma and stick close to her house and lay low," she said. "That's why I'm here. I don't need to go out and get a bunch of reminders about everything I left behind or miss, okay? I'll just…stay in my grandma's house and pretend it's in…Michigan."

"Why Michigan?"

"Because I don't miss anything about Michigan."

"Listen, I don't think your being here is a good idea. You know that. But Sapphire Falls has been affecting your whole life," Kade said, his tone a little gentler. "At first you were dealing with rehab and getting your shit back together. But it's *been* together. For almost two years. And you're not moving on. You don't date, you don't make new friends, you don't go out much."

"My best friend is essentially a hermit," she pointed out.

"Yes, you also have bad taste in friends," Kade agreed drolly. "But it's also because you can't get past everything you left here. You need to use this trip to get over this town and these people, and I don't think you can do that by hiding at your grandma's. I think it's possible that you're remembering things a little rosier than they actually were. Just get out there and prove to yourself that you're not really missing anything."

But she already knew how that would go. She *was* missing Sapphire Falls. She could not sit in the gazebo and watch the town go by without wanting to mail Christmas cards to every person she saw. She could not float down the river on an inner tube and not want to build a house on land that overlooked that very water. She could not take a drive down a dirt back road without wanting to do that every single night for the rest of her life.

And she could not be in this town when the Ferris wheel rolled onto Main for the annual summer festival. She was really praying that her grandmother's rehab would take more like four weeks, rather than the six predicted. She wouldn't be able to handle attending the festival without breaking down, pulling out her cut-off denim shorts, and slipping on her boots. And never taking them off again.

"You write gory, psychotic murder mysteries. Since when are you so into nostalgia and heartbreak and moving on?" she asked him crossly.

"Because this is the kind of thing that drives people into psychotic rages that result in gory murders."

She didn't believe that he actually believed that. She started up the steps to the porch. "Yeah, come to think of it, the longer we talk, the more murderous I feel."

"See what I mean?"

She let them in with the key they'd been given when they'd "checked in"—which had consisted of pulling the envelope that said "HANNAH" off the door where it had been taped, and opening it to find the key to the front door, a key to their room, their room number, and a note that said "Welcome".

There was a small lamp shining warmly from the table just inside the door and a light glowing from the kitchen at the end of the main hall, but the rest of the house was dark and quiet as they stepped through the front door.

She and Kade quietly ascended the staircase, trying not to wake their neighbors. There was a squeaky seventh step, but otherwise they made it upstairs without a sound. Until she stepped from the top step to the second floor. And ran directly into a chest. A naked, wet chest.

The only bathroom on the second floor was the first door on the left, and a tall, lanky male form in only a towel had stepped out of the bathroom just as Hannah turned the corner.

"Oh, I'm sorry," she exclaimed, jerking back.

"Hey," the man said with a slow smile. "I didn't know we had girls staying here."

Kade stepped off the top step just then. The man's gaze flickered to him, and then back to Hannah. "Oh. You're not alone."

She couldn't help but laugh at his obvious disappointment. "Nope."

"Right. Got it. I'm Chase. I'm in town doing some time at the dirt bike track."

"Racer?" Hannah asked. The dirt bike track was a new addition to town since she'd lived here, and she was excited to see it. She, like a lot of the girls in town, were fans of the sport. And that had a lot to do with the men who rode.

"Yep," Chase said. "You follow the sport?"

"Not as much as I used to," she admitted. "But yeah."

"Well, come out and watch me some time," Chase said, with a confident charm that said he didn't really care that the man she was with was standing right behind her. "You'll be able to say you watched me before I was famous."

"I'll have to do that."

"I'd give you an autograph, but I don't have a pen on

me," he said, running a big hand over his damp chest and down over a six-pack of hard abs.

Hannah laughed again at his less-than-subtle style. "Well, we'll be here for a while. I'll catch you sometime."

He gave her a wink. "You do that." Then he lifted his gaze to Kade. Who looked completely bored. "You a fan too?" Chase asked.

"Of?" Kade asked.

"Racing."

"Not even slightly."

Hannah elbowed him. This was the kind of shit Kade was going to do all over town if she didn't break him of it.

But Chase simply laughed. "Well, I'll give you an autograph anyway. Maybe it'll be worth money someday."

"Maybe," Kade said dryly.

Okay, so it was funny that an amateur dirt bike racer was pressing an autograph on a man who'd signed his name four hundred times at his last book signing. Hannah hid her smile.

"When do you race next?" she asked. She'd never been to a race here, of course, but she'd been to many in the past. And demo derbies. She loved those.

"Two weeks," Chase said. "But then I'll be back. I'll leave a note on your door with the date and time."

She was sure it would include his phone number too. Wow. He was something. It didn't bother her. Maybe because she and Kade weren't really a couple. Or maybe because the guy could leave his number if he wanted to—whether or not she called was up to her. Or maybe because she'd grown up in Sapphire Falls. They put cocky in the water here.

"Can you take the late-night talk show downstairs?" a gruff male voice interrupted from two doors down.

They all turned to look at the neighbor they'd disturbed. Hannah had her mouth open to apologize. But she froze, mouth gaping.

No, not frozen. Her entire body felt hot suddenly. With shock, with mortification, with…shock.

Because the man standing in the doorway, in only boxers, his hair mussed, scruff on his face, rubbing a hand over his chest, was Kyle Ames.

Possibly because he'd clearly been asleep, it took Kyle three more seconds to recognize who he was talking to. But she knew the instant that he did. He snapped upright, his eyes widened, and he said simply, "Hannah?"

That single word, in his voice, thundered through her. Her heart pounded, there was a rushing in her ears, and her whole body went numb. Shock. She realized what it was even as she knew she had no power to control it or reduce it.

Because Kyle was standing twenty feet away from her, mostly naked, looking sleep rumpled and gorgeous. His dark hair was sticking up on top, he had a line on his cheek where he'd been lying on his pillow, and he had more than a little sexy scruff on his jaw. He scratched said sexy, short beard and blinked as if trying to clear the confusion that was evident in his expression. And—well, he was mostly naked.

He'd always run religiously. The whole staving-off-aging-and-illness thing, at least in part. But he was also no stranger to manual labor. Helping people he knew build fences, load trucks, lay bricks, cut trees, and a million other things that people had to do on farms and even around town to keep things working. She remembered him saying how he missed being outdoors and working while he'd been in school. She also remembered, even then, wondering how he'd do as a physician, inside all day, lifting stethoscopes and pens rather than tools. But he'd assured her that he'd keep busy on the weekends with projects. There was always something going on in Sapphire Falls, and he'd intended to be a part of it.

It looked like he'd done that.

All of those thoughts tripped through her mind as her body reacted to the display of skin and hard muscles that she also remembered so very, very well. It all combined to shoot hot, hard yearning through her gut. She had always been attracted to Kyle, but never more so than when he'd been a little off-kilter and mussed and imperfect. She was the only one who had really gotten to see him like that, and even those times had been rare.

The realization made the desire coiling through her belly mix with a healthy dose of nostalgia and regret, and she suddenly couldn't pull in the good deep breath that her lungs were demanding.

"Whoa. Okay." Kade's hands wrapped around her upper arms, and he pulled her up against him, keeping her knees from literally wobbling.

She was so grateful for her friend who could read her, and her swaying.

"Breathe, babe," he said near her ear.

"Sorry, man," Chase said to Kyle. "Didn't mean to wake anyone up."

"You're staying here?" Kyle asked, having not taken his eyes off of Hannah. And Kade.

She nodded dumbly but couldn't unstick her tongue from the roof of her mouth. Or maybe she didn't want to unstick it. Because what was she going to say? *Dammit.* She had not been prepared for running into him like this.

"There aren't a lot of other options in town," Kade said smoothly. "We didn't want to put Hannah's parents out. She will, of course, be spending a lot of time with Alice initially."

Kyle's expression went from flummoxed to hard in a snap. As if Kade's voice had activated the reaction. "Right. Okay. Well, I have early rounds." And with that, he turned into his room, shutting the door hard.

Hannah winced. She felt Kade's hands squeeze her arms.

Chase ran a hand through his wet hair. "You guys know Kyle, I take it."

"We, um…" Hannah's mouth still didn't want to work.

"Hannah is from here. She and Dr. Ames went to high school together," Kade said, again smoothly stepping in while Hannah tried to make an ass of herself.

Okay, so maybe he was learning a few things about reading a social situation after all.

Though standing with two half-naked men in a hallway after midnight might not be the type of "social" situation she'd been imagining.

"Oh, got it, okay." But Chase looked like he might want to know more about what had just gone down in that hallway.

"We should get to bed," Kade said, turning Hannah toward their room and nudging her forward.

"Right. Well, I'll see you around," Chase said.

"It seems that it's nearly impossible *not* to see people around, here" Kade said.

Chase simply chuckled.

Kade opened their bedroom door and pushed Hannah inside. He shut it behind them quickly and then regarded her with a deep frown.

"You okay?"

"Yes. Great. Of course. Great."

But she only made it to the side of the bed before her knees gave out, and the adrenaline coursing through her made everything start shaking.

Why? She'd messed up—admittedly pretty big—but she'd cleaned up, she'd gotten her life together, she'd been good. So why did Kyle have to live at Ty's? Where she and Kade were sharing a room tonight? Where she'd hoped to stash Kade so that he wouldn't run into Kyle? Or anyone else. But especially Kyle.

But the answer was hard to ignore.

Karma was a bitch.

Chapter Two

Kyle called Derek on his way to his truck. He'd pulled on jeans and a T-shirt, stuffed his feet into his tennis shoes, and had been out the door in under five minutes.

"She's staying at Ty's," he said to his friend the second Derek picked up. He jammed the key into the ignition of his truck and backed out of his space quickly.

"Oh, fuck," was Derek's response.

"I'm taking your guest room," Kyle told him. There was no way in hell he was staying at Ty's. Maybe once Hannah was sleeping at Alice's. If Hannah slept at Alice's. If she stayed with Alice during the day and at night, went back to Ty's—and her boyfriend, who had pulled her up securely against his body the second he'd seen Kyle—then Kyle would be camping at Derek's until she was back safely in Seattle.

He wondered briefly if the house he was building would be enough of a shelter for the next six weeks. It was fully enclosed and the dry-walling was done, and the weather was getting warmer. He could camp out there. Or he could stay at the clinic. The medical clinic was a renovated house, after all. They had storage and offices in the upstairs bedrooms, but obviously the thermostats, plumbing and electricity worked. He could just put an air mattress in his office. Anything to avoid seeing Hannah with Michael Fucking Kade.

Oh yeah, he knew who the guy with Hannah was. He was the big shot author who was the reason why Hannah had stayed in Seattle. Alice had assured Kyle over and over that Hannah and Michael weren't involved romantically. But the guy had sure touched her easily tonight. As if he'd done it many, many times.

"I'll be here at the bar for a while yet," Derek said, "but let yourself in."

Hell, anyone could let themselves in at Derek's house. The guy never locked his door. "Thanks."

"So it's gonna be a long six weeks, huh?" Derek asked.

Kyle preferred to pretend that his friend did not sound amused by that. "Very long."

"Well, don't eat all my cereal in the morning."

Kyle wouldn't be touching Derek's cereal, and he knew it. Sugary cereals in a variety of shapes with prizes at the bottom were definitely not Kyle's thing. "Alice will feed me in the morning," he said.

He was making a house call. Actually, he was going over for breakfast and to help Alice with "something" she needed done before her surgery. She hadn't been specific, but it didn't really matter what she needed done—he was her guy for the job. Of course, he'd agreed to it before he knew Hannah was already in town. Because Hannah wasn't supposed to be here for *two more weeks*. But now that he knew for a fact that Hannah wouldn't be at Alice's in the morning, he was more than happy to linger over eggs and waffles with one of his favorite people in the world. Especially considering that after this, he'd be avoiding Alice's house as much as possible until Hannah left.

Kyle pulled into Derek's driveway, parking to the side so Derek could get his truck in next to Kyle's. He let himself in through the back door and headed for the guest room.

Thanks to learning to sleep pretty much anywhere, anytime he could during his residency, he fell to sleep quickly. But he did something he hadn't done in a really long time: he dreamed of Hannah.

And woke up totally pissed off about it.

Which was why he was standing at Alice's kitchen island, mixing the bowl of dough far harder than it required, eight hours later. Or it might have been because he'd just spent the past hour freshening up the paint in the bedroom Hannah had used growing up. The very pink paint.

So he was now wearing a bright green apron with ruffles, had streaks of pink paint on his face and arms, and was elbow deep in homemade pasta dough, while arguing with two seventy-three-year-old women who were drinking coffee that he knew was laced with RumChata in place of creamer.

And if this was the first time he'd worn an apron while arguing with the two of them, he might be questioning his sanity. But the truth was, this was typical.

"Stop encouraging her," he told his grandmother firmly.

Ruby gave him a wide-eyed innocent look that was complete bullshit. "She's my best friend, Kyle. If she wants to try to get her granddaughter to fall back in love with Sapphire Falls, there's nothing I can do but help her."

Kyle swallowed hard. Getting Hannah to fall back in love with Sapphire Falls? Sounded like a great plan. If he thought for one damned second it would work. Or if he cared. Because he didn't. At all. Not even a little.

Besides, how the fuck had Hannah fallen *out* of love with Sapphire Falls? It had been everything she'd wanted at one time. Yeah, yeah, people changed, things happened. But not to Hannah. She'd been the same person, with the same plans and dreams and goals, for nearly twenty-five years. Then suddenly it had all changed? Just like that? Because she was living in fucking Seattle and had met Michael Fucking Kade?

Sure, it was her big research project on chronic pain with the University of Washington that had kept her out there. Supposedly. And Michael Kade had been photographed with and linked to a number of women over the years—and none of them had been Hannah. Still, Kyle knew that Kade had been a big part of her life, the life *he* had not been a part of, and he hated the guy a little. Or more than a little.

"And what do you think Hannah is going to think or say when she finds out that you gave her the wrong date?" he asked Alice as the flour, water, and egg mixture squished between his fingers. He gritted his teeth. The Diabolical Duo had waited until they were two cups into their RumChata and coffee and his hands were stuck in the dough before bringing the topic up. Because they knew he wouldn't leave them now. Leaving Ruby's homemade pasta only partially finished would be a travesty, and they knew he'd never let Ruby drive home tipsy.

"I'm an old lady," Alice said with a shrug. "You know how my memory is."

"Sharp as a tack," Kyle said. "Which Hannah also knows, I'm sure."

"It will be fine. She can't stay mad at me."

No one could. Which was how the sweet little lady got her way. All the time. With everyone.

"So you tricked her into coming early. Now what?" Kyle asked.

"Now we bake, and garden, and take walks, and have a big family picnic, and go through scrapbooks, and any other damned thing I can think of," Alice said with a little frown. "It's a good plan."

It was a terrible plan. "You can't stand on your hip long enough to bake anything," Kyle said, thinking he surely didn't need to point out that *he* was the one with flour all over himself at the moment. "You can't kneel to garden and you can't walk more than a block."

"I'll make it work," Alice said, lifting her cup.

Kyle turned the dough out onto the counter and punched it. He was onto her. Alice wanted Hannah to do all of those things to instill some sense of nostalgia in her granddaughter. But, Alice couldn't do it all with her because of her bum hip. And Alice was assuming that, as with everything else, what she couldn't do for herself, *Kyle* would jump in to do.

But there was no way in hell he was gardening or walking with Hannah.

"I'm…concerned," he said, trying with everything he had not to say *you're bat-shit crazy if you think gardening is going to make her want to move back here.*

Alice waved her hand. "Don't be concerned. If I can't take a walk, we can take a drive."

Kyle sighed. "Not about the walking."

"Then what?"

"You're getting your hopes up."

He'd do almost anything for Alice. He'd help her in any way he could. Even if it meant wearing ruffles. Even if it meant spending the morning in the childhood bedroom of the only girl he'd ever loved; the bedroom where he'd actually gotten to third base with her for the first time; the bedroom that had always been bright freaking pink. Kyle squeezed the dough harder.

But the one thing he would not do for Alice was let her believe that Hannah was coming home to Sapphire Falls for good. Alice had already held on to that belief for three years. And it had hurt her a little more every time she spent a Christmas without Hannah, or had to mail Hannah's birthday present to Seattle, or heard one of her friends talk about spending time with one of their grandchildren. When Hannah left at the end of the six weeks—or sooner, if Kyle had anything to say about it—he did not want Alice to be heartbroken. Again.

"Hope is a wonderful thing," Alice said.

Kyle couldn't totally disagree there. In general. But in this case… "Realism is a good thing too," he said.

Alice finally met his eyes directly. "Don't tell me that you don't want her to come home as much as I do."

Kyle focused on the dough instead of on the blue eyes that Alice's granddaughter had inherited. He'd been a sucker for big blue eyes for a long time. "I realized after year one that what I want doesn't matter, Alice."

He'd hung on to the same hope Alice still had for the first year—that Hannah would miss home, realize what she'd left behind, and come running back to them. Year two he'd settled on being hurt and pissed off. Year three he'd decided he was glad that she'd realized she didn't want him, them, everything, before they'd gotten married and were a few years and a few kids into the whole thing.

"You don't mean that," Alice said.

He lifted his head. "I do mean that. I'm not saying I like it, but she's been gone for three years."

"You're still friends," Alice pointed out.

Right. He and Hannah were friends. Supposedly. They hadn't spoken in three years, but he couldn't tell Alice that. He nodded. "Of course. I've known her my whole life. I still care about her. I want her to be happy." And dammit, he meant that. Yes, she'd hurt him, and he was angry, and he hoped that being back in Sapphire Falls amidst all of the people and things she'd left behind tore little holes in her heart. But in all honesty, for three years he'd clung to the idea that she was happy. That her life in Seattle really was everything she needed and wanted. That was the only way any of this was okay.

In spite of everything, he wanted to believe that whatever she'd chosen instead of a life with him was fulfilling and happy and...better.

He hadn't been enough for her. He hated that realization, and it had affected pretty much every other relationship with a woman he'd had since Hannah, but it was clearly the truth. Hannah had helped him discover the one thing he wasn't good at. Being a life partner.

And that was humbling, if nothing else.

"If you want her to be happy, then you'll help me," Alice said. "Because Sapphire Falls is where she'll be happiest."

Kyle sighed and began rolling out the dough.

"Hannah's a grown woman. She can decide for herself what will make her happy."

Alice shook her head stubbornly. "Clearly that's not true."

"Alice," Kyle said, feigning patience. "She *chose* to leave."

"She didn't *leave* us, though," she said. "She just stayed away. That's different. Being away and never coming home, even to visit, has made it easy to forget or ignore everything she had back here. But once she's here for an extended period, she'll be reminded of everything she left behind and she'll want to stay."

Kyle just kept rolling, pretending to be totally focused on the task. He wouldn't admit that he'd had a similar thought a time or two. That it might have occurred to him it had been easier for Hannah to stay away over the past three years without a single trip home than it would be to actually leave Sapphire Falls, as she would have to do this time. And that when she was over a thousand miles away, she might be able to ignore everything she'd loved here, but once she was right in the middle of it, it would be impossible. Hannah had loved it here. This was home. Life here was what she'd always wanted.

He also wouldn't admit to her sweet, big-hearted grandmother that he hoped being home was hard on Hannah. Really hard. That he hoped Hannah was smacked in the face by everything she'd left behind every single day she was here. He hoped she regretted it. He hoped she missed it. He hoped that leaving at the end of the six weeks would tear her heart out.

Kyle realized he'd rolled the dough far too thin and forced himself to relax. Yeah, he was definitely not admitting any of that to Alice.

"So, what are you going to do?" Ruby asked.

"Whatever it takes," Alice said.

Kyle sighed. Alice was setting herself up for

heartbreak. She was going to show Hannah everything Alice loved about Sapphire Falls, and then Hannah was going to essentially say "yeah, no thanks" when she got in her car and headed for the airport.

"You have her bedroom repainted and looking like it always did," Ruby said. "You have everything ready for her favorite meal. What else?"

"I'm going to have her go through things in the attic," Alice said. "Tell her I need help cleaning some things out. All of my scrapbooks and her toys and things are up there."

"You're not going to throw any of that out," Ruby said.

"No. But she doesn't know that."

Ruby laughed. "You're going to make her nostalgic by going through stuff, and then really make her want to cling to it all at the idea of throwing it away?"

Alice frowned. "It's symbolic of the other things she should be clinging to."

"Wow, that's hardball," Ruby said, obviously impressed.

And that was just what Kyle needed—his grandmother getting ideas about how to manipulate the emotions of her grandchildren.

"If you really loved her and wanted her to be happy, wouldn't you just be supportive?" Kyle asked.

Alice frowned at him. "She wants to come home. I know she does. And you," she said, pointing a finger at Kyle, "knock it off with the supportive, do-whatever-you-need-to-do stuff."

Kyle blinked at her. "Excuse me?"

"You know if you'd begged her to come home, if you'd gone out there after her, she would be here right now."

"I was being a good *friend* to her," he said, ignoring the part of his conscience that said *yeah, how come you never begged or even thought of getting on a plane?*

But he *had* thought about getting on a plane. He'd just been way too hurt, and afraid of having her reject him to his face, to actually do it.

"You were *supposed* to be madly in love with her," Alice said.

Kyle set the rolling pin down and faced her more squarely. "Are you questioning how I felt about Hannah?" Because *that* was bullshit.

Alice lifted her chin. "Maybe. It just seemed that it was really easy for you to let her go."

Kyle felt his eyes widen. Oh no, *nobody* doubted that Hannah had been his One. Not even Alice. Maybe especially Alice. "You're *mad* at me because I was supportive of her following her dream and maintained our friendship in spite of the fact that she broke my heart?" Okay, so he hadn't maintained their friendship. And supportive was not exactly the right word for how he'd been. But he didn't know that Alice was upset with him. In fact, he'd been working really hard to be sure she *wasn't* upset with him.

"I'm *hopeful*," Alice said, "that you realize this is your second chance."

"My second chance," he repeated. Then he narrowed his eyes. "To *not* be supportive? To be clingy and pathetic and beg her not to leave again?" Because he was *not* doing that. Probably. Because he was going to be *avoiding* her as much as possible.

"To show her that you want her."

The words hit him hard in the chest. There had been doubt about him wanting her? In *anyone's* mind? Why did that make him a little crazy? "I wanted her, Alice," he finally said seriously. "Her not coming home tore me up."

"Good," Alice said.

Kyle cocked an eyebrow.

"And so now you'll help me convince her to stay."

He took a deep breath, then blew it out slowly. "Here's the deal, Alice," he said. This was really more for Alice than for him, but fine, she could think that these were his feelings too. "If I do that, if I help her remember all the things she loved here and show her what she could have again, and then she gets in her car and leaves at the end of the six weeks to go back to Seattle, that's going to *really* hurt."

Alice nodded. And then, like a knife to his heart, her face fell. Sadness filled her vibrant blue eyes and she sighed. "I know. But at least then, I'll know that she remembered everything. And I did all I could. Then there won't be any what-ifs."

Jesus. Kyle ran a hand through his hair, then grimaced as he realized he now had flour in his hair to go with the paint streaks on his arms and face.

But this was progress. Alice was at least admitting that Hannah leaving again was a possibility. She'd been pretty firmly stuck in her denial for a very long time now. He, on the other hand, had gone through the seven stages of grief, from shock and denial right up to reconstruction and working through. He'd adjusted to life and work without Hannah. He'd been dating for two years now. Sure, none of those dates went past number four and he wondered every fucking time if he was screwing everything up, and then he'd get out before he could screw them up for sure. But he was dating. That was a good thing.

Okay, so he'd gone through six of the stages. He wasn't quite through stage seven, where he really truly had moved on.

"I think it's really good that you get past the what-ifs," Kyle said to Alice, seriously. And if it seemed that everything he said to her could be applied right back directly to *him*, so what? "If you need to do all of this, and try to convince her that this is where she wants to be, fine. But," he added as Alice opened her mouth, "when it's over and she does leave again, you have to accept that and be done with it."

Kyle felt a kick in his chest as he heard those words out

loud. Yeah, yeah, so he needed to listen to his own advice.

Finally, Alice nodded. "Fine. If she gets on that plane in six weeks, I'll accept it."

"You promise?" Kyle asked.

"Yes. And to prove it…I'll give you the key to the clinic if that happens."

Kyle straightened. "Seriously?"

Alice didn't look happy but she nodded. "Yes. But you have to help me. You have to show her what could be if she stays. But if she leaves again after everything we do, then I'll give you the keys to the clinic and sign the papers."

The clinic was the house that sat next to the house that had been turned into Kyle's medical clinic. The two houses had belonged to Alice's twin sisters, who had lived next door to one another, from the night of their double wedding to the day the younger one passed away in her sleep— exactly two days before the older twin died. Alice had inherited both houses, and had given one of them to the town. The town had raised money for the renovations that had turned it from a home into a medical clinic. They had also raised funds to turn the other into a physical therapy clinic. Though a chunk of the money had come from Alice. That clinic was supposed to have been Hannah's. So, Alice had kept the deed to the house with the PT clinic. And the keys. She'd intended to give them both to Hannah when she moved home.

And since that hadn't happened, Alice still had both.

No matter how much begging and charming and sweet-talk Kyle had tried, she wouldn't give it up and let him recruit another PT. She'd insisted that Hannah was coming home, and that then and only then would that house be a PT clinic.

The city council had tried reasoning with her. The mayor, TJ Bennett, had tried making a deal with her. Hailey Conner Bennett, the woman who more or less ran the town and made all the important things happen, had tried. Levi Spencer, the millionaire who had transplanted from Vegas to Sapphire Falls, had made her an astronomical offer on behalf of the town.

Alice had held firm.

When another PT had come to Sapphire Falls and suggested putting a clinic somewhere else, he'd been unable to find anyone willing to sell or rent him a space or a plot of land. Which had seemed strange to him. Not so much to Kyle. Alice McIntire was one of the most beloved citizens in town, and no one would seriously entertain an idea that would go against her wishes.

Well, Kyle had. He'd asked Alice about letting another PT come to town and use another space. *His* grandmother had cut him off from his weekly allowance of sausage and gravy for a month. He wasn't doing that again.

Of course, it was all ridiculous. Hannah was supposed to come home. She hadn't. So they should get a new PT. But the town had put a lot of money into that clinic, trusting that Alice and Hannah would both do what they'd promised.

If Alice hadn't taught most of the town aged fifty and under in kindergarten, or been their piano teacher, or been their Sunday school teacher, or been their Girl Scout leader, people maybe would have leaned on her harder. But she had been all of those things. And Kyle knew that TJ Bennett had said, "Please, Alice," and she'd said, "No, I want that to be my granddaughter's clinic," and he'd said, "Okay, no problem, we'll wait."

It had surely been that simple. Because Alice always got what she wanted around here. Even with the grumpy, gruff mayor.

"I can recruit a PT? We can use that clinic?" Kyle verified.

"I'll sign the thing over to you," Alice said. "You can do whatever you want with it."

"And will you cry every time you go by it, or make me

feel guilty about that every time I come over for dinner?" Kyle asked, knowing full well both of those things were possibilities.

Alice frowned at him. "I might make you feel guilty for thinking I'm planning to guilt you for the rest of your life."

Kyle raised an eyebrow. "First, I didn't say rest of my life, but good to know the time frame in your mind. Second, you still guilt me about the lamp I broke when I was eleven."

Alice huffed out a breath. "Fine. I'll give you the keys and be happy about it."

He gave her a little smile. "You don't have to be happy about it. You just have to act happy about it. And not over-salt my food when I come to dinner."

She nodded. With an eye roll.

"Okay, this is good," he said, feeling optimistic about Hannah's visit for the first time. At least something good would come from it. Two somethings—Alice would finally move on and quit getting her hopes up and then dashed about Hannah moving home, and they would get a PT in town.

"So, you'll help then," Alice said.

"Help?"

"Convince Hannah to move home."

Kyle felt a big rush of *oh crap* go through him. "What are you talking about?" he asked, playing dumb.

"We have to make her miss it here," Alice said, a bit impatiently if he wasn't mistaken.

"I thought *you* were going to work on making her miss it here," Kyle said.

"I'll handle reminding her of her childhood and getting her involved with the family," Alice agreed. "And *you* will handle the romance side."

Oh, yeah, that was not happening. "Alice, that is the worst idea you've ever had," Kyle told her honestly.

"You have to," Alice insisted. "You're the main thing

that she'll want to come home for."

Kyle snorted at that. Yeah, clearly he was a huge draw. "She's known where I am for three years."

"But you've been *so supportive and understanding*," Alice said with more than a touch of sarcasm and a definite frown. "It's your own damned fault it was so easy for her to stay away."

Well, that wasn't true at all. He hadn't been supportive or understanding. If he remembered correctly, his response to her had been, "You've got to be fucking kidding me."

No, it hadn't been mature and supportive and loving. He'd been young and pissed off and hurt and stressed out. He remembered distinctly that he'd been standing in the hallway of the hospital where he'd been doing his family medicine residency when he'd taken her call. Three days after she hadn't shown up at the gazebo, hadn't returned any of his calls, and hadn't called him herself. He'd been running on about four hours of sleep a night, had a take-no-shit attending physician breathing down his neck, had a little girl dying of cystic fibrosis on his caseload that was tearing him up, and had every other person in his hometown asking what was going on with Hannah. He had not been in a good place to take her call and be supportive and understanding about her getting an "amazing opportunity" to stay in fucking Seattle.

He'd been worried and confused, too. So hearing her talking about how excited she was about the research project at the university over a thousand miles away, had done nothing to make him feel understanding.

And then she'd said, "I'm really sorry, but I'm not coming home. I have to stay here."

That was the part he'd said "You've got to be fucking kidding me" to.

"I got this really great opportunity to work on a research project."

He hadn't said anything to that.

Then she'd said, "Everything has changed. I can't...explain it. I just can't come home. I need to...be here."

And he'd said, "For how long?"

And she'd said, "For good."

And he'd said, "Fine. Do what you want."

Okay, that hadn't been *everything* they'd said. Of course. A person didn't end a ten year relationship in twelve sentences. But that was the highlight reel.

"So you think that if *I* want her to stay here, she will?" Kyle asked Alice.

"I think you're a huge key to her staying, yes," Alice said. "She needs to see her family and friends and the clinic and the town again, too, but without you, I don't think she'll want to be here."

Well, no pressure there at all. But he couldn't deny that there was a tiny, albeit stupid, part of him that thought *is she right?* Could he actually make Hannah want to stay? Not that he wanted her to, of course. He'd moved on. Or was working on step seven, anyway. He sure as hell wasn't going to go back to step one. But, though it probably made him an immature asshole, there was that thought of *she definitely should fucking miss me.*

"So if she leaves, you'll be mad at me?" Kyle clarified with Alice. "It's all on me?"

"Of course not," Alice said. "But I do expect you to give it a really good effort."

"It?"

"Romancing her."

Kyle shook his head. Diabolical. That's what Alice was. "You want me to *try to* romance her? Show her what she's missing and how it could be with us if she stays?"

Alice nodded. "I know you keep telling me that you're still friends, but I know you, Kyle. You're still in love with her. And I think she feels the same way."

Kyle realized in that moment that he was on the verge

of big trouble. He wanted Hannah to be happy and fulfilled in her life in Seattle. While at the same time wanting her to have her soul turned inside out upon leaving this town once again. But he couldn't tell Alice that he wanted Hannah happy and miserable at the same time. That was confusing, even to him.

"So you'll help win her over?" Alice asked. And she actually batted those blue eyes that made him say stupid things like *yes* and *sure* and *whatever you need.*

"Yes. Sure. Whatever you need." He was pretty sure that she missed the sarcasm. Or chose to anyway.

But he had a plan. He could help Alice get over this idea of Hannah coming home, he could come out of this still on Alice's good side, while not jeopardizing his pride. Or his heart.

Hannah took the walk from Ty's place to her grandmother's house with a weird mix of emotions swirling through her. Fondness for everything from the post office to the lilac bushes that lined her grandmother's street. Nostalgia as memory after memory flooded her mind. Tension over the idea of possibly running into someone and having to have a conversation. And agitation remembering running into Kyle the night before.

Basically, the same mix of emotions she expected to feel for the entire six weeks she was here.

Being worried about running into someone and having a conversation especially annoyed her though. She talked to people all the time. And was completely normal about it. No one who met her and had a casual, friendly conversation with her knew that she only had about seventy-five percent range of motion in her neck, slept on a ridiculous concoction of foam rollers and pillows that she needed so much, she traveled with them even if it was just overnight, and had for a time eaten Percocet like they were M&M's. No one in Sapphire Falls knew what her last three and a half years had been like.

But these people knew her. Had known her all her life. And she'd been put together, on top of things and organized. She'd been a great student. She'd been involved in countless extracurricular activities. She'd been on the honor roll. She'd never left her house without makeup on and her hair perfect.

And now there were days when blow drying her hair made her cry and matching her shoes to her outfits was just a little beyond what she could handle. Not all days, of course, but more than she liked. And she hadn't felt organized or on top of things in far too long to remember.

Put simply, she was a mess.

But in Seattle, she could get away with it. It was a big city filled with people she didn't know and who didn't really care if she hadn't washed her hair in a couple of days and if she didn't plan things more than three days out because she never knew how things were going to go, and that she stuck needles in herself on a regular basis. Acupuncture needles, but it was still weird to some.

She had pursued her training in acupuncture and massage therapy even as she was kicking her opioid addiction. It not only paid her bills, but she could now write off massage oil as a business expense. Not many people could say that. She was interested in and practiced it all, including meditation, essential oils, massage and yoga, in addition to acupressure and acupuncture techniques. Not to mention her relaxation techniques, such as adult coloring books and pottery.

But all of that was a little "out there" for Sapphire Falls. She wasn't sure people here even knew what essential oils were.

So, her plan was, for the six weeks she was here, to blend in. To be the girl they remembered. Because it would avoid a lot of questions, a lot of explanations she didn't really want to give, and a lot of talk about how weird she'd become.

But she still feared that one ten-minute conversation with her high school biology teacher, Mr. Black, or a visit at the diner with Gwen, the administrator at the nursing home where Hannah had worked all through high school, and they'd know she was different.

And not in a good way.

Hannah stopped at the end of her grandmother's front walk and took in the house that had been the site of so many Christmas mornings and weekend sleepovers and family picnics. This house was possibly dearer to her than the one she'd shared with her parents. Because here, she'd been able to be a kid. She'd been able to eat cookies she didn't have to shop for, make messes she didn't have to clean up, and play outside until dinnertime, because she wasn't the one making dinner.

The house looked great. The light yellow color with the white trim had always been so cheerful, and Hannah could swear that it looked newly painted.

Hannah started up the path, pulling her rolling suitcase behind her. It was just after nine thirty and they were due in Kyle's office at ten. She had no doubt that Dr. Ames operated on a strict schedule. The guy had never been late for anything as long as she'd known him, and she was not going to keep him waiting on them on her first visit to his office.

Her heart thudded at that. His office. The one he'd always dreamed of. The one that was in the huge, light blue house with the hardwood floors and enormous picture windows that let the sunshine stream in. Kyle had been thrilled when the town had announced their plans to convert the old beauty into his medical clinic. And it was next door to another beautiful house that had been remodeled and fully furnished and stocked as a PT clinic.

The clinic that was supposed to have been hers.

That thought sucked a little air from her lungs, and she had to work to pull in a long breath.

Yeah, the first couple steps through those doors might be tough. But she was ready for this. She'd gotten up early so she wouldn't have to rush. When she got stressed and in a hurry, her pain levels could shoot right up. Today, she wanted to be at her best. So she'd meditated, eaten a good breakfast, taken her time getting ready, putting on her makeup and doing her hair with extra care, and then taken the relaxing morning walk to her grandmother's house— one of her happy places.

Facing Kyle Ames wasn't going to get any easier than this.

And she really needed to get it over with.

"Grandma! I'm here!" Hannah called, stepping through the front door.

She paused as tears rushed to her eyes at the familiar smell of the house. Lemon furniture polish and shortbread cookies. It felt like a simple deep breath of the air in her grandmother's house and she was shot back to the past, and her heart ached.

"Darling!"

Alice emerged from the kitchen at the end of the hallway in front of Hannah, making her way across the hardwood floor, leaning heavily on the cane in her left hand.

Hannah frowned as she turned to set her suitcase out of the way in the corner. She'd known the hip was bad, but it hadn't occurred to her that her walk-four-miles-a-day, climb-up-and-down-on-step-stools, run-everything-at-her-church grandmother might be using a cane. Which was stupid. It made total sense. A physical therapist would have probably considered that. The meditation-loving, natural-supplement-peddling, massage-therapist-acupuncturist apparently hadn't, however.

"Hi!" Hannah pasted on a bright smile and met Alice halfway across the foyer, wrapping the other woman in a tight hug.

If the smell of Alice's house brought memories flooding back, being wrapped in her arms and hearing, "Oh, my sweet girl," murmured in her ear, brought the tears.

Hannah sniffed and just let herself sink into the feelings for a moment. Then she pulled back and gave her grandmother a genuine smile. "I'm so glad to see you."

Alice hooked her cane over her forearm, as if she'd been using the thing long enough to be used to doing that when she needed to free up her hands. She took Hannah's face between her palms and studied her eyes. "Are you okay?"

Whoa, she hadn't been expecting that question in the first thirty seconds. She swallowed. Her grandmother would see the truth, she knew. Finally, she gave a short nod. "I'm getting there." That was the truth.

That seemed to appease Alice, at least for the time being. "I'm so happy you're here, darling," Alice said, again moving her cane to her hand and turning toward one of the chairs.

The chair had been in that same spot in that living room all of Hannah's life.

"Don't get too comfortable. We need to head to your appointment in two minutes."

Alice frowned. "My appointment?"

"The one with Ky—Dr. Ames," Hannah said. Yes, Dr. Ames. That's what she should stick with when talking about Kyle. It was much less personal. It reminded her that her only dealings with him should be—would be—in his professional capacity in regards to her grandmother.

Except of course when he's half-naked in the hallway outside your bedroom. Or sleeping in the bed thirty feet away. Or showering in the same shower that you'll be using...

Yeah, so that had been her first thought when she'd stepped into the bathroom that morning. She was only human. And even if she shouldn't be in love with him anymore, that didn't mean her heart was listening. Or her libido, apparently.

She stubbornly shut down that nagging inner voice—that seemed to love the fact that Kyle had been sleeping two doors down all night—and focused on her grandma as Alice said, "Oh, that's not for a couple of weeks."

Hannah shook her head. Was her grandma confused? "We're scheduled to see Ky—Dr. Ames—in his office this morning."

Alice waved her hand. "I got the dates wrong. That's in two weeks."

"But your surgery is on Monday."

"In two weeks."

Hannah moved closer to the chair. "Grandma, what are you talking about?"

"I told you the wrong date," Alice said. "My surgery isn't for two more weeks. But it's so great that you're already here! We can spend some really quality time together before then."

Hannah stared at the woman who was blinking up at her innocently. With a little twinkle of mischief in her eyes. Alice didn't get dates wrong. "You lied to get me here early?" Hannah asked.

"Well, I wouldn't put it that way."

"But you did—"

Suddenly there was a loud clatter in the kitchen, and Hannah heard Ruby's voice, and then a low, deep rumble that made goose bumps dance up her arms.

How could she recognize and react to the muted, unintelligible sound of his voice? That was ridiculous. But those goose bumps were real.

"Kyle's here?" she asked Alice, forgetting for the

moment that her own grandmother had duped her. *"Now?"*

"Yes, he came over to help me with a few things," Alice said.

Hannah frowned. *"I'm* here to help you with things."

"Oh, these are things he does all the time."

"What does 'all the time' mean?"

"He comes over at least twice a week. Sometimes we just have dinner together, but he mows my yard and whatever else I need."

Of course he did. That sounded exactly like Kyle. And Hannah would love to know why hearing that a man mowed her grandmother's lawn made her nipples tingle. *That* was ridiculous.

But she'd always been turned on by Kyle's do-everything-for-everyone side. Which was strong. And constantly obvious.

Hannah was torn between the sudden desire to bolt and to stomp down the hallway to confront him. Just knowing he was in the other room made her feel jumpy. But she'd known she was going to see him. She'd just hoped that it would be in the professional setting of his office with Alice as the focus of their attention and conversation. They simply had to be comfortable enough around one another so that she could call with any questions or concerns after Alice's surgery, and so that he could be totally honest with her about any complications that would arise. Would it be a little awkward at first? Yes. The hallway at Ty's last night had proved that. But of course it would be. So they needed to get that first uncomfortable, how-do-we-act, what-do-we-say stuff out of the way so they could concentrate on Alice.

Well, no time like the present. She was in her grandmother's house. He was on her turf. This would maybe be better in some ways than seeing him in the clinic that was very much his territory—and a huge reminder of how Hannah had let him down.

She leaned over and kissed her grandmother's cheek, again breathing in the familiar and beloved scent of lemon and vanilla. She got choked up and found herself saying, "I'm really sorry I haven't been here before now."

Alice cupped her cheek lovingly. "But you're here now."

Hannah nodded and straightened, blinking against the wetness in her eyes. "I'm just going to go have a word with Dr. Ames. I have a couple of questions." Like *can we act like grown-ups and not avoid each other entirely for the next six weeks for my grandma's sake?* And *can we please just avoid each other for the next six weeks for my grandma's sake?*

Hannah knew it would be hard for Alice to see her and Kyle together, but not *together*. But surely Alice would rather have them be friendly than…not. It was no secret Alice and Ruby had been over-the-moon delighted when Hannah and Kyle had fallen in love. And now it would be hard to keep her grandma from hoping for a rekindling of those feelings. Which would be hard for Hannah, considering it wouldn't really be a *re*kindling of anything. You couldn't rekindle a flame that had never gone out. At the same time, she knew Alice would hate it if she and Kyle couldn't get along at all.

Hannah swallowed hard and started down the hall toward the kitchen with other questions in her head. *Is there any way you could ever forgive me?* And *Do you ever still think about me or are you totally over it all?*

The expression on his face last night was not the look of a man who was totally over it all, but she'd surprised him, woken him up, had showed up with another man…it probably wasn't fair to judge him on his reaction under those circumstances. He could very easily be over her. He could have moved on. He could be dating someone seriously.

And, contrary to the cramp in her gut—and her heart—

at the thought, she wanted that for him. She wanted him to have moved on. She wanted him to be happy.

If his girlfriend was a PT, even better. He could have everything he'd ever wanted.

Hannah tried to chalk up the churning in her stomach to butterflies over seeing Kyle. But while those were very prevalent, that was not the only reason she felt a little sick as she approached the kitchen. Six weeks was going to be *way* too long to see Kyle out and about with another woman.

"Hannah! Darling!"

The moment she stepped into the kitchen, Hannah was enveloped in a huge hug from Ruby, her grandmother's best friend and the woman Hannah had always considered her adopted grandmother. Again, Hannah felt her eyes stinging as she hugged the other woman. But her eyes were firmly on the man who'd just turned from the sink.

He was wearing a green ruffled apron, had something pink streaked on one arm, his neck, and cheek, had flour in his hair, and was drying his hands on a bright yellow towel with blue teacups on it.

And he looked completely masculine, at ease, and…hot. Very, very hot.

Her stupid nipples, that thought him mowing the lawn was attractive, definitely liked the apron look. She knew exactly what that was—it was their past coming back to bite her in the ass.

This wasn't the first time she'd seen him in an apron. And it wasn't the first time the sight had turned her on. Since most of the chores and jobs around her parents' house had fallen to her, Kyle had realized the best way to spend more time with her was to help with all of it. They hadn't gone to the movies much, or to parties, or dances. But they'd had a ridiculously fun time cleaning the house. And cooking. And doing yard work. It seemed that Kyle could make anything fun. And sexy.

There had always been a lot of touching, stolen kisses, and innuendos thrown back and forth as they worked. Just being with him had been all she'd wanted, and knowing that he felt the same way and was willing to scrub floors with her—and kiss her over a bucket of dirty water—had been more romantic than any bouquet of flowers he could have sent or jewelry he could have given her.

But if he'd been helping Hannah all those times, what was he doing painting Alice's house now? Just being a nice guy? That was possible. But he was also a very busy guy. Being the only physician in town didn't give him a lot of time off.

It felt like she'd been frozen, hugging Ruby, staring at Kyle for about ten minutes, but it only took a few seconds for all of those memories to flash through her mind.

Ruby pulled back and cupped Hannah's face. "Our beautiful girl. I'm so happy to see you."

Hannah felt her throat tighten and she couldn't quite make her mouth curl into a smile. She just nodded. "Me too," she said, her voice scratchy.

Then Ruby stepped aside, leaving nothing to focus on but Kyle.

"Hi, Hannah."

His voice, expression, body language—everything was completely different from the night before. He looked completely relaxed now. Maybe even slightly happy to see her. Not overjoyed. That would be a lot to ask, of course. But he didn't look angry or tense. Or surprised.

So he'd known she'd be here. And he hadn't made a point of avoiding being here himself. That was…interesting. Maybe he had already decided they should act mature about this. Or maybe he really was over it all. Maybe his stomach wasn't knotted and his chest wasn't tight and his mind wasn't spinning with memory after memory. And maybe his nipples weren't tingling at all.

Hannah cleared her throat. "Hi."

"Welcome home."

And that certainly didn't sound like a guy who was angry or tense. Or uncomfortable.

This was *her* grandmother's kitchen. Why did it feel like she was the guest?

Oh yeah, because she was. It was clear that Kyle was not only comfortable in the kitchen, but that he'd been here for a while. And that he had no problem seeing his ex-girlfriend/almost-fiancée while dressed in an apron. Which meant, this was nothing unusual.

"Thanks," she finally replied. And realized she really needed to work on not sounding breathless when she talked to him.

But then it got worse.

He crossed to stand right in front of her. "It's good to see you," he told her. And pulled her into a hug.

Hannah felt like her body exploded with sensations. She got hot and tingly and jumpy and melty, and that was all before she took a deep breath and pulled Kyle's scent into her lungs. That so-familiar scent that made her feel safe and loved and happy and like anything was possible, and like she was the luckiest girl in the world, and like she would never be alone, never be scared or worried, because Kyle was there and hers and would always take care of her.

And then, low in her ear, she heard him say, "We need to talk."

She had no idea what to say or do with that. But he let her go before she had even managed to process lifting her arms, putting them around him, and returning the hug. That just seemed like way too much to accomplish with all of the feelings and memories and just *Kyle* washing over her. So there was no hope for her forming words.

Holy shit. She was in huuuuuge trouble.

"Can I help you with your bags or anything?" he asked, as if Hannah wasn't on the verge of crying, melting, and hysterically laughing all at once.

She shook her head. "I just—" She had to stop, clear her throat, and start again. "Have one. I can take it up. I just came to take Grandma to her appointment. With you. Later. Well, in a few minutes. I thought. But I guess not."

All of those actual words made sense, but she was babbling and sounded like an idiot. Hannah closed her eyes briefly, making herself breathe.

It's Kyle. Pull yourself together. Be grateful he's being friendly and civil. Stop acting like a twelve-year-old with a stupid crush.

She'd never been a twelve-year-old with a crush. Not even on Kyle. When she'd been twelve, she'd been into books and movies, and the only crush she'd had was on Brad Pitt. And that only lasted until he'd dumped Jennifer Aniston. She'd never looked at Kyle that way. They'd grown up together and were friends, nothing more. And then one day when she was fifteen, she'd sat next to Kyle in a committee meeting and within ten minutes, realized that she'd been missing the perfect guy right under her nose.

They'd clicked. He'd checked every box on her Mr. Right Checklist. And that had been that.

Interestingly, she'd never been breathless or had a hard time forming words around him before. He'd always been Kyle. He'd made her happy, he'd made her feel loved, he'd turned her on. But he'd done it all with things like…well, mowing the lawn. As stupid as that sounded. Kyle being Kyle had been what made her head over heels. Not things like smiles or a husky voice or hugging her or how he smelled.

At least, she hadn't thought so.

"Well, if you need anything, let me know," Kyle said.

Alice came into the room, saving Hannah from responding. "Oh, you're done with the pasta. Thank you," she said to Kyle. "Did you want to clean up here before you go to the clinic?"

Hannah's eyes flew to the counter behind Kyle. The counter that was covered with homemade pasta. "You made the pasta?" she asked, before she realized that the question sounded stupid.

He nodded. "Hope you like it."

"You made it for *me*?" Hannah asked. She immediately wondered if it was possible for her to run her questions through her stupid-filter before she said them out loud. Apparently not.

"Well, for Alice," he said. "But she wanted it for you."

"Kyle's been doing the pasta, and a lot of other cooking, for me for a while," Alice said.

"Why?" Hannah asked. Just being within ten feet of Kyle, and his hard chest and wide shoulders stretching the soft blue cotton T-shirt he wore, was distracting her. She made a conscious effort to focus on her grandmother. "You're not enjoying cooking anymore?" The kitchen had always been Alice's haven.

"I can't stand very long on my hip," she said. As if to emphasize the point, she moved to one of the kitchen chairs. "And when Kyle found out I was eating frozen dinners, he said there was no way that was going to continue. And he started coming over to cook."

The look Alice gave Kyle was so full of affection that Hannah felt her chest tighten.

She looked at Kyle. He was leaning against the counter, his arms crossed, the stupid apron doing absolutely nothing to detract from his confident masculinity. And now that she knew he was wearing it because he cooked for her grandma so she didn't have to eat frozen dinners…stupid tingling nipples.

"She won't admit how long she was eating that stuff before I found out," Kyle said. "Every time I came over for dinner, she had something homemade and amazing."

"Those meals took her *hours* to make," Ruby piped up.

"She'd have to do part of it and then sit and rest."

"Big mouth," Alice said, shooting her friend a glare.

Ruby shrugged. "Like that's news."

Kyle chuckled and Hannah felt her stomach flip. Cooking for her grandma, wearing an apron as if it was the most natural thing in the world, sporting streaks of flour and whatever the pink stuff was without a care…that was all bad enough. But the affectionate way he was looking at her grandmother and that soft laugh was knotting Hannah up. And she'd been here for less than an hour.

Huuuuuge trouble.

"Well, I'm glad I caught on to what you were up to," Kyle said to Alice. "I think we can both agree that with all the practice this past year, my scalloped potatoes and ham is as good as yours, and my zucchini bread is even better than yours."

Alice gasped. "It is *not* better than mine. Though I agree that your teriyaki chicken is better than mine now."

Kyle laughed. "My teriyaki chicken has always been better than yours."

Hannah knew she was watching this with her mouth hanging open. Finally, she asked, "For the past *year*?"

Kyle looked over at her, almost as if he'd forgotten she was there. "Maybe a little more." He looked at Alice. "It was last March or so when I stopped over and found you with that frozen pizza. I almost fell over."

"You've been cooking for my grandmother for over a *year*?" Hannah said. "Because her hip bothers her too much?" She was aware that Alice was sitting right there, but Hannah couldn't look away from Kyle.

For just an instant, she thought she saw something harden in his eyes. Then he nodded. "She's been pushing through for a long time."

Hannah looked at her grandmother. "I thought you've been putting it off for just a couple of months."

Alice didn't meet her eyes as she said, "Oh, it hasn't

been too long."

"Alice."

All three women looked over at Kyle.

"You have to be honest with her." His tone was soft but firm.

Alice sighed. "It's been bothering me for a long time. Kyle's been trying everything, but it finally got to the point where there aren't any other options but surgery."

"It's been to that point for about five months," Kyle said. He met Hannah's eyes. "She's been suffering for a while."

Hannah didn't have time to be amazed by how influential Kyle clearly was with Alice. Hannah could *feel* his disappointment. In her. She swallowed. "I didn't know." She looked back at Alice. "You didn't tell me."

"I didn't want you to come home because you had to. I wanted you to *want* to be here."

Okay, that hurt. "I *want* to be here to help you." Though it seemed that Kyle had been more than helpful. For over a year.

"Well, you're here now," Alice said brightly. "And I couldn't be happier."

Hannah bit her tongue to keep from commenting on the fact that she was here *early*. Clearly Alice still needed help, even if she hadn't had the surgery yet. Hannah wasn't entirely sure why Alice had given her the wrong date, but technically there was no reason Hannah *couldn't* stay longer. Her boss was currently only six blocks away, and as long as he was around, she could do her job. She might, however, have to let him out of the room at some point.

"So, I'm going to wash the car quick and then head to the clinic," Kyle said, pushing away from the counter.

As he slipped the apron over his head, his shirt rode up on his stomach, revealing the six-pack that made Hannah have to stifle a groan. She could have looked away, she supposed, but she had no idea where she was going to find *that* willpower.

But when Kyle caught her looking, and cocked an eyebrow, she determined to work on it. Hard. She could not go around staring at Kyle and getting all worked up over him. That was a horrible idea. In fact, now that she'd seen him again, she realized that she desperately needed to just avoid him as much as possible. Not because it would be awkward or because he'd be cold and unfriendly. The opposite. Not only did he give her tingles just being *him*. He was also being friendly and acting as if there was nothing strange at all about them being in her grandmother's kitchen together.

That was, strangely, worse than if he'd been angry. Angry, she'd been expecting. And angry would keep them apart.

Friendly and warm was not just a surprise. It was too hard to resist.

She'd truly expected him to be distant and…hurt. She supposed that was the best word. She'd expected that he'd be angry with her, and hurt, and that he'd want to avoid her too. But here he was, making pasta for her grandmother for *Hannah*. And hanging out. And hugging her. And telling her they needed to talk.

What did he want to talk about? Alice? Her hip? Her surgery? Hannah could hope that was what it was. But maybe he wanted an explanation for their breakup. Maybe he wanted to know what the hell had happened in Seattle. Or maybe he wanted to yell at her for ruining his life.

But he wasn't acting like a guy who wanted to yell at her.

She frowned. Why didn't he want to yell at her?

It wasn't that she wanted him to. Exactly. But what had happened between them was surely yell-worthy. Wasn't it? She'd lost so much sleep, had worried so much, had missed him so badly…

And he wasn't even going to yell at her?

Kyle crossed to the table and kissed Ruby on the cheek, then Alice on the top of her head. Then he turned to Hannah.

She straightened at the look in his eyes. Though she could not have labeled what she saw there for anything. Was he thinking about kissing her too? Cheek or top of her head or…somewhere else? That was not okay. Probably.

"Definitely good to see you," he said. He lifted a hand and cupped her cheek. For just a second. Then he dropped his hand and headed for the back door.

Hannah lifted her hand to her cheek as she watched him. That had been strange. The gesture had seemed almost affectionate. But his eyes had been filled with something else.

"I'll see you ladies later," he said from the doorway.

Just before stripping his shirt off and stepping out onto Alice's back porch.

Hannah's nipples were not the only things tingling then.

She watched him cross the yard toward Alice's detached garage. Hannah had no idea how long she watched him, but it was well into pulling Alice's car into the driveway, hooking up the hose and soaping up the car. Shirtless. With lots of muscles bunching and skin getting wet.

She became aware that Ruby and Alice were still at the table talking.

Hannah managed to move away from the spot where she could see Kyle perfectly, cursing the huge windows in her grandmother's kitchen. "So, Kyle comes over a lot?" she asked.

"Oh, yes. All the time."

"You need that much help?" That made Hannah's heart hurt. No, Alice's well-being wasn't Hannah's sole responsibility, but she'd always known that she would be part of the team taking care of her grandmother. Actually, the captain of the team. Her father could only do so much manual work, and her mother didn't have much time.

Alice shrugged. "Kyle does more than I need him to, but that's just the kind of guy he is."

Well, if he was anything like the man she'd known three years ago, Hannah couldn't argue with that. "What kinds of things does he do besides cook?"

"Fixes leaks and puts in new light fixtures and dusts the top shelves. Anything to keep me off a ladder. He and Derek painted the house last fall. He also tries to save me money whenever he can. And, washes my car." Alice glanced toward the window, and Hannah couldn't help that her eyes followed too.

Kyle was bent over, scrubbing one of the tires. Yeah, it wasn't just his abs and chest and shoulders that were worth ogling. That ass…

"Just kind of whatever I need," Alice said.

Hannah pulled her attention from the window. Dammit. "He does all of that for you? Why?"

Alice looked mildly offended. "Because he likes me."

"Of course he does," Hannah said apologetically. "I just don't know how he finds the time."

"He says he likes being around here. And around me. Brings back good memories. And he wants me to be able to stay in my own house as long as possible and not need to move to an apartment or assisted living if all I need help with is the yard and such," Alice said.

And yeah, that made sense. Kyle Ames, protector of the status quo. But it was sweet, she had to admit.

Hannah took a deep breath. "I'm um…going to…I have a question for Kyle."

She did. She was pretty sure. It seemed there were things she'd planned to ask him when she'd thought they were meeting at his clinic. It seemed now that all she was really wondering was why he wasn't more upset about seeing her again. Because *she* was certainly feeling upset. Anticipating their first meeting had made her anxious, and then, after the surprise of running into him last night, she'd been even more worked up about seeing him today.

And then all he'd given her was a smile, a hug, and a "it's really good to see you". What the hell did *that* mean?

Alice smiled. "Of course, dear. Take your time," she said. "I'm sure you have a lot of catching up to do with him."

Well, Hannah wasn't so sure about that. She knew exactly what Kyle's life had been like. She was sure it was going exactly according to plan. Everything always went according to Kyle's plans. Okay, maybe not the marriage and family bit. Or at least not with her. But he was probably right back on track. Yeah, she definitely needed to find a few things out—like who he was dating—so she knew how to prepare for the next six weeks.

That was something she loved about Seattle. She didn't have to prepare or be on guard or know what she was doing three weeks from next Sunday. She could just take it day by day. But for the next six weeks…or more…she was going to have to be on her game. If she could remember anything from the Hannah McIntire Perfectionist Extraordinaire Handbook. She'd lived it for eighteen years. It would come back to her. Surely.

But as she approached Kyle and all of his hot, solid muscles and his slick, lickable skin—*lickable?* She *had* to stop thinking about Kyle and licking in the same sentence—she was pretty sure she was missing a few pages from that handbook. Because *that* Hannah had always been confident and upbeat and prepared for anything, even when it came to Kyle. In fact, Kyle had been one of the most predictable things in her life.

But when he turned and saw her coming and gave her a slow, almost knowing smile, Hannah realized she had no idea what to do.

But she did know she was in huuuuuge trouble.

Chapter Three

"You're late," Kyle said, feeling the satisfaction of seeing Hannah crossing the grass toward him expand and inflate at the look on her face.

She looked ruffled.

That was a very good thing. Because no matter what else Hannah felt about being back in Sapphire Falls, back with her grandma, back around *him*, it was not going to be calm, cool and collected.

Fuck no. Hannah was going to be riled up, stirred up, worked up, if he had anything to say about it. And he thought that he just might. She'd certainly seemed off-kilter in the kitchen earlier.

He'd figured pretty quickly that she would expect him to be cold and angry toward her. She hadn't been expecting a smile and a friendly greeting and a hug.

The hug had been completely spontaneous. He hadn't even thought about touching her. Actually, he had, and had decided *against* it, knowing that would be a bad idea for *him*. And he'd been right. Having her in his arms again had sent a shock wave of emotion and longing through him that had nearly sent him to his knees.

But he'd powered through. Not let it show. Kept his cool. And it had been worth it. She'd been shaken by the whole exchange, and he loved that. Being back in her hometown, with her family, with her ex, with the life she'd given up, *should* shake her up, dammit.

"Late?" she asked, lifting her hand to shield the sun from her eyes.

"I'm almost done." He gestured toward the car, though couldn't help but notice the way her eyes seemed to reluctantly leave his chest to follow his hand. "Figured you might want to help me out. For old times' sake."

They'd washed plenty of cars together. In part because it had needed to be done. In part because it was a damn good time. He'd never really thought about it, but while his friends had been taking their girls out for pizza and to river parties and concerts, he and Hannah had been working, taking care of their families. They'd cleaned and cooked, done yard work, shopped. But it had never felt like work. It had always been a lot of fun.

And he intended to remind her of that. Along with other things.

As long as they had some rules in place. And a plan.

That was key.

But Alice and Ruby were watching from the kitchen, so now wasn't the time to fill her in. Besides, he needed to know a few things before they really got started. Like just how difficult this would be. For her. Of course, for *her*.

He rounded the front of the car and she immediately backed up. Yep, that's what he'd expected.

He looked her up and down. "You remember the old times, right, Hannah?"

She frowned and planted her hands on her hips. "What are you doing?"

He glanced up at the kitchen. Sure enough, their grandmothers were watching. And not even trying to be sneaky about it. "Alice won't like it if we argue."

Hannah bit her bottom lip but dropped her hands. Her back was to the window so Alice couldn't see her watching him suspiciously. "What are you doing?" she repeated.

"What do you mean?"

"Seriously? The big, happy smile, the hug, the 'let's relive old times'?"

"What did you expect?"

Her eyes narrowed further. "You almost proposed to me. I didn't show up. I didn't come home for three years. And you're *happy* to see me?"

Kyle felt emotions rock through him, and he fought to keep his expression neutral. "I wouldn't say happy, no."

She sighed, as if relieved. "Okay, that's better. So what's going on?"

He still held the hose, the water splashing softly onto the driveway. He looked her over. She looked...exactly the same. She wore a dress that hit just above her knees. It was white with tiny blue flowers. It had short sleeves and four tiny buttons up the front, cinched at the waist and hugged her breasts, but was completely modest and sweet looking. She was wearing blue sandals that, of course, matched the flowers on the dress perfectly. Her hair was straight and shiny. Her lips were also shiny, the pink gloss applied flawlessly. Her makeup was picture-perfect, looking so natural he could barely tell she had any on.

When they'd been together, he'd loved how put together she always looked.

Now he wanted her messy.

He wanted her dress wrinkled, her hair mussed, her lip gloss smudged. And he wanted to be responsible for all of it. He didn't really understand what all of that meant. Except that neat and tidy were not words that accurately described anything he felt about all of this—her being here, all the feelings she stirred up, the complications she presented for Alice.

He moved the hose just slightly, the water splashing closer to her toes peeking out from her sandals.

She saw the motion, and probably felt a few cold drops. "Kyle."

"Yeah?"

"You're not going to get me wet."

His eyes locked on hers. "No? You sure about that?"

She licked her lips and he felt a surge of satisfaction. He was affecting her. He shouldn't like that so much. But he definitely did.

"Okay, *why* would you do that? I come out here to talk

and you want to have a water fight?"

"Maybe."

"Really?"

"Or maybe I just want your grandmother to see us having a water fight."

She looked confused. That was okay, since her back was to the house—where Alice and Ruby were still blatantly watching from the kitchen window.

"Why would you want that?" Hannah asked.

"Because it will make her happy to see us getting along and being like we used to be."

Hannah swallowed hard. "That's...dangerous."

"Oh? How so?" Would she find it tempting?

"I don't want to get her hopes up."

Okay, maybe not tempting. Or at least she wasn't admitting that. But they were, actually, on the same page, even if she didn't know it yet.

"Yeah, remember that," he said.

"Remember what?"

"That you don't want to get her hopes up." Then he moved the hose, splashing water over Hannah's feet.

She shrieked and danced from one foot to the other, trying to avoid the water stream. "Kyle!"

Yep, he wanted her messy. And wet. In so many ways. But he shut that thought down. Then started it up again. *Wet.* In many ways. Yeah, he wanted that. He wanted her affected. He wanted this, being here, with him, to *do* something to her. He followed as she started around the car, trying to get the vehicle between her and the water stream.

"Oh, come on, you always ended up wet when we did this in the past," he said. And he absolutely meant the double entendre. It was an easy one, of course, but no way was he going to pass it up.

"Kyle!" she gasped, and he knew it wasn't from the cold water that he managed to splash on the backs of her calves. She was surprised he'd said that.

And he could understand. It wasn't like he'd *never* said anything dirty to her, but it was usually in the heat of the moment. And even then, it had been rare. Hannah just wasn't the type of girl you talked about sex with in her grandmother's driveway.

"This is going to happen, Hannah," he said. "I've got the hose."

She whipped around when he thought she was going to continue around the car. The water stream hit her right in the stomach, drenching her from the waist down. She gasped at the cold and he quickly diverted the water. He hadn't been intending to spray her like that.

But before he could say so, she planted her hands on her hips. "You've got the hose? I always got wet? What are you, twelve? What are you *doing?*"

He couldn't help it—he grinned. She was clearly pissed off and she looked…adorable. Half of her wet and messy, half still perfectly styled and put together.

"I didn't mean the hose comment like that," he said honestly.

"That doesn't answer my question. What's going on?"

"This isn't the place to talk about it."

She looked around. "Why not?"

"Because one of us is going to end up yelling. Maybe even both of us. And that will upset your grandma."

Hannah's eyes flickered to the house over his shoulder. "They're watching."

"Exactly."

"And you want them to think that we're getting along."

"Yes."

"So that Grandma isn't upset about us *not* getting along."

"Right."

She sighed and dropped her hands. "But we're not going to be getting along?"

"I didn't say that."

She frowned. "I'm not following."

Yeah, he knew that. He was still formulating the plan, but he knew how it needed to go. And this little water fight—and her irritation about it—had given him a solid idea.

"Just play along for now," he said. "I'll fill you in later when we have a minute alone."

Her eyebrows rose. "We're going to have a minute alone?"

He raked a hand through his hair, annoyance rising in his chest. "Jesus, Hannah, don't you think we need at least a minute or two?"

She swallowed. "I'd kind of…hoped…we wouldn't," she finally finished weakly.

And that pissed him off. He shifted so his back was fully to the kitchen window. "Really? You thought you'd be here for six weeks and we wouldn't talk?"

For fuck's sake. This was the first time they'd seen each other in *three years*.

She gave a little shrug. "I was planning on laying low, sticking around here, not really stirring anything up."

Now it was his turn to lift his eyebrows. "Not stirring anything up? Seriously?" Hell, the *thought* of her being back in town had had him stirred up for almost a month now.

"I know we would have talked about Grandma and her surgery and stuff, but yeah, I guess I was thinking maybe it wouldn't have to…get personal."

A hot knife of disbelief, anger, and *oh fuck that* went through Kyle so fast that he had to suck in a quick breath. She didn't want to get personal? Yeah, that wasn't going to happen. Everything about this felt personal. And he was going to make sure she felt the same damned way.

"The last time I saw you, you were soapy and wet in my shower. I went down on you, made you come in my mouth, then turned you around and fucked you from behind before I had to get to the hospital. Then you went back to Seattle and broke things off with almost no explanation. And now, three fucking years later, you think you're just going to stay here for six weeks and things *won't get personal?*"

He couldn't believe how difficult it was to hold himself still and keep his body language casual for any onlookers. He wanted to shout, he wanted to shake her, he wanted to punch a fist into Alice's car hood. And Kyle never got worked up like this. He felt like his whole body was vibrating.

Hannah was also holding herself tightly, her arms crossed, her cheeks flushed, and her eyes wide.

Kyle was also having trouble fighting against the visual memories of everything he'd just reminded Hannah of. He could picture the way the soap bubbles had clung to her breasts, he could taste the intoxicating combination of soap and Hannah on his tongue, he could smell the shampoo and the sweet scent of her arousal mingling. His body was reacting to it all too. His blood was pumping from anger and red-hot desire.

"I can't believe you just said that," she finally managed.

"Yeah, well, there's more where that came from."

There were *years* of memories like that. And not just the naked ones. Memories of them on the porch swing talking about the future, family dinners where it had felt like their families were already meshed into one unit, even simple things like him learning to braid her hair. Intimate, sweet moments. Blow-his-mind hot moments. Moments full of laughter and family and love.

Dammit, she'd *loved* him. He would put everything he had on that. It had been real. There was no way in hell he was going to let her stick around here for six weeks and *not* think about all of those things.

Alice wanted to remind Hannah of all these things in an attempt to keep her around. Kyle knew that wasn't going to happen. But he wanted to remind Hannah of all of these things because it was wrong for her to have forgotten or to pretend they hadn't happened. And he wanted leaving here this time to be the hardest thing she'd ever done.

"So *this* is what this visit is going to be like?" Hannah asked. She was breathing faster than she was before.

He nodded as more of his plan came together in his mind. "Yeah, this is what this visit is going to be like." Definitely.

"Then I'll absolutely be avoiding you," she decided. She started to move around him.

Kyle stepped in front of her. He didn't touch her, but he wasn't letting her go that easily. "Good luck with that," he said. "This is Sapphire Falls."

"You're going to harass me?"

He lifted a shoulder. "I wouldn't call it that."

"What *would* you call it?"

He gave her a slow smile. "I'd call it a seduction, Hannah."

Her entire body went hot.

Holy crap. She wasn't sure she'd ever heard Kyle Ames use the word "seduction" before. Because she was really sure she would have remembered it.

She was squeezing her hands so tightly into fists that she felt her nails digging into her palms. "Wha—what do you mean?"

"Seduction. Temptation. Enticement. Pursuit."

"Stop just giving me synonyms," she interrupted.

"But we haven't even gotten to my favorite yet," he said.

She did not want to hear it. He wasn't even touching her, in fact there was about a foot between them, but she felt her nerve endings jumping and snapping like she was covered in the candy that popped in your mouth. Yeah, he was shirtless and that wasn't helping anything, but how could she feel this hot and bothered? It had been a while since she'd had sex. In fact, the last time had been that time Kyle had described in his shower. That had to be it. It had to just be her body and hormones remembering him.

Or something.

"Don't you want to hear my favorite synonym for seduction, Hannah?" he asked.

Had he ever said her name with that rough, husky edge to his voice? Good Lord, she would have never kept her panties on around him if he had. And yes, they'd spent a lot of time naked together over the years. But she didn't remember feeling this…stirred up. Dammit.

That was exactly what she did not want to be.

"Hannah," he said softly, his eyes locked on hers. "Ask me what my favorite synonym for seduction is."

He really needed to stop saying *seduction*. She shook her head.

But he gave her a slow, sexy smile. "Conquest."

He said it anyway.

And damn…that one sucked the air right out of her lungs.

Conquest. *Conquest?* Kyle Ames had just used a very dominant, very alpha, very unlike-him word with her.

And…yeah, damn.

"I don't understand why you would do this," she said.

"You could just walk way," he said.

For some reason, that hadn't even occurred to her. Which was a huge problem.

"Yeah, I guess I could." But she didn't move.

"Which would be perfect, actually," he added.

"You want me to just walk away?"

"That would be awesome. And if you could work on looking a little pissed off, that would be great too."

"You want me to try to look pissed off?"

"*Are* you pissed off?" he asked.

She thought about that. She should be pissed off. Maybe. Though she wasn't sure why. He hadn't really done anything except…tease her. Tempt her. And she should probably be more pissed off at *herself* for that. "I'm annoyed," she finally answered.

"Well, that will work, but pissed would be better. So yeah, you'll have to work on that."

"You want me to be pissed off?"

"I want you to *seem* pissed off. At least."

She took a deep breath, then blew it out slowly. "What are you talking about?"

"I'll explain later. When we can talk it out. Alone."

That talking alone thing again. She really didn't think that was a good idea at all. Of course, he'd said at least one of them would be yelling. She'd definitely entertained the idea that airing things out, getting it all out in the open, letting Kyle have his say about what she'd done—and not done—could maybe be good.

But she didn't want to hear it. She owed it to him. He deserved a chance to say all the things he wanted to say. But she didn't want to hear it. She didn't really want to hear all of this either. This tempting, crazy-hot, *seductive* stuff. Just not talking to him, seeing him, listening to him, watching him interact with her grandmother, would be so much easier.

But maybe she didn't deserve easy.

And besides, as he'd said, there was no way she was going to be able to avoid him entirely while she was here. It was Sapphire Falls. And he was a part of her grandmother's life. As her doctor and more.

Hannah finally nodded. "Fine. Explain later."

"Now look pissed off and stomp around me and into the house and tell them how annoying and immature I am."

She frowned. "Why?"

"Later."

She huffed out a breath. "Well, I'm not *pissed off*. Don't worry. I'll just…go change and…find you later."

"Yes, do that. But you need to be pissed off now."

She didn't understand this. "But I'm *not*."

He sighed. "Okay. But you're going to have to work on your acting after this." Then he lifted the hose and doused her with water.

And not just a splash. Not just a spray of water over her legs and feet. This was a full blast of water that started at her hair and drenched her from head to toe.

And it was freaking freezing.

"Kyle!" She wiped the water from her eyes and glared at him. "What the hell?"

"Just like old times," he said with a grin.

"This is *not* like old times!" She'd never worn a nice dress and sandals to wash the car. She would have had her hair pulled up. She would have been barefoot. And she would have been giving as good as she got and enjoying it. Because she would have known what he was thinking, and she would have been completely comfortable. Because the car washing—just like doing the dishes with him, and mowing the lawn, and folding laundry—had all been a sweet kind of…love. They'd been connected. They'd been a team. And every one of those activities had enforced that.

But comfortable was the last thing she felt right now. And she had no idea what he was thinking.

He just stood grinning at her. "There are definitely some advantages to this plan." His eyes traveled over her and Hannah looked down.

The dress was white, of course, and was now clinging to her like a second skin.

She glared harder. "You have a plan?"

But of course he did. This was Kyle. She should have known. He'd probably calculated the exact amount of water he'd soaked her with.

"I do," he said with a nod. "But you're still not walking

away."

Dammit. She wasn't. "This is all really...not like you."

Something flashed in his eyes, and he dropped the grin and the playful demeanor. He tossed the hose onto the grass, took two big steps forward, and wrapped an arm around her waist, bringing her up against his body, soaking his jeans in the process. "No, it's not," he said. "I always treated you like a princess. I was polite and chivalrous and a fucking gentleman."

Up against his hard, hot, half-naked, now-completely-wet body, Hannah's thoughts seemed to scatter like a handful of confetti tossed into the air. "You...you were..." she mumbled. Kyle had always been sweet and thoughtful toward her. Even when he'd been sexy, even when they'd taken those hot, slippery showers and he'd done the things he'd reminded her of a few minutes ago, he'd been...sweet. As strange as that sounded. Until right now in her grandmother's driveway, he'd never said anything like "I turned you around and fucked you from behind."

She shivered with the memory of him saying that...and doing that.

"Well, that didn't exactly work out for me, did it?" he asked, his eyes on her mouth.

It took her a second to realize he was talking about being sweet not working out, not the shower sex. Because that had definitely worked out for them both.

"I don't..." She licked her lips that were suddenly dry in spite of the fact that the rest of her was dripping wet. From the hose. And from Kyle. "I don't know what you mean."

"I mean, treating you romantically didn't really work out for me," he said. "So I think we're going to try something new this time."

And then he kissed her.

Except, it was nothing like the kisses she was used to. He didn't just touch his lips to hers. He *took* her mouth.

That was the best description. He took her chin between his thumb and fingers, tipping her head and then holding her still. He opened his lips over hers immediately, slicking his tongue along her bottom lip and then slipping inside to meet hers with firm, hot strokes. He held her tightly to his body, turning her and walking her backward until her butt was against the side of the hot, wet car.

Hot and wet seemed to be the theme here.

Because then he was pressing his body against hers so that she could feel every inch of him. Every. Single. Inch.

He kissed her until she couldn't breathe, she couldn't think, she couldn't *do* anything except let him. Let him do pretty much anything he wanted.

When he did finally lift his head and stare down at her, his first words were, "Dammit, Hannah."

She felt her eyebrows rise. "What?"

"You weren't supposed to let me do that."

"I'm sorry, what? I *let* you do that? You just kind of did it." But she'd totally let him. And she would likely do it again.

"Push me back."

She frowned. "Wh—"

"Just fucking push me back," he said, sounding like he was talking through gritted teeth.

She put her hands on his chest and pushed.

He moved back away from her. "Now frown at me."

That was not a problem. "You're crazy, you know that?"

"Very likely," he agreed, shoving a hand through his hair. His gaze ran over her again, head to toe.

And her stupid nipples not only responded, but now with the wet, clinging dress, Kyle definitely noticed.

He lifted a brow, then met her eyes. But he didn't say anything. At least not about the nipple thing.

"Now stomp inside like you're pissed off."

She pulled in a breath and pushed away from the car.

"Well, this time I am." She started for the door.

His chuckle floated after her. "Yeah, you're definitely going to have to work on your acting."

"Um, Dr. Ames?"

Kyle looked up from the file he was reviewing at his desk. He'd been having a hell of a time concentrating since getting into the office. He'd run home to shower and change clothes, but the shower had done nothing for his ability to push Hannah to the back of his mind. In fact, she'd been very much in the forefront of his thoughts—and actions—in that shower. Reminding her of the last time they'd been together had been stupid. Because it reminded him too.

"Yeah?" he asked his receptionist and lab tech, Bailey. In a small clinic like his, even with the whole on-call-constantly thing he had going on, he could only keep so many healthcare professionals busy, so Bailey, and his nurse, Lila, both took on extra jobs that kept the clinic running and, when put together, worked out to full-time hours. Bailey ran the lab, was going to school to be a radiology tech, and answered the phones. Lila helped with the insurance paperwork and filing, along with Donna, the part-time coding specialist who worked from home while she babysat her grandkids.

"Albert is here," Bailey told him. "Early, as usual."

"Okay, great." Kyle pushed back from his desk, grateful for the older man's tendency to show up thirty to forty-five minutes ahead of time for his appointments.

Bailey turned out the door. Kyle started around his desk as his phone buzzed in his pocket. He glanced at the screen and saw Alice was calling.

"Hey," he greeted, just as Bailey stopped on the third step down.

"I forgot to tell you," Bailey began. As Alice said, "I saw that kiss. Well done."

He frowned, hating that he was getting Alice's hopes up on purpose. It was going to be up to Hannah to be sure that those hopes did not stay up. And Hannah didn't know that yet.

"Thank you," he said to Alice. As Bailey continued, "Hannah McIntire is here."

He grinned. That hadn't taken long.

Then Alice said, "Well, she's very happy to be home. So thank *you*."

His grin died. He sincerely doubted that Hannah had told her grandmother that she was happy to be home because of Kyle or his kiss. But Hannah was here. Already. He'd told her to come and find him later. She'd taken about an hour and a half.

Hmmm. Maybe she was happy about that kiss. It had been an especially good one. He'd lost his mind for a little bit there, in fact. He'd actually expected her to push him away immediately. Or at least after a couple of seconds. He hadn't expected her to let the kiss go on and on. And on. And he definitely hadn't been prepared for her to melt in his arms, open her mouth, and make that little moaning sound she'd made.

He cleared his throat as his body responded to that memory.

"You shouldn't thank me for that," he finally said to Alice.

"Should I tell her to wait or leave or what?" Bailey asked.

"How's my day?" he asked Bailey. Just as Alice said, "I knew that I could count on you to help, but I didn't think you would jump right in like that."

Right. He hadn't meant to jump right in. He hadn't meant to kiss her, and he definitely hadn't intended to push her up against the side of her grandmother's car. That had not been the plan. And that was a huge red flag. More than ever, he needed to stick with the plan where Hannah was concerned. Not that he'd been the one to fuck it up before…

"She'll never be able to resist you," Alice said in his ear. As Bailey confirmed, "You're pretty busy today."

Kyle pulled in a breath. Okay, the plan. The plan to make Alice happy while getting a little revenge on his ex while getting to kiss her again while not getting his heart broken. It was a solid plan. It was an important plan. It would work. If he just kept his focus. And didn't mind being a vengeful asshole for a few weeks.

And he didn't think he did, as a matter of fact.

He'd worry about what that said about his character after Hannah left again.

He looked at Bailey and said, "I'll be right down." And then he put his plan into motion when he said to Alice, "It's up to Hannah how this all goes. Don't forget that."

Bailey nodded and descended the stairs in front of him.

Kyle started after her.

"Well, just be yourself, honey," Alice said. "Follow your gut—"

"Follow your *heart*," he heard in the background from his own grandmother.

"Yes," Alice agreed, "just follow your heart."

"Girls, that is not—" Kyle started, but just then he stepped off the bottom step and looked into the waiting room. Hannah's eyes were the first ones he met, and his ankle wobbled.

She was lying on her back on the floor, her feet on the wall beside the tall potted plant that occupied the corner by the window, with Albert and Bailey looking on.

And he realized a very important fact: He was screwed.

"Following your heart is not what?" Alice asked in his ear.

Kyle took a deep breath. "Not going to be a problem."

Totally. Screwed.

Hannah couldn't, for the life of her, remember what she'd been telling Albert in the first few seconds after Kyle walked into the room. She was instructing him on something having to do with the back pain he was coming in to see Kyle about. And it had occurred to her that one of the things she'd learned in her last continuing education class might help. So she'd explained it. And he hadn't understood. So she'd gotten on the floor to show him.

Okay, *whew*. That's what she was doing.

"Morning, Albert," Kyle said, coming into the room.

"Mornin', Doc."

But Kyle hadn't taken his eyes off of Hannah as he crossed to where she still lay on the floor. He stopped and looked down at her with a small smile. He didn't greet her specifically, but he held out his hand.

She wasn't sure touching him was a good idea, but she didn't really see any reasonable way around it. At least not with an audience. And as she slipped her hand into his, she thought, for just a second, that maybe that was part of Kyle's plan. To only touch her when there were people watching so that she couldn't avoid it or pull away.

As he hauled her to her feet, she also realized that didn't make complete sense either, though. In her grandma's driveway, he'd told her to push him away and act pissed off.

What was going on?

Kyle gave her hand a little tug, and she took the step that brought her nearly up against him. Hannah sucked in her breath, then pressed her lips together. But Kyle heard it. She knew because his gaze dropped to her lips. And Hannah was interested to find that Kyle looking at her lips could also make her nipples tingle. They stood staring at each other for a very long moment that was full of…expectation. Or memories. Or something.

Dammit.

Then it got worse.

"Hey, Albert?" Kyle asked, still looking at Hannah. "You think we could reschedule? I think this pretty lady needs some of Dottie's hash browns. It's been three years, you know."

"Oh, yeah, I can definitely come back later," Albert said quickly.

Hannah managed to look away from Kyle and over at the older man. He was watching them with wide eyes.

Oh, crap.

Hannah stepped back quickly. What was Kyle thinking? Looking at her like that? Saying they were going to breakfast together? *Rescheduling appointments?* And with one of the biggest gossips in town? Albert was one of the older men who met for coffee every morning at six a.m. at Dottie's Diner. Nothing happened in Sapphire Falls that they didn't know about. And talk about. And speculate about. And exaggerate.

There were a few things about Kyle Ames that were obvious within about five minutes of knowing him—he loved schedules, he hated change, and he planned *everything.* Albert had known Kyle longer than five minutes. So had all of the people Albert was going to tell that Kyle had changed his schedule around to spend time with Hannah.

Why did Kyle want to have breakfast with her? She was here for whatever this talk was that they needed to have. He'd made it pretty clear at her grandma's that something was going on and he said he'd fill her in later. Well, this was later.

"I was hoping you could show me the PT clinic," she said quickly.

That would be a place where they might be able to have

a private conversation. She had no idea how busy they were over there, but if it was a typical physical therapy clinic, there would be music, conversation, and the whirring of machines and clacking of weights. Maybe they could duck into one of the private treatment rooms.

There was no way they could huddle up for a whispered conversation—or a loud argument—anywhere else in Sapphire Falls without everyone knowing about it. They couldn't duck into one of Kyle's treatment rooms or head upstairs to his office. Bailey and Albert had already witnessed more than Hannah was comfortable with. Mostly because she didn't know exactly *what* they'd witnessed. The PT clinic was the only place in town run by someone who hadn't grown up in Sapphire Falls.

That thought made her chest ache. It wasn't that they purposely kept other people out of Sapphire Falls or didn't want them starting businesses. And plenty of those businesses started by hometown folk ended up bringing new people to town. Like Mason Riley's huge company, IAS. He employed a huge number of people and many of them were from other places. And then there was Mason's wife, Adrianne, who owned the bakery. She was not a Sapphire Falls girl originally, but the town—and Mason— had won her over. It wasn't really a specific business plan for the town. It just kind of worked out that way. People grew up in Sapphire Falls and they didn't really leave very often. Or if they did, they came home eventually. The ache intensified, and Hannah rubbed the spot over her heart.

"You want to see the clinic?" Kyle asked. He seemed surprised.

Hell no, she didn't want to see the clinic where she was supposed to be working right now. Walking through the doors to Kyle's clinic had been a kick in the gut. Seeing the PT clinic, her dream clinic, would be even worse. But she wanted to know what was going on with Kyle, and she couldn't drag him down the hallway and lock him in a room with her *here*. At least not without feeding the gossip machine that was going to be going nuts anyway. So she nodded. "Sure."

She needed to be cool about it though. She needed to be happy for the town and for the PT who was working there. She'd never even been brave enough to ask who it was. Because it didn't matter. That person was lucky to be here and Hannah was glad the town had a therapist. That's all that mattered.

Kyle was studying her, seemingly searching for something in her face. And she wasn't sure she wanted him to find it.

"When do you want me back here?" Albert asked Kyle, edging toward the door.

"Bailey, what have I got later on?" Kyle asked.

"You're booked all afternoon," Bailey said.

"Oh, then you need to talk to Kyle—Dr. Ames—now," Hannah said quickly to Albert.

She wanted to talk to Kyle and find out what was going through his mind, but she could not come in here and disrupt his whole day.

"But I've got this new exercise to do now," Albert said.

"I do hope that helps a little bit," Hannah said. "And let me know if you want any other tips. The yoga seems intimidating at first, I know, but it can really be a great adjunct therapy." She glanced at Kyle. "In addition to whatever Dr. Ames has you doing, of course." She didn't actually fully believe that. Yoga and massage and meditation and acupressure and acupuncture could, in fact, replace a lot of the things that Western medicine prescribed for pain, but standing in the middle of Kyle's clinic, in front of Kyle, didn't seem like the time to tell one of his patients that.

Kyle looked even more surprised now. "You were talking to Albert about his pain?"

"She knew as soon as I walked in that there was

something wrong with my back," Albert piped up. "She could tell which side even."

He beamed at Hannah, and Hannah couldn't help but smile back. She'd known Albert all her life. He seemed to have not aged at all in the time she'd been gone. But he was moving slower.

"Albert had some back surgery about a year ago," Kyle said. "It didn't go as well as we would have liked. We're working on management right now so he doesn't have to have another."

Hannah nodded. Albert had told her all of that. And her neck had spasmed in sympathy. She knew all about spinal surgeries that didn't go as planned. And only a small portion of her knowledge came from her physical therapy textbooks.

"We were talking about management," she said. "It's important to recognize early pains and stiffness so that we—you—can prevent those really bad days." Though the bad days sometimes came anyway, for no apparent reason.

Kyle gave her a small frown, but he didn't seem irritated. It was more of an interested look. "Maybe you need to chat with Hannah a little more, Albert. Maybe we should see if we can set up an appointment with *her*."

Hannah felt her cheeks heat. She had no business setting up appointments with anyone here. And she hadn't meant to open her big mouth and talk to Albert about his aches and pains. But they'd been sitting there together, alone in the waiting room, and it had, actually, been obvious to her that he was having back pain. And she knew some things about managing that kind of pain. Why should she stay quiet?

Oh yeah, because it would complicate everything if she started talking about what she really did for a living.

Still, if she was a practicing physical therapist, surely she would have spoken up to help a man she knew well who was obviously in pain.

"I'm happy to give you some websites," she said.

"I don't use the internet," Albert said.

Kyle snorted. "How do you email Coach Riley then?"

Mike Riley was the head coach for the football team at the University of Nebraska. Which made him the leader of the main religion in Nebraska.

"Well," Albert said, "I can email. I don't know about the other stuff."

Kyle was giving the other man a knowing smile that Hannah didn't fully understand, but she said, "That's fine, Albert. I'm happy to show you some things." That wouldn't hurt. It was yoga. That didn't require a special license. And the chances of her and Albert being someplace together where a yoga instruction was appropriate were slim anyway. But she'd make the offer. That was the least she could do since she was getting in the way of his appointment with Kyle.

"Maybe we could meet up at Hope's place," Albert suggested. "She's obviously got space."

"Hope's place?" Hannah asked.

"Hope Bennett. She's married to TJ. She does yoga and has a place on Main," Albert said.

Hannah looked at Kyle. He shrugged. "She does. She's also into herbs and oils and massage."

There was a yoga studio in Sapphire Falls? And someone who knew about massage and oils? Hannah was stunned. "Oh, well, you could just ask her for help then." That was a relief. Less pressure on Hannah and more ongoing help for Albert.

"Oh, yeah, Hope's sweet. But she's not you," Albert said.

Hannah swallowed. It was nice that Albert trusted her simply because she was from here and he'd known her for years. It was also a little crazy. Being born and raised in Sapphire Falls in no way made someone an expert in anything other than maybe building bonfires, telling tall tales, predicting weather patterns based on things like the fuzz on caterpillars, and country music. "But she's from here now."

"Sure," Albert agreed. "And she's great. But if my doctor has a favorite, I should go with her, right?"

Hannah shot Kyle a glance. She didn't like the butterflies Albert's comment kicked up in her stomach. And Kyle was neither confirming nor denying that Hannah was his favorite. He just mostly looked amused. "I'm sure Kyle likes Hope."

"Of course, everyone likes Hope," Albert said. "But he's never suggested I talk with Hope about my back."

"He hasn't?" She frowned at Kyle. Why wouldn't he suggest some of Hope's services to someone in pain? Maybe Hope wasn't very good. Hannah would hate to think that Kyle was one of those physicians who was closed off to ideas that were a little outside the tradition medicine box. But he really might be. Kyle liked tradition and plans and predictability. Alternative health options probably didn't fit in his mold.

"Nope. So I think you're the one I should talk to," Albert said.

"Well, I'll tell you whatever I can," Hannah said. She'd stick with the easy-to-understand, basic stuff. Even some clumsily applied trigger-point pressure could relieve a little pain, and that would be something.

"We do have a whole clinic next door that has *actual* therapy equipment," Kyle commented casually. "You don't need to go to Hope's."

Right. The PT clinic. "Yes, Albert, you've tried physical therapy, I assume?" Hannah asked. Maybe Kyle didn't refer patients to Hope, but she knew he would recommend PT.

"Eh," Albert said. "I did it for a while. But it was a long way to go."

Hannah frowned. She didn't know enough about his

condition specifically and really had no business talking to him about PT. She could show him stretches and talk to him about acupressure. She could also maybe, carefully, bring up acupuncture. But there was no one in town who could offer him those services on an ongoing basis anyway. And people tended to get weird about being stuck with needles.

"Well, if nothing else, I can certainly wait on those hash browns until you and Dr. Ames talk."

"Oh, don't be silly," Albert said, waving her concern away. "This back's been bugging me a long time and it's not going to get better in the next few hours. Or worse, for that matter."

"Are you going to be at Mary's tonight?" Kyle asked him.

"Yep." Albert waggled his eyebrows. "It's date night."

"I'm stopping by to check on her rash. I'll give you a look then," Kyle said.

"Sounds good to me," Albert told him. Then he winked. "Really glad that rash isn't contagious."

Kyle grinned and shook his head. "Too much info, Al," he said. "But tell her to save me a piece of apple pie."

"You got it." Albert started for the door.

"But you can stay," Hannah protested weakly. Now Kyle was making a double house call? And Albert was waiting several hours to talk to his doctor about his pain? This was ridiculous.

"Nah, now you've got me thinking some hash browns sound really good. That might just fix me right up."

Kyle chuckled as the door thumped shut behind Albert. "Haven't seen him move that fast in a while."

"Those hash browns *are* really good," Hannah said. In fact, they were almost magical.

"Yep, *that's* why he's hightailing it over there," Kyle said with a grin.

Hannah knew Albert would have been heading straight

for Dottie's whether he was hungry or not. That's where all the other gossipy old men congregated, and anyone who brought in new gossip and news got their first cup of coffee free. Of course, the coffee was only about fifty cents a cup, but it was all about the honor of knowing something first. In Sapphire Falls, that was quite a feat.

Hannah lifted an eyebrow at Kyle. "You think he's going to share his new exercise for back pain? He might just get right down on the diner floor and prop his feet up on a booth?"

Kyle's smile grew, and for a second Hannah forgot that she was annoyed about her and Kyle being the newest piece of gossip in town when she didn't even know what was going on.

"I think the floor of the diner is one of the cleanest places in town," Kyle said. "And I think that Albert loves knowing things other people don't. And I think there are about six guys in there who are also having back pain. And I think hearing that he got the information from *you* will make a huge difference."

Hannah didn't know if Kyle was intentionally rubbing in the fact that she would have been a very welcome and well-respected part of the health care team here, or if he was just talking, but it worked to intensify her regret. She couldn't practice PT, here or anywhere. And the accident hadn't been her fault. But that didn't mean she didn't wish it was different.

"They don't listen to the PT here?" she asked. She'd actually wondered about that in the past. Sapphire Falls was a very tight-knit community. They accepted new people and loved seeing the town grow. But patients had a hard time liking their PTs sometimes anyway. The hallmark of physical therapy was healing, of course, but to get there sometimes required tough love. And pushing. And nagging.

Kyle's smile died almost instantly, and Hannah blinked at the sudden change.

"Come on," he said. He started for the door. "Bailey, I'm heading out. Call me if you need me."

"You know it," Bailey told him.

Kyle took Hannah's elbow as they stepped out onto the porch, almost as if he felt the need to keep hold of her.

"Kyle, I just—"

"Save it," he said. "We can say whatever we want to in about two minutes."

She let him lead her down the porch steps and to the sidewalk in front of the house. Then he took her hand.

She stiffened slightly, but let him hold it. It felt...nice. She had no idea what was going on, but she hated to make a big deal out of holding the hand of her childhood friend and one-time boyfriend. Maybe he'd done it without thinking.

He looked over at her. "You're going to hold my hand?"

Or maybe he hadn't done it without thinking. "Yes. I guess. I don't know." She frowned. "*You* took my hand."

He pulled in a breath. "I know. Pull away."

"But I—"

"Holy shit, Hannah," he said through gritted teeth as he gripped her hand tighter, even as he smiled and waved at a car passing by. "Can you just fucking go along with me for two minutes?"

Chapter Four

She sighed. She didn't really understand what was going on, but could she go along with Kyle and do something just because he asked her to? Yes. She could do that. She owed him that much. So, she yanked her hand out of his hold.

Hannah took a deep breath, then let it out. It did no good to let this get her worked up. She was the one who'd hurt him. She could let him deal with this however he wanted to. And her neck couldn't stand the tension that pent-up frustration caused.

She consciously worked to relax her neck and shoulders and took another breath as they started down the sidewalk that ran the short distance between the two immaculate lawns. Clearly the city had done some work here. The grass was lush and green, the smooth, white sidewalk had been newly paved, and the flowers lining the paths were a bright explosion of colors.

The house-turned-medical-clinic sat on Main Street but was off the square a couple of blocks, so the tree-lined street was quieter than the one that ran in front of the diner and other businesses. Not that *that* was a busy street by Seattle standards, but it was the one where she and Kyle would be noticed. For now, they were pretty much alone.

And, stupid as it was, it felt weird to be walking next to Kyle and not holding his hand.

They only had about fifty feet to go to get to the house next door to Kyle's clinic. Okay, it was the Sapphire Falls Medical Clinic officially. The city owned it and it was overseen by a medical board, on which her grandmother sat. But it was Kyle's clinic. It had been remodeled with him and Jason Gilmore in mind. Both were from Sapphire

Falls and both had intended to return home to practice. Jason had, however, fallen in love and moved to California, leaving Kyle the sole physician in town. But Kyle was handling it. Because it was Kyle. And because he was willing to make house calls at all hours of the day. She had no doubt that he answered questions while picking up his mail and called in prescription refills while in the midst of eating a burger at the Come Again and checked vitals while digging new flower beds at the park.

He never stopped. He never had. And being needed by everyone for everything 24/7 was right up his alley.

He stopped at the end of the path that led up to the PT clinic and gestured for her to go ahead of him. She did, flouncing up the steps to the porch. She wasn't even sure why she was flouncing, but he'd told her to stomp inside like she was pissed earlier at her grandmother's, and now he'd told her to pull away from his hand-holding. She could only assume that flouncing was the right move.

But at the top of the steps, she realized Kyle hadn't followed her up onto the porch. He disappeared around the side of the house. She went to the edge of the porch and leaned onto the railing, trying to see where he'd gone. "Kyle? Hey!"

"Hold on!"

She heard a door open and then shut, and a minute later, Kyle opened the front door from the inside.

"What's going on?" she asked.

"I don't have a key for the front. But she doesn't realize that the side door has the same lock it's always had and that I got the key from Ted."

Hannah didn't understand any of that explanation. "What do you mean?"

"Come on in," he said, not answering her question. He stepped back and let her get her first look at the clinic. "I'll show you around."

She took a deep breath and stepped across the

threshold. The threshold to the very quiet, very empty house that was supposed to be a busy, noisy PT clinic.

The check-in desk was an actual desk, in a warm oak that looked completely at place in the wide foyer with the twelve-foot ceiling and huge window above the door that let in lots of sunshine. The hardwood floor in the entryway and down the main hallway glowed in the light, and the place smelled like the wood polish someone had obviously lovingly used on the old floors.

"You can work with Alice over here for her rehab," he said, flipping on the overhead light in the foyer. "Might as well use the equipment. Sounds like Albert will sign up too."

"I'm not licensed in Nebraska," she said weakly. Of course, she left off the "or anywhere else in PT".

"I'm not too worried about Alice suing you or you charging her insurance company," Kyle said. He turned into what had been the living room of the old house.

"I was planning to work with her at home," Hannah said. She'd pulled out her home health notes from school and dug into her memory from one of her internships that had included home health visits. "A lot can be done in her own environment and that makes it more functional, really. Learning to go up and down her own steps is more valuable than up and down steps in a clinic setting…"

But she trailed off as she stepped through the arched doorway into the living-room-turned-waiting-room. Because it really still felt like more of a home. It was exactly as she'd pictured it. And she loved it immediately. It was clearly meant to be the waiting room, but the couches and end tables and lamps were much more inviting than those in a typical clinic waiting room.

She turned and looked across the foyer into what would have been the dining room. But rather than a glass-fronted china cabinet and a huge table surrounded by high-backed chairs, the room held a treadmill, a recumbent bike, some weight equipment and a large, padded-mat table for exercising set up near the tall windows.

"The other equipment is this way," Kyle said, starting down the hall.

Hannah might have protested, but she couldn't force any air for words past the tightness in her throat. She followed him wordlessly, displeased to find that she couldn't keep her eyes off his ass in blue jeans.

Blue jeans. Doctors in Seattle didn't wear blue jeans with their lab coats. But damn, on Kyle it worked. It didn't do one thing to detract from his take-charge attitude or the feel that he was fully professional and brilliant. Of course, in high school, he'd always been take-charge and brilliant, and he'd worn blue jeans, shorts, and football and baseball pants. And all of those had definitely worked for her.

He stopped in the hallway in front of the open door to what had once been a bedroom and the one that was still a small powder room. The bedroom now held an examination table and an ultrasound machine as well as a large set of shelves and cupboards. This was where evaluations and private treatment sessions would be held.

"We turned the den into two more exam rooms," Kyle said. "It was a great room, but we decided dividing it made more sense. Now one exam room has a fireplace though."

Inexplicably, Hannah's throat tightened to the point that she had to cough and simply nod. Kyle focused on her for the first time since he'd stepped into the house. For just a moment, something flickered in his eyes, but he quickly looked away.

He gestured down the hall. "The kitchen is still a kitchen. We can store icepacks and stuff in the freezer, and Kelsey thought it was the perfect setup for helping teach proper bending and lifting and compensatory strategies for people in their own homes."

"Is Kelsey the PT?"

He frowned. "She's *a* PT. She consulted with the

medical board on ideas for the clinic."

Ah. Hannah nodded. Mimicking real-life situations for patients learning to compensate either temporarily or permanently for injuries and disabilities was important and sometimes difficult in a clinic setting. The house here was…pretty much perfect.

"The laundry room is also still as is," he went on. "With the exception of new appliances. Obviously, it would work for doing towels and sheets used in the clinic, but it's also good for having patients work on balance and reaching and weight bearing and stuff." He gave a little chuckle. "Or so I've been told."

By Kelsey, no doubt. Hannah didn't respond. The house was a wonderful combination of warm and homey and functional. It had been set up perfectly. Sapphire Falls needed a PT in town. She could not be jealous of whoever got to work here. Or, at least, she shouldn't be.

"You and Alice are welcome to use it anytime."

"So you oversee the PT clinic too?" she asked, focusing.

"No. The medical board does. But it just sits here, so there's not much to oversee."

She frowned. "No one's practicing here?"

His eyes hardened slightly, then he seemed to visibly relax his shoulders. "No. Everyone's driving to York."

"Have you tried to hire someone?" she asked.

Kyle's jaw definitely tightened with that. "Kind of a long story," he finally said.

And his tone clearly indicated that it was none of her business.

Which was true.

But they could either talk this thing out or pretend she was just a random classmate back in town for a visit. Or more, a random patient's random family member.

She wasn't either of those things, and pretending she was would not make any of it different.

"Just because I'm not the one here, doesn't mean I don't care who is," she said quietly.

Kyle's head snapped up and he stared at her. His expression clearly said that he couldn't believe she'd gone there. She met his gaze directly. Yes, she was to blame. She got it. But she kind of wanted to hear him say it.

"No one's practicing here," he said, "because your grandmother has convinced the city council to hold off letting anyone else in because you might come home."

Hannah blinked at him, processing his words. Or trying to. Finally, she just said, "What?"

"Okay, more specifically, your grandmother has convinced Hailey and TJ," he said, referring to Hailey Conner Bennett, who pretty much ran the town, and TJ Bennett, the current mayor.

"But…why would…" But it wasn't really hard to believe that Alice would do that. She would never fully believe that Hannah wanted to be anywhere else for good. Because Hannah didn't really want to be anywhere else for good. "Why would they listen to her?" she finally managed to ask.

"Because it's Alice," Kyle said with a sigh. "Your grandmother has more friends and favors stored up in this town than Kathy Bennett."

Hannah couldn't argue with that. Not only had she taught and volunteered for years, she was, flat-out, beloved. If Alice McIntire asked someone to do something, they would bend over backwards to do it.

Hannah felt her chest tighten. This was even worse than she'd thought. Not only had the town put money into the clinic that wasn't being used, they were now keeping it open as an option for Hannah. "I didn't know she'd done that."

Kyle gave a single nod. "Now you do." He brushed past her and started for the front of the house again.

She hurried to keep up with him. "I never asked her to.

I've never given her any indication that I was planning to come back."

Kyle swung around in the middle of the foyer. His expression was tight. He didn't reply immediately and when he did, all he said was, "I know."

Hannah swallowed. She was never going to get used to that look from him. Kyle had always only looked at her with affection and respect and passion and love.

She hated this cool, hard stuff. She sighed. "I'm sorry. I'll talk to her."

"If talking worked, we wouldn't be here," he said.

"What do you mean?"

"I've been telling her for three years that you're not coming home."

Hannah flinched slightly. There was a bite to his tone, but more, it was the words. The way he seemed absolutely certain of them. And was pissed by the truth.

She nodded. "She's stubborn."

"Especially if you've never actually said that you're not coming back," Kyle said.

"I just…" She hadn't been able to say those words. As unfair as that might have been to her grandmother.

"You just led her on because that was easier on *you*," Kyle filled in.

"Hey, I didn't mean to hurt her," Hannah said, crossing her arms over her chest.

"But you did. By making her hope for something that was never going to happen."

Hannah was sure she was imagining things when she thought for an instant that maybe Kyle wasn't talking about Alice being the one that was hoping. She shook her head. "Whether or not you believe it, for a long time, I kept hoping too."

His eyes narrowed. "Hoping for what?"

"To come home."

His eyes widened, then narrowed again as his jaw

tightened. "But you didn't."

She shook her head. "I couldn't."

"Right." He paused, as if he was going to say something. Then he turned. "We should head to the diner."

"Hang on." She reached out quickly, without thinking, and grabbed his arm. He stopped but didn't turn back. She felt his muscles tensing under her hand, but she held on. As if she could keep him there if he didn't want to stay. Still, he waited. "You can say whatever you want to say to me."

She didn't want to hear it, of course. But she knew he had a right to be angry with her.

"You don't really want that."

Her mouth suddenly felt dry. She nodded. "I do. You said at Grandma's that you were done with being chivalrous and polite to me. And I think that's good."

"Do you?"

She'd been shocked by his words, and actions, in her grandmother's driveway. But in retrospect, she wanted more emotion from him than pleasant and polite. Because seeing him again, being around him, having him touching and kissing her, was very, very emotional for her. And she wanted to know that it was stirring him too. *She* was a mess. She'd fallen from perfectly put together to barely holding it all together, and she resented the fact that he was still as perfect as ever. "Why would you be nice and friendly to me? After everything that happened?"

She instantly realized that she'd said the wrong thing. Or maybe it was the right thing.

Kyle advanced on her and Hannah quickly backed up. But he kept coming. She bumped into the wall behind her, and Kyle didn't stop until he had his hands braced on the wall on either side of her head. He leaned in, his nose centimeters away, his dark eyes boring into hers. "You're over the nice-guy thing? Got your fill? Did you discover that you have a thing for not-nice in Seattle or something?"

She wet her lips. He had her backed up against the wall

and he definitely looked angry now. But she wasn't scared.
She wasn't intimidated. She didn't regret it. Her heart
pounded and her whole body felt tingly.

His gaze dropped to her mouth, and Hannah didn't
know what possessed her—clearly a big shot of crazy—
because she said, "Yeah, maybe I *am* over the nice-guy
thing."

She wasn't. What woman got over a guy being nice to
her?

But then Kyle muttered, "Damn you." And took total
possession of her mouth.

And yeah, if this was *not* nice, she'd take a double,
thank you very much.

His mouth was hot and demanding as he kissed her,
pressing then letting up, pressing and letting up. He licked,
he stroked, he even nipped her bottom lip, and Hannah felt
every nerve ending in her body burn.

That went on for at least a full two minutes. Then he
slid one hand from the wall to the back of her head,
tangling in her hair. The other slipped to her lower back
and he pressed her forward, into him. And the hot, hard
length of his thighs and his fly.

Hannah sighed, and he tugged on her hair, urging her
head back. She instantly stiffened, expecting a jolt of pain
from the angle. It didn't hurt, but her sudden rigidity alerted
Kyle to the change in her demeanor. He lifted his head. His
eyes were dark and he looked a little dazed.

She licked her lips and worked to take a deep breath.
Finally, she said, "I don't know. That was pretty nice."

He pushed away from the wall, taking a huge step back.
"*That* is a problem," he said.

Okay, so it was unexpected and maybe a little
complicated. But *problem* seemed like a stretch. "I'm not
upset by it, if that's what you're worried about." She pulled
her fingers through her hair.

"Exactly," he said. "That's the problem."

"That I'm not upset?"

"Yes."

"Why?" And then she remembered how he'd wanted her to act pissed off and push him away at her grandma's. How had she forgotten that? But then again, she'd felt off-kilter since stepping foot into his clinic. Overwhelmed by the reality of his dream come true...that had nothing to do with her. And then *this* clinic and the dream that she'd thought she'd let go of. That she clearly hadn't. "What is going on?"

"I kissed you because Helen Cooper and Betty Canton were walking by."

Hannah glanced out the window. No one was out there now, but she certainly hadn't noticed anyone earlier. She'd been fully dialed into Kyle. "Why would that make you kiss me?"

"Same reason I kissed you at your grandmother's."

"You said that was because *she* was watching and it would make her happy."

"Exactly."

Hannah had gone inside after the car-washing incident and gone straight to her room to change clothes. Her grandmother hadn't said anything about the water fight or the kiss and Hannah was grateful. She couldn't explain it, or how she felt about it. And she appreciated that her grandmother's only reaction was to smile. A lot.

"How did kissing me just *now* make my grandmother happy?" But he didn't have to answer. She got it as soon as she said it out loud. "Helen and Betty are her friends and will tell her all about it."

"They've probably already texted her," Kyle said.

Hannah couldn't deny the tiny stab of disappointment at realizing that the kiss had been motivated by something other than just *wanting* to kiss her.

"What's going on?" she asked. "This is the second major kiss you've laid on me because of my grandmother."

"And the second time you haven't reacted the way I expected," he said with a frown.

"How did you expect me to react?" Melting into a puddle of lust at his feet hadn't been his intention?

"I expected you to push me away, to be shocked, or offended, or…something."

"I was shocked." Hannah thought about that as she said it though. She'd been surprised but maybe shocked was strong. She had expected there to still be some attraction between them. A lack of chemistry had, in no way, been a part of them breaking up. And after seeing him in the hallway at Ty's, she wasn't at all surprised that once his mouth was on her, she'd lost track of the fact that kissing him shouldn't feel so natural.

"But you weren't offended."

"No." That was the true.

He sighed. "Okay, so we need a plan."

A plan. Of course they did. "A plan for what?"

"You realize that Alice is planning on launching a whole campaign to convince you to come home, right?"

Hannah felt her heart thump. "She is?"

"Yes. She thinks that all you need is to be reminded of everything you left here. That after six weeks, there's no way you're going to want to leave."

Oh boy…

"So over the next six weeks, I'm going to try to win you back."

Hannah froze at that. She stared at Kyle. "Back?"

"Yes."

"You mean…romantically?"

"Yes."

"You want me back?"

"No."

Oh. Okay. Right. She blinked at him. That kind of hurt. But she was also completely confused. "I don't get it."

"Your grandmother wants you back. And she thinks *I'm*

the key to getting you to come home."

Hannah blew out a breath. Wow. That was…not as easy as it sounded, but not as off base as it should be. If Kyle could adjust his plans, imagine a different life, forgive her for messing everything up, and love her in spite of her no longer checking all of the boxes on *his* Ms. Perfect List then…

But no, that wouldn't happen. One thing she had figured out while in Seattle and away from everything here was that she and Kyle had been drawn together more by practicality than by passion. Oh, things had been hot sexually between them. There was definite chemistry. But if she'd wanted to travel the world as a belly dancer or go into botany or open a winery, he would have never asked her out on that second date. Because yeah, they'd talked about their plans and aspirations on date one. That was how Kyle Ames rolled. He'd known what he was looking for, she'd answered all the questions correctly, so she'd gotten the job of girlfriend and future wife. Not that she'd ever doubted for one second that she wanted that job.

"I'll talk to her," Hannah promised. "I'll convince her that I'm happy in Seattle."

Kyle's jaw ticked again at that, but he just said, "Talking to her isn't enough. I've tried that. My grandma's tried that. Your mom and dad have tried that."

Ouch. Hannah didn't know that her parents had been telling her grandma that there was no way Hannah was coming home. She wasn't sure how she felt about them believing that. Especially since it was the truth. Or was supposed to be anyway.

"She thinks that she knows you best," Kyle continued. "And that you actually want to come home, but something is keeping you in Seattle. She also thinks that if I forgive you and show you that you can have everything you left behind again, you'll change your mind and move home."

Hannah's heart stuttered. "But you don't want to give

me everything I left behind."

"No. You made your choice, and *I* understand that. I'm over it."

She nodded. "Got it."

"But I'm going to help Alice get over it too. She has this idea that we're fated to be together, and that it's only a matter of time before we're back together. I'm going to help you *show* her that you don't want Sapphire Falls, and that none of that is going to happen."

Hannah knew that the painful thump in her chest at the idea that she and Kyle were *not* fated to be together was ridiculous. Her grandmother had always talked about fate, had loved fairy tales, and believed in soul mates. Hannah, on the other hand, knew that things happened and people made choices—and mistakes. Hannah crossed her arms. "How?"

"I'm going to do exactly what she wants me to do— give you a second chance."

There's more to it, don't overreact, she told herself, but she still felt her heart flutter. Stupidly.

Kyle frowned. "And you're going to turn it all down."

See? More to it. "What does that look like exactly?" Hannah asked.

"I'm going to be the freaking ghost of Christmas past, present and future. Except that it's not Christmas."

She lifted an eyebrow.

"I'm going to remind you of your past here and show you what your future could look like."

She cleared her throat. "How? Exactly?"

"We're going to relive the good old days. And I'm going to romance you. And I'm going to seduce you."

There was that word again.

Hannah felt her breath catch in her chest and she struggled not to show it. But it was futile. The man in front of her knew her better than anyone. He saw it all in her eyes.

"And you have to resist it all."

Resist. Seduction. Kyle. Yeah, those three words didn't really go together for her.

"And what does *that* look like?"

"I ask you out, you say no. I sit next to you at the Come Again, you scoot your chair over. I try to kiss you, you push me away."

"Ah, the kissing thing."

Something flickered in his eyes. "Yes. With the pushing-me-away thing." He said it firmly as if to be *sure* she heard that part.

"Is that really the only way to do this?" she asked. Almost desperately. Because she was kind of feeling desperate. He was going to romance her—even *seduce* her—for *six weeks*? She wasn't going to survive that.

"Yes," he said resolutely. "This is what Alice wants."

"She wants us together," Hannah pointed out.

"But me pursuing you is the first step in that."

"She'll be disappointed when it doesn't turn out the way she wants it to."

"And that's on you," he said bluntly.

A long silence stretched. Hannah thought it all over, and she suddenly, completely, understood. "Why would you do this? Set yourself up for rejection and all of that?"

Those same eyes hardened almost instantly. "Because I've already been rejected. *I* have no delusions here. This is like the difference between telling your friend there's no such thing as Big Foot, and going out camping with him to *prove* there's no such thing as Big Foot. *I* know there's no Big Foot, so I'm not worried about running into him while peeing in the trees."

Hannah blinked at him. "This is like proving there's no Big Foot?"

"You coming home is Alice's Big Foot. It's not real, it's all in her head, but she needs proof."

"You can't just tell her that *you* don't want me and

don't want that future anymore?"

Something flickered in his eyes again, but it was gone when he blinked. "I want to be on her good side. Which means *not* telling her how I really feel about her granddaughter. Alice wants you home. I'm going to do everything I can to make that happen for her."

"While filling me in on the plan and telling me to resist it all?"

"If there was even the slightest chance that I thought you wanted to come home and these things were the key to that, I'd rethink the plan. But there is no Big Foot, is there, Hannah? There's no homecoming in your future."

Hannah tried to swallow but couldn't quite make her throat work.

Kyle nodded as if she'd just confirmed everything. Which, she supposed she kind of had.

"So, I will do what Alice wants," Kyle said. "I'll stay on her good side, and also show her that she needs to let go of this hope and move on."

"And all you get out of it is knowing that you helped my grandma?"

"And the keys to the clinic."

"What do you mean?"

"Your grandmother is holding this clinic hostage. She won't let anyone else practice here. A PT from Lincoln wanted to put a clinic here, but Thomas Jenkins wouldn't sell or rent him the office space he wanted, and the council denied his request to build."

Hannah felt her eyes widen. "Are you kidding?"

"I wish," he said flatly. "It sucks that your grandmother is the most beloved woman in this town. Everyone is willing to do her any favor she asks."

"Yeah. Like you. Willing to kiss me and get pushed away over and over just to show her that *I'm* the bad guy and you're the good guy."

"Yep. Like me," he said. "Though," he went on,

moving in a little closer and dropping his voice. "It's not like I think any of this will be a hardship."

Hannah swallowed hard. "No?"

"Kissing you? Always been one of my favorite things."

"Getting rejected over and over? Not really something you're all that familiar with."

"Nope. Just you. And like I said, already went through it for real so my actual ego won't suffer. As far as the town's concerned, I predict that I'll have plenty of cakes and cookies and…company…to comfort me after you leave."

Oh, she was sure that was true. No doubt that company would be female, local, brunette, somewhere between the ages of twenty-six and thirty-six, and a Tim McGraw fan. And she hated the little surge of jealousy she felt at the thought. She blew out a breath. This was completely complicated by the fact that the idea of kissing Kyle was far, far too tempting. And the fact that she wasn't sure she'd be able to push him away.

"The only problem would be if there *is* a chance this could work," he added.

"To win me back and get me to come home?"

"Right."

"You think you're that good?" she asked with bravado she was sure he saw right through.

He frowned. "I'm counting on *you* having made the decision to stay in Seattle based on real, solid, important things. Things that were, and are, real and solid and important enough to make you upend your entire life, my entire life, your family's entire lives, and leave this town hanging without the health care they'd been planning on." He leaned in. "You better be fucking happier than you've ever been in Seattle, Hannah. I mean it."

Whoa. Okay, so *there* was the bitterness and blame she'd been expecting. She pressed her lips together. He'd counted on her once before. To come home. Now he was asking if he could count on her to *not* turn his life upside down again. Finally, she nodded. "No worries. I'm definitely going back to Seattle."

"Okay." He took a deep breath. "Good."

Right. It was good. Mostly good. Pretty good.

"So, this should be simple," he said. "I'll flirt, romance you, ask you out. All you have to do is say no."

Simple. Sure. "Got it."

He looked at her for a long moment. Then stepped close, cupped her face, and kissed her. This time was sweeter than before, but just as hot. The feel of his lips, his hands, the taste of his mouth, the scent that surrounded her when he was against her…it was all so familiar that Hannah felt tears sting her eyes, and her chest actually hurt with the ache.

She rose on tiptoe, threading her hands through his hair as well, arching close.

His mouth opened over hers and his tongue stroked along her lower lip. But as she parted her lips, he pulled back.

He still held her face, and he was breathing hard, but he was frowning down at her.

"You're supposed to push me away."

Crap. Right. Of course she was.

"That was a test?"

"Yes."

"Well, I wasn't expecting that." She put her hands on his chest and pushed now.

He stepped back and dropped his hands. "You aren't always going to expect it."

"We can't come up with a signal or something?" she asked with a scowl. This was probably the worst idea she'd ever heard and agreed to.

She was strong, dammit. She'd kicked her addiction, she was healthy and focused now. And one freaking kiss from a guy who didn't even like her anymore, and she felt weak and vulnerable and…pissed off.

"A signal?" Kyle asked. He almost seemed amused. "Like I pull on my earlobe before I'm going to kiss you?"

"Yes. Or at least keep your damned tongue in your own mouth." She wiped her thumb over her lower lip, her gaze fastened—in spite of herself—on his mouth. Where her lip gloss now was.

"It has to be believable," he told her, seeming not only unfazed by her irritation, but by the kiss as well. "And I would never *not* tongue kiss you, Hannah."

Yeah, *long* six weeks ahead. She was hot and bothered by one kiss. One kiss fueled mostly by revenge, no less.

"And I assumed that since all of this was a big show for Grandma, that this stuff would be happening when she was around," Hannah said, wondering if there was an essential oil that would *decrease* libido. There were a few that could be used to increase it. But there were calming oils. Maybe she needed to carry around a bottle of lavender oil. Or bathe in it. Or something.

"Oh, no," Kyle said. "She's going to be expecting to hear people talking about this—you and me back together will be big news. This is for the whole town."

Hannah sighed. "I can't believe I'm going along with this."

Kyle's expression grew immediately serious. "You are because you owe her. If you don't do this, she's going to be heartbroken when you leave again. If you don't do this, she'll be hanging on to a false hope that you will change your mind. I don't know what you've said, or not said, to her over the past three years, but I'm not going to have her putting off any more surgeries or keeping other PTs out of this town or giving me a hard time about the women I date because she thinks you're on your way home."

"She gives you a hard time about the women you date?" Hannah asked. Stupidly. That wasn't her business, and she certainly didn't want to talk about the other women in

Kyle's life. No, scratch that...the *women* in Kyle's life. There was no "other" about it. Hannah wasn't in his life. "She does."

"Is that why you don't have a serious girlfriend?" Was her grandmother *that* big of a meddler?

"She doesn't give me a hard time until after I break up with them."

"What does she say then?"

"Basically, 'I told you so'." He gave a small smile. "Though she uses more words than that."

Of course she did. Alice didn't really know the meaning of the word "concise". "What about when they break up with you?" Hannah asked. She was proud of herself for not asking how many girlfriends there had been. That didn't matter. Or, it shouldn't matter.

Kyle drew himself straighter and said simply, "They don't break up with me."

They just looked at each other for a moment. Finally, she said, "I was the only one. You can say it. I was the only one who let you down and broke a promise."

"How about you keep *this* promise, and we'll call it even," he said.

"This promise? You mean pretend that you're trying to get me back and I'm resisting?"

"The promise to help Alice know that you're leaving, and not coming back to stay, ever," he said.

Oh, that one. She understood where he was coming from. She knew that her grandmother had never fully believed Hannah wasn't coming home. Probably because Hannah had never *fully* believed it. In her mind, she knew it was the right choice. Her heart was a different matter. But she hadn't known that her grandmother had been putting off her surgery for that long and keeping other PTs out of town. She had to help fix this. "Okay. I promise." But her heart hurt saying it.

"And for the record, I'm pretending to try to get you

back," he said. "But you're *actually* resisting."

"Yeah, I got it."

"I mean it, Hannah," he said firmly. "You can't let me or Sapphire Falls get to you."

She lifted a brow. "Yeah, I *got it*."

He studied her eyes for another moment, but finally gave a short nod. "Fine." He turned toward the door. "Let's walk. It's a beautiful morning."

"Walk?"

"The diner. We're having hash browns, remember?"

She sighed. "I came down to find out what you wanted to talk to me about. Maybe I should just head back to Grandma's."

"Oh, no." He pulled the door open. "Albert and Bailey both heard me invite you to breakfast and you accept. Albert's already told the entire diner. We have to show up."

"But I'm supposed to be resisting you," she pointed out. This might be okay. If she resisted being around him, she wouldn't have to worry about those kisses that were already messing with her head.

"Yes you are. In public. In front of people. Which means that occasionally we have to be in the same place at the same time."

This was going to suck.

"And we can stroll through the square. I bet you've missed that too," he said.

Stroll? When had go-go-go Kyle Ames ever strolled anywhere? They certainly hadn't ever strolled together. They had been a power couple even at age sixteen. The clubs she was president of, Kyle was vice-president. The organizations he was president of, she was his VP. It had become a joke that they were a set and you couldn't have one without the other. Not that anyone really minded. They got stuff done.

But if Kyle wanted to stroll as part of his plan to make her grandmother happy, then she couldn't fight it. She hated the idea that Alice would be heartbroken when she left. And Kyle's plan might seem extreme, but it had merit. Alice could be stubborn. And, as much as Hannah hated to admit it, there was a good chance that Kyle knew her grandmother better than Hannah did now.

So this would be, well, pretty much torture. But she owed them.

"Okay, fine," she finally agreed.

Kyle gestured for her to move past him out the door. Then he turned the lock and followed her out, pulling it shut behind him.

At the bottom of the stairs, he took her hand. Hannah hesitated for just a moment, still amazed by how good that felt. Then she pulled her hand away.

"Good girl," he told her.

She gave him a tight smile. Pulling away from him should have been easier. But it made her sad.

Chapter Five

They started up the sidewalk toward downtown without speaking. Giving Hannah way too much time to think.

Well, Kyle was her ex. Big deal. People had exes and went on with their lives. He was really her only ex. He'd been the first guy she'd ever dated and the only she'd ever slept with or talked about a future with. That was probably why she was having trouble shaking him. It was nothing more than that.

Except that it was painfully clear she wasn't over him. She wasn't surprised that she still had feelings for him. It wasn't like he'd done anything to make her fall out of love with him. But she'd hoped to be more over him than she evidently was.

And there was also the tiny detail of her ruining everything for him. Some of her feelings toward Kyle were absolutely guilt.

But as they crossed the street that put them officially on the main part of Main and at the heart of Sapphire Falls' business district, she had to admit that it didn't seem like she'd ruined everything. Kyle lifted a hand and waved at some of the passing traffic. He had a little bounce in his step. She wouldn't have been surprised if he started whistling. He seemed the very picture of contentment.

And why wouldn't he? He was practicing in the clinic in the town he'd always dreamed of. He was here with his family and friends. He was a part of the community.

Okay, so she'd messed up the marriage and family thing. And he wasn't living in a house he'd designed and built on the ten acres out east of town. But she hadn't ruined that. He could still have that.

Just with someone else.

And she hated that her heart ached a little with that thought.

"Have you seen your parents?" Kyle asked, seemingly out of the blue, as he raised his arm to wave at yet another friendly soul.

Hannah shook her head as they hit the final block to Dottie's. "Not yet. They're coming over to Grandma's for dinner tonight."

"Oh, great. I know your dad is eager to see you."

She snapped her head around to look at him. "What?" He'd talked to her dad?

"Your dad is glad you're home. He's eager to see you," Kyle repeated as if she hadn't heard him rather than not understanding what he'd said.

"How do you know that?"

"He told me." He stopped and pulled the door to Dottie's open, stepping back for her to precede him.

Her next question—or twelve—was swallowed up by a chorus of "Hey, Doc!" and "Dr. Ames!" and "Hide the tomatoes."

You could tell the time in Sapphire Falls inside of Dottie's without ever looking at a clock. From six to eight, the place was packed. The farmers came in for breakfast after feeding their livestock and before starting their other work for the day. All the main businesses in town, including City Hall, surrounded the square, and everything opened at eight. So everyone stopped here for coffee and news before unlocking their doors and flipping their signs to "open". At eight, the hubbub died down and the diner filled with retired residents who wanted to linger over their coffee and conversation. The place was usually pretty quiet by ten. And then the lunch rush hit, and the tables were again filled as people grabbed sandwiches and soup and shared any gossip that had happened since eight. Which wasn't usually much. So they'd rehash old gossip. Or speculate over what the next topic of gossip would be.

That was where Hannah and Kyle would fit around noon today, she was sure.

It was easy to take attendance of the dozen or so people in the diner at this time of the morning. There were three in a back booth who looked to be actually doing something other than drinking coffee and gabbing. The other nine were gathered around four tables that had been pulled together into one large one right in the center of the diner. Six of the nine had been meeting there for morning coffee and gossip since Hannah could remember. It looked like two new retirees had joined them in the past three years. And then there was Levi Spencer. Sapphire Falls' own millionaire philanthropist.

Levi Spencer was a hard guy to forget once you saw even a photo. Incredibly good-looking, charming, funny…he had it all.

Hannah stared a moment longer than was strictly polite, she knew, but Levi was a sort-of local legend. She'd heard all about him from Alice. He and his brother both lived in Sapphire Falls now, but they came from big Las Vegas casino money. Money that Levi spread around Sapphire Falls and the surrounding area like the farmers spread fertilizer. The money had a similar effect too. There were numerous businesses and charities and restoration projects in the area that had sprung up or grown, thanks to Levi Spencer.

He and Hailey Bennett were actually quite a pair evidently. Hailey had the crazy go-big-or-go-home ideas and Levi had the crazy go-big-or-go-home money. They both loved Sapphire Falls with a passion and they both liked to make a splash.

The table in the midst of the men was covered with coffee cups, two carafes, spoons and sugar packets, and a huge basket of fried green tomatoes. The basket had quickly been covered with napkins and slid behind the collection of coffee cups, but Hannah was sure Kyle had seen it. He'd likely been expecting it. She grinned. Apparently, they didn't want their doctor to see their morning snack.

Hannah could admit that the tomatoes weren't the healthiest option for breakfast, but Dottie made some of the best. And they were, after all, tomatoes. And of the nine men around the chipped Formica tabletops, only two were under the age of seventy. Clearly they were doing something right.

Kyle nudged her forward and she took a step deeper into the diner.

She'd known every person in here all of her life, including Dottie and the head waitress Vi—who had been the head waitress and had the same exact hair color and style for as long as Hannah had been alive. Well, except for Levi. But she suddenly felt shy as their collective attention settled on her. And Kyle. She'd purposefully avoided the diner earlier when she'd gone looking for coffee on her way to her grandma's that morning. She was sure everyone knew she was home. It was hard to even buy a new pair of jeans in Sapphire Falls without everyone knowing what size they were.

She'd been at the Come Again last night with Kade. But this...this was her first real public appearance. In front of men who were self-appointed guardians of the news in Sapphire Falls. Meaning, the biggest gossips in town. And this time she was without Kade. And with Kyle.

"Morning, everyone," Kyle said, pressing a hand against Hannah's lower back to move her toward a booth to the right. There was no sense in going too deep into the diner. Everyone would want to talk to them so they might as well stay up front.

Hannah gave everyone a small smile as she slid gratefully into one side of the booth. It made her feel less center stage. And it meant Kyle had to move his hand off of her. That simple touch, one he probably hadn't thought about at all, made Hannah want to cry. She had felt that hand on her back hundreds of times. It had always felt caring and protective. Now it was clearly an automatic reflex. An indifferent gesture.

It was going to be a very long six weeks.

"Nice of people not to get sick until after you've had breakfast, huh, Doc?" Vi asked, bringing two cups and a carafe to the table.

Kyle gave her an easy smile. "Everyone here is just so considerate," he agreed with a nod.

"You don't want to piss off the guy with the needles," Frank called from the center table, blatantly nosing into the conversation as if it involved everyone in the diner.

And in all fairness, you didn't have private conversations at Dottie's. Everyone just knew that.

Kyle poured Hannah and himself coffee and nodded. "You're catching on," he said without looking at Frank. "And it's only taken four needles."

"Slow learner," Conrad, another of the men, said. "I figured it out after one."

Kyle smiled and lifted his cup. His gaze was on Hannah instead of the gathering of men.

"Those cortisone shots are bitches though," another, Larry, said. "I got one too, and those are worth like three flu shots."

Conrad looked over at Kyle. "You gave me a cortisone shot *and* the flu shot."

"Well, interestingly," Kyle said. "Cortisone shots don't actually prevent the flu."

"And you bruised me!" Conrad said.

Again, Kyle didn't look at them as he lifted his shoulder. "You disparaged my golf swing."

"Your golf swing is atrocious," Conrad told him. "And I got the flu anyway."

"You got a sinus infection," Kyle said, sipping his coffee and smiling at Hannah. "Not the flu."

That smile made her stomach flip. But not because it was flirtatious. It was full of pure amusement and affection.

"Felt like the flu," Conrad told him.

"Sinus infection," Kyle repeated. "I know because I also got the pleasure of swabbing your nostrils."

"That was wholly unpleasant," Conrad agreed.

"For us both," Kyle said.

"Hey, it's better than other things he could swab," Frank said.

"I'm sure he's swabbed it all," Jerry, one of the newer additions to the group, said. "You have to practice swabbing stuff in med school, Doc A?"

"Can we stop talking about infections and swabbing things?" Vi asked, returning to the table to take their orders.

"Oh, come on, Vi," Larry piped up. "How many times have people puked in here? Stuff happens."

Vi pointed her pen at him. "One more mention of infections or puke and I'm cutting off the coffee."

They all groaned good-naturedly.

Hannah sighed, cradling her cup in her hands, thankful that there wasn't a single place to input anything because she wasn't sure she'd be able to get words out. It was just so...nice. They were talking about infections and puking and it was nice. Wow.

"All I'm saying," Jerry said, "is that Doc A has probably seen a lot of very...interesting...things."

"And disgusting," Kyle said with a nod. "Farmers are the worst. They hate coming in, so stuff is bad by the time I see it. And they mess around in dirt and worse. Lots of potential for infec—" He cut himself off when Vi pointed her pen at him. "Sorry," he said. Then waited a beat and said, "Lots of potential for...pus."

"No," Vi said. "No, no, no. You're not getting strawberry jelly with your toast this morning, Doc. That is also a topic not allowed in here."

"But, Vi," Kyle said, clearly fighting a smile, "these are

just normal, everyday things for me. I forget that they sometimes make people a little uncomfortable." He gave Hannah a wink and then said to Vi, "Maybe we should make a list of things that come up at my place of business that wouldn't be appropriate here. Maybe the guys can help."

And just like that, the nine grown men in the middle of the diner became a group of kindergartners who had been told they had to make a list of naughty words. All with grins as they watched Vi's reactions.

"Well, obviously there's shit."

"He'd call it something more official than that."

"Yes, true."

"What about snot?"

"He'd probably say mucus, right?"

"Hey, Doc, is it snot or mucus?"

"How about menstruation?"

"Is someone actually writing this down?"

"Vi, you writing this down?"

"Oh, fecal material."

"Definitely a good one."

"Ejaculation."

"Is that bad?"

"In a diner?"

"Yeah, okay maybe."

Vi looked down at Kyle. "Now you're not even getting toast," she told him under the hubbub that continued.

Kyle laughed. "Totally worth it."

That laugh. Hannah felt heat curl through her belly at the sound. And at the amusement on his face. And at the familiar taste of Dottie's terrible coffee. And the smells, and the faded apple wallpaper border that hung above the window where Dottie handed the food to Vi, and the napkin dispensers. Yes, even the napkin dispensers were exactly as she remembered them.

Hannah drew a shaky breath and sipped her coffee.

Dammit she was in trouble. She missed this place with an ache that was only growing. And she'd been in town less than twenty-four hours. She'd been with Kyle for only a couple of *hours* altogether, and she was feeling a similar ache about missing *him*. No, not similar at all. Much, much stronger.

She rubbed her head. She couldn't believe her grandmother had hung that much hope on Hannah coming home. And yet...she could. Why would anyone, least of all the grandmother who had spent her life in Sapphire Falls, believe that Hannah had found something better? Hannah's life plan had always been to stay here. Even before she'd fallen for Kyle, Hannah had pictured her life in her small hometown, living the life her grandmother, and even her parents to some extent, had lived. Her parents had had a rougher time, with her dad's injury and money being tight. But honestly, Hannah knew they would have never chosen anywhere else to live.

Yes, Hannah had to go back to Seattle. But she wasn't sure she could convince her grandmother that she *wanted* to go back.

This was going to be very complicated.

It seemed clear that the easiest way of handling being back here—and not buying a house and calling dibs on this booth...and the man across the table from her—was to stay away from the public places and social times as much as possible.

That could work. Alice wasn't going to feel up to much for a while, so Hannah would just lie low at her house for as long as possible. She'd make short trips out, she'd take Kade with her when she could, and she'd just avoid as many things as possible that would remind her of how much she loved it here.

That meant no races at the track, no get-togethers at the river, very little time at the Come Again—though if Kade was writing there, she needed to be there to keep an eye on him—and nothing to do with the summer festival.

"How do you want your eggs, honey?" Vi asked.

Hannah snapped back to the moment and the fact that they were now ordering breakfast. She looked up at Vi. The warm, friendly, familiar face that had served her more French fries than all other waitresses combined.

"Hash browns," Hannah said.

Vi tapped her order pad. "Got 'em. With brown gravy. But do you want fried eggs or scrambled? You always went back and forth on those."

And Hannah felt tears well up. Vi remembered her order. After all these years. All she could do was nod.

"Fried," Kyle said, glancing from her up to Vi, "It was usually fried."

"Got it." Vi made a note. Then she put a hand on Hannah's shoulder. "Good to see you, honey."

She moved off to place their order. "No toast for Doc!" she called to Dottie through the window.

That pushed a soft snort out of Hannah.

Kyle gave her a grin. "Some things never change."

The words could have felt like a jab, a reminder about the things that *had* changed and the fact that it was Hannah's fault, but in that moment, with the scent of bacon and toast and coffee swirling around them, and the sounds of the older men now arguing about whether it was okay to say penis and vagina in the middle of the diner, and those stupid napkin dispensers that had always been there, and it felt more like they were just reminiscing.

She nodded. "Thank God for that."

And she meant it. The unchangeable, the steady, the dependable meant so much more to her now than it had even when she was young and just sensed that she wanted that in her life. Now she knew how valuable it was to have things to hold on to when you were adrift in the sea of the-shit-that-sometimes-happens-in-life.

The accident had changed her whole perspective about

plans. She'd had a whole to-do list of plans that day. They'd even been written down. In Sharpie marker in her planner. And nowhere on that list had been an ambulance trip or a fractured C5 vertebra. She knew now that plans were no guarantee about how things would go, and that you couldn't make the universe bend to your will.

Kyle's gaze hadn't wavered from her face. "Some people find it boring. Or too easy. It's not very exciting around here."

Hannah met his eyes directly too. She had known this guy all her life. Maybe more importantly, he knew her. Did she feel guilty about leaving and not coming back? Yes. But dammit, she'd learned a few things while she'd been gone. Things she was glad to have learned. Like how to not get so hung up on perfection and how not to take things for granted.

"I guess it depends on your definition of boring and easy and exciting."

Kyle opened his mouth to reply, but just then Jerry got up from his chair to go the restroom. One of the other men gave him a hand up, almost automatically, as if he did it all the time. Within the first three steps, it was obvious that some things *did* change.

"Jerry had a stroke?" Hannah asked Kyle quietly.

Kyle glanced at Jerry and nodded. "About ten months ago."

Jerry was a lifelong farmer, on and off farm machinery, lifting and carrying and pushing and pulling...even a moderate stroke would change his life, and from the way he was having to lift his leg to move his foot and not trip, this was a little more than moderate.

She swallowed as she watched him. "Is it hard?" she asked.

"His boys took over the farm but yeah, it's hard for him to not be able to do all the things he loves."

She shook her head and focused on Kyle. "Is it hard for

you? To see people you've known your whole life aging and getting sick and going through things that change everything?" She knew she was treading close to a topic that was far too personal for her that she didn't want to talk to Kyle about. But his answer mattered. A lot. Maybe Kyle had learned something about how life changed in spite of your best efforts sometimes, and that it was okay to adjust your plans.

"Of course," he replied, keeping his voice low. "But it just makes me all the more determined to help things *not* change when I can."

Right.

"Hey, Doc, what time are you and Butch going fishing next Saturday?" one of the men from the table called out.

"Early," Kyle said. He glanced over at the men. "You want to come?"

"Thinkin' about it."

"Let me know. I've got Brady and Hunter coming over to collect night crawlers before that," Kyle said.

"Will do."

"You go fishing with these guys?" Hannah asked. "That's new." She liked thinking there were new things in Kyle's life. Maybe things he hadn't expected.

"I go because it's the only way Butch will go," Kyle said, lifting his cup.

"Why's that?"

"He had a heart attack fishing last year. He was alone and he barely got the phone dialed before he passed out. Scared the shit out of him. Now he won't leave the city limits without me."

"You specifically?" she asked. "Not just any friend?"

Kyle shrugged. "I'm a doctor. I make him feel safe."

That made some sense. But what she loved most was that Kyle was willing to do it. "But you don't even have time to dig your own night crawlers. I think it's sweet that you take time out to make sure Butch still gets to fish."

He gave a half grin. "I could buy night crawlers at The Stop. Brady and Hunter are doing it for me because they owe me."

She couldn't help it. She was intrigued. She didn't even know who Brady and Hunter were for sure, but she loved this peek into Kyle's life. His *happy* life. She wanted him to be happy. Needed for him to be. "For what?" she asked, with her own smile in place.

"Well, technically because I loaned them money to buy their mom a birthday present," he said. "But the purse they got her was like forty bucks. I don't think they can dig that many night crawlers in a summer. But they feel like they're paying me back. I'm actually doing it because I like that they're spending time together doing stuff other than playing video games or watching TV. Brady's about two years older than Hunter and has been hanging out more with his friends, and I know Hunter misses him."

Hannah knew she was staring, but…wow. "Are you making this stuff up?" She glanced around. "Did you plant all of this?"

He lifted an eyebrow and looked around. "Plant what?"

"All these people who love you and who you help with all this stuff that's so much beyond just being their doctor," she said frankly. "This is a little…do-gooder, even for you, isn't it?"

He frowned slightly, set his cup down, and leaned in. "You think I'm trying to impress you?"

She lifted a shoulder. "I don't know. It just seems like…a lot."

Kyle huffed out a laugh that didn't sound particularly amused. "Well, this is my life. So yeah, it's a lot. But I'd hate for my life to be anything *but* a lot."

She looked at him for a long moment. The thing was, this *wasn't* above and beyond the possibility for the man she knew.

He reached out and ran the pad of his finger over the

back of her knuckles where she had her hands folded around her cup.

"I sure as hell hope *your* life is a lot," he said, his voice a little lower. "Dammit. I really do hope that." He looked a little pained by that admission.

"You're not secretly wishing that my life is miserable in Seattle?" she asked.

"I probably should be. I guess no one would blame me," he agreed. "But no. I would hate to think that anything short of amazing got you to stay out there."

Hannah felt her chest tighten. There were lots of things about her life that she did like. But no, it wasn't *amazing*. Not really. Some of the moments, the people, the things she did were. But overall, that was not why she'd stayed. But in that moment, she realized she couldn't tell him that. No matter what had happened, or not happened, between her and Kyle, she knew it would hurt him to think she was less than incredibly happy. And even while that was sweet and made her feel humble, she also knew she couldn't hurt him with the truth.

Just like after the accident had happened; she couldn't have put that on him. Kyle fixed things. He took care of people. He couldn't have fixed that for her. And he couldn't have come to take care of her. So it would have only hurt him to know what had happened.

The stroking of his finger on her hand sank in at the same time she realized they were being watched. So, she pulled her cup away, removing her hand from his touch.

And she hated doing it. Very. Long. Six. Weeks.

"Hey, Larry," Kyle said as Vi set their breakfasts in front of Kyle and Hannah.

"Yeah?"

"You know that elbow that's been bugging you? Maybe you should ask Hannah about it."

Hannah stopped unrolling her silverware from the napkin that Vi had set down. "What?"

"Oh, yeah? Albert said she had some ideas about his back."

"Yeah," Kyle said with a nod, shaking hot sauce over his eggs.

God, even that made Hannah feel nostalgic. And she thought hot sauce on eggs was disgusting.

"You wanna take a look?" Larry asked Hannah.

"I…um…" She sighed. If Kyle was going to keep doing this, she needed to tell him—all of them—the truth. "I'm happy to talk with you about what I do for pain," she said. "But you should know that I'm not practicing PT."

Larry chuckled. "Well, I hope you're past the point of practicing."

All the guys laughed with him. Kyle just rolled his eyes at her. That was possibly not a new joke. She smiled at the men. "I mean, I'm not a physical therapist."

Man, she hadn't said those words out loud very many times. They sounded very strange.

Kyle frowned. "What are you talking about?"

But she addressed the information to Larry. "A couple of years ago, I got very interested in treating chronic pain." That was true enough. It was *her* chronic pain, but she'd definitely been interested in treating it. "I wanted to know what techniques could be used besides prescription drugs." Because she'd been an addict who was trying to get clean while still suffering from the pain she needed the pills for. She thought it was okay to not share *every* detail. "So I found myself learning about massage therapy and essential oils—"

"Like what Hope does?" Levi asked.

For a second, Hannah was flustered by having Levi Spencer's attention on her. That was ridiculous of course. He was one of the guys… Oh, who was she kidding? He was not just one of the guys. He was a minor celebrity and, okay, she was a little starstruck. She smiled, though she was sure she looked nervous. "Yes, I guess so. From what

Kyle and Albert told me anyway. But I also practice acupuncture."

"No way," Levi said. "That's amazing. Hope has done some massage stuff on me, but I'd love to try acupuncture. You setting up appointments? I have this spot in my shoulder blade that kills me sometimes," he said, reaching behind his back as if to indicate the spot.

"You get that from rolling the die at the craps table or pulling the lever on the slot machines?" Conrad asked him with a huge toothy grin.

Levi laughed. "I think it's from hoisting all those gold bars around in my money room."

Conrad thought that was hilarious. "Yep, that's probably it. I could come over and help you get rid of some of that."

Levi clapped Conrad on the shoulder. "And you know that just makes me want to spray-paint a bunch of bricks gold for you to come over and haul them around for me."

"Well, now I know they're fake," Conrad said. "I wouldn't fall for that."

"You would if I told you that *one* of them is real and you have to figure out which one."

Hannah watched the exchange, torn between saying *hell yeah* to Levi coming over, taking his shirt off, and letting her work over his muscles, and saying *hell no* to the whole thing. The idea of sticking any of these people with needles made her jumpy.

"Hey," Kyle said from across the table. He snapped his fingers in front of her. "Hey."

She focused on him again. "Um, yeah?"

"You're picturing Levi without a shirt on, aren't you?"

She was pretty sure her blush confirmed it without her having to say a thing.

Kyle narrowed his eyes. He didn't seem to find that funny. "You do acupuncture? Really?"

Oh, right, back to the big confession. She nodded. "I

do. And massage. And yoga and meditation."

"No PT?"

"Nope."

"Because of the big pain research study you stayed out there for?"

"Right." That had been part of it. Of course, she'd been one of the subjects of the study. They'd needed people with a narcotic addiction who were willing to try alternative pain-control techniques. She'd been treated with acupuncture and had been grateful ever since that it had worked for her. It was the best thing for managing her pain when it got bad. "I became fascinated with it when I saw what it could do."

"And you just gave up on the PT?" Kyle looked pissed off.

She knew that he wouldn't necessarily embrace the alternative medicines that she was passionate about, but why did he care? She wasn't doing it here. And she wasn't trying to convert anyone. He was the one who had told Larry to ask her about his pain. "Yes," she said. She hadn't given it up, exactly. She couldn't do it anymore. But she couldn't tell him that without going into all the details.

"I found something else I was passionate about," she said.

It looked like he was gritting his teeth.

Levi Spencer suddenly slid into the booth beside her. Man, the guy even smelled amazing.

"So," he said, giving her a big, charming grin. "Tell me more about the acupuncture. I'm intrigued."

"I can't imagine anything that you do that would actually cause a muscle strain," Kyle said, frowning at the man.

"Oh, there's lots of things," Levi told him. "There's writing checks. Making all those zeroes could technically be a repetitive-motion injury. Or there's flying my private plane. That's not as easy as I make it look. Or it might be shifting the gears in my Porsche," he said thoughtfully.

"You're an ass," Kyle told him.

Levi grinned. "And you're jealous. But don't worry, I really do just want her to stick me with needles."

"I'm going to tell Kate you're flirting," Kyle said.

Levi laughed. "Call her right now." He shifted and pulled his phone out of his pocket. He hit the number one on his speed dial and then pressed the button for the speakerphone.

Hannah looked over at Kyle, but he just gave her an exasperated look.

A moment later a woman's voice answered, "Hi, honey."

"Babe, I'm at the diner," Levi said.

"I'm shocked."

"Hi, Katie!" a few of the guys called.

She laughed. "Morning, guys."

"Hey, I was just calling to tell you that I'm being accused of flirting with another woman, but I don't want you to worry."

"If you were conscious and around another woman, I'd be concerned if you *weren't* flirting. That's the sign something is wrong."

Levi grinned. "It's actually mostly because it seems to be riling Dr. Ames up a bit."

"Ah, yes, the trifecta—you're conscious, there's a woman, and it will irritate someone else if you do it. Of course you're flirting."

Hannah could swear she could hear Kate's grin...and her eye roll.

"Oh, and she's an acupuncturist, so she can stick needles in my sore shoulder," Levi added. "That okay with you?"

"Honey, I'm just glad it's not a jealous husband wanting to stick his fist in your face," Kate said.

Levi nodded. "You're the best."

"I know."

"See you later."

Kate disconnected and Levi grinned at Kyle. "So, I have permission to get half-naked with Hannah. Are *you* okay with that?"

Kyle scowled at him. "Not even a little."

He couldn't have surprised her more. Hannah flashed Kyle a look, and then said to Levi, "Don't worry about Kyle. We're just friends."

"That's not what I hear," Levi said.

"Oh?"

"I know the whole story."

Hannah's gaze flickered past him to the men perched around the center table, watching them. "Oh." Yeah, he probably did.

"So." Levi looked back and forth from her to Kyle. "This will be interesting."

"I'm trying to talk Hannah into staying," Kyle said, flashing *her* a look.

She read it loud and clear—no time like the present to put the plan into motion. Fine.

"But I have a life in Seattle," she said. "So, while it's great to be home to visit, I'll be going back."

"Well, we'll see," Kyle said.

And damn, that sounded real. Real enough for her stupid nipples to tingle anyway.

Levi was studying them both. He finally focused on Hannah. "As a guy who came to this town to visit for Christmas and now can't imagine home being anywhere else, I think it will take a mighty strong something to pull you back to Seattle after being here again." Then he glanced over at the older men. "Did you guys hear that? Mighty strong. I'm sounding more like you all the time."

He got a thumbs-up, a couple of eye rolls, and several chuckles. While Hannah worked on not feeling like he'd just kicked her in the stomach. A mighty strong something?

Like fear? Like weakness? Like not wanting to hurt anyone any further? She looked across the table at Kyle. He was watching her closely.

But there was something strong that would make her go back to Seattle at the end of this visit—the desire to do what she'd promised Kyle she would do. This time.

"Anyway, I actually came over to talk to you about Michael Kade and his new book," Levi said.

"Oh?" That surprised her.

"I want to be in it. How can I go about that? Send him a gift? Offer him cash? Take him out for a drink?"

Hannah laughed. "You want to be in his book? Really?"

"Eccentric-playboy-millionaire-turned-small-town-philanthropist. I think that would be a great protagonist."

"You know that he writes thrillers, right?" Hannah asked.

Levi's eyes actually sparkled. "I know. I'm thinking I could be...a zombie."

"Oh, for fuck's sake," Kyle muttered. He scooted to the edge of the booth. "I have to get back to the clinic." He looked at Hannah. "You coming with me?"

Well, there was an eccentric-playboy-millionaire-turned-small-town-philanthropist blocking her way. For one thing. For another, she was supposed to be resisting Kyle. And that seemed like a really good idea.

She shook her head. "I think I'll stick around and talk about zombie millionaires and acupuncture, actually."

Kyle narrowed his eyes, then looked around the diner. "You all behave, okay?" he asked.

They all gave him wide-eyed innocent looks. He rolled his eyes.

"I'll see you later," he said to Hannah. And it seemed like there was a lot of meaning in those words.

The only problem was that she didn't know if that meaning was fake, for the sake of the onlookers, or if he meant it.

No, that wasn't the only problem. The *other* problem was that she didn't know if she wanted it to be fake or for him to mean it.

Very. Long. Six. Weeks.

Chapter Six

"So you do actually stick people with these needles?" Conrad asked Hannah, pulling his sleeve down and rubbing his elbow where Hannah had just done a basic massage with some of the oil she'd brought from Seattle.

"Yep." She held up one of the acupuncture needles. "They're small. You don't feel them like you do the needles used for cortisone or flu shots," she said with a smile, thinking back to the conversation at Dottie's.

"Can I touch it?" Conrad asked.

She handed it over and watched as the man tested the tip of the needle against his thumb.

She'd shown Albert a stretch for his knee at the grocery store yesterday and Frank some range of motion exercises for his neck when he'd stopped her in the bakery. Both men had asked more about the acupuncture so she'd decided to bring some of the needles into the Come Again tonight, knowing at least a couple of the guys would show up. They'd hinted—okay, they'd flat-out told her—that this would be a great place to tell everyone more about what she did because Dr. Ames didn't come in after hours.

Apparently this after hours' thing, where Derek served coffee and soda to the crowd that hung out after his usual closing time, was catching on. It had started with Peyton Wells coming in to study while Derek, Mitch and Andi—lifelong friends and now partners in the best contracting company in the area—worked on expanding the bar for the Come Again's upcoming brick oven pizza business. Now there were a handful of people who showed up with laptops and plugged in after hours, working away in the only public spot in Sapphire Falls open past midnight.

But meeting here made it easy to avoid Dr. Ames.

Reportedly, Kyle went to bed around ten p.m. every night in case someone needed him in the middle of the night. And it didn't surprise her a bit that everyone in town knew Kyle's habits and routines. For one, his patterns would be easy to keep track of. For another, he probably flat-out told everyone who depended on him—which was everyone—where and when to find him.

Though, as she talked to the men about their aches and pains, Hannah was becoming convinced these underground consultations with her were not because Kyle wouldn't like the idea of her treating his patients with acupuncture and teaching them self-help techniques. The men just liked the challenge of trying to keep a secret from him. Much like the fried green tomatoes. There was no way these men actually thought Kyle wouldn't find out about these clandestine meetings in Kyle's best friend's bar.

So she was going along with it. Because the men were clearly entertained and because she did believe she was helping them.

"Here, let me show you." She took the needle back from Conrad and watched as Frank leaned in closer from the table next to them. "Kade, let me have your arm."

Kade kept typing, completely oblivious to her conversation with Conrad.

She nudged his foot under the table, and he blinked up at her. "Can I use your arm to show Conrad how the needles go in?"

Kade looked at the other man as if just realizing he was there. "Um."

"I do acupuncture on Kade's arms to help prevent carpal tunnel from all the typing," she said, giving her friend a frown. He couldn't act tentative or the other men would also hesitate. "I'm sure he wouldn't mind if I showed you on one of the points we often treat."

Conrad narrowed his eyes at Kade. "Does it help?"

"It does," Kade told him.

"Does it hurt?"

Kade gave Hannah a look. "My work flow, yes." He'd told her he was at a sticky point in the book and really wanted to get through the chapter tonight.

Conrad frowned. "Just stick out your arm, boy."

He did. With another heavy sigh. Hannah gave him a sweet smile that she knew did nothing to soothe his irritation. She palpated along his forearm to find the spot she knew helped him most and carefully inserted the needle.

Conrad pulled back slightly, his eyes wide. "Are you okay?" he asked Kade.

"Mostly."

"What's not okay?" Frank asked, leaning in, clearly fascinated.

"I'm annoyed," Kade said. "Acupuncture doesn't help with that."

"That's not true," Conrad said. "I read something yesterday that said that acupuncture can help with mood and mental health."

Hannah looked up at the older man with what she was sure was clear shock. "You read about it?"

"Sure did," Conrad told her. "Google you know."

She nodded. "That's…great." She was surprised, but delighted that he'd been interested enough to look it up.

"Well, be careful about what you're reading," Kade said. "You want to be sure it's from a trustworthy site. There's a lot of crap out there. If you have questions you need to talk to Hannah. Don't avoid it because of something you read. Just let her explain whatever you're worried about."

Hannah turned her shocked expression toward Kade this time. She knew that he believed in what she did, but she wasn't sure she'd ever heard him defend it before. Of course in Seattle they rarely ran into anyone with whom her practice needed to be defended.

"Oh, I'm not worried," Conrad said. "I trust Hannah. We were just talking at the diner about whether or not acupuncture could help with," he glanced at Frank, then Hannah, then said, "certain issues. We were looking it up and I got interested in some of the reading."

"Which issues?" Kade asked.

"Just some more personal things," Frank said. "Other than pain and stiffness."

Conrad snorted. "Well, kind of stiffness."

Hannah lifted a brow. "Erections?" she asked directly. "You all were talking about acupuncture and sex?" Of course they had been. After that first morning with Kyle in the diner, she probably should have seen this coming.

"And where you'd have to stick those needles," Frank added.

Kade nodded. "*That* is a very good question to ask."

And Hannah grinned. She couldn't help it. This all made her feel good. Even if the older men of Sapphire Falls acted like twelve-and thirteen-year-old boys, she loved that they were interested in and talking about acupuncture in any capacity. She really did believe that there was a place for alternative medicine and healing in the lives of the people here.

She'd been cutting through the square the day before yesterday, when Ty Bennett had stopped her to say that his lower back had been feeling amazing since the quick acupuncture treatment she'd done on him when she'd been at the house to see Kade. Ty, an Olympic triathlete, had apparently had acupuncture treatments in the past. When he'd learned from Kade that Hannah was a practitioner, he'd even offered to knock money off of Kade's rent if her friend could get Hannah to work on him. As if seeing Ty Bennett without a shirt and having a chance to massage the well-defined back muscles of a world-class swimmer wasn't payment enough. There were definite perks to her job.

Albert had shown her how he could walk up and down aisle three in the grocery store, carrying a gallon of milk in each hand, without limping on his usually sore hip after she'd taught him how to use a tennis ball to work out a tight spot. Martha Biggley had called Alice to tell her that Martha's arthritis was so much better since she'd started using the peppermint oil Hannah had given her. Hannah had even had a chance to do an acupuncture treatment on Ruby that morning, when Ruby had complained of a terrible headache. Ruby had gotten up from the bed in Alice's guestroom reportedly feeling ninety-percent better.

Hannah couldn't deny that it all made her feel incredibly fulfilled. She loved helping people alleviate pain, and yes, there was definitely something special about doing it for people she knew and loved.

But it was also bittersweet. This was part of the dream she and Kyle had shared. Helping and healing their hometown. Treating people over the past few days had been rewarding and depressing at the same time. It was like getting a taste of your favorite dessert and then being told you couldn't ever have it again.

"And then you leave them in for a little while?" Albert asked, eyeing the needle in Kade's arm with more curiosity than skepticism.

"Right. It depends on what we're treating," Hannah told him.

"And you move them around?"

"Sometimes. A little bit. But mostly you just lie quietly with them in. Most people feel no discomfort and if they do, it's very mild."

Conrad scoffed at that. "I'm hardly worried about it hurting. You know what I did to this knee in the first place?"

She did. He'd told her twice already. "Yeah, jumping off a tractor and landing in the back of a truck probably wouldn't be good for anyone's knee."

"And that was when I was sixty-eight," Conrad said. "I screwed this thing up jumping off a horse when I was a kid, and then again when I was working for the railroad and jumped out of a moving car."

"You need to stop jumping off of things," Kade told him dryly.

Conrad laughed. "Probably."

"Heads up, everybody." They all looked up to see Derek standing by the table. "Dr. Ames is on his way in."

"How far away is he?" Conrad asked, his expression one of a little kid caught with his hand in the cookie jar.

"Probably pulling into the parking lot now," Derek said.

"You could have given us a little warning," Frank said with a frown.

"Yeah, I could have, but it's way more fun to watch Dr. Ames wonder why you're all here so late and you try to act natural," Derek said.

"It's because of you," Frank said to Hannah. "Gotta be."

"What's because of me?" she asked. All she could think was *crap*. She'd been avoiding Kyle for four days now. She had a perfect record. She'd *heard* all about him, and how amazing he was, everywhere she went. But she hadn't seen him. She wondered if she could sneak out the back door.

"Doc coming down here so late at night," Frank said.

"He and Derek are friends," Hannah reminded them.

Derek laughed. "Yeah, he's not coming down here because of me."

"Maybe he wants to see his sister," Hannah said, nodding toward Riley Ames, Kyle's little sister, who was hunched over her laptop at a corner table.

Derek shook his head. "Nope. Sorry. This one's all on you."

Crap.

"We should just get out of here," Frank said. "He'll be suspicious when he sees us here so late."

"No time to leave," Conrad said, glancing toward the door. "He'll be here any second."

Hannah reached over and removed the needle from Kade's arm. He rubbed the spot then straightened and focused on his computer screen again. Which was not an act for Kyle's sake. Unlike Conrad and Frank, making a big commotion while getting up and changing tables so they were farther from Hannah.

"Oh good, you're done with Conrad." This came from Tessa Sheridan, who had just come over to their table. Tess was another lifelong Sapphire Falls resident and the fiancée of the Come Again's owner, Bryan Murray. "I was going to have you take a look at my foot. I have some plantar fasciitis and was wondering if you thought acupuncture could help."

"It definitely could," Hannah said.

Tessa brightened. She started to pull a chair closer, but Frank hissed, "Not now. You can't talk about her needles with Kyle here."

"Why not?" Tess asked him. "I have to sneak around behind his back too?"

"Definitely," Frank said. "All this hocus-pocus stuff will make Dr. A nervous."

Tess grinned. "Why do you think that?"

"Dr. A is as straightlaced as they come," Frank said.

Well, that was true. "It's not hocus-pocus," Hannah felt the need to protest.

"He'll think it is," Conrad said. "It's better that we just keep this on the down low."

Hannah wasn't sure if it was the almost-eighty-year-old using the phrase "on the down low" or how adamant he and Frank both were about keeping up this game of don't-get-caught-by-Dr.-Ames, but she couldn't help but grin. They both looked like they were having so much fun, she just couldn't take it away from them. She winked at Tess.

"Maybe we could meet sometime tomorrow. Maybe around

ten? At the bakery?"

Tess nodded. "And we'll probably have to get muffins and coffee to keep up our cover, right?"

"Absolutely," Hannah agreed.

"Got it." Tess glanced around. "I'd better get back to the back then. I don't want to tip Kyle off that anything funny is going on here."

Frank and Conrad nodded in agreement.

Tess slipped behind the bar and through the swinging door to the kitchen, just as the door to the Come Again opened.

Is Hannah there?

Kyle sent the text to Derek as he stomped out to his truck. He hadn't seen her in four days. He wouldn't typically care—okay, he shouldn't care—except that he was supposed to be making her miss Sapphire Falls. How the fuck could he do that without seeing her?

She'd been doing what she'd said she would do—lying low at her grandma's. He knew from Alice that Hannah had been there every day, all day. They'd played cards, baked, and talked. Alice seemed thrilled. Which was great. But he already knew that Hannah had missed her grandma. How could she not? It was the town, the life here that she also had to miss. And *him*, dammit. And he'd explained why it was important that she get out and see people and do things so that Alice felt she'd given Sapphire Falls a fair chance.

Thought you said not to text you about where she is anymore, was Derek's reply.

Kyle started his truck. He was stuck with this guy as his best friend? Where was Scott when Kyle needed him? Oh, yeah, wrapped up in love—and his bed sheets—with Peyton Wells. And good for Scott. He'd wanted Peyton for a long time.

But he'd chosen a really crappy time to finally make it happen.

Kyle texted Derek back. *You better hope you don't come down with some terrible disease anytime soon.*

I feel great. Never better.

It wouldn't take much for me to start a rumor that links you and ED in the same sentence.

ED? I'm not familiar with that.

Erectile Dysfunction.

I know what it is. I'm just not familiar with it myself. If you know what I mean.

Kyle ground his teeth. *Is. She. There?*

Just remember, you told me not to tell you this stuff. And yes.

Kyle shifted into drive. It was after closing time, but Derek had been letting a few people hang around after it got quiet in the bar, and according to the rumor mill, Michael Kade was one of them. Kyle could only assume that, since Hannah was *nowhere else* in town, she was there with him.

Kyle sighed. If he walked through that front door, he was going to have to tell Derek about this plan to make Hannah miss Sapphire Falls. And Derek would assume that Kyle also wanted her to miss Kyle. And Derek would be right. The most annoying thing about Derek was that he had a scarily accurate bullshit meter. Kyle couldn't lie to him. Not that Kyle ever had much need to lie to him.

Until now.

And only because Derek would tell him that this was a really stupid idea and a dangerous game. And he would be right about that too. And Kyle really hated when Derek was right about something that Kyle was wrong about. And he had definitely been wrong thinking he could get by with kissing Hannah even once and not want it over and over again. Forever.

And he'd kissed her three times. Already.

Fuck.

Kyle pointed his truck for the Come Again anyway. Sure enough, Hannah was at a table on the far side of the bar. With Michael Fucking Kade.

She saw Kyle the second he stepped through the door. He gave her a simple eyebrow raise. She rolled her eyes. So Kyle decided to plant his butt at the bar.

It wasn't like he could avoid Derek anyway. And maybe he'd just wait and see what Hannah did with him here. He'd been working, of course, the last few days. But he hadn't run into her at the diner or the bakery or the gas station. He'd stopped by Alice's each evening after work as well, but Hannah had already left by the time he got there and didn't come back during the hour or so he'd hung out. But she also wasn't at Ty's when he'd stopped over there. Not in the hallways or the bathroom or the kitchen or even in her room, at least according to the ever-helpful Chase. He hadn't seen her, or so he'd reported.

So that left only one conclusion. She was avoiding Kyle. And he thought he'd been pretty clear that she wasn't supposed to do that.

"She's been in town less than a week and you're already up to your ass in trouble?" Derek asked, pushing a cup of black coffee across the bar to Kyle.

"I'd appreciate it if you could act even a little surprised," Kyle muttered.

Derek scoffed at that. "I don't blow sunshine up your ass. That's one of the things you love about me."

Kyle scoffed at *that*. It was true, of course, but he tried to keep from telling Derek he was right as much as possible.

"I wouldn't exactly call this trouble. I know what I'm doing."

"You're coming up with excuses to torture and kiss Hannah McIntire," Derek said.

Kyle couldn't stop his grin. "You heard about the

kissing?"

Derek gave him a don't-be-a-dumbass look. "You did it in a big picture window on Main."

Kyle nodded, suddenly feeling a little better. "That's the point. I did it that way on purpose. As part of my plan." He wanted to be sure his friend knew that he was on top of this. "The whole town is supposed to know and talk about it."

"To remind her that you can't do anything here without everyone knowing your business?"

"So it gets back to Alice, so she knows I'm doing my part to make Hannah stay."

"You want Hannah to stay?"

Well, that wasn't the right question. Or at least not the question he wanted to answer. "I want Alice to *think* I want Hannah to stay."

Derek nodded. "Because Alice wants her to stay."

"And because Alice needs to get over that."

"Got it."

And Kyle had a feeling that Derek really did. His friend was laid-back and no fuss, but he was insightful as hell.

"And how do you want Hannah to feel about all of this?" Derek asked a beat later.

"I want… I want her to want to stay," Kyle said, honestly. "Of course. I think everyone who comes to Sapphire Falls should want to stay."

"You know," Derek said with the tone of voice that indicated he'd been thinking about something and was about to impart his version of wisdom.

Kyle steeled himself. Because sometimes Derek really nailed it.

"I'm pretty sure Hannah knew when she decided to stay in Seattle that you were never going to go out there to be with her."

Kyle frowned. No, he'd never had any desire to go to, or live, in Seattle. Not that she'd asked. And he'd been way too pissed and hurt to think about going after her. He shifted on his seat. "So?"

"So maybe she was trying to just make a clean break. Maybe she knew that coming back here, or even having you ask her to come back here, would have been too hard to say no to. And maybe, if you weren't willing to go after her, maybe she thought that what you guys had wasn't really true love."

Kyle felt his scowl deepen. "You're an expert in love? The guy who thinks spending a major holiday with a woman is a deep commitment?"

Unfazed, Derek shrugged. "Look, Hannah was the perfect woman for you. I'll give you that. But…maybe that was the problem."

"Meaning?" Kyle asked, wondering why he was encouraging this.

"Meaning, on paper, you and Hannah were the perfect match. And that's how you both always did things…on paper. You write them down and cross them off. You had your whole life plan laid out, but in the "marriage and family" space, you needed a name. You saw Hannah's perfect hair and matching everything and her daily planner, and you immediately put her in that blank. And then, when things veered off course a little, you crossed her off."

Kyle didn't reply. He gritted his teeth, though. Because he was coming off as an ass here, and he didn't like that.

"And I don't think you can be pissed that she might have crossed you off her list too," Derek said.

Kyle felt surprise ripple through him. Hannah had crossed him off her list when things hadn't gone according to the plan? Her plan had changed, and she knew that he wouldn't change with it, so she'd found a new name to write in the "marriage and family" space?

Dammit. He really hated that this woman was making him continue to question things.

He glanced over to where Hannah and Michael were

sitting together. They were each working on their laptops, across the table from one another. They weren't talking. They weren't even touching. The guy was sitting right there and he wasn't looking at her, wasn't asking her what she was reading online that was making her frown, wasn't watching as she lifted her coffee cup and dipped the tip of her tongue into the whipped cream on top. He didn't even have his leg pressed up against hers under the table.

What a fucking idiot. Supposedly they weren't a thing, but that meant Michael Kade was a complete dumbass.

"You know, you were very insightful with Scott about Peyton the other night," Kyle said, swinging back to face Derek.

Derek nodded. "I'm awesome."

"That wasn't the word I was thinking of."

Derek tipped his head. "You two are just annoyed that I notice things that you don't."

"Why don't you quit noticing things about our girls?"

The second he said it, Kyle knew he was in trouble.

"*Our* girls, huh?" Derek said with a smirk. "Does Michael Fucking Kade know?"

Kyle hadn't even known until that moment.

No, that wasn't true. He'd known. On some level. Always. Fuck.

"Shut up," Kyle told Derek.

But Derek's grin said there was no way this was over. "Speaking of your girls, did you notice who's in the corner?" he asked, jutting his chin.

Kyle looked in that direction. He hadn't noticed anyone but Hannah. And what's-his-fucking-name.

He saw who Derek was referring too instantly then, though. And he groaned. It was his little sister, Riley. Peyton was also here, sitting with her friend Heather. And, for some reason, Conrad and Frank sat at a fourth table, drinking coffee.

"What's Riley doing here?" he asked. She was bent

over her computer, tapping away earnestly. "She hacking the bank or something?"

His sister back in Sapphire Falls was just what he needed. He'd seen her for about ten seconds at their mom's house the other day, but she'd looked at him, said, "I don't want to hear it," and had disappeared into the basement where she'd spent most of her teens, gaming and online. So they hadn't really talked, and that was fine. They'd talk eventually. And she still wouldn't want to hear it.

He couldn't have been more opposite of someone than he was his own sister. Of course, most of that was because Riley had done everything in her power to be the opposite of her good-grades, good-kid, good-attitude older brother. She was the other Sapphire Falls girl who didn't care about his opinions or feelings. Riley had always been way smarter than everyone around her. She'd been into computers from a young age and had oscillated between wanting to be a graphic designer and a video game developer. She'd headed for California the second she was done with high school and had eventually ended up in cyber security.

And then she'd ended up in jail.

She'd hacked some big Fortune 500 company and had gotten caught. She'd been released when they'd proven that she'd been set up and hadn't known what she was doing. But she was now having a hard time getting a job in anything related to security. What a shock.

Derek chuckled. "She doesn't have to hack them. She could walk in there, bat her big blue eyes and get Jonathan to open the safe for her."

Jonathan was the bank vice president now that his grandfather had retired and his dad had moved up to president. He was young. And Riley had a way with men. Kyle knew it was her flame-red hair and her tattoos and her piercings and her sassy attitude. Because Derek had told him that's what it was. Because Derek loved rubbing in the fact that Kyle's little sister was hot.

Now she had a record—kind of. That would probably really do it for the guys around here. Riley wasn't a typical Sapphire Falls girl, that was for sure. It came from trying to not be known only as Kyle Ames's little sister. But it drove Kyle nuts. He did not get the attraction to the troublemakers.

His gaze flickered over Peyton. Peyton was trouble with a capital T, and had his friend Scott all wound up. Peyton was beautiful and definitely had a sweet streak to go with her troublemaking tendencies, though. He liked Peyton. But he could never be involved with her. She was way too unpredictable.

Nope, Kyle didn't get it. His eyes landed on Hannah again. He definitely went for the good girls, the girl-next-door type. The Hannah type. She'd been a good student, a leader, driven, steady, all of the things he was.

They'd been two peas in a pod.

Until she'd done the most unpredictable thing of his life. He wasn't sure anyone had ever surprised him as much as Hannah had.

Shouldn't that have cured him of his attraction? Steady, man-with-a-plan, never-waver, never-falter Kyle Ames shouldn't still want the woman who had pulled his very carefully, tightly woven rug out from under him.

But seriously, how could Michael Kade just sit right there and not even look at her?

"Chin up, Doc," Derek said. "You're not the most whipped guy in town."

Kyle looked over his shoulder where Derek was focused and saw Scott had arrived. Well, Peyton was here. Scott was never too far away from wherever she was. Unless he'd been shot. And clearly it had taken him only a few days to get back in the habit.

Scott barely spared them a glance as he met Peyton halfway across the room. They talked briefly, and then

Scott turned back to join them at the bar. With a big, stupid, in-love grin.

But what really hit Kyle in the chest, was Peyton's big, stupid, in-love grin.

So, she'd finally come around. The troublemaker had fallen for the cop.

Scott took a seat at the bar across from Derek and next to Kyle. Derek pushed a cup toward Scott.

"Is that cinnamon?" Scott asked, looking up at his friend.

"Nutmeg, actually," Derek said, "though I'm not sure you, or I, could really tell the difference."

"So, this would be a…" Scott trailed off, intending Derek to fill in the blank.

"You don't know what cappuccino is?" Kyle asked. "Really?"

He didn't know why he was feeling surly, but he was. Maybe it was his best friend being annoyingly in love. Maybe it was his little sister being back in town and not acting even slightly remorseful about the things that had gone down in California. And not wanting Kyle's advice or help. But he knew it wasn't either of those things, really. Not that they were helping his mood, but his surliness definitely came from Hannah. Or more specifically, not seeing Hannah for the past four days. Which was idiotic. He hadn't seen Hannah for the past three years, and he'd managed to be happy and go through his life like a normal, patient, friendly guy. Just a few days ago he'd been determined to simply avoid her as much as possible while she was in town. Now he was crabby because he hadn't seen her?

"I just wanted to be sure that my friend who's a bartender is actually making cappuccinos and then sprinkling shit on top," Scott said, picking the cup up and taking a sip. "Not bad," he said after he'd swallowed.

Kyle picked up his cup of black coffee. "Spoken by the

guy who uses flavored creamer," he muttered. Scott's penchant for vanilla creamer was funny. Usually. Tonight, even that annoyed him.

Scott laughed and looked at Derek. "Maybe Doc here needs something stronger than coffee."

"Bar's closed," Derek said. "Coffee, tea, cappuccino, soda, water."

"Yeah, what exactly is going on here?" Scott asked, swiveling to take in the room again. "Frank and Conrad are out kind of late, aren't they?"

"They're here getting advice from Hannah," Derek said with that stupid grin that made Kyle want to deck him.

Kyle focused on his coffee. The two older guys had come in because of Hannah? Well, so what? And so what if, apparently, after Kyle had left the diner the other day, feeling cocky and sure that he was going to get his way on everything, she'd told the guys more about her massage therapy and acupuncture practice and had given them her cell number? And so what if Frank and Conrad had decided that they wanted to have a pretty girl stick needles in them?

Oh yeah, he'd heard all about it. From the other guys who had been there, from Dottie, from Vi, from some of the people that all of *those* people had told. The person he *hadn't* heard it from was Hannah. Which was the most annoying of all.

"What's up with that?" Scott asked Derek.

"They came in because they heard Hannah's been in here the past couple of nights. They wanted to ask her some questions but didn't want Dr. Ames to find out."

Hannah had been in here the past couple of nights? Kyle gritted his teeth. It was amazing the things that Derek did and didn't listen to. But Kyle wasn't going to give him the satisfaction of reacting to the news that Derek had kept *that* information from him.

Scott looked at Kyle again. "And yet, Dr. Ames is right here."

"Yep," Derek said. "Here he is. Weird, when he has rounds at the hospital bright and early in," Derek glanced at the clock on the wall, "a little over six hours from now."

Scott turned toward Kyle and rested his elbow on the bar. "Yeah, that is weird."

Kyle drank more coffee. He was going to need it tomorrow. And it kept him from giving anything away in his expression.

"But I guess if someone's in town trying to take some of your business away, you'd probably want to keep tabs," Derek said.

"Hannah's trying to take some of Kyle's business?" Scott asked.

She wasn't trying to take his business. She'd have to freaking stay here to actually do anything for anyone long-term anyway. And he wasn't annoyed by her giving the guys advice or by the guys letting their curiosity convince them to give something new a try. He was annoyed because she wasn't giving them physical therapy advice.

He couldn't dictate what kind of advice she gave people, of course. He did believe there was a place for massage therapy in pain management, but he wasn't as gung ho about someone sticking needles into his patients. Still, that was their choice. And he trusted that Hannah was as good at that as she always had been at everything else. Which was interesting—he trusted her.

Still, the whole not-physical-therapy thing did annoy him. A lot. Yes, massage and acupuncture were probably good adjunct treatments to physical therapy. Yes, the guys had both tried physical therapy and could do that anytime. Acupuncture was a little less common around here and was something new to try. It wasn't going to hurt them and it wasn't going to hurt Kyle's business.

It still bugged him.

Because Hannah was supposed to be a physical therapist. Next door to him during the day. And next to him in bed at night.

But she'd chosen another city, another lifestyle and, apparently, another profession. Pretty much rejecting everything she'd always planned with him.

Yeah, it bugged him. To put it mildly.

"Well, it didn't really start out that way," Derek said, leaning on the bar with both forearms. "It's actually kind of a funny story."

"It's really not that funny," Kyle said.

"Well, it's probably in how the story is told," Derek said.

"He has a point," Scott agreed.

"It was Kyle's idea that they talk to her," Derek said.

"Shut up, Derek."

But they all knew there was no way Derek was going to shut up. "Kyle wanted to show her that it's really nice to be involved in taking care of the people in your hometown. You know, kind of rub it in that she didn't come home to practice like she'd promised. But he wanted her to talk to them as a physical therapist."

"Because she *is* a physical therapist, right?" Scott asked.

"Yeah, but Hannah's not talking to them about physical therapy. She's telling them all about acupuncture and massage and immersion therapy and stuff," Derek told him.

"Immersion therapy?" Scott repeated.

"Oh, you'll have to have Hannah explain it. She gets really excited talking about it," Derek said with a smirk.

Kyle rolled his eyes. Obviously, Hannah and Derek had been talking about her new passion. That didn't bother him. Exactly. Though he hadn't seen her really excited about anything. And he wanted to. Hell, he'd like for her to talk to him about anything at this point. And this mild sense of desperation was making him nuts.

Derek went on, "She's very anti-pain medication and, well, pills in general, it seems. So she's telling our old guys with arthritis and gout all about how to change their diets and to use meditation and massage and other stuff instead. Which, of course, kind of rubs our doc the wrong way. Pun totally intended."

Her advice to the other men did not rub him the wrong way. Her not talking to *Kyle*—about her life and career and practice, or about anything at all—was rubbing him the wrong way.

Scott seemed to be thinking about all of that. "So," he said to Kyle. "She came to town, you sent people to talk to her to show her what she's been missing, and now she's telling them the opposite of what you've been telling them. And on top of that, they're sneaking around and meeting her after hours to avoid you."

Kyle just lifted his cup. He really wanted to lift his middle finger. But that wouldn't faze either of these guys anyway.

It wasn't the advice that she was giving—exactly. Then again, it was kind of a moot point. Where would these people go for immersion therapy? And yeah, okay, he was going to look that up. He knew the basics, but being the primary care physician in a small town of mostly farmers and manual laborers, he read a lot about arthritis and traumatic amputation and the flu and infections and other things that affected the general population. Immersion therapy and meditation and acupuncture were not in his wheelhouse. And he didn't like that either. She wasn't talking to him, but he also knew nothing about what she was talking to everyone else about. He didn't like feeling left out of her life.

And that was the stupidest thing of all. He'd been left out of her life for three years now.

Of course, he'd never liked it.

"Pretty much," was Derek's response to Scott's summary.

Scott laughed. "How long is she back?"

"Her grandma is having her hip replaced, so she's here to help with her rehab. I guess she'll be here for, what, about six weeks or so, Doc?"

Kyle nodded. "Or so."

"And Riley's back, too?" Scott asked. "When did that happen?"

Kyle felt his scowl increase. Speaking of women who were keeping him out of their lives and away from any details about those lives.

"A few days ago too," Derek said. "She's staying with her parents while she gets back on her feet."

"I heard all the charges were dropped," Scott said. It was no secret that Riley had been in jail, but Kyle had asked Scott about some of the legal things surrounding Riley's arrest and release, so Scott knew even more than most. He had connections across the country because of his work with a task force battling sex trafficking along the major interstates that went through the Midwest, so he'd made some calls and gotten Kyle a few extra details.

"They were, but it's hard to get a job in the computer world after something like that," Derek said.

"But she didn't do anything wrong," Scott said.

"Well, she did—it just wasn't her fault," Derek said. "She was set up." He grinned. "But everyone now knows that she's capable of hacking the biggest, most secure companies. Her skills make potential employers nervous in spite of her intentions."

"Got it," Scott said.

"So, she can't get a job," Kyle said flatly. He was far less impressed with it all than Derek seemed to be. "Which means she can't pay her rent or buy food or, you know, take care of herself, so she's back—living with my parents and doing web design until she can find something else."

"And she hates every minute of it," Derek added. "Well, except hanging out in here, because her family isn't here being judgmental and giving her unsolicited advice.

Until now, of course." He gave Kyle a look. "But Dr. Ames just couldn't stay away. I just haven't figured out which girl he's here for."

Riley hated every minute of being back in Sapphire Falls too? Great. Two of the most important females in his life were back in town, both hated being back in the town he loved, and were shutting him out. Perfect.

"Both," Kyle muttered, pushing his cup toward Derek for a refill.

"You could leave," Derek suggested, pouring the coffee.

Kyle didn't reply. He could. But that would mean not being in the same place Hannah was, and now that he'd managed to get in the same place as her, he didn't want to leave. Which was so pathetic, he almost couldn't choke down his first drink of the blessedly strong brew.

"You know," Derek said, wiping up a wet ring on the top of the bar. "I've decided that your plan with Hannah makes total sense."

"Does it?" Kyle liked hearing that. A lot. Because he was thinking he'd made a huge mistake. Already.

"Sure. This way you can flirt with her—which you never would have been able to avoid anyway. You can also kiss her—which you also probably wouldn't have been able to avoid. You can even sleep with her—which God knows you need. And you stay on Alice's good side the whole time. And you avoid heartbreak at the end because you know what's coming. You have a plan. That's all you really need."

"Right," Kyle agreed with feeling. Derek wasn't wrong. A plan was always good. But there was something Derek had mentioned that Kyle wanted to go into a little further. Or a lot further. "You think I should sleep with her?"

Derek shrugged. "I haven't known anyone who needs to get laid more than you do, man. And this *is* the woman who's basically kept you from getting seriously laid for three years. Might as well do what you can with her while she's here."

"I've gotten la—I've had sex in the past three years," Kyle said. Getting laid was such a crude term for it. He liked to think that he was a nicer guy than that.

"Yes, but you haven't gotten seriously laid," Derek said.

"What's the difference?" Scott asked.

Kyle really wished he hadn't. Because he wasn't sure he wanted to hear this. But there was no way he could walk away now.

"Seriously laid is that holy-shit-now-*that*-was-fucking-amazing sex. The kind that makes you feel satisfied to your fucking *bones*," Derek said, with an enthusiasm that was unusual for him. "The kind that can tide you over for a long time because you know it's gonna be tough to get anything that good again."

Kyle lifted a brow and glanced at Scott. Derek was full of shit. But Kyle found Scott nodding.

"Yep, I get it," Scott said. "The kind that makes you feel like you're totally wrung out. And at the same time makes you willing to give up food, water, and air to keep getting it."

Kyle looked back to Derek. Derek was nodding at Scott's words.

Okay, so Scott was in love. But Derek? "You've had this kind of sex?" he asked Derek. "You've been *seriously laid*?"

Derek nodded. "A couple of times. But the keyword is *seriously*. You have to be seriously into the girl."

"And that's happened to you a *couple* of times?" Kyle asked. He couldn't think of a girl that he thought Derek had been serious about.

"Well, I do serious differently than you and Scott," Derek said. "But yeah, I've been into a couple more than most. And that sex is unbelievable."

Scott nodded. "I'd never had it until Peyton. But yeah."

Kyle shook his head. "I've had that. With Hannah."

Derek laughed at that. Then he realized Kyle wasn't laughing. "Oh. Well, okay, maybe."

"What the fuck does that mean?" Kyle asked.

Derek looked at Scott, but the cop shook his head as if to say *you're on your own*. Derek sighed. "You haven't had that with Hannah, man."

Kyle scowled at him. "Excuse me? I was going to marry her."

"Right. Because she's organized and neat and on time and shit."

Kyle quickly went through all the cons to punching his best friend and the Come Again's manager. There were several. But he wasn't sure he cared. "There was more to it," he said tightly.

"I know you think so," Derek agreed. "But you and Hannah weren't ever…passionate. Like, I never saw you watching her the way Scott watches Peyton."

Kyle looked over at Scott. Who was, at that very moment, watching Peyton across the room and looking very much like a guy who was imagining her naked. He'd never looked at Hannah like that? Come on.

Then he really made himself think about it. When he'd looked at Hannah, he'd felt…affection. Satisfaction. Pride. Happiness. All of which were very nice. Probably the way a guy *should* look at the woman he wanted to marry. But had he ever looked at her and imagined her naked? Surely he had.

But in the next moment, Kyle admitted that if he had, he would have reeled it in. Not behind closed doors—or in the back of his pickup or on the couch in her parents' basement—but in public where others might notice? Yeah. Hannah was a nice girl. If he'd looked across a public room and had thoughts of messing up her perfect hairdo and smudging her perfect lip gloss and wrinkling her perfectly ironed skirt, he would have stopped them. He'd respected her. Liked her. Appreciated things about her other than her body and the sex.

But Scott was now looking at Peyton with a hunger that everyone in the bar could feel. And it didn't make Kyle think for one second that Scott didn't respect or like or appreciate her. He simply *wanted* her. In that primal, natural, she's-mine way that a man should want a woman.

Kyle looked over at Hannah now. She had her hair up in a twist at the back of her head, but there were tendrils escaping. And that made his fingers literally itch to pull more of it free. And then he straightened as he really took in her appearance for the first time. When he'd first walked in, he'd noticed her. Just her. And the man she was sitting with. But he'd been focused on her reaction to seeing him more than how she looked.

But now...

Holy shit. She wore sparkly pink flip-flips, short denim shorts, and a button-up shirt. But the shirt was untucked. And she'd missed a button. And, if he wasn't mistaken, there was a dollop of whipped cream on her shirt.

She looked hot as hell. She'd preferred dresses and skirts, so he'd rarely seen her in denim shorts, though they were a staple for girls in Sapphire Falls. Hannah had worn them from time to time, of course. Summers were hot here and they were far more practical than dresses for things like yard work. But when she *had* worn them, they hadn't been I-can't-think-straight short. And even if the shirt did have buttons and should look proper, it hugged her breasts, and that one undone button showed a hint of pink satin underneath when she shifted.

She looked a little disheveled, actually. And he knew without a doubt that he wasn't leaving this bar until he'd messed up her hair, smudged her lip gloss, and wrinkled that shirt.

"I stand corrected," Derek muttered.

Kyle focused on him again. "What?"

"I have now seen you look at Hannah the way Scott looks at Peyton."

Kyle frowned. It took denim shorts and spilled whipped cream to make him look at her that way? But that's not what this felt like. This felt like she'd somehow given him permission to look at her that way. By being a little less than perfect, she'd flipped a switch in his brain.

Scott cleared his throat and turned back to the bar just then. Clearly, he'd missed several minutes there. Kyle was sure he was giving Scott a look that mirrored Derek's I-know-what-you're-thinking-about look.

"Shut up," he told them, lifting his cup.

Derek chuckled. "I don't know which of you is more entertaining. Calm, cool, to-do-list Kyle being all grumpy and wrinkled and annoyed, or by-the-book, all-his-shit-together Scott being all gaga over a girl."

Scott and Kyle looked at each other.

"We really do have our shit together," Scott said.

"Absolutely. You're as calm and cool as I am," Kyle said.

"So why are we friends with Derek again?"

They both looked at the bartender.

"Beats the shit out of me," Kyle said.

But Derek wasn't bothered. He straightened from the bar and gave them a smile. "Fine. Just remember that I also know how to make you *not* calm and cool. Scott, ask Kyle who the guy is at the computer over in that other corner."

Right. That's what he wanted to talk about. "You bastard," Kyle said.

Scott glanced at the guy. "Why? Who is he?"

"He came to town with Hannah. They're even sharing a room over at Ty's," Derek said.

They weren't exactly sharing the room. Hannah had been staying at Alice's. As far as Kyle knew. From what Alice said, that was the case. But he hadn't actually asked, "what bed is Hannah sleeping in?" And he hadn't been back to Ty's except to change clothes. He wasn't even using the shower there because he knew Hannah might be, and he wasn't sure he could handle seeing her bodywash sitting on the edge of the tub. That's how worked up he was.

He hated being worked up.

"Why isn't she staying at her mom and dad's?" Scott asked.

"Seems that when she didn't come home as planned, Kyle wasn't the only one she ticked off," Derek said.

That was...true. Her family had been hurt and upset. They were okay now and had invited her to stay, but Hannah had insisted she wanted to be with Alice as much as possible. Kyle knew that because her dad had told him, not because Hannah had. And again, he was annoyed. This was ridiculous.

"And she brought this guy with her?" Scott asked. "Boyfriend?"

Derek shrugged. "We're assuming. Right, Kyle?"

"I don't fucking care." He really wished he meant that. He didn't think that Michael Kade was her boyfriend. He was sitting at that tiny table with her and seemed hardly aware she was even there. If he *was* a boyfriend, he sucked at it. And she hadn't mentioned him as a reason why she couldn't go along with Kyle's seduction plan. But Kade *was* the man who got to see her every day. In fucking Seattle.

"But you know who that is, right?" Derek asked Scott.

Scott looked at the guy again. "No, should I?"

"You ever heard of Michael Kade?" Derek asked.

Scott nodded. "Sure. The writer. He does thrillers and stuff, right?"

"Yep. And that's him."

Scott looked again. "No shit?"

"No shit. That is Michael Kade, the *New York Times*

bestselling author, and he's here in Sapphire Falls with Hannah for as long as she's here. He calls her his muse."

Before Kyle had to respond to that, Peyton slipped in between Scott and Kyle. And Kyle kind of wanted to kiss her for it. Having one of his friends watching all of his reactions—and commenting on them—was bad enough. Though he should probably be glad to have Scott around. At least the big cop knew a little of what Kyle was going through. Because it was clear that he was as wound up over Peyton as Kyle was over Hannah.

"Hey."

"Hey yourself," Scott said as he swiveled his stool and Peyton moved between his knees.

Okay, so what Scott was going through wasn't exactly what Kyle had going on. Scott had the girl.

Kyle knew he should just concentrate on his coffee, but he found himself looking at Hannah again. And thinking about the seriously laid thing. Sex had been great between them, but it had been pretty straightforward. They'd done it in a truck, on a blanket by the river, on a couple of couches, and various beds. They'd tried out some different positions. But there hadn't been anything even remotely kinky about it. It had always been…making love. Cheesy maybe, but true. It had been sexy. But there had always been an underlying sweetness.

But *sweet* was the last word on Kyle's mind when Peyton stretched up and laid a hot kiss on Scott that had Kyle shifting on his stool and shooting Derek a look. The bartender was watching with wide eyes. He glanced at Kyle and mouthed, "Damn."

Yeah. Damn. Because now Kyle wanted that. Not with Peyton, but that unabashed passion and can't-hold-back-how-I-feel that was palpable between her and Scott.

Finally, Peyton settled back on her heels, running her tongue over her lip and smiling up at Scott like he was her everything.

And yeah, Kyle wanted *that* too. He wanted to be the reason that a woman smiled with that combination of affection and naughtiness. And not from just anyone. His gaze flickered over to Hannah again. She was still staring at her computer screen, but it almost looked like she was trying too hard to seem enthralled with whatever was on there. Had she seen Scott and Peyton's kiss?

He looked over at Riley. She was watching the spectacle with eyebrows up. Peyton's friend, Heather, was also watching with a huge grin. And sure enough, when he glanced back at Hannah, her eyes had lifted from the screen and she was looking at Scott and Peyton. But her gaze shifted to him a moment later. And her cheeks got pink.

He couldn't actually see that from where he was sitting clear across the bar, but somehow, he knew it. And he felt a strange surge of *yes* go through him. She'd seen the hot kiss, but she was thinking about *him*.

Suddenly he felt a lot better about everything. Well, almost everything. He still hadn't seen or talked to her in four days. And she was telling everyone in town *but* him about her life in Seattle. And he didn't even want to know about her life in Seattle, but he wanted to know *her*.

Crazy. He was going crazy.

Scott and Peyton were heading for the door a minute later, and Kyle was relieved. He had too many fucking *emotions* going on right now, and they weren't helping with the one he'd best label *cock-swelling lust*.

"So she's been down here the last two nights?" he asked Derek.

Derek grinned. "You caught that huh?"

"And you didn't tell me."

"You're not supposed to care."

Right. "Well, that's not really working out."

"So I see."

"What the hell has she been doing for the past four days, anyway?"

"Are you talking about Hannah?" someone asked behind Derek.

Kyle looked around his friend. Mitch Dugan was helping himself to a bottle of water from behind the bar. His arms were covered in sawdust, and he had a tool belt slung low on his hips.

"Yeah. I've been…" *Needing to see her*. But that sounded stupid. And maybe creepy. "…wondering how she's doing," he finished, nearly wincing at how stupid *that* sounded.

"Seems like she's doing great," a female voice added to the conversation.

Kyle looked over to see that Andi had joined them.

"Everyone's talking about her acupuncture and stuff— hey!" She frowned up at Derek who had elbowed her after "stuff".

Kyle frowned, but before he could ask what Andi was talking about, Tessa Sheridan stepped around Mitch. "She's been out by the river just about every afternoon," Tess said as she grabbed the coffee pot.

"The river?" Kyle asked.

"Yeah, I've seen her out there walking and…meditating, I guess, when I've been on my runs," Tess said.

Tess was a marathoner and, unlike other people in this town, followed a pretty strict schedule. Kyle liked that about her. He also liked that when she came in to talk to him about muscle strains and other things that she listened and did what he told her to do. "She's been meditating by the river?"

"If I had to guess," Tess said with a shrug. "That's what it looks like."

What else did he not know? And why did it matter *at all*?

"I need to talk to her," he said, swiveling on his stool.

"Whoa there," Derek said. "She's here with Michael."

"So?"

"So, you'll be interrupting if you go over there," Derek said.

"So?"

"That might irritate Hannah."

Kyle didn't really give a crap. Her avoiding him for four days irritated *him*. Now they would be even. "I'll risk it," Kyle told him.

"Come on. Just be patient for a change."

He narrowed his eyes. "Hey, you said the first night they were in here that you made them leave and made it really clear that the after-hours thing was friends only."

"So?" Derek asked this time.

"So, you're being really supportive of Michael Kade being in here after hours now. For the past *few days*." Yeah, he wasn't letting that go.

Derek scrubbed at a nonexistent spot on the top of the bar.

"Why?"

Derek shrugged.

"Don't give me that," Kyle said. "Why the change of heart?"

Derek sighed. "His new book."

"So?"

"So, he said after he gets through the next chapter, he's going to let me read it."

Kyle stared at his best friend. "You're a Michael Kade fan?"

"Well, yeah," Derek said as if it was a really stupid question. "And he's setting this book here."

"Here? In Sapphire Falls?" Kyle asked.

"Yep. He's calling it Aquamarine Ridge though," Derek said with a grin.

Kyle grimaced. "That's horrible."

"I know." Derek's grin grew. "It's this funny, tongue-in-cheek, serial killer thriller."

"A serial killer thriller that's funny?"

"Yeah."

"I didn't know he did funny," Kyle said. The guy didn't even look that interesting, not to mention funny.

"He doesn't," Derek said. "This book is something new for him. And it's awesome."

"I can help you get Hannah alone for a bit." Yet another voice joined the conversation.

Kyle looked over to see Levi Spencer coming through the door from the kitchen. Bryan was right behind him. Bryan went to Tess, wrapping an arm around her and kissing the top of her head as Levi came around the end of the bar. Levi was helping finance some of the remodel, and it looked like they'd had a meeting of key people tonight.

"Yeah?" Kyle asked.

"I want to talk to Mr. Kade about this book. From what I hear, the loveable, eccentric millionaire zombie has yet to be introduced," Levi said. "And I don't mind interrupting them at all." He gave Kyle a grin, and Kyle knew that he meant it. Levi was one of those guys who got away with stuff most people couldn't. Yes, his money helped, but the man pretty much dripped charm. Even the guys around here were suckers for it.

"Excellent," Kyle said, sliding off his stool. "Lead the way."

Chapter Seven

As Levi Spencer appeared next to their table, Hannah found herself slightly tongue-tied for a moment. Again.

"Okay, Kade, I'm willing to talk about the millionaire being the sidekick." Levi pulled out a chair at the table and took a seat without invitation. "And okay, he can be completely alive. But maybe he could still be morosely interested in brains."

Michael Kade regarded Levi with an expression that was partly amused and partly exasperated. "The protagonist's sidekick is completely alive but still wants to eat brains?"

"I'm just saying that it might be worth talking about."

"Do you know what authors like even less than negative reviews?" Kade asked.

"Readers who tell them how to write their books?" Levi guessed.

"You got it in one."

"I understand," Levi said, nodding. "Regarding *most* readers."

Kade sighed. "I think I know my next victim."

"The loveable, eccentric millionaire?" Levi asked, his eyes lighting up as if being a murder victim was even better than getting to help solve the murders.

"Let me guess, you have an idea about how he should die. And it involves something about his brains."

"You really are good at this," Levi told him.

Suddenly Kyle was next to Hannah. He wrapped a big hand around her upper arm. "We need to talk."

Yep, she'd known she wasn't getting out of this bar without talking to Kyle tonight. As it happened, however, this was great timing. She couldn't listen to Levi and Kade talk about murder and brain matter.

She looked up at Kyle and nodded. "Yes, great. Okay. Let's go."

Kyle was clearly surprised. "Really?"

"I *hate* when Kade talks about his murder scenes," she said, shooting Kade a frown. "Derek can totally read *that* scene," she said.

"Derek can read it," Kade agreed. "But you have to, too. You know the deal."

Hannah groaned as she got to her feet. "Then no extra detailed descriptions of the brains."

"Oh, come on," Levi protested.

"That's a good point," Kade said. He looked at Kyle. "You willing to give me some insight into how brains look and feel?"

Hannah grabbed Kyle's arm and pulled him away from the table before he and Kade could make a stupid coffee date or something. "Over here?" she asked, starting for the juke box.

Kyle stopped. "Kitchen," he said simply. He took her hand and headed in that direction.

There were several people gathered around the bar with water, coffee, and soda, discussing remodel plans, but Kyle pulled her around behind the bar and through the swinging doors that led to the kitchen, without a pause. No one seemed to give them much notice. Except Derek. And he gave Kyle a wink.

Hannah wondered about that wink for a second, but quickly another thought occurred to her.

"Oh crap," she said as the doors swung shut behind them. "Was I supposed to say no to talking privately?"

Kyle shook his head. "No."

"But I'm supposed to be resisting you."

"Yes, but not avoiding me entirely." He looked and sounded totally frustrated suddenly. "Like you've been doing since our breakfast at Dottie's."

She focused on his chin rather than his eyes. "I haven't really been avoiding you," she hedged. She had been. Completely. Because that was way easier than pretending she didn't want his attention and pushing him away when he touched her.

He stepped close and tipped her head up with a finger under her chin. "You have. It makes it very hard to romance you when I never see you."

She swallowed. "Yeah, well, sorry if I haven't been making it easy for you to torture me."

She said it with a frown but Kyle grinned, his frustration seemingly fading. "Torture?"

"Like that's not your intention?" she asked, looking into his eyes.

"If you mean do I want to make it extremely hard for you to go back to Seattle, yes, I do," he said, his expression serious now. "If you mean do I want you to hurt a little bit being back here and realizing everything you've missed, I definitely do." His voice went a little husky and he leaned in closer. "If you mean do I want you wound tight and wanting it all back, absolutely."

Holy crap. She just wasn't used to this intense side of Kyle. Yes, he'd always been focused and determined and driven when it came to things like grades and taking care of his family—and hers—and accomplishing his goals. But he'd never turned this edgier side on *her*. But then, he'd never needed to. She had always gone according to plan. There had been no trying really necessary.

That thought jolted her. She'd never been the subject of his intense, slightly frustrated, determined focus because she'd been easy for him and fallen in line and hadn't needed any extra attention or effort? But a second later she had to admit that yeah…pretty much.

And she also had to admit that she liked the extra attention and effort. And that was really dangerous.

"You really want me sorry?" Hannah asked softly.

"I really, really do."

"Can I just tell you that I'm sorry?"

"Show, don't tell, Hannah," he said. "Just like with your grandma. You have to prove stuff sometimes."

Yeah, she supposed that was true. And she found herself going up on tiptoe, gripping his shoulders, and kissing him.

It took less than a second for Kyle to respond. He took over the kiss, his hands tangling in her hair, his mouth opening, his tongue demanding her surrender. Which she gave without a single qualm. He gripped her head and flat-out plundered her mouth. For nearly two full minutes. Then he pulled back, rested his forehead against her, and asked raggedly, "What was that?"

"I thought I heard someone coming," she lied.

"Oh?" He didn't believe her, she knew. "But you're supposed to be *resisting*."

"But I can't push you away if you're not up close to start with," she said.

He stared into her eyes for a long moment. Then he shifted and took her hands in his. He put her palms against his chest. She could feel his heart hammering and it sent a thrill through her. "Okay. Push me away."

"In a minute," she said, her voice husky. She just wanted to *feel* him for a second.

"God, you look…so different."

And she remembered what she was wearing. And that she had a spot where she'd dropped whipped cream. And that she had no makeup on. And that her shoes didn't match her outfit at all.

She stiffened, but Kyle didn't relax his hold. "Hey, I like it," he told her.

Her hand went to her hair. She'd pulled it up because she hadn't been able to wash it that morning. It had been a rough couple of days. She'd been having pain that she attributed to stress and to sleeping in a new bed. Kade had done some treatment on her a few hours ago and she was better now, but still definitely not the put-together girl Kyle would remember. "I'm kind of a mess today. I just couldn't...get myself together."

He frowned, clearly concerned. "You okay?"

"I'm..." She pressed her lips together. She wasn't sure how much to share with him.

But for some reason, she wanted him to know that she hadn't been avoiding him because she hadn't wanted to see him, but rather because she just wasn't what he would expect. Yeah, maybe that was a good thing to let him in on. "I have some neck issues," she said carefully. "Ongoing. They flare up from time to time and the last couple days have been a little rough."

His frowned deepened. "Neck issues? Like what?"

"Do you remember the car accident I had a few years ago?"

"The one when you were doing your last rotation?" he asked. "Yes." Then his eyes narrowed. "It was worse than you said it was, wasn't it?"

How had he known that? But she nodded. "It was. It took me a lot of therapy and I still have...issues."

"What can I do?"

Exactly what she'd expect from him. And it was sweet. But there was nothing. She shook her head, swallowing past the tightness in her throat. "Nothing. It's fine. I manage it."

"It doesn't sound like it. You've been hiding out for four days and you're wearing cut-off denim." His eyes tracked over her legs and then came back to her face. "Not that I'm complaining."

The combination of heat and concern in his gaze made her heart wobble in her chest. Denim was practically a requirement to live in Sapphire Falls, but she'd always preferred dresses. Dresses were easy. They looked nice with little effort, and they were easy to make. Once Alice had taught her to sew, Hannah had been in heaven, making her own dresses and skirts. Now she could buy her dresses, but she still wore them primarily. Maxi dresses were her favorites. So comfortable, and yet they gave the illusion of being a little dressed up.

But she hadn't packed much for the trip to Sapphire Falls since she hadn't planned on being overly social, and knew she'd have a washer and dryer at her disposal. And now she needed to do laundry. She hadn't been quite able to work up the energy for the cookie-baking session Alice had wanted to do *and* do her laundry, so she'd rummaged in her old dresser for clothes. And this was what she'd come up with.

"That's one way I manage," she confessed to Kyle. "I let go of things like worrying about how I look, doing my hair and makeup and stuff."

He clearly didn't totally understand that. "I can help, Hannah. We can check things out. I can get some x-rays set up while you're here. And we can go from there."

"I've had all of that," she said quickly. She didn't need Kyle seeing the fusion in her neck. "I've been dealing with it for three years." Well, minus the months she'd spent hooked on painkillers. That hadn't exactly been dealing with it. "I know what works. And sometimes just chilling out is what I need to do. Decrease the pressure and stress, just relax."

"Like meditating by the river?"

She shouldn't have been surprised that he knew about that. This was Sapphire Falls. "Yeah. Like meditating by the river."

"And avoiding me."

"Yes," she said honestly. She blew out a breath. "But that sounds worse than it is. There's just this pressure of putting on this show for Grandma, and I thought that I needed to be in a little better place."

He ran his thumbs over her jawline. "I hate that I made

you hurt."

And that made her heart squeeze. He did. Even that little bit. Imagine if he knew everything she'd been through and that she hadn't been able to tell him. Yes, he was hurt and angry about the breakup, but he still cared. And he would be completely pissed to know that there was something she had thought he wouldn't be able to handle. Kyle Ames handled things—all things—and he was very proud of that. "It's not your fault," she told him.

His eyes tracked over her face and hair. "Damn, I really want to run my hands through your hair. Is that weird? But I love this tousled look."

He probably couldn't have said anything that would have surprised her more. "Really?" Because if tousled did it for him, she could so deliver on that. Tousled was a really nice term for her new normal. Of course, she then had to immediately remind herself that she didn't want it to "do it" for him.

"Really. I can't explain it. But seeing you not quite perfect is…different. And…hot."

Oh boy. Well, not quite perfect was totally her. Crap. He was supposed to like and want the Hannah he remembered. Because that was an awesome mental barrier she could keep up between them.

Instead, she heard herself say, "Well, you're probably going to see a lot of my not-quite-perfect in the next six weeks." Because it was true.

Without a word, he lifted his hand to the back of her head. She felt his fingers on the clip she had holding her hair up, then she felt the clip give. The twist loosened and her hair fell to her shoulders.

He pulled his fingers through it. "It's curly."

She nodded, her mouth dry suddenly. "I let it air-dry yesterday."

"You always wear—wore—it straight."

"Yeah." She'd always dried it straight and then

smoothed it with a straightener. Her natural curls could get pretty frizzy in the humid Nebraska weather. He'd seen it curly, of course. Like when she'd been in a pool or at the river. But she would then always pull it up into a braid or ponytail to keep it under control

He was fingering one curl that laid against her shoulder. "This is so different," he said.

"Things change."

His pupils dilated and he took a deep breath. "Yeah. I've never had such an urge to go wild with you."

She sucked in a quick breath. She wasn't sure what exactly he meant, but the look in his eyes and the gruffness in his tone told her that he wasn't talking about her curls and denim.

He skimmed a hand over her shoulder, down her side, resting on her hip. "I was always really sweet to you."

She nodded.

"Romantic. Considerate. A gentleman."

She couldn't disagree.

"And look what that got me."

Okay, that hit her directly in the chest. "Kyle. You were…an amazing boyfriend. We were good, right? For a long time."

"Maybe. But maybe good wasn't all we needed. Maybe we needed more. Maybe we needed hot. And wild."

Oh, Lord. Hot and wild. Two pretty simple words with lots of meanings, but Hannah felt her stomach flip. "What does that mean?"

"I think it means that this idea to romance you might not be complete." He was studying her lips, and Hannah wasn't sure she'd ever been as aware of her mouth. "I think maybe I should do more than remind you of what you left behind. I should show you what you could have here now instead."

"But you don't want me to stay," she said softly. She'd said it before too, and she wasn't sure why she kept saying it. To remind him? To remind *her*? To hear him change his mind? The last thing she needed was more reason to not want to leave.

"I want leaving to be the hardest thing you've ever done."

Already there. She hadn't exactly left Sapphire Falls but not coming home had been hard. Very hard.

"And you managed it pretty easily when I was sweet and gentlemanly," he went on. Now he lifted his hand and ran his thumb over her bottom lip. "So maybe I need to step things up."

She didn't have a chance to reply or ask what he meant because he leaned in and took her mouth again in a hot, wet kiss that made fire lick along her limbs.

The limbs that he was now running his hands over. He slid his big palms up and down her arms, tangling with her fingers and then pressing her hands back against the wall behind her. She laid her hands flat on either side of her hips. It was a small sign of submission, she knew. It wasn't pulling him closer, but it certainly wasn't pushing him away. Kyle definitely understood. His hands gripped her hips as he deepened the kiss, holding her as he pressed into her, his erection obvious against her fly. Her body felt like it was melting at the evidence of his reaction. He stroked lower, his fingertips meeting her bare thighs, and she sighed.

He ran a finger under the edge of her shorts on both sides, and she felt the sensations shimmying straight to her clit. Oh, boy. It had been a long time. And Kyle had been the last man to really make anything shimmy right there.

He trailed his lips down her neck, licking a path that made goose bumps skitter down her arm. "Damn, you taste so good," he said roughly.

Hannah tilted her head back to rest against the wall, not to give him better access, but because her body was quickly losing the ability to do anything but just *be*. The wall would hopefully keep her upright.

A clatter sounded from the front of the bar, reminding her that there were people just on the other side of the door. She started to lift her head, but Kyle already had her hips in his hands again and was sliding her along the wall and around the corner.

"If they come in and I push you away, they won't see it here," she said, her voice hopelessly breathless.

"I know. So no sense pushing me away just yet."

Then he put his mouth back on her neck, and she decided that his ideas were brilliant. Maybe even this one about turning things up from sweet and gentlemanly to hot and wild.

He was cupping her butt now, and she felt herself arching her hips closer to his as he kissed her in that one especially sweet and hot spot. She'd never understood why that spot just behind her earlobe made her crazy, but it did. And he'd clearly remembered. In fact, five seconds after he put his lips there, she was grinding against him. She still had her hands against the wall though, so she could tell herself that he was making her do it. She was a complete liar, of course, but as long as that pressure stayed right *there*, she was good.

"Unbutton for me."

It took her a second to process his words. Her eyes flew open—the first time she'd realized they were shut—and she looked up at him. "What?"

"Unbutton." His hot gaze dropped to the front of her shirt.

Why couldn't *he* unbutton her? "You do it," she urged. Okay, that was definitely the opposite of pushing him away, but she didn't care. Every inch of her skin seemed to be anticipating his touch, *craving* it.

"*You* do it," he said firmly.

She swallowed. Okay, actually, *that* was the opposite of pushing him away. Not just letting him touch her, but encouraging it, *helping* him do it.

Was he testing her? Was he trying to see what she would do?

Well, had he not kissed her behind her ear, she might have kept enough sense to try, even halfheartedly, to return to the plan of resisting him. But he *had* kissed her there and so this was all his fault.

She lifted her fingers and undid her buttons quickly. She'd buttoned them up wrong anyway, she realized. As the buttons parted and Kyle's expression grew more and more heated, she remembered she was wearing a pink bra with light green panties. They didn't match at all, and she wondered briefly if Kyle was going to find that out. And if he'd realize that she'd *always* worn matching panties and bras.

She liked when things matched. Back when she could expend energy on things like that. She hadn't considered herself uptight or Type A, but she had been. Definitely. But nothing in her house growing up had matched. Their furniture had been a hodgepodge of new and old. They hadn't had matching towel sets. Their pots and pans had been a mix of things they'd gotten on sale or had been given clear back when her parents had gotten married. Even the storage containers in the fridge had been a mix of tops and bottoms. They were small things that didn't really matter, but they'd somehow seemed like a lack of organization, or caring, to Hannah. And truthfully, it *had* been a lack of caring. She got that now. Matching up the lids on the Tupperware was an unimportant detail when you were worried about paying the electric bill to keep the fridge on in the first place.

As the final button parted, she went one step further and spread the two sides apart.

Frankly, if Kyle didn't like a pink bra with green panties, she didn't really care.

"Holy shit." He traced a finger along the upper edge of

the bra, heating her skin with that single touch. "You're so fucking gorgeous."

Hannah felt her eyes widen. It was a heartfelt, and hot, sentiment…that he'd never said before. He'd told her she was beautiful. He'd probably even used the word gorgeous. But he'd never said *fucking* gorgeous. He'd never said *fucking* to her period. Not even if he was swearing about something else entirely.

He was right, he'd always been sweet and considerate of her. He'd given a mischievous look here and there. He'd kissed her with heat. He'd let his hands wander at times he shouldn't—under the edge of a tablecloth or in a corner where they might get caught—but he'd always kept himself just this side of indecent. And while he'd certainly seen and touched every inch of her, they'd never really talked about it. It had been a lot of sighs and moans, but very little actual words.

He slipped the tip of his finger into one bra cup and tugged gently. "Unhook."

Hannah couldn't believe they were doing this. She was going to unhook her bra in front of him, in the Come Again kitchen, with the very bright lights above and the crowd of people only a few feet away?

But she was already reaching behind her back. They were around the corner. She'd have time to pull her shirt closed if someone came in.

The hooks slid free and the bra went slack. Kyle tugged again, pulling it away from her breasts.

Her nipples were already hard, but they puckered further the instant his gaze hit them.

"Oh, damn, yes." He ran the pad of his thumb over one of them, and Hannah gasped softly, her thighs squeezing together as heat and want shot straight to her core.

They'd mostly had sex in the dark while they'd lived in Sapphire Falls. They'd been teenagers after all. But when they'd gone off to college and had two dorm rooms to use however they wanted to—within reason—they'd done it with the lights on and in broad daylight.

But this felt different.

Because in the past, they'd had sex as most people did most things they thought they were going to get to do over and over again for the rest of their lives. They'd enjoyed it, but they'd also taken it for granted.

He'd never studied her before. He'd never licked her nipple and then pinched it gently while watching her carefully for every reaction. He'd also never said, "Playing with your nipples always made you so wet."

She sucked in a breath. Apparently talking about it also did. He'd never talked about her being wet before. He'd *felt* it, of course. He knew how to make it happen. But they'd never talked about it.

"Say it," he told her, tugging gently on one nipple. "Tell me you're wet for me."

"I'm—" She cleared her throat. "I'm very wet for you." Wow, it was crazy how hot it was saying it out loud herself.

He kissed his way to the other breast and licked and sucked there for a moment, making her squirm against the wall.

Then she heard herself say, "But I thought this was all about showing, not telling."

She froze for a second. She couldn't believe those words had come from her mouth.

Similarly, Kyle stopped moving, then slowly looked up at her. And she was really glad she'd said it. That look in his eyes was worth it.

Okay, she wasn't sure exactly what had gotten into her, but it was time for him to be a little shocked and hot too. She kept her eyes on his as she popped open the button on her shorts and slid the zipper down.

Kyle seemed to be holding his breath as he watched her part the front panels, showing off the, yes, green panties. It was so hot watching him watch her, and she wondered why they'd never done this before and why they were doing it now and if they could maybe go somewhere else and *really* do it. She was shocked that she wanted Kyle to watch her touch herself, but she so did.

She slid her hand into the front of the panties, then lower, her middle finger gliding over her clit. She gave a little shiver. Then kept going. She slid her finger through the wet heat he'd caused, feeling the insane urge to lie down on the tile floor and spread her legs for him. Who cared who was on the other side of the swinging door? Who cared that the floor in the kitchen of a food service business was the last place she would have ever imagined lying down? Who cared that this was Kyle and she was supposed to be resisting him—for some admittedly good reasons—and that getting naked for him was probably the opposite of that?

"Definitely wet," she told him, her voice barely audible.

There was a pause where there was no sound, no motion, no nothing but hot anticipation in the air. Then he growled and took her face in his hands and kissed her. And she felt tears pricking at the back of her eyes because even in the midst of the intense desire she saw in him, *felt* in him, he was still holding her head gently, clearly remembering her neck.

She found herself gripping the front of his shirt, her whole body pulsing with need and wanting his hand where hers had been between her legs so badly, she was on the verge of telling him.

"Oh, yeah, we're definitely stepping this up a notch," he said against her mouth, his voice like gravel.

Hannah felt the urge to cry, and laugh, and moan all at once. This was torture, for sure. And he intended it to be. But he wasn't immune. He was tortured too, and for some reason that made her feel horrible and wonderful at the same time.

Finally, Kyle dropped his hands and pulled in a deep

breath. "Okay." He seemed to take a second to gather himself, then he said, "Now, push me away."

Those had to be the last words she had been expecting. "What?"

"You still have to resist…at least in the end. We can't forget that."

Right. They couldn't forget that. In the end. When this all ended.

She forced a smile. She was hot and tingly and confused and disappointed and pissed off. She flattened her hands on his chest and pushed, though she definitely didn't want to. Then watched him as she re-hooked her bra, re-buttoned her shorts and shirt. He watched every bit of it, looking a little like someone who was starving and was watching someone wrap up a gourmet meal to save for later.

"Tomorrow night. You need to be here," he said.

"Here?"

"At the Come Again."

"But—"

"Hannah," he cut her off. "This thing," he gestured between them, "needs to be public for the plan to work." He paused and added, "At least some of it."

And her stupid heart flipped at the way his voice got a little huskier when he said those last five words.

"If your pain is an issue, let me know, I'm happy to prescribe something."

And that was like dumping ice-cold water on her head. She knew he'd be happy to give her whatever he thought she needed. He might even insist on it. Because Kyle loved to fix things and in his mind, that was what medication was for. He'd hate the idea that she was right there, hurting, and he wasn't able to do anything for her.

She needed to suck it up. "Fine."

"Okay, I'll see you then."

"Okay."

He took a huge step back, shoved a hand through his hair, gave her one last look—which focused on her mouth and made heat and electricity shoot clear to her toes. "And now you need to head back into the bar and act like we just argued."

Hannah looked at the door and back to him. "What?"

"You're not supposed to be letting me do the things I just did, remember?"

Like kissing her and touching her and unbuttoning her shirt and… She cleared her throat. "Yeah, I remember."

"Then get your pissed-off face on," he told her, gesturing at the door.

"You know, maybe we really should argue," she said. "Instead of…" She waved her hand in the direction of the wall where he'd kissed her and partially undressed her and—okay, so she'd partially undressed herself, but still.

"Okay," he said agreeably. Maybe too agreeably. "What should we argue about?"

They had honestly never argued. At least not about anything major or with any real heat. They'd gotten along famously, because they'd been on the same page about nearly every topic of any importance.

"How about I tell you that I don't like Kade's books?" Kyle asked.

She actually snorted at that. "Yeah, me either."

He looked surprised for a moment, then gave a half smile. "Okay, so not that. How about how I think acupuncture is a little hokey?"

She shrugged. "You're not the only one. I can get you some articles."

"That doesn't tick you off?" he asked.

"I don't need to justify it to anyone," she said honestly. "I know it helps me and the people I work with, and that's all that really matters."

"But I could tell people that I think the acupuncture is hokey," he commented. "My opinion and recommendations mean a lot around here. If I tell them not to do it, they won't."

She crossed her arms. He was trying to start a fight. But she knew there was truth behind what he was saying. "You mean like Frank and Conrad?" she asked.

"Frank and Conrad are only two of my patients. And they don't listen to *anyone,* so don't get your hopes up for somehow changing their habits."

Well, now she *was* a little irritated. "I find that when you do things that actually *help* people, they tend to stick with it. Pain isn't always something you can fix or heal completely, but there are definite ways to manage it."

His eyes narrowed and he took a step forward. "Are you challenging me?"

She lifted her chin. "I don't know, maybe." She had never done that before either. She'd...gone along. Ugh. She hadn't really thought of it that way before, but yeah, she'd definitely gone along. No wonder Kyle had this thing about control. He'd always had it. But the truth was, Kyle Ames was not always right. No matter if he believed that or not.

"So, you're saying that you can convince Frank and Conrad to stick with *your* plan and it will help them feel better?" Kyle clarified.

He didn't know how into it the men already were, but she didn't mind having a slight advantage. She nodded. "Yeah, that's what I'm saying."

Kyle gave her a grin. "You're on."

Hannah managed to stomp out into the bar as if she was annoyed, but she had to admit that she felt more confused than anything. Kyle had rattled loose some major emotions, and annoyance was a very mild one, about seventh down the list. She felt a little excitement at the idea of helping Frank and Conrad, actually. Some of her advice had already helped them, but she hadn't even started on the acupuncture yet.

And then there was something...fun...about shaking up

Kyle's preconceived notions about, well, everything. Especially her. She hadn't felt put together for three days, but suddenly that wasn't bothering her at all. He liked her hair wild and curly and certainly didn't seem to mind the denim shorts. At all.

Which brought up the number one emotion on her list. Lust. Pure and simple. She wanted more of his hands and his mouth and his...other stuff.

So she'd been back in Sapphire Falls for six days. Only five weeks and one day to go.

Chapter Eight

"Not cowboys. Farmers," Hannah said to Kade as she flipped the last page of his latest chapter.

"What?"

"You're calling the guys cowboys. They're not cowboys here. They're farmers."

"There's a difference?"

Hannah rolled her eyes. "Well, yeah. The cowboys are out in western Nebraska. Wyoming. Montana."

"Texas."

"Texas," she agreed. "You seem intent on writing characters that should be Texans. Why don't you just move your setting?"

"Because I like Aquamarine Ridge, Nebraska," Kade said.

They were on the bed in Kade's rooms at Ty's place. Hannah was propped up on pillows against the wrought iron headboard, and Kade was facing her, leaning on pillows stacked against the footboard.

Hannah shivered. That name was more horrible every time she heard it. "Well, then you can't call them cowboys."

"You still haven't explained the difference."

"Cowboys are more like ranchers. They raise cattle and sheep. They have ranches. Farmers live on farms and raise crops…and some animals," she said. "And they drive trucks. And tractors."

She winced as she finished, knowing exactly what Kade was going to say next.

"So there are no horses around here?"

She sighed. "Yes, there are."

"And cattle…those are cows. There are no cows here?"

"There are definitely cows here," she admitted.

"And I didn't realize that cowboys don't drive trucks."

"I'm sure that they do drive trucks sometimes," Hannah said.

"So…"

"Just shut up." Hannah rolled her eyes at his smirk. "In the middle of the country and this state, where the land is better for crops, they're farmers. If you want cowboys, you need to move your stupid book."

"I'm not moving my book."

"Please," she tried.

"No way. That gazebo is the perfect place for them to find the first body."

Hannah shuddered. "I can't believe you're bringing a psychotic serial killer to town and offing beloved pillars of the community."

"I haven't decided if he'll be a serial killer," Kade told her.

"But you're leaning that way."

"We'll see how the good citizens of Sapphire Falls treat their author-in-residence."

"Author-in-residence," Hannah repeated with a snort.

"That's what Hailey Bennett called me in her email."

Hannah looked up at him. "Excuse me?"

"Hailey was very excited about it. She wanted to put me up on the website."

"You're on the Sapphire Falls website?"

"No." Kade frowned. "Mark didn't want some big press release sending a bunch of people running to Sapphire Falls where there are only two cops and no one locks any doors or keeps any secrets. Like where their author-in-residence is working, having breakfast, and sleeping at night."

Hannah laughed. "He was worried about a stalker showing up here?"

"Hey, I could be stalked," Kade said. "I've gotten really nasty letters and emails. And two death threats. And the police force in Laramie thought they had a guy who was copycatting *Blood Peril*." He said it with the pride of a new father who'd just witnessed his child's first steps.

Hannah gave him her you're-not-in-touch-with-reality look. "Yes. They thought they did. For about five minutes. Because the one deputy had just read the book, and the guy they found had a roll of mints in his pocket and died— sadly, by the way—from carbon monoxide poisoning. But there was no foul play. Or psychotic basketball coach. Or voodoo priestess. And that was Wyoming." Sometimes Kade forgot that people dying in real life was sad and often tragic.

"You don't think people kill each other in Wyoming?" Kade asked, whipping his phone out again.

He was going to Google it. Hannah's hand shot out to grab his phone. "Please don't remind me that I sometimes think you're a bad bagel away from becoming one of your sociopathic characters," she said.

"All I'm saying is that letting people know I'm staying here in Sapphire Falls could be dangerous."

She nodded. "Okay. You might be right. You do have a rabid fan base." Who had put him on all of the bestseller lists several times. Even if Hannah didn't get it.

Kade often reminded her of how cool she should think it was to be the best friend of someone so famous. After which, she would remind him that she really knew far too much about him to be impressed anymore. And it had nothing to do with his addiction to narcotics and everything to do with the fact that he listened to Elvis when he wrote his creepy, gory novels and ate oranges like he was trying to ward off scurvy. Not that she had anything against Elvis or oranges. Actually, she thought it was kind of sacrilegious to kill people off while listening to the King. Kade said that all that optimism and cheese and happiness in the songs made him homicidal. And the oranges...well, oranges were fine. But he ate four of them a day. That was just weird.

"Hailey said they'd keep it on the down low," Kade said with a grin.

"You saw Hailey?"

"She stopped over here yesterday. With Levi."

Well, of course they'd stopped over. "And let me guess, you're putting the guy in your book." Levi and Hailey together? No one could resist that.

"I'm basing a minor secondary character on him," Kade agreed. "But he wants a bigger part."

Hannah grinned. "Well, watch yourself. Those two are downright scary in their ability to get people to do things."

Kade seemed to consider that seriously. "I can see why. Hailey's gorgeous. And so sweet."

Hannah felt her eyes widen. Sweet? She wasn't sure that was an adjective many people used for the ex-mayor and current Queen of Everything. Though Hailey did always have the best interests of Sapphire Falls in mind. And yeah, she was gorgeous. But Kade could be a challenge for her. He wasn't from here and lacked a general give-a-shit that was, Hannah knew well, incredibly frustrating to go up against.

But there was no way Kade being here was on the down low. Nothing in Sapphire Falls was ever on the down low. Lucy, the owner of the little bookshop in town, had probably already placed an order for Kade's newest release. There was a sort-of-but-not-really-secret book club in Sapphire Falls. They mostly read erotic romance, from what Hannah had gathered since she'd been back in town, but they might have thoughts of inviting Kade to a meeting.

Wait 'til the sweet—and even the not-so-sweet—ladies of Sapphire Falls got a glimpse inside the mind of the author who had been called "a more twisted Stephen King". Yeah, that would be fun.

"I hate your book," she told him, tossing the pages onto the bed beside her and flopping back against the pillows behind her.

"Well, what's new?" Kade asked. "But I don't think that's why you're being like this."

"Like what?"

"Bitchy."

She sat up. "Hey. I'm telling you that the guys here aren't cowboys. That's just a fact, Kade. That's not about my mood."

He continued to type on his laptop without looking at her. "It was more your tone of voice."

She rolled her eyes. "You're such a baby."

"Yep, definitely your tone."

And suddenly Hannah wanted to cry. She couldn't really say why. Things just felt…not right. Kade noticed when he glanced up a moment later.

"What's going on?"

And with his question, she suddenly knew. "Kyle."

Kade nodded. "Well, that was bound to happen."

"I'm worried about him."

That was clearly not what Kade had been expecting to hear. He stopped typing. "Worried? Why?"

"He hasn't changed at all."

"And?"

"Actually, that's not totally true—he's gotten even *more* uptight. He's crazy busy, but he spends all his free time with our families. He doesn't socialize much. He barely dates and none of that is serious. It's like he's taken his inner circle and pulled it in even tighter. So there are changes, but they're not good."

Well, except some of the changes she'd noticed when they were alone. She shivered a little, remembering the kitchen of the Come Again two nights ago. When it was just the two of them, he seemed to be…hotter. Naughtier. And it made her want to be alone with him a lot.

Which actually fed nicely into a plan that had been forming in her mind since Kyle had laid out *his* plan to

convince Alice that Hannah wasn't staying around. But
Hannah kind of needed to hear her best friend tell her it
wasn't crazy. Or at least not totally crazy. She sat forward
on the bed. "He has no life of his own—it's all about other
people. *All* the people. He's on call 24/7, he's helping our
families in all his off time, everything is about this town.
Everything is on a schedule and planned out."
"How do you know all of this?"
She sighed. "Well, besides spending every day with my
grandmother and seeing my parents three times already
since I've been home, I've also been to the bakery, the gas
station, the grocery store and the diner to pick up a carry-
out order."
"So?"
"So everyone is intent on telling me how great Kyle is."
It was absolutely a planned attack that Alice had put
together. Hannah knew it. People were eager to find ways
to work Kyle info into conversations. And when they
couldn't find a way, they just blurted it out. And clearly,
they'd each been assigned a specific topic under the
umbrella of Kyle-is-amazing. Some told her about his
work—how he was always there for everyone, how hard he
worked, the hours he put in, the dedication he showed.
Some told her about his social life—that he rarely went out,
that he hadn't dated anyone seriously since Hannah, that it
was too bad he hadn't settled down yet, and how Hannah
had always been perfect for him. "He's so dedicated, so
accessible, so generous, so kind, blah, blah, blah," Hannah
said.
"And?" Kade asked after a beat.
"I just…I'm not sure he really has any *fun*. He's never
spontaneous, never does anything just because." The only
people she'd encouraged the Kyle conversations with were
her family members, but the more she heard about him, the
more she wondered. It was quickly clear that Kyle was
organized and scheduled and routine-oriented and…rigid.

And that a lot of his social time was spent with people twenty to fifty years older than him, often involved manual labor, and seemed to be a perfect way for him to avoid socializing more. Her dad had commented that he seemed to sometimes make up reasons to be busy at their house.

"Why is this your problem?" Kade asked.

"Because it's my fault."

Kade lifted a brow. "How?"

"He was always a very routine-oriented, predictable guy," she said. "But he'd relax with me. At least as much as he ever did. But what little bit of go-with-the-flow he did have…broke…or something…when I didn't come home and changed the plan." She sighed, feeling a definite sense of sadness. "I proved to him that always knowing what's coming and what to expect is the safe way to go."

Kade seemed to be thinking that over.

"And everything that he thinks will remind *me* of life here—the Come Again, the town square, hanging out at Grandma's house—is way more than a memory for him. It's his life. Every day."

"Okay," Kade finally said. "Is that bad?"

"If it's keeping him from trying new things and taking chances, yes."

"And you feel the need to fix that?"

"Of course," she said with a frown. "Just like he wants to be sure that Grandma goes on with her life without me here," and there was the pang near her heart again, "I want him to go on."

"And you have to be the one to show him this."

She took a deep breath. And nodded. "Yeah. I think I do. I think I might be the only one who can."

If anyone could coax Kyle into doing something off-plan and out of character, she thought maybe it could be her. She didn't know if that was something to be proud of or worried about though. Just like she didn't want Alice to be putting so much stake in Hannah and her thoughts and feelings and actions, she didn't want that for Kyle either. It was…sweet…or something…that he still cared about her to that extent, but she wasn't sure he was aware of it. Or if he was, if he was glad about it. Surely he didn't want to be stuck thinking about her and what could have been after she left again.

"And I think I have a plan."

"Oh boy."

She frowned at Kade's clear lack of enthusiasm. "Seriously."

He shut the laptop and folded his arms over his chest.

"Okay."

Wow, a shut computer. He was taking this seriously now. "I want to remind him about having fun. Give him some positive spontaneity."

"Positive spontaneity," Kade repeated. "Okay."

"And I also think I could maybe introduce him to some of my practices with massage and maybe even acupuncture."

"I thought he was skeptical about all of that."

She nodded. "But he cares about my pain. It bothered him to know I was hurting." She felt a warmth in her chest, remembering how concerned he'd been. "I think I could at least teach him more about it."

Kade sighed. "You want to sleep with him."

She scowled. "How did you get from acupuncture to sleeping with him?"

"Positive spontaneity. Massage. Seemed like a natural path."

Yeah, well, *maybe* that had occurred to her too. Kyle's hot kisses and sudden willingness to say all kinds of not-so-gentlemanly things had her thinking about a lot of things she hadn't expected when she'd planned this trip home. "There's definitely still chemistry between us," she admitted. "Maybe even more in some ways." She frowned. "Which is strange."

"Why?"

"I'm a very different person than I was before."

"First, you're not very different," Kade said. "You've had some experiences, but you're still basically you."

She wasn't so sure about that. But she could admit that over the past few days in Sapphire Falls, she'd felt more like her than she had in three years. In her heart of hearts, love and home and history were important to her.

"And secondly," Kade went on, "it's very possible for chemistry to increase over time. Experience and hurt and challenges change us into better, deeper people. Those wounds can make us even more attractive to the right person. And they make it possible to appreciate real chemistry and love over the superficial stuff that we all have when we're younger."

Hannah knew she was staring at him. But, as far as she knew, Kade had never had a deep, serious relationship that involved chemistry. He had physical relationships and he had meaningful relationships, but they were never the same relationships.

He noticed her look of incredulity. "I write a lot of psychologically complex and disturbed characters, so I read a lot of psychology books and I pick up positive things too sometimes. Accidentally, of course."

"Of course," she murmured. But it all made some sense. The changes—the wounds—she sensed in Kyle definitely made her feel more protective of him. Like she wanted to make it all better. Like she wanted to fix him. They certainly had *that* in common—wanting to fix things for the people they cared about.

"It really is more about fixing the things I broke," she said.

"That you broke?"

She nodded. "This trip is about Grandma getting her hip fixed, but there's more. Now my parents know I'm fine. And the town's seen me and knows I'm okay, but not coming home to stay, so they can move on with a new PT. Just like Grandma will realize I'm really in Seattle for good and she'll give the town the PT clinic. So the last thing is Kyle. I need him to remember how to have fun. To not be scared of letting go and having a new relationship."

Her heart ached with that idea, but she knew that she had to help him get over this idea that everything had to be predictable to be good.

"That's going to be really hard after he falls back in love with you," Kade said.

Her heart tripped. "He's not going to fall back in love with me."

"You're right. I think he's already there. But now you're going to remind him of it and reinforce it."

Yeah, well, she was right there too. But she shook her head. That could *not* happen. Because leaving Sapphire Falls was going to be hard enough. If she thought Kyle had those feelings for her, she might have to admit that she had those feelings for him too, and it would be all the harder.

"Well, then this is good," she said, meaning it about eighty percent. Or maybe fifty percent. "He'll definitely be over me after this."

"This?"

"If I can be here, involved with my family, and reminded of all the things I love about this town, and I also have a fling with him and *still* leave, then he'll really hate me and will get over me. He knows I'm leaving. I promised."

"And you have to keep a promise to him this time," Kade said.

He knew her well. She nodded. "Absolutely."

"So you *are* planning on sleeping with him."

She sighed. Okay, fine. "Kind of." And yeah, she felt a little pulse of pleasure between her legs at even the thought.

But *mostly* she had to help Kyle break free of the idea that everything had to be planned and forecast. He needed some spontaneity in his life. He needed to go with the flow and see that it could turn out. Or maybe even more; if things veered off course, he was perfectly capable of adapting.

"So what are you going to do exactly? I guess just taking your clothes off would be spontaneous and fun and would result in sex."

"Sex isn't the *goal*," she insisted. But Kade wasn't wrong about the fun part. "I need to show him that having fun is important and that being spontaneous can be fun. That not always having a plan can still be a good thing." She'd been thinking about this since Kyle had told her *his* plan to publicly seduce her. She had some ideas for what was going to happen in private.

And ironically, reminding Kyle how to be spontaneous was going to require a solid plan.

Holy shit.

Kyle drew up short in the doorway of Alice's kitchen. Alice was sitting out on the porch and had asked him to get her a glass of lemonade. She hadn't mentioned that Hannah was in the kitchen. He'd hoped to run into her, of course, but she'd been so good at avoiding him that he wasn't sure he'd see her. Of course, she hadn't known he was coming over here today. Exactly why he'd stopped by without warning.

But even if he managed to catch her by surprise, he really wasn't sure how she was going to react after their little kitchen tryst three nights ago. He knew how *he* was reacting to it. A mix of smugness, burning desire that had kept him up a lot of the night, and confusion. She'd been so hot. There had been some tentativeness there too, like she wasn't sure what she was doing—or couldn't believe she was doing it. But she'd kissed him back, she'd pressed close, she'd unbuttoned when he told her to. And damn, that had been the hottest thing he'd ever seen.

Until, of course, she'd slipped her hand into her panties. He'd been with other women in the past three years. Admittedly, for the first few months after his breakup had actually sunk in, he'd fucked his way around the county in a quest to banish Hannah from his thoughts. Then after that first year, he'd actually given some effort to finding someone he could be serious about. He wanted to move on. He wanted the whole marriage-and-family thing. But he hadn't found anyone who made him think that forever was possible. Then sex had turned into nothing more than a fun, sometimes necessary way to blow off steam. But those hook-ups had been a lot less frequent. Still, he'd seen plenty of women wearing denim shorts and unbuttoning blouses for him and touching themselves.

It had never made him as hot and hard as watching Hannah. Hell, she'd barely been undressed. And he'd only seen her hand in her panties. He hadn't seen the really good stuff. And he'd never felt the wave of got-to-have-her that he'd felt with her.

Because he'd pushed her. He'd gotten her hot enough that she was doing things she never would have done before. Other women wanting him had always felt good, of course. But pushing Hannah to that point had been the next level.

She was now up on the counter in Alice's kitchen, scrubbing the high shelves in Alice's cabinets. She was wearing another pair of short-shorts and a pink spaghetti-strap tank top that reminded him of the color of her bra she'd had on at the Come Again. These shorts weren't denim, though. They were a soft gray color and looked like sweatpants that had been cut off. But they rode high on her legs, gaped around her thighs, giving peeks at tantalizing shadows, and hugged her ass. And she was cleaning cupboards. Which shouldn't have been erotic at all, but it shot him back to the past when they'd worked together to take care of their parents and grandparents, their school, and their town.

His body tightened at the entire picture, and he stopped to take a deep breath so he didn't stalk right over there, yank her down into his arms, and repeat that kitchen scene on her grandmother's white Formica countertop. Without any panties in the way.

As he watched, Hannah lowered her arms, rolling her shoulders and neck as if they were stiff. She reached up and kneaded her right shoulder, then ran her hand up to the side of her neck, squeezing the muscles.

His gut tightened, and it wasn't about how delicious her ass looked in the shorts now.

She'd told him that she still had neck issues from the car accident she'd been in at the end of her last internship in Seattle. He remembered the phone call. She'd been hit by a car in a crosswalk and had been taken to the hospital. She'd had all the tests done and she was starting physical therapy the next day. That had been the report. He'd been worried, of course, but she'd assured him she was fine. She'd sounded normal. And her parents and grandmother knew nothing about it. And she'd begged him not to tell them. She'd told him there was nothing to worry about.

So he hadn't. He'd been buried in his residency and was relieved, honestly, not to have one more thing demanding attention and energy. But if she was still having issues three years later, it hadn't been quite a no-big-deal event.

And suddenly he felt a surge of concern and protectiveness that made him nervous. She wasn't his problem. She'd taken herself away from being his problem.

He still didn't like knowing that she was in pain of any kind.

But this was physical pain. That he could help her with. He was a freaking doctor. All she had to do was say the word and he'd do whatever he could to make her better. Hell, maybe she didn't need to say a word. Maybe he needed to insist. Like telling her to unbutton the other night. Maybe she just needed to know what he wanted from her—for her to let him take care of her.

Yeah, that was definitely concerning.

As was the surge of irritation he felt toward Alice. Why did *those* cupboards need to be cleaned? That was ridiculous. Alice didn't need to be making Hannah get up there like that.

And *that* was crazy—he was as protective of Alice as anyone.

Or so he'd thought.

He frowned, moving forward. "She has you scrubbing her cabinets?"

Startled, Hannah gave a little yelp and swung to face him.

Kyle moved quickly so that when her foot slipped off the edge of the counter and into the sink, he was there to steady her. Of course, that required a hand on her leg. Her smooth, warm leg. His senses instantly registered everything about touching her, and he had to fight the urge to stroke his palm up and down.

"You got this?" he asked, his voice rough.

"Yeah."

Her voice wasn't normal either. But it could have been because he'd scared the shit out of her. He took a moment before looking up at her. And even with that moment of preparation, he was slammed by memories from the night before. The way her hair had curled wildly over her shoulder, the silky heat of her mouth, the sight, feel, and taste of her breasts, her dipping her hand into her panties, the heat in her eyes, the sound of her voice and the little gasps and moans.

He swallowed hard. And backed away from the thigh he desperately wanted to lick. He looked up and their gazes collided. "Sorry I scared you. I should have thought of that before I said anything."

She shook her head. "It's fine."

He felt his brows slam together. "It's not. Why do people say things are fine when they're not?" Like when she'd said she was fine after the car accident that now, three years later, still bothered her?

She frowned, clearly confused by his sudden irritation. "I didn't fall on my ass and you didn't mean to scare me, so it *is* fine. What's with you?"

He shoved a hand through his hair. Nothing was with him. Except that he was worried about a neck problem he knew almost next to nothing about in a woman who had quite clearly wanted him out of her life.

"Nothing. I'm fine too." See? People lied about that all the time. "Does your grandma know that your neck's been bothering you? She shouldn't have you cleaning her cupboards out."

Hannah's surprised expression matched the surprise he felt shoot through him. He was dissuading Hannah from helping Alice? When had that ever happened?

"I mean, she should have asked me to do it," he said. It wasn't like he thought Alice should be climbing up there.

"She didn't ask. I was looking for her ice cream maker and realized that it's been…a while since these cupboards were cleaned and organized."

Those high ones? Yeah, probably three or four years. Kyle hadn't ever given them any thought. If Alice had tried getting up there or had asked him to, he would have realized they needed attention and would have taken care of it, but he spent his time putting out the little fires—catching her doing things she shouldn't or anticipating the day-to-day things that would be tough for her. That ice cream maker? He hadn't seen it in years, and he knew that if Alice wanted ice cream, she headed to The Stop.

But watching Hannah now, the smell of soap in the air

brought back a wave of memories. They'd done these kinds of chores together all the time. To spend time with her, he helped her clean the house or do dishes or make meals. It fit them—they were together, but they were active and productive. Neither of them were really the sit-on-the-couch-for-a-two-hour-movie type. If they weren't at Hannah's house, they were at Alice's or Ruby's, or doing something at school—bake sales, fundraisers, club meetings.

Hannah hopped off the counter.

"The ice cream maker?" he asked.

She blushed slightly but nodded. "It just seemed…like something fun. We used to make homemade ice cream all the time."

Ah, being home was stirring up memories for her and making her nostalgic. That was excellent. Right on plan. "I remember," he said, wishing that the nostalgia wasn't as contagious as it seemed to be. He really wanted to make homemade ice cream with her. Fuck.

"I don't suppose you could help me for a minute?" she asked.

Kyle felt his eyes widen.

"What?" she asked.

"You just…never ask for help."

She started to reply, but pressed her lips together and nodded. "Yeah, you're right. I didn't used to be very good at that."

"And now?" Kyle knew it was ridiculous to hate that there were changes in Hannah's personality. Of course there were changes. It had been three years. She'd been living a totally different life in a big city far from home. And hell, learning to ask for help wasn't some terrible thing. *He* hadn't learned how to do it, but in general, he understood it was a good thing.

"I've gotten a lot better at it," she said. "It was hard. I was used to being the one that helped everyone else, did everything." She was watching him closely. "It always felt good to be the one that everyone could depend on."

He gave a short laugh. "If you're asking if I'm still that guy, the answer is absolutely yes."

"I figured. Even before my dad told me that you take care of their lawn and snow removal. And before I found out you repainted my grandma's house. And my bedroom." For a second her voice got a little husky.

Did knowing he'd been in that bedroom, fixing it up for her, make her feel the weird sense of connection and strangeness that he'd felt doing it?

"And even before I found out you did all of the landscaping at the park—after paying for all of the new equipment. Not to mention everything you do for *your* parents and grandmothers."

So she'd been talking about him with…people. Presumably her parents. It wasn't like the things he did for all of those people were a secret. But he didn't expect them to sing his praises.

"To be fair," Kyle said, feeling like maybe she wasn't entirely impressed by all of that, "my dad doesn't let *anyone* touch his lawn. And Derek helped me with the landscaping at the park."

"You're the only doctor in town," she said. "How do you have time for all of that extra stuff? You're at my mom and dad's once a week and here with my grandma more often than that."

"Careful planning," he said with a shrug. "Not much sleep."

"And not spending any time dating."

He didn't think that was a question. But had she been asking about his dating habits? But no, with her grandmother, his grandmother, and her parents around, she wouldn't have had to ask. He was sure they were all very happy to share his status with her. His single-and-hasn't-seriously-dated-anyone-in-months status. Or, as her grandmother would have put it, his single-and-has-never-dated-anyone-worthy status.

"I don't date much," he acknowledged. He climbed up on the counter, needing to be busy. And not look at Hannah. And she had asked for his help, after all.

"Why not?" she asked, right on cue.

He bent to retrieve the rag she'd been using to wipe down the shelves. Reaching to the back of the highest one was no problem for him.

He debated how honest to be with her. Finally, he realized he had nothing to lose. "Because I haven't figured out what I did wrong with you, yet."

There was dead silence behind him. As expected. He wiped the next shelf down and then bent to put the serving bowls and platters back in their places.

It was nearly two minutes before Hannah spoke. "You had a plan. And I messed it up."

Kyle's spine stiffened, and he stopped with the Thanksgiving mashed potato bowl in hand. And yes, he knew Alice used that bowl for mashed potatoes at Thanksgiving. He'd been to several Thanksgiving dinners at her house over the years. Even when Hannah hadn't been there.

"You had these…expectations for how things should go," she went on. He set the bowl on the shelf carefully. "And I couldn't meet them anymore."

"So there *was* something I did wrong." He didn't turn around. "People in Seattle don't have expectations?"

"They don't have expectations of *me*," she said softly.

Kyle blew out a breath. Then he swung around and jumped to the floor. "So no one expects anything of you? And that makes it better there? You couldn't take the pressure?"

She shrugged. "Right."

Her agreement with what he'd essentially meant as an insult made him pause. "What pressure?" he asked. "No one could know you or love you as much as we—the people here do."

She nodded. "A lot of it was self-inflicted pressure. I know that now," she said. "But yeah…doing the right thing all the time, not just for me but for my mom and dad, for Grandma, for you…it was a lot to feel bad about when I *didn't* get it right."

"You didn't have to do everything right for us," he said. But he heard the lack of conviction in his voice. And knew she did too. It wasn't that she had to do everything or be perfect, but yeah, they'd all depended on her. *He'd* depended on her. Not to be perfect, but to be…steady. Predictable.

She gave him a small smile. "But I always did," she said. "That's not ego. That's just fact. I did everything right. I made plans and carried them out. I set goals and I met them. I made good choices. I mean, even when we started having sex, we used the pill *and* condoms. And we were…"

He shifted his weight at the subject of sex between them. She was just stating a fact, but it was extremely difficult to take the emotions out of that topic. "We were what?" he managed.

"We took a long time to get to that point. And we were so sure by then that we were going to get married. It never felt like we were just horny teenagers or doing something wrong." She sighed. "It felt like sex inside a marriage, I swear."

He knew that should sound strange, but he knew what she meant. The first time he'd slept with another woman after Hannah, it had felt like he was cheating. Okay, the first few times. He'd kept going, thinking it would get better. It took a long damned time to not feel, if not *wrong*, then just *not normal* to be with someone else.

"Yeah," he agreed. And the only fucking reason that any of that had been an issue was because *she* hadn't come home. He worked to rein in his emotions. "I don't expect perfection," he told her. At least, he didn't from other people. From himself, maybe. And yeah, okay, maybe at one time he'd come to expect it from her. Because she delivered. "But you never gave me a reason to doubt that you weren't...perfect."

She gave him a smile that almost seemed sad. "I know." He didn't know what to say. He really didn't. He hadn't expected to get into all of this today when he'd stopped over. "And we were kids, basically. I've grown up," he said. "I deal with illness and injury every day. I know perfection is unattainable."

"And because of that, you try to make everything you can control as close to perfection as possible," she said. She was rubbing her shoulder again, though it seemed subconscious.

"And you think relationships are one of those things I try to control?" he asked.

"I know about the landscaping at the park," she said. "Do you really think I didn't find out that the longest relationship you've had in three years was seven dates? And that there are long stretches between women."

He sighed. "Six dates."

"Ellen said seven."

And he understood why Hannah believed her. Ellen, the owner of the Bang and Blow salon, was one of their lead gossips.

"Well, it was six. I don't count the first meeting at the bakery that was completely set up...by Ellen, by the way."

"And you started comparing them all to your checklist on date one, right?" she asked.

"I don't have a checklist." He totally did. Derek had said the same thing. And they were both right. It wasn't actually written down or anything like that, but he knew what he was looking for. Was that so bad?

"You do too," she said with a little laugh. "Don't you

remember giving me the list of reasons you loved me on Valentine's Day?"

He huffed out a breath. "That's not a checklist."

"More or less. It's what you want. And it's what you measure all these women against, right?"

"I measure all these women against *you,* Hannah," he finally snapped. "You should be flattered by that." Though his tone was hardly complimentary.

She nodded, not looking happy. "You compare them to the old me. To the me who was young, and loved taking care of everyone else, and who could get by on five hours of sleep, and whose biggest problem was studying for a chemistry exam on the same night that I had to paint the Homecoming float and do all the family's laundry."

"You don't love taking care of people anymore?" he asked, irritated and not even fully sure why.

"It's easier not to," she said. "Then you can't let anyone down."

"Clearly I don't feel the same way."

"Clearly."

They just stood looking at each other, memories, hurt, regret filling the air between them. Finally, she said, "Other people are the hardest things to predict. I think that's why you've been avoiding relationships."

"Well, considering my last serious relationship with a woman took the most unexpected turn of my life, yeah, probably." What the hell was the point of arguing that?

She didn't flinch or grimace. Instead she frowned. "And that's made you avoid *all* new relationships?"

"No, I—"

"You treat a town full of people you've known your whole life. You hang out with the same friends from high school. You eat the same favorite dinners—at *that* same table," she said, pointing to the kitchen table behind him. "You do the same odd jobs, drive the same roads, you have the same phone number you've had for ten years, Kyle."

She was now digging her fingers into her shoulder, and wincing as she did it.

He sighed and moved closer. He knocked her hand out of the way and turned her with his hands on her upper arms. Then he began kneading the muscles. Her skin was soft and warm, but it was the little groan she let out as his thumb rubbed circles over a spot just above her shoulder blade that got to him.

He swallowed and concentrated on massaging her muscles. "I don't need a new phone number," he said softly. "I don't need a different job and I have the best friends I could ever hope for. I take comfort in knowing the full history of everyone who comes through my clinic door, and in eating my grandmother's chicken and cheese bake once a month. I love that when I go to a birthday party, it's almost always one of several I've attended for that person. I love that I know if I go to the post office at one p.m., Helen will have her after lunch Oreos out of the cupboard."

"You have a lot of food options around this town," she said, her head dropping forward.

She reached up and moved his hand an inch to the left then pressed down on top of it. He increased his pressure on the spot and she groaned again.

"I found the life I love early," he said, after taking a big breath of her scent. His rubbing seemed to release it from her skin. "I think I'd be foolish to not hang on to it."

He opened his mouth to continue, but she reached up again and grasped his thumb, moving it down slightly and pressing again. "Feel that?" she asked.

There was definitely a hard ball under his thumb. "The knot?"

"Yes. That's a trigger point. That one flares up a lot. Can you press right into it? You have to hold for about ninety seconds to release a trigger point."

"Um, yeah, sure."

She kept her hand on top of his as he pressed. He didn't

count, far too distracted by just the simple act of touching her. But after about a minute, the knot of tissues softened. He was surprised to actually *feel* that.

"Ah," she sighed. "Thank you."

Something in her voice, or maybe just the realization that he'd done something for her that had helped, made him lean forward and press his lips to the spot. It was slightly reddened and a little warmer than the rest of her skin. He felt her sigh and lean back slightly.

"So much better," she said softly.

He lifted his head and she turned. He'd given this woman a lot of touches of all kinds over the years, in a lot of places, but he didn't know if he'd really ever taken pain away. And doing it with his own two hands was a very intimate thing, as he thought about it.

And as much as he wanted her, he had the urge to do something else. He wrapped his arms around her and pulled her in for a hug.

"I'm sorry your neck hurts," he said against the top of her head. "I want to help."

She seemed surprised for only about a second. She wrapped her arms around him and her body softened against him. "I know," she said. "I really do know that."

"Just tell me what you need."

She hesitated. "*This* actually feels really good."

He squeezed her a little tighter. It didn't feel like enough, but he could definitely be happy holding her for as long as he could. His time was limited. He knew that. And he knew that even being prepared for her to leave again wasn't going to help a bit.

"Are you growing the lemons for the lemonade?" Alice asked as she came into the kitchen.

Hannah didn't pull back immediately. But she did take a deep breath, and then slid her hands up between them and pushed.

Just like she was supposed to.

Of course, Alice missed it completely. She'd crossed to the fridge and had her head ducked behind the door, looking for the pitcher of lemonade.

Kyle let Hannah go anyway. They stood staring at each other for a long moment. And in that moment, it became clear that this plan where he pretended to want her and she pretended not to want him wasn't working. Because he wasn't pretending.

"Sorry, Alice," Kyle finally said.

"Oh, was he on an errand for you?" Hannah asked. "I got him roped into helping me with the cupboards."

He'd actually forgotten about the lemonade completely.

"Of course he helped you," Alice said, turning from the fridge with the lemonade.

Hannah and Kyle both started for her. Carrying a pitcher and using her cane wasn't easy. Hannah took the pitcher and Kyle steered Alice to a chair at the table.

"Did I give you a chance to steal a kiss?" Alice asked Kyle, not at normal volume but hardly in a whisper.

Kyle gave her an eye roll.

She elbowed him, though from her seated position, her elbow connected with his thigh. "I stalled outside as long as I could."

"I was thinking about lemonade," he said. "Not kissing," he added in an actual whisper, to make a point.

"Well, that explains a lot," Alice told him. "Kissing should always be the first thing on your mind."

Yeah well, *she* had a point.

"Hello!"

Everyone turned to see Hannah's dad coming in through the back kitchen door.

"Hi, Dad."

Kyle felt a catch in his chest at the look of sincere happiness on Hannah's face as she greeted her father. Crap, he wasn't supposed to care this much about her pain and her being happy and all of that. *She* had left *him*.

"You're just in time," Alice informed her son.

"Does that mean there are cookies?" Ben asked. He crossed to Hannah and kissed her cheek.

She pointed at the cookie jar. "What a silly question." He headed straight to the jar. "What are you just in time for?" she asked.

"I'm going to take Mom to York," Ben said, biting into what looked like oatmeal raisin.

Hannah was really good at oatmeal raisin. Then again, Hannah had always been really good at just about everything.

"You didn't say you needed to go to York," Hannah said to Alice.

"I don't need to go, but I want to. We're going to shop a little and have dinner."

"You're going shopping and to dinner," Hannah repeated. "You're feeling up to that?"

"To having my son help me pick out a new TV and buy me dinner?" Alice asked with a laugh. "Of course."

"I could take you," Hannah offered. "That's why I'm here, right? To help with things."

"Oh, yes, absolutely," Alice said. "I was hoping you could do some of the work over at your dad's that needs done."

"What do you need help with?" Kyle asked.

Ben glanced at Alice, and Alice gave him a little nod. Kyle sighed. That wasn't obvious at all.

"I needed to get the windows washed," Ben told them. "The outside. I got one of those spray things that go on the hose and my shoulder has been feeling really good, so thought I could get them done." He glanced at Hannah with a smile. "That treatment you did on me really helped."

Hannah looked pleased. "I'm so glad."

So, she'd worked on her dad. That was great.

"I can definitely do the windows," Kyle said. "No sense in testing your shoulder just yet. Let Hannah work on it a little more before you get too gung ho."

Ben nodded. "Whatever you say, Doc. But the bottom ones will need to be dried. They say that stuff doesn't leave streaks, but it does."

"Got it. I'll take care of it," Kyle said.

"And I can help."

Kyle glanced at Hannah. Scrubbing cupboards was bothering her neck. He could only imagine what washing windows would do to it. And she'd told him at the Come Again that one of her coping mechanisms was just letting things go and relaxing. She should take advantage of the time to sit back and put her feet up. Or something.

But he was a selfish bastard and he wanted some one-on-one time with her. He'd just make sure that he did most—or all—of the work. She could sit back and put her feet up outside in her dad's yard. Maybe in a lawn chair. With a bikini on.

"We can do it together," he said. "Of course. We're a great team." Not only would that make Alice happy—which was confirmed by a quick glance in the older woman's direction—but if Hannah needed any more massages, he would be right there. Willing and able.

Hannah looked from him to her grandmother and must have read the same pleasure in Alice's face that he saw. Hannah nodded. "Yeah, that's true. We work really well together."

"Everything is out in the garage," Ben said happily. "We'll be gone for…a while."

Kyle caught *Hannah's* eye roll that time and couldn't help but grin. Yeah, Ben and Alice were really subtle. They were clearly trying to get him and Hannah stuck together for a period of time, just the two of them. He could hardly complain about that.

"You ready to head over there?" he asked her.

"You sure you don't have any other plans?"

"I took the afternoon off because Alice said she needed

some help," he said, shooting the older woman a look as he outed her lie. "She's clearly in good hands, so now, I'm all yours."

Yeah, he'd used those words on purpose. For Alice. And for Hannah.

Hannah's cheeks were a little flushed as she pulled her gaze from his. She looked down at what she was wearing. "I guess I'm dressed for window washing. Might as well."

"Or you could put on a swimming suit," he said. "I wouldn't mind."

He caught Alice's little grin and knew he was playing right into her plan. But his comment was less to please Alice and more to make Hannah aware that *he* was aware of her body. And wanted to see more of it.

The pink in her cheeks got a little deeper, but she gave him a look. "That's a great idea, but I didn't bring a swimming suit. Guess I'm stuck in this."

"There's probably an old suit in the dresser upstairs," Alice suggested helpfully.

Hannah shook her head quickly. "They'd only be bikinis."

"That's fine," Kyle said. "Less to get wet." Except for all of that beautiful skin.

He knew that she was thinking of their conversation the other night at the Come Again, about her being wet for him. And he'd bet that right now she *was* a little bit too.

And he hoped that he could make that little bit into a lot more. Later. When they were alone.

He knew this was all dangerous, but he was beyond caring. Knowing she had pain from that fucking car accident had brought a huge surge of protectiveness out in him and a need to *do* something, to somehow heal her, or at least make her feel better. Somehow. And the fact that she was still willing to get up on Alice's countertop to clean was making him feel a little... He wasn't sure. Restless. Irritable. Frustrated.

"Doing work in a bikini can be risky," Hannah said. "Things shift and slip when you're reaching and bending."

Kyle almost groaned. Especially when her cheeks got pink again. She hadn't meant for it to sound dirty. But it totally had. And now he couldn't wait to get started.

"So I think I'll stick with this," she added on hastily, indicating what she wore.

They'd washed windows together before, and she'd never dressed quite like this. She would have worn a tank top, maybe, but it would have been paired with regular shorts, not cut-off sweatpants. And she would have still had her hair done and makeup on. Now her hair was in a messy bun, and she had no makeup on that he could see.

And she looked gorgeous.

She'd never been afraid of hard work or getting dirty or breaking a nail. But she would have redone her manicure right after the job.

They helped Alice get settled in Ben's car and watched them disappear at the end of the block.

"I feel like walking, how about you?" Hannah asked.

It was only about four blocks. But more, there was something in her eyes that had him nodding. "Sure."

Chapter Nine

They started across the backyard without a word, taking the old familiar path between the two houses that included cutting through yards rather than using the sidewalks and streets. And if that walk didn't bring memories back for Hannah, he didn't know what would. He never had been able to smell lilac bushes without thinking about stealing kisses from her in the far corner of her grandmother's yard before it turned into Mr. Carlson's yard.

The big old oak that took up most of the southwest corner still held the swing that he and Hannah had sat on, holding hands, stargazing and talking so many summer nights. At least, that's what Alice thought they were doing back here. And they'd done a little bit of all of that. But Hannah had also lost an earring, a button, and a pair of panties back here. Not all at the same time. And she'd come back and found the earring and the panties the next day when the sun came up. A lot more than hand-holding had gone on back here.

But a lot more than sex had too. They'd been in love. Yeah, it might have been kids' love, a little unrealistic, and a lot full of dreams, but it had been real.

"Oh, wow." Hannah headed straight for the swing that Kyle had been hoping to walk right past. She sat to one side, leaving room for someone else, and pushed off with her foot. "I haven't been on this thing in forever."

Kyle propped a shoulder against another tree and tucked a hand in his pocket, watching her. She looked…different. It was the same yard, the same swing, but she was different. And his heart ached a little with that thought.

She smiled at him. "Come sit with me."

He shook his head. "You're fine without me."

Her smile faltered, and he cursed his choice of words. But then...they were true.

"You don't have to swing with me because I'm *not* fine without you. Maybe just because you want to," she finally said.

It felt like there was a lot of meaning there, and he paused.

"Does everything you do with anyone else have to be about helping them or doing something *for* them?" she asked. The swing came forward and she pushed off again with a toe in the dirt.

He shook his head. "Of course not. I go to games with my friends and have dinner with my family and sit at the Come Again and chat."

She nodded. "Good. It's okay to do things just for fun. For no real reason except that you want to."

"Thanks, Dr. Phil," he said dryly.

She didn't look offended. "I'm just saying that it's okay to not always be everyone's hero."

"I like being everyone's hero. That's what I want." And up until she came back to town, he'd felt pretty damned good about that.

"But if you wanted to sit and watch a game on TV and eat a pizza, but a friend needed help digging fence posts, you'd be digging," she said.

He sighed. "Yep." And dammit, that was a good thing.

She just nodded at that. Then she hopped off the swing. "Okay, let's go."

She started across Mr. Carlson's yard and Kyle followed, falling in step by the time they got to Carlson's clothesline. She ducked under the line. "I haven't seen someone hang clothes out to dry in forever," she said. She shot Kyle a smile. "Nothing smells better than sheets and towels just in off the line."

Kyle would beg to differ. That spot just behind her ear,

the one that made her moan like no other, smelled better than anything.

They kept going, rounding Carlson's house and hitting the sidewalk. Hannah turned west when they typically headed straight across the street and through Mrs. Perkins' side yard.

"You lost your way?" he asked.

She swung around, but kept walking backward. "I want to make a stop on the way."

"If you're going that direction, it's not really on the way."

She shrugged. "I can meet you over at Dad's. Or, you can come with me."

He didn't know what she was doing, but he found his feet turning in her direction, almost as if they couldn't help it. Wow, big shock.

Hannah was surprised by the easy silence between them as they walked. And by how easily he'd just fallen into step beside her when she changed direction. Maybe there was hope for him.

But she couldn't read too much into it. An unplanned walk downtown with her was not the same as being spontaneous with bigger things. He definitely needed to go off-script once in a while.

"I do get why you love it here," she said after they'd walked a couple of blocks.

"I know you do."

She looked over. "Do you? You don't think I've abandoned everything because I didn't appreciate it adequately?"

He shrugged. "I did think that for a while. But that's not you, I know that."

That surprised her, honestly. "I'm glad. I do love this

town."

"It's just not enough for you."

She would not put it like that. "It's not that it's not enough. It's probably…because it's too much." She almost regretted the words, but it was the truth and at this point, she wasn't sure it hurt anything more for her to tell him what truth she could.

He didn't reply right away to that. They walked another block and turned toward Main. Finally, he said, "And I was too much, right?"

Oh boy. She hadn't expected this walk to turn into some deep conversation. But she couldn't shy away from it. They needed to talk. She thought about her response. Okay, time for some honesty. She stopped walking and turned to face him. "You were…you. You were exactly who you have always been. You knew what you wanted and you made no secrets of it. So, actually, you were…easy. In a way." That much was definitely true. There wasn't any question what her life here would have been like.

"Because I'm predictable?"

"Yes." And God knew that there was a lot to be said for predictability. "I knew exactly what you wanted and needed and…I realized I wasn't it."

"On your own. You decided for me that you weren't what I wanted and needed." He definitely sounded angry.

She took a deep breath. Here went nothing. "I'm not a PT because I can't be. Not because I'd rather do acupuncture—though I do love it—but because I don't have a PT license and I can't get one. Even if I could, I wouldn't be able to do the work. I can't lift and transfer patients, I can't handle squirmy kids, I can't do the manual work with the orthopedic patients. I also can't be *here* and do the scrubbing and window washing and lifting and helping that my family needs. I can't help repaint the gazebo or build parade floats or help haul tree branches out of the park. And I'm scared of sex."

Kyle was watching her. Not staring exactly, but also not frowning. He was watching and listening. There was a little flicker of *something* in his eyes at her last few words.

She took a deep breath. "My neck is fused at two levels and my C5 is held together by a metal plate. I was in therapy for months, and even after all of that, the pain continued. I wasn't able to finish my last rotation, so I couldn't graduate and I couldn't get my license. They offered to let me come back and repeat that last rotation so I could graduate, but I needed so many pain pills to get through that...it wasn't worth it." Okay, maybe not the *whole* truth. She wasn't sure why, but she didn't want to share her addiction story. It was behind her. And she sure as hell wasn't proud of it.

He was staring at her. Hannah was vaguely aware that there were people driving by and possibly looking out the windows of their homes, seeing them standing here talking like this. Well, it would hopefully just perpetuate the story about Kyle trying to win her back. And her resisting.

"So," she went on when he still didn't respond. "I couldn't be what you all needed me to be. It was easier to stay where no one really needed or expected things like that. And where I didn't have to face disappointing all of you," she added softly. "I took so much pride and reward in *doing* things, like you do. It was such a part of my identity, very much how I thought of myself. And when I realized I couldn't do it anymore, it was really devastating. I didn't think I had anything else to offer all of you."

Kyle didn't even respond to that.

So, again, she kept going. "If you think about it, we never just talked. We planned and plotted. We analyzed our plans. We talked about the future. But we didn't just sit and chat. Or sit and *not* chat. We were always *doing* something. Same with my parents. I was always working around the house while my mom was working outside of the house. We didn't just sit around and talk. I don't know my mother's television habits—or if she even watches TV—but I know that she gets up every morning at five thirty a.m. and puts a load of laundry in the washing machine, makes her coffee and lunch, and takes only about forty minutes from shower to walking out the door to work. I don't know my grandmother's favorite memory of my grandfather. But I know where all of her cooking utensils are and that she loves rosemary and that she always plants four rows of petunias and four rows of marigolds in her garden every year. I don't know your favorite class from med school and why, but I know that you went to the gym five mornings a week and were in class until four and took a half hour to watch the news each night before starting to study and were in bed by eleven. I know how to *do* things with and for the people I love, I know their schedules and routines, I know favorite things if they have to do with something like food, or flowers I made or planted. But that's it."

"And you know Michael Kade?"

Those were Kyle's first words, and she definitely noticed the flash in his eyes. But she had to nod. "I do. We were in a pain support group together. That's how we met."

"You still go to the group?"

"Sometimes. And I don't know if we just got in the habit or if we actually learned that talking can help or what, but we still talk even outside of the group."

"You didn't tell me about your surgery. Or your therapy. Or your pain," Kyle finally said.

"You were in residency. And there was nothing you could do. And I knew that would kill you. That *not* being able to be there and fix it would be so hard on you. So no, I didn't tell you."

"Or your parents or Alice?"

She laughed humorlessly. "God no. They would have been beside themselves. For one, what could they have done? And for another, they were never the ones that fixed things, you know? That was me. I was the one that held stuff together. They wouldn't have known what to do."

"It's bullshit that you didn't tell us," he said, scowling.

"Really?" she asked. "*Really.* I'm right about all of it, Kyle. You couldn't have done anything and you would have gone crazy."

"But you didn't even give us the chance to be there for you."

She stopped and let those words play in her mind. She hadn't given them the chance. Because she'd thought that it would be too painful, for all of them, if they failed to really understand what she was going through and to be there for her. But…he was right. She nodded. "I know. I didn't give you a chance. And maybe I should have. But I was trying to protect you."

"Protect *me*? From what?"

She swallowed hard. "From being worried and frustrated when you couldn't be there and help me."

"All I fucking do is *be there* for people! I figure things out when it can't be me directly. I would have done whatever I could, Hannah."

She hadn't intended for them to get into all of this here and now. Or ever. But okay… "You're there for people you can fix things for."

"Not all of my patients can be fixed. I get pain. I understand chronic conditions, for fuck's sake." He looked extremely pissed off.

And she understood that. She'd taken this chance to be her hero away from him. And it probably wasn't fair for her to be the only decision maker, but in the midst of everything—the pain, the fear, the sorrow over giving up her dreams, the addiction—she simply hadn't been able to face anything else. Like disappointing Kyle, or Kyle trying and failing to help her, or getting her hopes up that they could work things out and then breaking up later on.

"I know you understand pain and chronic conditions,"

she said. "But you make things better for those people anyway. Even when you can't take their pain way. You make their town gazebo look great, and you plant flowers for them to see when they walk through the square, you joke with them at the diner, you go to a guy's girlfriend's house for dinner so you can do a check-up on *his* time, you go fishing with them so they're not scared."

It was strange how all of that had been in her mind, but she hadn't really put it to words before. But it was all true, and she realized now that all of that was one of the reasons he kept doing the things he did. It was his way of making things better even when he couldn't directly fix something. And, in spite of the fact that she wanted him to have some fun—felt that was really important, actually—his dedication to making everything around him as good as they could possibly be was also kind of hot.

"And I could have done other things for you if I couldn't fix your neck," he said, moving in close.

She'd expected his anger to continue, but there was something else in his eyes now. A softer emotion—concern, maybe. Or protectiveness. Yeah, that seemed right. And heat. There was definitely heat. Which surprised her, but she didn't mind it a bit.

He put his hand on her shoulder and rubbed gently. "I could have massaged your neck, kissed it better." His voice had dropped to a husky lower note.

And she realized, yeah, that would have made her feel better. Or at least, if she was in pain, she'd rather be in pain with Kyle trying to make it better, than be in pain alone. Crap. He was being too nice about this. It would all be easier if he was still a little angry.

She wet her lips. "I know you would have done anything you could. But it would have been hard on you, on both of us. You would have been frustrated. I would have felt bad making you frustrated."

"I would have been," he admitted. "But that doesn't

mean I wouldn't have wanted to be with you."

"It would have been a regular thing," she said. "With the people here, when something doesn't get better, you can still do other things—the flowers, buying a round of coffee or beer, making them laugh. But then you can go home and they go home and you can get away from it. With me, it would have been in your face, all the time, every day. There would have been no escape." She paused. "Believe it or not, I was trying to take care of *you* by keeping you away from this."

He stared at her. Then he squeezed her shoulder gently before he dropped his hand. But he didn't move back. "I guess you have a point," he said.

She felt a strange mix of relief and disappointment at that. She wanted him to understand why she'd made the choices she had. Maybe she could have come home. Maybe. But it would have been hard. And she had not been in a good place for anything hard three years ago. Maybe she could have handled it a year ago. Maybe even eighteen months ago. But by then she'd been sure it was too late.

She wasn't *un*happy about her life in Seattle. It was good to get out of your comfort zone sometimes. Her life there, her new normal, had taught her things she wouldn't have learned if she'd stayed in Sapphire Falls. Like getting everything checked off her to-do list was not what was most important at the end of the day. And how perfection was just an illusion. And how strong she was. That was the most valuable of all.

And sadly, she wasn't sure Kyle would appreciate it. Leaning on people, it takes a village, love your neighbor, were all things that were woven into the fabric of Sapphire Falls so inherently that you didn't even really notice it until you were somewhere else. She didn't think people here, Kyle in particular, wanted people to be *weak*, but there wasn't a lot of suck it up, dig deep, what doesn't kill you makes you stronger here.

And leaning on people and helping others certainly weren't bad things. Of course. While she'd felt that she'd been helping hold the fabric of her family together at times, she'd never felt alone. But she'd never had to stand on her own and really find out what she was made of either.

"So tell me more about the sex thing," he said, lifting his hand again. This time he just cupped the back of her neck in an almost protective gesture.

She swallowed hard. She'd kind of blurted that part out, of course. But she'd been trying to tell him all the ways she wasn't who he wanted and needed. And surely sex was part of that.

Of course, since she'd been home, she was feeling a lot less worried about or scared of it. She was feeling a lot like she needed to give it a try, in fact. Like soon. With the guy right in front of her.

Hannah put her hand over his and moved in closer. "There's a lot of jostling that happens during sex. Lots of…"

She felt his hand tighten on the back of her neck slightly, and it sent heat shooting through her body.

"Lots of?" he prompted.

"Um…" She was really trying to think of a word besides the one she'd been about to use.

"Hannah," he said, low and gruff. "What is there lots of? I mean, I can give you a list of words, but I'd love to know what you were thinking."

"Pounding," she said softly, almost without sound.

Heat flared in his eyes and a slow, sexy half smile tugged at the corner of his mouth. "There sure as hell can be."

Lord, that gruff, low voice was enough to get her ready to go all on its own.

"But…" He stroked his thumb up and down the side of her throat. "I can be very gentle if I need to be. I don't want to hurt you."

"You won't," she said, breathless suddenly. She didn't know how she knew, but sex with Kyle would not be painful. She could *feel* it.

"Is there anything that definitely hurts or definitely doesn't?" he asked.

She shook her head. Then cleared her throat. "I don't know. I haven't…done it…since."

He took that in, and then slowly his eyes widened. "You haven't had sex at all since your injury?"

She wet her lips and shook her head. "No." It was practically a whisper. "You were my last. And my first. And everything."

Kyle took a deep breath that seemed to shudder through his body, then he leaned in, putting his forehead against hers. "Damn, you can't tell me stuff like that when we're standing on a public sidewalk."

Hannah could hear the desire in his voice, and his need made electricity dance along her limbs. "And I'm supposed to be pushing you away," she said, her voice husky.

"Yeah."

"I don't think I can." She needed him to know that.

"Good." That single word was incredibly heartfelt. And very hot.

Then he straightened. "We have windows to wash."

She blinked at him. "Oh."

"And I have the afternoon off," he said.

"Right."

He gave her a little smile. A very sexy, very promising little smile. Even if she wasn't sure what he was promising.

"The sooner we wash those windows, the more time I have for…gentle pounding."

Two words that were a little ridiculous together, but Hannah had never been more turned on in her life. "Okay, let's go."

He chuckled as she took his hand and started up the sidewalk in the direction they'd come. "Hey, hang on." He tugged her to a stop.

"What?"

"Where were we going?" he asked, nodding in the direction they'd been walking.

"Oh, just to Hope's."

"Hope's shop? Why?"

"I was thinking about massage oil and stuff," she said, touching her neck almost subconsciously. But she saw his eyes follow her movement. She dropped it. "I was going to seduce you."

He tugged on her hand again, this time bringing her up against him. "Damn, I think I would have enjoyed that."

"Well, the whole rejecting-you thing was in public," she said, suddenly feeling a little vixen-ish. She'd never felt like a vixen—or anything even close to one—in her life. In Sapphire Falls, she'd always been the good girl, the girl next door at best. In Seattle, she'd been…in pain and lost and confused, frankly.

Now, back in her hometown, with Kyle, she felt like so much more than any of that. She felt powerful in a way she never had before. Because Kyle would take care of her.

The irony of that was not missed on her. Not only that it made her feel powerful—or like she could risk trying to be powerful anyway—because Kyle would be there to back her up. But also that she was here now feeling something she hadn't before…because he was being exactly who he'd always been.

Kyle was the rock. *The* rock. Everyone's rock.

And if she'd learned anything over the past three years, it was to cling to the things that were steady and solid because life, the universe, and everything could shift and change in the blink of an eye.

Speaking of blinking eyes—suddenly Hannah was blinking back tears. She gave him what she was sure was a wobbly smile. "I was thinking that in private there could be a lot less pushing."

He did that thing again where a simple curl to his mouth made her stomach swoop.

"But I really want to push you, Hannah," he said, the huskiness in his voice sending an arrow of need straight through her core.

"You do?"

"I do. I want to push every button and every boundary you've got."

"Yes," she breathed. She shook her head. "This is so…different for us."

"I know." But he didn't seem apologetic.

Which was good. Because she so didn't want him to be sorry for any of it. "And yes," she said, "let's do some pushing."

He gave her a wink, and she felt her heart, her stomach, and pretty much everything else flip. And maybe fall a little. She felt it. It was familiar. But she hadn't expected to feel it here. Not because Kyle wasn't fall-worthy. Not at all that. But because she didn't know she could fall again. Or further.

"But let's go to Hope's first." He started down the sidewalk again toward Main.

"Wait, what?"

"The massage oil. That could really help your neck, right?"

"But…" Well, yeah, it could. And she did want to give him an education about some of the alternative health options. If Hope was knowledgeable and right here in Sapphire Falls, Kyle needed to know about what she had to offer. And Hannah was curious. "Okay," she agreed, falling into step beside him.

And she kept her hand in his. Sure, she was technically supposed to be pulling away, but no one had driven or walked by, so she was going to enjoy it as long as she could.

A little bell tinkled overhead as they stepped into

Hope's shop a few minutes later. The aroma, of course, was the first thing that made an impression. The air was scented with lavender, cinnamon, sage, lemon, sandalwood, and dozens of others. Hannah knew it could be overwhelming at first, but she filled her lungs with the air and sighed happily.

Kyle gave her an amused and slightly affectionate look. "I like that sound."

"I like making it," she returned.

"Challenge accepted."

She wanted to respond—by pulling him in for a hot kiss—but just then a woman with pale blonde hair with purple streaks came through the curtain that covered the doorway behind the counter. "Hi," she said brightly. She gave Kyle a big smile then looked back at Hannah. "You must be Hannah."

Hannah laughed. "Hi, Hope, it's nice to meet you."

"I was wondering when you were going to stop by. If it wasn't soon, I was going to send a thank-you gift to your grandmother's for you." Hope came around the counter, and Hannah took in the picture of one of the women in Sapphire Falls who, by all accounts, was delightful and fit right in, but who was nothing like a "regular" Sapphire Falls girl.

She was average height and build, with long hair and big green eyes and an easy smile. But she was dressed in a billowy white top and wore multiple rings and bracelets that tinkled as she moved. She also wore a multicolored wraparound skirt that fell to her ankles. And she was barefoot. She gave off a very hippie vibe, and Hannah liked her immediately.

"A thank-you gift?" Hannah asked.

"I've had more business in here since you've been back than I've had in the last six months put together," Hope said with a grin. "This is a very part-time, just-for-fun mostly thing for me anyway, but it's been so nice to have new faces in the door, asking questions and trying new things."

"And you're thanking me for that?" Hannah asked. Then it dawned on her. "Oh, you mean Albert and Conrad and Frank?" She was glad they'd stopped in to check out some of the oils she'd talked to them about.

"Oh them, and most of their friends, and Albert's girlfriend and her best friend and daughter, and Frank's granddaughter, and Conrad's sister's card club." Hope gave Hannah a wink. "You've stirred up a lot of curiosity."

"I'm so glad," Hannah told her sincerely. "I'm a big believer."

"Well, I'm so happy you came in. And if you feel like teaching any yoga classes or if you need a massage table," Hope gestured to encompass her shop and the rooms that were, apparently, down the hallway to her left, "please let me know. I'd love to have someone to share this with."

"Hope's a new mom," Kyle said. "Peyton was going to come in and do a few evening classes for Hope, but now she's working a lot more with her party-planning business."

"Yes. And Peyton's version of yoga was less," Hope seemed to be searching for the right word, "relaxing than mine."

Hannah laughed. "I remember that Peyton is…energetic."

Hope nodded but she was smiling affectionately. "She's one of a kind."

"Hope is Peyton's half-sister," Kyle said.

Hannah nodded. "Grandma told me about that. I'm so glad you found each other."

Hope took a deep, satisfied breath. "I'm so glad I came here and found my home and family," she said.

Hannah's breath caught in her chest, surprising her. She was, strangely, a little jealous of Hope.

Hope was running an alternative medicine shop, essentially, right in the midst of Hannah's hometown.

Where she figured people would hear "meditation" and turn and walk in the other direction. Not to mention oils and yoga. But Hope was making it happen. And she'd found Sapphire Falls and fallen in love and was now living a life that was so much like the one Hannah could have had, for a moment she felt tears stinging.

But she couldn't actually be jealous. Hope hadn't taken any of this away from Hannah. She could have had it all. Probably the key to the shop was that Hope hadn't worried what these people would think of her because she wasn't from here, and they had no preconceived notions. That wasn't true for Hannah.

But not only could Hannah have had all of this. She still could. She could stay. She could…

Then she looked at Kyle.

She couldn't stay. She'd promised him she'd leave. He was getting close to her, letting his guard down a little, because he knew she was leaving. He was spending this time with her because he knew they had a plan. She'd already turned his world upside down once. Now he had things back together and knew, maybe even more now, what he wanted. She couldn't change everything again. He might go along with an impromptu trip to Hope's shop, maybe give in to some kissing later, maybe even more, but all because it was still within the defined context of what he'd laid out from day one.

She couldn't tell him she was rethinking things. That wasn't fair. His words and actions and reactions might be completely different if he knew *that* was the plan. Or even a possibility.

And she shouldn't be thinking all of that anyway. Sure, Sapphire Falls had "let" Hope open a yoga studio, do a few massages, and sell some little bottles of oils. It didn't sound like the entire town had fully embraced it anyway.

More would come if you were in here too.

She tried to ignore the voice. But it was clearly true.

Since she'd been in town and talking about the oils and such, Hope's business had increased. It was a little silly, but there was something to be said for being a hometown girl, born and raised.

You would love this. You've loved working with Albert and Conrad and Frank and everyone else.

"So, just let me know about the yoga," Hope said.

Hannah forced herself to concentrate.

"Do you know anything about acupuncture?" Kyle asked Hope.

Hope looked as surprised as Hannah felt at his question.

"I know a few practitioners and I've had it done," Hope said. "I loved it. I think it saved me from carpal tunnel."

"Hannah could probably use a space to do some of it here," Kyle said.

Hannah looked at him in surprise. He was volunteering that information? And not cringing?

"Really? Oh my gosh, would you work on me sometime?" Hope asked, fully sincere.

"Oh, I don't know..."

"You'd rather do it on the park benches and picnic tables?" Kyle asked.

He looked mildly amused. Hannah narrowed her eyes. "I don't know what you mean."

"You found out all about my dating history and God knows what else without even asking. Do you really think that I haven't heard about the acupuncture and massage and stretching you've been doing at the diner and bakery and the Come Again and down at the park?"

Hannah swallowed. She'd really been trying not to step on his toes. But dammit, people were coming to her with questions, and she was not only qualified to answer them, but she was passionate about what she did. "I haven't done any acupuncture in any public places," she said. Sticking a needle in Kade's arm at the bar the other night didn't count. She might have done one—or four—treatments in people's homes, but that's not what they were talking about. And he probably knew about it anyway.

"But you've done some massage," Kyle said. "And given lots of advice."

She shrugged. "Completely conservative suggestions. And I always encourage them to talk about it with their physician."

"That's strange that it seems whenever I walk up on a conversation in a public place in the last several days, all talking stops," Kyle said dryly.

Hope laughed. "Well, everyone is taking your kissing as a recommendation, Dr. Ames."

"Our kissing?" Hannah asked.

"I heard you were heating up the kitchen at the Come Again," Hope confirmed.

Well, so much for sliding around the corner. Hannah felt her cheeks heat and decided to just not think about who had seen what in that kitchen. Other than Kyle of course. And thinking about what *he* had seen—and touched—her cheeks got even hotter.

"I already owe you thanks," Hope went on. "And now I'm going to hound you until you can work on me," Hope said. "Please look around and let me give you some things as a thank-you." Hope waved toward her shelves and the little round tables she had set up throughout the shop that held various displays.

"Oh, that's not—" Hannah started.

"I insist," Hope interrupted. "Really."

"Well…" Hannah looked at Kyle. "I was thinking about some lavender, chamomile, orange and ylang-ylang."

"Someone needs to relax a little?" Hope asked, moving toward her shelves.

"He does," Hannah confirmed.

"Who?" Kyle asked, frowning slightly. "Kade?"

"You. I was going to sneak into your room at Ty's and spray it on your sheets and pillows," Hannah told him.

He grabbed her wrist as she started to follow Hope. "If you're sneaking into my room and doing anything to my sheets and pillows, you better be naked and planning to stay for a while."

The tingly *yes please* feeling tickled through her and she gave him a smile. "I don't know if I'll sneak in naked, but I can get that way quickly once I'm through the door."

His eyes darkened and he said, "Or you can just start the night in there with me and there will be no need for sneaking."

"Even better. I—"

"I think these would combine nicely with this oil," Hope said from across the shop, clearly not realizing she was interrupting.

Hannah gave Kyle a wink and joined the other woman near the chamomile oil.

They talked shop for a few minutes until Kyle came up next to her again and asked, "Would this be good for your neck?"

She looked at the little bottle he held, then up at him. "Yes. How did you know that?"

"She has little cards all over that talk about the benefits of each oil and stuff," he said, glancing around the room. "It's amazing that all of these things can do all of that."

Hannah grinned and shared a look with Hope. It was always fun to bring in someone new to the world of essential oils and aromatherapy and the other natural, healing things she'd spent the last three years on. She'd just learned that Hope had pretty much grown up around all of this, and that her shop reminded her a lot of one her mother had owned in Sedona.

"That would be great for her neck," Hope confirmed. "But it's best if it's mixed in an oil and applied by someone else."

Hannah caught the twinkle in Hope's eye. "Oh, yes, that's true. No problem. Kade's done this a lot of times."

"Yeah, well, too bad Kade's not going to be seeing you for a while," Kyle said. He handed the bottle of oil to Hope. "We'll take it. Mix it up however it needs to be to help Hannah."

And in spite of how sweet and funny and hot it was when Kyle got possessive, Hannah felt a little prick of tears behind her eyelids again. He was doing this because he did care about her. He wasn't pushing his medicine on her. He was willing to do it her way.

"You bet," Hope told him. "I'll mix this up too," she said to Hannah, indicating the four vials Hannah had chosen for Kyle's relaxing room spray, and the sweet marjoram she was going to make into a cream for Alice. It would help with inflammation and muscle pain after her surgery.

The moment Hope disappeared through her curtain, Hannah turned to Kyle. She put her hands on his forearms and pulled him close, then she rose on tiptoe and kissed him. Just a sweet, not-too-short, not-too-long kiss.

"You thought you heard someone coming?" he asked when she pulled back.

She smiled up at him, remembering her excuse for the kiss at the Come Again. "No. That one was completely because I couldn't help it."

"Well, if we can use that excuse…" He cupped the back of her head and lowered his lips to hers again.

This kiss was much less sweet, and much longer, than Hannah's, and she felt like she was vibrating from head to toe by the time he lifted his head. His hand slid down to the back of her neck again and he just held her there. He was gentle, touching her head and neck, but he didn't shy away from it and didn't touch her as if she would break. It was almost protective the way he held her.

And she loved it. She loved that he knew about it now and wasn't intimidated by it. Sure, it might be in part because he was a doctor, but she loved that he was still

comfortable touching her and trusting her to tell him if he
needed to stop or do something differently.

"Let's get those windows washed," he said gruffly.

She nodded. But she already had other ideas. Those
windows could wait. Showing Kyle how much fun
spontaneity could be…naked spontaneity, to be
specific…could not wait.

Chapter Ten

He was barely keeping his shit together.

Hannah's neck…God. She had a metal plate holding one of her vertebra together, for fuck's sake. And she hadn't told him. She'd been "fine" when she'd called to tell him about the accident.

She wasn't even close to fine.

And she hadn't fucking told him.

He'd been right about being bad at relationships with women. Clearly. His own girlfriend, practically his fiancée, had been in a major accident, had surgery, endured therapy and pain, was *still* dealing with pain issues, and she hadn't told him a thing about it.

Kyle forced himself to say a nice goodbye to Hope. He even managed a smile. But it seemed like all of the things Hannah had told him on the sidewalk on Teal street were suddenly sinking in.

And she hadn't had sex in three years. Since him. Jesus, *that* was enough to rip apart absolutely *anything* that had been holding his emotions back. He was beyond thrilled that she hadn't been involved with anyone else. He was also worked up about her being scared of it though. He so wanted to help her find that pleasure again. But he so did *not* want to do one damned thing that might hurt her.

All of the relaxing/energizing/healing/positive aromas he'd just been inhaling in Hope's shop weren't doing shit to help his emotional turmoil.

But then Hannah slipped her hand into his as they stepped out of Hope's shop.

He took a deep breath, worked on not squeezing her hand too hard, and absorbed not just the feel of her, but that she'd initiated it and how natural it felt.

"Endorphins can also be really good for pain," she said as they walked along Main. She said it matter-of-factly, looking in the window at the clothing shop.

But Kyle's reaction was hardly matter-of-fact. "You need some endorphins, Hannah?" he asked.

"I think we both need some endorphins." She looked over at him.

"What makes you say that?"

"You're wound tight," she said. "I can feel it."

Wound tight was an understatement. "It's been an interesting day so far."

She nodded and kept walking. But he pulled her around to face him, stepping close. Right on Main Street. And she definitely did not push him away.

"I don't get worked up like this about things," he told her. "I handle stuff. I'm the go-to guy when other people get worked up."

She nodded again.

"But you—you make me feel things that I don't know how to handle. And it's messing with me." He lifted a hand to the back of her neck. "I *hate* that you're hurt."

She gave him a little smile and said, "Well, while I really want to show you that you don't have to be everything to everyone all the time…I'm going to tell you something that I think will help you a lot right now."

"Lay it on me." He'd love to hear this.

"A lot of people could be doing the things you do for other people—painting bedrooms and washing windows and making pasta and stuff—but there's something you can do for me that no one else can."

He felt his heart expand painfully. Damn, he really did have a thing for being The Guy. And being The Guy for Hannah, in any way, was dangerously enticing. "Tell me," he said, his voice low and firm.

"You can give me an orgasm. Or ten."

Heat ripped through him. "That idea isn't exactly

helping me feel *less* wound up," he said. "But yes. Absolutely. I'm your guy. Let's go."

He started down the sidewalk, pulling her along behind him. She laughed and jogged to catch up.

Wound up didn't begin to describe it, actually. And it was a combination of so many things. It was the fact that she'd trusted him with her secrets. It was the fact that he wanted to take care of her and protect her and make her feel good, and be whatever she needed him to be. But also that she was feeling a little like healing him too. She was worried about how much he did for other people, how much of his life was spent on other people's lives, and how he needed to relax—apparently. And while he certainly didn't think there was really anything to *worry* about, he did like that she was trying to take care of him.

They hadn't done that for each other before.

They had both been kicking ass and taking names and setting goals and mowing them down. Hannah had never really needed him. Sure, she loved when he worked beside her and they turned manual labor into something fun and flirty. But it wasn't like she couldn't have gotten it done without him. She was the most capable person he'd ever met, next to himself.

Now it was different. They were seeing things in the other that needed some TLC. And they wanted to be the ones giving it.

That felt…awesome. He could admit it. In all those years of taking care of other people together, they'd never really taken care of one another.

It was time that changed.

They turned off of Main onto a sidewalk leading north and a minute later were in a quiet residential area. Not that Main Street Sapphire Falls was loud and crazy and busy, but it was truly the hub of the businesses and where the majority of what traffic they did have could be found. Even a block north of Main, things got quiet and slower.

They cut through yards, making their way to Hannah's mom and dad's house. They weren't talking. But they didn't need to. They'd already said a lot and, frankly, Kyle's mind was a lot more focused on *showing* Hannah how he was feeling very soon.

As they came around the corner of the Warners' house, just a block over from the McIntires' house, they were hit in the face with drops of water and they pulled up short. The Warners were watering their lawn.

The spray arched away from them, and Kyle said, "We'll have to cut this way." He started to skirt the wet yard and head through the space between the shed and the neighbor's yard, but Hannah pulled him to a stop.

"Or," she said, giving him a big smile. "We could just go right through here."

There was a mischievous twinkle in her eyes that made Kyle willing to do anything. It was strange, but he wasn't sure he'd ever seen Hannah mischievous before. He'd seen plenty of other emotions, of course, over the years, but definitely nothing that had to do with trouble or naughtiness.

He liked it. A lot. Which was also a little unusual for him. And worth exploring. He liked predictable. Mischief was not predictable. And Lord knew he should be careful about letting things with Hannah be unpredictable. But he couldn't help himself, it seemed.

"Through the sprinklers?" he asked, eyeing the fountain-like spray that bowed over the yard, leaving silvery drops on the grass.

She nodded and started walking backward, tugging him with her.

"But we'll get wet," he said. It was a weak protest at best. But honestly, neither of them had ever been big into getting messy in the past. Then again, things had gotten messy anyway.

"Yeah, but you like it when I get wet."

Kyle stopped. Hannah had never talked dirty. Not to him. And frankly, if he thought about her doing it with anyone else, a possessive anger filled his chest. Suddenly, with that single, still-not-even-all-*that*-dirty sentence, he wanted to hear so much more. "Yeah, I really do," he told her with a nod.

"And if our *clothes* get wet, we'll just have to take them off and put them in the dryer when we get to my house."

Yep, he was all in here.

He pulled her to his body, wrapped his arms around her, and lifted her off the ground. She gave a little shriek as he headed into the cold spray. Within moments, they were both soaked. They were also laughing. And Kyle felt like his heart was beating harder than it ever had, looking into her eyes as they spun through the sprinkler like two little kids. He wasn't sure he'd ever seen her quite like this. And, hell, he'd seen her as a little kid. But even then, she'd been more…reserved. He'd seen her happy, of course. But this was different. This was just pure happiness on her face. It wasn't about some accomplishment or some big family event or a parade or the annual festival. It was simple and spontaneous and…absolutely gorgeous. They hadn't done this—this silly, in-the-moment-just-because fun. Not enough, anyway. Not nearly enough.

Their skin grew wetter and slippery, and Hannah's grip on his neck grew tighter, until almost instinctively, she wrapped her legs around his waist to keep from sliding. His hands went to her ass to keep her up against him and their mouths ended up only millimeters apart. They stood under the spray, just looking at each other, not caring that rivulets of water were running down their faces and that their clothes were plastered to their bodies.

Well, he cared about that a little. Her tank and shorts molded to her body, and she looked like a freaking water goddess.

"I wish I could keep this look on your face forever," he

told her, not even aware he was going to say the words until he had.

Her expression softened. "Really?"

"Really. God, maybe if we'd done more of this—" He cut himself off before he completed the sentence.

She pressed her lips together, staring into his eyes. Then she said, "I know. I think that too."

"I'm sorry. For not being what you needed." His voice sounded tight, which made sense since he practically felt his throat squeezing the words as they went past.

She took a shaky breath. "Don't be. We were us, Kyle. We were what we both wanted us to be then."

He nodded. "Yeah. I know. I just— We missed some stuff."

She nodded. "But we're here now. We can do that stuff now."

"Anything," he said, completely serious. "Anything to make you look like that."

Maybe he should be strong, nurse his hurt feelings a little longer, remember the pain and regret. But this didn't feel weak. This felt like…healing. It felt like things that had been broken were getting put back together. Maybe even stronger than before.

"What's going to keep me looking like this is you holding me, just like this, but without any clothes between us."

Kyle immediately pivoted in the direction of her house and started across the lawn.

She laughed. "You can't carry me all the way there."

"Watch me."

She leaned in and put her mouth near his ear. "We can get there faster if you put me down and we run."

He dropped her to her feet immediately, grabbed her hand and, laughing, they ran to her mom and dad's. The back door was, of course, unlocked. As were all back doors in Sapphire Falls. Which was a little crazy and a little great.

They burst through the door and into the kitchen. Hannah stripped her shirt over her head as she started for the laundry room, but Kyle reached out and snagged the back of her shorts.

He pulled her to a stop, spun her, and backed her up against the door. Then he kissed her. And kissed her. And kissed her. He held the back of her neck in one hand, the other squeezing her hip as he poured his passion and regret and affection and concern into the kiss. This had to be good for her. He had to be gentle, even as he wanted to rip every stitch of clothing from her body and run his tongue and lips and hands over every inch of her.

She was wiggling against him now, and he felt her hands slip under the edge of his shirt and start rolling it up his body. The wet cotton definitely didn't move as smoothly as when it was dry. When she got it to his armpits, he leaned back only enough to help her peel it off. She ran her hands over his pecs and shoulders, down his sides, and over his stomach. The muscles jumped under her touch, and he felt a shiver go through him—desire, anticipation, and yeah, that pure happiness again.

He brought her in for another kiss, thoroughly exploring her mouth, a little lazier this time, but she started wiggling almost right away and making those sighing-moaning sounds that shot straight to his cock.

He felt her hands at his fly and realized he needed to catch up a little. He moved his hands to the waistband of her shorts, grateful for the baggier cotton. He quickly sent them to her ankles, unable to keep from looking down and taking in her plain white bra and the purple polka-dotted panties.

"I don't match my underwear and bras anymore," she said, lowering his zipper.

Her knuckles skimmed over his erection and he sucked in a breath. "I don't care about matching bras and panties, Hannah."

"It just seemed so silly to be worried about stuff like that."

"Totally silly. Doesn't matter if they match once they're on the floor," he agreed.

She started to pull his jeans over his hips but, as everyone knew, wet denim was a bitch to get off. She yanked and tugged for a few seconds but finally let out a breath. "You're going to have to do it."

But he had a better plan at the moment. Keeping his pants on for a little bit seemed like a good idea. So that he could take the time to do some other things they hadn't done before.

"Laundry room," he told her, turning her and nudging her in that direction.

She went without argument, grabbing their shirts and her shorts from the floor on her way. Kyle took a second to appreciate how fucking amazing her ass looked in the unmatched purple polka dots. He ran a hand through his wet hair, then started after her.

Hannah tossed the clothes into the dryer, then turned to face him. She watched him watch her unhook her bra and toss it in too. Then she slipped her panties off.

Kyle could have sworn he actually felt his blood rush to his cock.

Damn. She looked exactly as he remembered her, and yet different. It was as if his memories of her had dimmed. Real-life, high-definition 3D was...fucking amazing. "You're gorgeous," he choked out.

She gave him a smile and said, "You've still got clothes on."

"Yeah, it's staying that way for a while."

She lifted a brow. "Oh?"

"I need some control. Wet denim might be my only hope."

"You don't need control." She frowned slightly. "I'm not fragile."

"That's not the problem."

"You're sure? I don't want you to go easy on me."

Christ. She sure as hell wasn't going easy on *him*, talking like that. "I intend to go just exactly the way you need me to go," he told her. "But if I take my pants off, I'm going to thrust first and think later."

She laughed at that. "I wouldn't mind more thrusting and less thinking right now, Dr. Ames."

That didn't help either. There was something dirty about her calling him by his title while bare-assed naked in front of him. And he really fucking liked it.

"Hannah," he said, his voice gruff.

"Yeah?"

"Get up on the dryer."

Her eyes widened slightly, but she boosted herself up on the machine without any questions or protests.

And that was maybe the hottest thing he'd ever seen.

He'd never been bossy, per se. They'd always been on the same page. Honest to God, with every damned thing. It was as if they could read each other's minds and finish each other's sentences. Of course, he hadn't known that she was actually hurt after her accident. Or that all the pressure here was what had kept her away.

He tamped down those feelings and thoughts. Now was definitely not the time to get into that. He was going to be fully focused on her and what she needed at *this moment*.

He'd stew about the other moments later.

Kyle stepped closer, but not quite close enough to touch her. Yet. "I want this to be so good for you."

"It will. I know it will. I'm not worried, Kyle."

"You said you haven't had sex in three years," he reminded her.

"Right. But it's not like I've forgotten."

Well, that was good. "But you've been scared of it."

She nodded. "With anyone but you."

He felt himself frown before he caught it. "I know it

makes me kind of an ass to be glad you haven't been with anyone else."

Looking at her now, he absolutely couldn't imagine another man ever touching her. She was his. That had never felt truer. Even when he'd been taking it for granted that he'd always have her.

It was crazy to be thinking that way, he knew. She was home to visit. This was...a fling? A fluke? Neither of those seemed right. And yet, how could this be anything more?

"I thought it was about my neck," she said softly. "And it was. In part. But even going on dates felt weird." She ducked her head. "It always felt weird being with anyone but you."

He crossed the space between them quickly and tipped her chin up. "Good," he growled, then he covered her mouth with his.

She gripped his shoulders, pressing close, and he groaned at the feel of her nipples against his chest. He lifted a hand and cupped one breast, rubbing his thumb over the tip. She gave a little half cry, half moan. He tugged and rubbed, then lowered his head and took the nipple in his mouth, sucking hard.

"Yes, *Kyle*," she gasped, her hand going to his head and curling into his hair.

"You know those buttons and boundaries I want to push?" he asked, panting against her breast.

"Yeah."

"I want to push right now."

"Okay."

He stepped back, somehow. "I want to watch you come."

"Yes. Okay." She reached for him, but he stepped back again.

"With *your* fingers first."

She paused, as if needing to process his words. Then her eyes widened. "What?"

"Please tell me that in three years of no sex with anyone else, you've at least been getting yourself off," he said.

She wet her lips and seemed to be contemplating her answer. Finally, she said, "Of course."

He let out a breath. "Do you have a vibrator?"

She nodded.

"Damn, I want to see that too," he practically muttered, his gaze raking over her body. He stepped in again and shut the dryer door. Then he reached past her and pushed the *on* button. The machine became to rumble under her and he watched her eyes widen. "Touch yourself, Hannah."

She sucked in a quick breath. "Wha—what?"

"Touch yourself. Take that hand that I can't wait to feel wrapped around my cock, and make yourself come."

Her pupils dilated and her cheeks flushed. But it wasn't embarrassment. He knew that. She was incredibly turned on.

"I've…we've…never done that," she said.

He leaned in, took her wrist, and moved her hand between her legs. "Please." He knew there was no way she could doubt how worked up he was. How much he wanted this. How much he *needed* it.

Hannah flexed her fingers and took a quick breath.

"Go on, honey," he urged.

She moved her hand, running her middle finger up and down in the sweet folds between her legs. It was a gorgeous, hot, amazing, dream-come-true sight. And it wasn't enough.

Kyle reached down and grasped one of her feet. He stretched her leg to put her heel up on the edge of the dryer, spreading her open. She gasped, but her hand kept moving, and the sight nearly buckled Kyle's knees. He kept his hand on her foot, holding it there. She circled her clit, then ran lower, dipping just inside before moving up again, this time pressing harder on her clit, and he could see every bit of it.

"Damn, Hannah, that's so fucking hot."

That seemed to spur her on. She slid her finger deeper the next time, moving in and out a few times before returning to her clit. He groaned, watching her nipples grow harder and all of that beautiful pinkness glisten behind her hand. Her breaths were coming faster and her toes curled slightly as the machine continued to vibrate under her.

He felt himself squeezing her foot, but she didn't seem to mind. He gripped his other hand into a fist at his side. He wanted so badly to touch her. To help. And he decided to tell her.

"You have no idea how badly I want to drive two fingers deep and feel all of that tight, hot, wet goodness," he told her. "There's no way you can understand how fucking amazing your pussy feels. I want to dive in there and not come up for years. I'm actually jealous you get to feel that gorgeous pussy clamping down on your fingers as you come."

She gave a little whimper and her hand moved faster.

He couldn't help it then. He reached up and pinched her nipple.

"Oh, God," she moaned.

She needed to be warmed up before he took her—and he was about thirty seconds from saying to hell with it and doing just that. He needed to be sure she was ready and relaxed from at least one good orgasm. And this was a great time to take things up a notch between them. Whether this was a fling or a one-time thing or a…whatever else it might be…he wanted this to be different from how it *used* to be.

He leaned in, put his mouth against her ear and squeezed her foot, while tugging on her nipple. "Come for me, Hannah. I want you to feel what my cock's going to feel in about two minutes. I want you to understand how all I really want is to be buried deep inside you. How nothing else—food, water, sleep, work—*nothing else* matters when I'm fucking you."

She cried out at that and came with the most beautiful look on her face and his name on her lips.

She was still shaking as he grasped her hand and lifted her fingers to his mouth. He licked up and down her middle finger and then sucked on it hard. She moaned again at that, her eyes locked on his mouth.

"I wanted to do that the other night when you teased me with this," he told her. "I remember everything about how you taste and smell and feel."

He had let go of her foot, and she quickly shifted so that she could wrap her legs around his waist and pull him close. She kissed him, almost desperately.

In spite of the orgasm, it seemed she was just as worked up now as before. He struggled out of his jeans, loving the way she clung to him even when he needed both hands and a lot of twisting and yanking and jerking to get out of the wet denim. He added the jeans and his boxers to the dryer, still kissing Hannah through it all.

Finally, he took both of her hips in his hands—and then froze. He groaned and lowered his forehead to hers. "Son of a bitch."

"What?"

"This is why being prepared for things is good," he told her. "I don't have a condom."

"I'm on the pill," she told him, tightening her legs around him. "I've always been on the pill, remember?"

She had, for bad periods. But they'd always used condoms too. "We've never—"

"I haven't been with anyone else," she interrupted. "And besides being the most careful person I've ever met, you're also a doctor. I trust that you're clean."

He dragged in a deep breath and nodded. "I am."

"Then no problem," she said, digging her heels into his ass.

He cupped her chin and made her look directly into his eyes. "I've *never* had sex without a condom."

A little shiver that was clearly desire went through her. She nodded. "I understand if you don't want to." But she dug her heels into his butt again and wiggled her hot, wet center against him.

Kyle cursed. "I've never wanted anything more." His hands splayed over her ass and he squeezed. "God, I can't say no." She hesitated then for just a second. But he kissed her before she could say anything. "It has to be with you," he said against her mouth after she'd melted into him again. "This is how it should be. Nothing between us."

She moaned into his mouth and tightened her grip on him. And Kyle couldn't hold back any longer. He pulled her forward on the dryer at the same time he flexed his hips, sliding into her.

He could tell she was holding her breath as she took him. He rested a hand on the back of her neck. "Easy, honey, I've got you," he said, locking his gaze on hers.

She bit her bottom lip and nodded.

Moving slowly to let her adjust was the most exquisite torture. Her pussy gripped him like a hot, slick glove that was never coming off. He felt her muscles milking him even from the first thrust, and he knew it wasn't going to last long.

"Hannah," he said hoarsely. "You okay?"

"So good," she breathed.

He loved, *loved*, that she had never been with another man, that all of this was his, and had always been only his. He felt a primal need to beat his chest, to crow to the world that he was the only one to ever know her like this, while also hugging her close and never letting anyone else even have so much as a smile from her. Both extremes were…well, extreme. And crazy. And completely unlike him. Kyle was unruffled, cool, collected, confident. Until it came to this woman. She'd made him feel things he not only was unfamiliar with, but that he half-loved and half-hated. He didn't like feeling out of control. He didn't like not being absolutely sure. He wasn't extreme, he wasn't crazy.

But this was Hannah.

That's all the explanation he could really give. Or that he really needed.

He pulled back, sliding out of her tight sheath. He had to grit his teeth against the sensations of being bare inside of her. Holy shit, the friction and heat were so much stronger this way. And with his second stroke, Hannah McIntire ruined him for all other women.

"More," she breathed against his neck.

"You sure?"

She smiled up at him. "You need me to take over?"

He grinned, surprised. "You think you can do better?"

"I can do faster," she said, shifting against him, taking him deep all at once.

"God, Hannah." And it was as much a prayer of thanksgiving as anything.

She moved back, and then, using her legs around him for leverage, took him in again.

"You're playing with fire, girl," he told her, trying to hang on to his sanity.

"Burn me, Kyle," she said, looking into his eyes.

He groaned, and grabbed her thigh. He still held her neck too, and he used what tiny bit of rational-not-Neanderthal-caveman he had left to hold her gently there, supporting her head. Because they were getting really close to pounding territory.

He thrust in and out, watching her the whole time, taking in every detail of her reaction and gritting his teeth against the sensations streaking down his spine with every thrust. He was climbing toward his climax quickly, and he wanted her there with him.

"Hannah, honey—" But before he even finished the sentence, she clamped down on him with a cry.

He let go with a roar, coming harder than he ever had,

emptying himself inside of her. The first time he'd ever done that with a woman. And it was the most blissful, I-can-never-go-back experience he could have imagined.

They slumped against each other, the dryer rumbling underneath her.

It was several minutes before Kyle could even lift his head off her shoulder.

Before he could figure out what exactly to say that didn't come out as *holy shit* or *please don't ever leave*, Hannah smiled up at him.

"Chalk one up for spontaneous," she said.

He chuckled. "Don't think for a second that I wouldn't have written *hottest fucking sex ever* in my planner if I'd known."

She shook her head. "Part of the hotness was that it just happened."

"This didn't just happen," he told her, stepping back, the sensation of pulling out of her equally *hot damn*. "This has been building since you got back."

She tipped her head. "Yeah. I mean I figured we'd sleep together. But I kind of thought there would be some scheduling, wintergreen breath mints, and some Tim McGraw involved."

He watched her hop off of the dryer and grab a towel from the pile on the table to one side. She handed him one as well, then wrapped the huge, fuzzy yellow thing around her body. And he instantly wanted her uncovered again.

"Scheduling, wintergreen breath mints, and Tim McGraw?" he asked.

She laughed. "Sex always involved scheduling, wintergreen breath mints, and Tim McGraw."

He frowned. But she was right. He'd always kept mints and condoms in his glove box, bedside table, stashed behind his video games in the basement, and had stuck some in the side pocket of Hannah's purse. So they were never caught without. Of course, generally, they both knew exactly when it was going to happen. Thanks to the scheduling. Fortunately, he'd pretty much always had his iPod with him—and Tim McGraw's greatest hits.

"I can't even smell wintergreen without thinking of you," she told him, watching him wrap the towel around his waist. "One sniff and I want to cry."

That hit him right in the chest. He had hoped that she'd missed him. But hearing that she'd cried hurt now. Maybe because he now knew about her neck and her physical pain. Dammit. She was even making him feel bad about her feeling bad—something he'd *hoped* for even up until the other day.

He reached out and pulled her against him. "Well, now you can smell it, eat it, whatever again. Because I'm right here. Nothing to miss."

She gave him a smile, but it wobbled at the corners, and he knew exactly what she was thinking.

For now.

Chapter Eleven

Kyle cupped the back of her neck with both hands and looked into her eyes. "You okay?"

God, the way he touched her, the way he cradled her neck and head, got to her. She didn't need that careful of a touch. She was feeling great. Endorphins for the win. And some of it was relief as well. Relief that she could have hot sex and her neck wouldn't seize up. And just pure happiness over being with Kyle again.

But Kyle's hands on her like that felt incredible. Just his hands on her neck. It wasn't sexual, but it was as intimate a touch as any other. And it hit her that they hadn't really taken care of one another before. They'd been partners in taking care of everyone else.

He'd helped her with chemistry and she'd helped him with geometry. He'd called her every night when she'd been sick with mono, but their conversations were mostly about the things he needed to do to take over the plans for the student council dinner she'd been putting together. She'd held his hand during his grandfather's funeral, but he'd been more worried about his grandma and mom than himself. Hannah had ended up helping to clean the kitchen at Ruby's house after the visitors all left while Kyle went through the sympathy cards with his family. And that's how they'd both liked things. They liked being the caretakers and having the other to help them out.

But it had been rare that they'd focused their energy just on each other.

And now, in these few minutes, she already knew that if Kyle would make her one of the people he took care of, she'd never want to leave.

That wasn't fair, of course. He'd fallen in love with her

because she was a partner, someone who would be beside him, not because he needed anyone else to take care of. In fact, that was the last thing he needed.

She did wonder, though, who was taking care of *him*. He had lots of people who loved him and who would do anything for him. But she knew he didn't ask them. Or let them. He was the doer.

So, it couldn't last; it could only be a brief, stolen period of time where they both let go of their previous roles and ideas. But she was selfish enough to steal that period of time.

"Play hooky with me," she said, grasping his wrists where he held on to her.

"What?"

"Play hooky with me," she repeated. "Blow off the things you think you need to do today and just stay naked with me the rest of the day and night."

His pupils dilated, but he said, "Your mom will be home at seven."

"How do you know that?" Hannah asked. He was right, but she was surprised he knew.

"It's the third week of the month," he said with a shrug. "So she works seven to seven this week."

Well, of course he would know that. She shook her head. "So we won't stay here. Let's go…to Omaha. We'll get a fancy hotel room and room service."

"I can't go to Omaha," he said. "I need to stay close."

Damn. She should have expected that. She'd seriously consider kidnapping him to Hawaii or something, but she knew *that* would be a little too spontaneous. "Then let's go camp out at the river," she said. "We'll have sex under the stars."

He swallowed. "The windows."

"They'll still be dirty in a couple of days, we can do them then."

She wasn't sure why she felt so desperate that this had

to happen *now*, but there was something here she wanted to grab on to. She wanted his full focus, his full attention. In the past, she'd been as guilty as he was of multitasking no matter what they were doing. Making to-do lists while watching a movie. Planning some big family barbecue while they were sitting on that swing in her grandmother's backyard. They'd always been on the go.

Now she wanted...just him. She was jealous of all the things and people that got his attention and time and energy. She'd never felt that way before. She'd been giving all of hers away too. But now she needed him, with just her, for as long as she could have him. Which wouldn't be long, she knew. It wouldn't last. Couldn't. That was who Kyle was, and as much as she wanted him to relax and have fun too, she knew he would never be able to fully let go of all of his responsibilities and schedules.

But maybe for one night. Tonight. Maybe she could have him all to herself.

"Please," she said, moving in closer and contemplating for about one second if she was actually willing to use his concern for her to get her way. Then his gaze dropped to her mouth, and a ribbon of heat curled through her and she decided that yes, she was willing to do that. She could feel bad about it tomorrow while she was washing windows.

"I'm so relieved, so happy, that the sex worked," she told him. "And now, I just want more. More of you. Everything you can give me." Okay, there, she was giving him something to take care of. That would surely work. "We could just go back to your room at Ty's, turn off our phones, and hide out together."

He pulled in a deep breath and moved a hand to cup her cheek. "No."

Her heart plummeted.

"Not Ty's," he said. "But I know the perfect place."

For a millisecond, she thought her heart had stopped, but then it kicked against her chest, and she took a huge breath. Oh my God, he'd said yes. He was going to escape the world with her for one night.

She stepped to him, wrapped her arms around his neck, and kissed him. One hand dropped to her ass and he pressed her close.

"Thank you," she whispered against his mouth. "I just need you tonight."

"I'm all yours," he answered gruffly.

She pulled back to look into his eyes. "You promise?"

He nodded. "I do."

She stepped back. "I get it's a big deal to just disappear," she told him. She did need him to know that she understood his effort here. "I'll call Derek and give him my cell. If there are any emergencies, he'll know and can get ahold of you."

"I really have to turn my phone off?" Kyle looked a little panicked at the idea.

She smiled. "Only my grandmother, my parents, Kade, and now Derek have my number. So we know if it rings, it's important. Whereas, if *yours* rings, it could be any one of about five hundred people."

"Yeah, okay."

"If there are any issues you need to be aware of, Derek or my family will let you know."

He took a breath. "Okay."

She kissed him one more time, then said, "I promise this will be good."

He cupped her face. "I know it will."

And her heart skittered again.

"But," he added.

Crud, she didn't want any buts tonight.

"Our clothes aren't dry yet."

"Oh." She glanced at the dryer. "True."

"So, how about this… I go do some of the windows while we wait for them to dry. When they're done, we'll head out. Then it's you and me and no work for the rest of the night."

Hannah shook her head. "I should have known you'd find a way to get some more work done first." But she said it with affection. He was such a great guy. A great guy who needed to have more fun in his life, but definitely a great guy.

"You pack us a picnic, maybe grab some pillows and sleeping bags, and maybe some candles, okay?" he asked.

She liked the sound of all of that. "Where are we going?"

"It's a surprise." He gave her a grin, and it hit her hard that she would happily look at that grin for the rest of her life. Kyle wasn't big into surprises—giving or getting—so this was a huge deal.

"Okay," she said, returning his smile. "I'm game."

"And do you think your dad has some shorts I could borrow?" he asked, looking down at the towel he wore.

She reached out and hooked a finger in the top of the towel and tugged. But he caught her wrist—and the towel—before she got it undone. "Don't start something you can't finish right now," he told her huskily. "I'll put you back up on this dryer."

She wanted that. Even more than she would have expected. "I'm not arguing."

"Well, now you've got this new idea in my head. I think I'd rather have you all to myself with no risk of interruption," he told her. "Because I'd really rather you just stay naked until sometime tomorrow morning." He leaned in and put his lips against hers. "Sometime *late* tomorrow morning."

She was even going to get him to sleep in and go in late to work? She nodded. "Okay. Yes. Hurry with the windows."

"I might not even clean every corner."

She mock gasped. "You? Kyle Ames?"

"I know. This is what you do to me."

She grinned, then pointed behind him. "There's clean laundry right there. Probably some shorts of Dad's in there."

He dug through the laundry basket and pulled out a pair of workout shorts. "These will do."

She didn't even bother to try looking like she wasn't watching as he dropped the towel and pulled the shorts on.

"Hannah," he said, his voice low.

She let her eyes travel slowly up his torso to his face. "Yeah?"

"Do you think your mom has any chocolate syrup in the fridge?"

"Probably."

"Be sure to pack that too."

She lifted a brow. "Yeah?" They had never used chocolate or whipped cream or anything like that during sex before. And suddenly that seemed like a damned shame.

"Definitely."

"Got it."

She watched him turn and head out the back door to the garage where the window-washing supplies supposedly were. She didn't feel bad putting the chore off. Her father had clearly made it up as an excuse to put her and Kyle together while he and Alice were out of town. And knowing Kyle, he'd sneak back over here in the night after she fell asleep and do it by flashlight.

Of course, that depended on where he was taking her. A little shiver of excitement danced through her, and she spun toward the kitchen. A romantic picnic, pillows and sleeping bags, and candles. Check, check, and check.

She found a small cooler on the back porch and filled it with cheese and crackers, some sliced ham, fruit, and the chocolate sauce her dad no doubt used on ice cream. She'd have to replace that before he noticed—and hopefully he would be too full from dinner with Alice to want ice cream tonight—because she wasn't going to explain why she'd taken that. She also added a couple of bottled waters, a couple of sodas, and two of her mother's wine coolers. Her mom and dad weren't fancy and didn't have expensive tastes. They were salt-of-the-earth people and, frankly, when it came right down to it, it wasn't the champagne that made a romantic evening romantic. She knew Kyle wouldn't care at all that they had ham instead of caviar and the chocolate syrup was an off-brand. And she loved him for that.

Hannah froze with a wine cooler in hand.

She loved Kyle for being down-to-earth and appreciating the important things in life.

Her loving him wasn't really a shock. She'd always loved him. But she realized in that moment that she'd been full of shit for about three years now.

She was not happier in Seattle, where she'd been exposed to new things and had to get out of her comfort zone. Sure, that was great. She'd grown up, learned some things, experienced some things that she would never forget and that she was grateful for. But she *wanted* to be in her comfort zone. Maybe that wasn't liberated or evolved or worldly or whatever. But one of the things she'd learned was that comfort was valuable and easily taken for granted. And she wanted it in her life. She wanted things to be simple and straightforward. She wanted things to depend on. She wanted to know that, no matter what else happened, tomorrow and the next day and the day after that would be full of family dinners and laughing with neighbors and holiday celebrations and falling asleep in the arms of someone who loved her and would take care of her.

Hannah felt tears gathering, and she blinked rapidly as she stored the last bottle and shut the cooler.

The cooler that she would love to borrow again and again when she and Kyle made plans to head to the river or out on a road trip. They could, of course, buy their own cooler, but it would be fun to stop over and see her parents and have her mom insist they take stuff for sandwiches too. And then when they dropped the cooler off again, they could give her mom and dad a bunch of the extra stuff she and Kyle had picked up at the roadside produce stand they would find...

She heard a thump against the side of the house and it pulled her thoughts from that crazy daydream.

But this whole thing—doing laundry and washing windows and raiding the fridge at her mom and dad's—just seemed so damned...awesome.

Okay, so maybe she was going to have a hard time going back to Seattle. Kyle would love that. That had been his goal all along. To make leaving the hardest thing she'd ever done.

But there was something in how he looked at her. And how he touched her. And how he was willing to run away with her tonight—at least a little—that made her think maybe she wasn't the only one with a change of heart. Literally.

She needed to get that man to wherever their hideaway was.

Now.

Kyle looked over as the back door banged shut.

And dropped the hose.

Hannah had come out of the house to help. Apparently. And her clothes weren't dry yet. Apparently. Or she was just trying to drive him crazy. And she'd been rummaging through the dresser in her old bedroom. Apparently.

"I didn't know you actually had bikinis," he told her, crossing the grass quickly.

"I only wore them to lay out in the backyard," she said as he got close enough to practically stand on her toes. "Not really appropriate for river or pool parties."

He didn't touch her. Once he started, he wasn't going to stop. But he definitely let his gaze roam over every inch. "We didn't really go to river or pool parties." He wasn't sure why he said it, but he realized it was true.

Hannah nodded. "I know."

"And we never really went to the Come Again," he said. They hadn't been old enough for most of the time they'd lived here, but they just hadn't socialized the same way other people their age had. There had been bonfires at the river, and parties at people's houses while their parents were away, and make-out sessions on Klein's Hill and in the dark corners of the haunted house. They'd gone to school dances and some of the festival events, of course, but most of their time had been spent at home. One of their homes. Along with their families.

"Just that one New Year's Eve when we were home from college," Hannah agreed.

The first New Year's Eve they'd both been twenty-one. He nodded. "Yeah. We weren't really party people."

"We were more home-and-family people," she said.

Exactly. They really had been. He still was. Very much so. Which made tonight feel very...perfect. They were at her parents' house doing some work while her dad took her grandmother out and her mom worked. And then he and Hannah were going to go home together.

"You ready to go?" he asked.

She glanced over at the garden hose that was still gushing water. She smiled. "Are *you* ready?"

"Girl, I'm not sure I've ever been more ready for anything in my life." Which should have maybe given him pause. He was ready to leave a job not yet done? He wasn't sure he'd ever done that before.

But his answer made Hannah's pupils dilate. "You didn't get very far."

"I ran over to Alice's to get my truck," he said,

gesturing toward the driveway.

Hannah grinned and stepped closer. "You didn't even start on the windows yet?"

"I needed to be sure that truck was ready to go the second those clothes were dry."

"I don't think they're quite dry yet."

"Well, it probably doesn't matter they're a little damp...we're going to be taking them off soon anyway."

She nodded. "Good point."

Five minutes later, he had his not-quite-dry clothes on, Hannah had pulled a T-shirt on over her bikini, and the cooler and sleeping bags were in the truck. Unable to keep from touching her, Kyle reached across the seat for her hand as he pulled out of the driveway.

"I left Mom and Dad a note that we're going out and to let Grandma know," Hannah said.

Kyle nodded. "Don't want her to worry."

But neither of them mentioned how thrilled Alice would be, or that she would now absolutely have her hopes sky-high. Of course, Alice wasn't the only one.

Kyle gripped the steering wheel tightly and worked to not squeeze Hannah's hand just as hard. The sex had been...too good. As Derek would say, Kyle had now been seriously laid. He wasn't sure there was any getting over it.

"I need to text Derek my number," Hannah said.

"I already did." Kyle didn't mention the *you sure you know what you're doing?* that he'd gotten in reply.

He knew exactly what he was doing.

Whether or not it was a good idea was another question.

It only took a right turn, a left, then another right for Hannah to figure out where they were going. She looked over, clearly excited. This was their spot. The place they'd first had sex. The place where they'd dreamed of their future home.

"Camping?" she asked. "You still have that blow-up mattress for your truck bed?"

He shook his head and brought her hand up to his lips, suddenly feeling emotional. This was either the biggest mistake he'd ever made—or the best decision.

"Better," he finally told her.

"Better?" She glanced behind them as if the answer was in the truck bed now.

"Look up ahead." He pulled onto what looked like a narrow dirt road but was, in fact, his driveway.

They bumped along for a few yards then crested a small rise, and Hannah got her first look at his house. The one he was building—or mostly *having* built, since he had no time to spend on it.

But as Hannah gave a little gasp and turned to look at him with wide eyes that looked a little shiny, Kyle realized that he hadn't given up on working on the house because of time. It was because he wasn't sure he wanted it.

It was supposed to have been his and Hannah's house. They'd drawn the sketches, made the lists and plans together. He loved the land, the view of the river, the wraparound porch, the skylights—all of which they'd talked about, dreamed about, together.

But he wasn't dying to get it done. Because he wasn't sure he wanted to live here without her. That seemed obvious now as he pulled up in front of it and watched her get out, almost as if in a daze.

He shut the truck off and sat behind the wheel, just watching as she made her way up onto the porch, running her hand over the railing almost lovingly, then crossed to the swing he'd hung. He couldn't even decide what kind of flooring to put in the bathrooms, but he'd hung a porch swing. He knew it was because they'd said they wanted a swing like the one that hung in Alice's yard. But they hadn't talked about bathroom floors.

He knew—and had done—the things like a fireplace with a stone hearth and a huge mantle big enough for photos and Christmas stockings. He knew the kitchen had to have an island and a double oven for when they had the family holidays at their place. But he had no idea what color the walls should be or what the cabinets should look like. Similarly, he knew they'd need a dining room big enough for an enormous dining room table for their family and friends to gather around. But he didn't have a clue what light fixtures to choose. He'd even known they'd wanted five bedrooms—for the kids they'd wanted to have. But he didn't know what type of tub to put in the master bathroom.

Because teenagers in love, dreaming in the backyard, only made big plans. Like porches and fireplaces and dining room tables. Not details like cupboard door handles or carpet colors. And they didn't plan on things like one of them getting hurt and having to change their career and alter their lifestyle.

Kyle ran a hand through his hair. Yeah, they'd made a solid Plan A. Not so much a Plan B. Neither of them had ever needed a Plan B before.

He finally got out of the truck and followed her onto the porch. He pulled out the key and unlocked the door. He pushed it open without a word and stood back to let her pass. But she stopped in front of him.

"Are you sure you want me here?"

Kyle looked down at her. So she realized that once they spent the night here together, he'd always think of her here. But he nodded. He had to. "You're the only one I want here."

No other woman would feel right here, and now he knew that if Hannah went back to Seattle, he'd have to sell this place.

Hannah gave him a nod and started to step through the doorway, but Kyle grabbed her at the last second, pulled her around, and kissed her.

When he let her go, he said, "It's kind of…not put together very well."

She laid her hand against his face and smiled. "Not put

together very well is my new normal."

Yeah, maybe. And it looked beautiful on her. He nodded and let her go. "See what you think."

"I love it already."

Before he could respond, she stepped through the door. Kyle followed. He led her through the rooms. There wasn't much to explain. Most of it was still just big, open rooms with nothing in them but tools and sawhorses.

Mitch and Andi were working on it for him part-time, but he was holding them up with his inability to make decisions.

He and Hannah ended the tour in the kitchen.

"It's amazing," she said. She seemed a little choked up.

"You okay?" he asked, moving close.

"Yeah, I'm—" She nodded. "Yeah." But her voice was thick.

And Kyle made a decision. The idea all along had been to make it harder than hell for her to leave. It had been about revenge in the beginning, or at least about him being right that she should want to be here instead of Seattle. But now, he really wanted leaving to be—impossible for her.

He put a hand on the back of her neck and brought her in, touching his forehead to hers. "This is about as far as I could get without you," he confessed. "We never talked about what kind of countertops we wanted."

Hannah sucked in a quick breath then sniffed. "I know I shouldn't say this but..."

"Please say it," he said softly when she trailed off. He had to hear what it was.

"I was thinking back at Mom and Dad's how I've been considering Seattle good because it's out of my comfort zone. But now it's hit me since being home—just like Grandma said—that I want to be *in* my comfort zone. And this—this house, with you, all of this—*this* is my comfort zone come to life."

Kyle absorbed all of that. Then he took a big,

shuddering breath, and covered her lips with his. He kissed her possessively, pouring his relief, his happiness, and yeah, the love he hadn't let himself admit until now, into the kiss.

And she returned every bit of it.

Finally, he bent, swung her up into his arms, and said, "Which room do we christen first?"

And when he expected her to say "right here, right now" or even "the master bedroom of course", she surprised him by saying, "the family room." Which was the perfect answer.

He carried her into the room off the kitchen at the back of the house. This room had the fireplace and the huge windows that overlooked the backyard where kids and dogs would play. It was the room where the Christmas tree with the homemade ornaments would be, the room where family movie night would happen, the room where people would gather to laugh and chat while final meal prep went on in the kitchen only a few yards away.

Kyle put her down, kissed her hard, and said, "Do not move." He'd set the sleeping bags and pillows down on the porch, and he grabbed them quickly, jogging back to Hannah. But she hadn't listened. She'd moved. Enough to take all of her clothes off.

The sun was sinking and the warm orange glow from the windows behind her made her look like she'd been dipped in gold. He quickly unrolled the sleeping bags, tossed the pillows in that general direction, then toed off his shoes while reaching to grab a handful of shirt between his shoulder blades, pulling it over his head. He'd barely tossed it away when Hannah was in front of him, her fingers undoing his fly. He helped her push his jeans and boxers off, but instead of straightening, Hannah knelt. She took his already aching cock in hand.

"Hannah." He cupped the back of her head. Just having her on her knees in front of him was hotter than anything any other woman had ever done. Because this was sweet, good-girl Hannah McIntire, willing to be naughty—and very nice—just for him. She hadn't done any of this with any other man. Kyle couldn't begin to describe how hot and possessive and fucking *happy* that made him.

She looked up at him through her lashes and flicked out her tongue, running it over the tip of his cock. "Yes, Kyle?" she asked, innocently.

All thoughts evaporated from his mind. "Make sure I don't hurt you," he rasped.

"Hurt me?"

He tightened his fingers in her hair and tipped her head back slightly. "If you're going to make me crazy like that, you gotta promise to let me know if I get carried away."

"Oh. I want you carried away," she said huskily.

"Promise me," he repeated, looking into her eyes.

She licked her lips and he groaned. And she smiled.

"Hannah," he said firmly. "Promise."

"I promise."

Without another second of hesitation, he took his cock in hand and rubbed the tip over her lips. He wasn't going to pretend he didn't want her mouth on him. He wanted every intimacy there was. He intended to have his mouth in lots of places on her too. He wanted to mark her, claim her, make sure she had everything she needed sexually. And in every other way.

He couldn't fix her neck or make that all okay, but he sure as hell could ensure she had no sexual urge or fantasy that went unfulfilled.

Hannah didn't remember blowjobs being so hot. For *her*. She'd done it, she'd loved making Kyle feel good. But now she *had* to do it. She'd gone to her knees with every intention of bringing Kyle to his.

She opened her mouth and he slid inside. She loved his hands in her hair, loved the way he cupped her neck, as if protecting her, and the way he'd made her promise to communicate. She also loved the hot, thick feel of him against her tongue.

She felt that vixen thing again and it gave her a rush. She felt like she was willing to do just about anything to and with this man. And where did that come from? Her sexual experiences certainly hadn't been expanded or varied since they'd been together. She'd practically been a nun. But she knew what it was—it was again that soul-deep desire to grab whatever good she could. Pleasure and happiness and yeah, dammit, orgasms. Because there were no guarantees for tomorrow.

She took Kyle in her hand and slid him deeper into her mouth. She licked and sucked and stroked, wanting more and more of his groans, the *Hannah*s he kept breathing, the feel of him holding her to take him and yet seemingly to protect her too. She felt him thrust a few times as she moved her head up and down, and then suddenly—faster than she could register what was happening—he pulled back and tipped her over onto the sleeping bags. He came down with her, bracing himself on his hands.

He stared into her eyes. "You good?"

"Very, very, very."

"Then I need to be inside you."

Heat flooded her system. "Can I be on top?" She wanted to take care of him this time.

He groaned. "That's not something you ask, honey. You just say, 'I'm going to be on top now.' I'll never say no."

"Good to know." She put a hand on his chest and pushed, rolling with him as he turned onto his back.

She swung a leg over and climbed on. She didn't need any further prep. The blowjob had made *her* hot and wet and ready, and she immediately moved to position him, then sank down on his steely shaft.

"God, Hannah," he groaned. "You're so damned tight. Be careful."

She laughed. "I'm really good right now." She wiggled her hips and flexed her inner muscles, dragging another groan from him. "You sound like the one that's not feeling well," she teased.

"I feel like I might die," he said. "But," he gripped her hips and moved her up and down, eliciting a grown from *her*, "death by pussy seems like a great way to go."

Hannah felt her pelvic muscles squeezing hearing him say *pussy*. She did love that Kyle had turned into a dirty talker.

She lifted and lowered herself slowly, her hands going to her breasts, cupping them, trying to relieve some of the fullness and tingling. Kyle gave a growl of approval at the sight, lifting a hand to help. He teased one nipple, tugging gently.

"*Yesss*," she hissed, that pressure exactly what she needed.

He did it again and her clit throbbed. She continued to move on him, putting a finger to her clit, where she circled as she rocked against Kyle.

"Holy hell, this is the best position," he praised through gritted teeth.

Hannah hadn't realized how much she'd like him just watching her. She circled faster, and, when he pinched her nipple, the electric bolt went straight to her clit, and she rocketed into her orgasm.

Kyle squeezed her hips, thrusting up into her, and within minutes was growling her name as he came.

When the shudders had stopped shaking him and he'd pulled in a deep breath, Kyle pulled her in to lie on top of him. She lay with her cheek on his chest, his hand stroking her hair. The position was a little tight for her neck, but the endorphin high was definitely a real thing—she felt boneless. And totally happy. And like this was exactly where she wanted to be. For good.

And she wondered how to break it to Kyle that she was considering messing up another of his plans—the one that sent her back to Seattle.

Hannah awoke with her head on Kyle's chest, her legs tangled with his on top of the rumpled sleeping bags. And she knew instantly she'd made a mistake.

Her neck was screaming at her.

Sleeping on the floor, after having sex three times on that floor, with her head propped up on the very nice and firm, but hardly orthopedically sound chest of Kyle Ames? Yeah, she was going to pay for this.

And that pissed her off. She couldn't have a spontaneously romantic night in the house that she and Kyle had dreamed up together, including rock-her-world sex, without regretting it the next day?

Dammit.

She started to sit up, but a big, hot hand squeezed her ass, keeping her in place. And she didn't want to move. Really, ever. Because up against Kyle in the middle of what should be their family room seemed like exactly where she should be.

And because as sore as her neck was now, it was likely to be worse once she tried to move it.

"Morning," he said, his voice rumbling through his chest in her ear.

She didn't look up at him—because she couldn't. She trailed a finger over his chest though as she said, "Morning."

He palmed her butt, pressing her against his hip. "I could get used to this."

Hannah had to force herself not to crank her neck to see

into his face. That sounded like a lot more than just a quickie because they couldn't help it. And it definitely didn't sound like he regretted it.

Or if he did, he was ready to regret it even more, because the next moment, he rolled, pinning her underneath him and looking into her eyes.

God, he looked good like this. His hair was mussed, his jaw sported morning stubble; his eyes were soft and sleeping, and he exuded a relaxed, happy air that she didn't see very often. Happy, yes. But happy in a driven-and-rewarded kind of way, not happy just because.

In this position, she could look at him without protest from her neck. She was still dreading getting upright and trying to move, but this was great for right now. She threaded her fingers through his hair and smiled up at him. "I could get used to this too," she said honestly.

Was this all incredibly complicated? Yep.

Had she been hoping to avoid complicated? Yep.

Had she really thought that was possible? No way.

Kyle lowered his head and kissed her deeply, and she was soon shifting her legs against him, his hot erection pressing into her belly and the deep rumbles of desire from his chest ratcheting up her own need. She spread her knees and he settled in between them as if made to be there. A few minutes later, when he slid into her, she wrapped her legs around him and held tight. He moved against her slow and easy, a much lazier pace than any of the times the night before, and she relished the feel of him against her.

"God, Hannah," he said against her lips. "I can't let you go again."

She stiffened in his arms. Had he meant to say that? Was this just the sex and pleasure? Or was it more?

"Need you," he muttered, as he picked up the pace.

Hannah didn't know if it was the deeper thrusts or the words or the way he was looking at her, but her body tightened around his, and the next moment she was shooting through the orgasm ether and never wanting to float back to earth.

He was right behind her, pumping deep, and saying, "God, yes," in her ear in a deep, gravelly voice that made her inner muscles squeeze again.

She didn't know how long they lay there tangled up in the sleeping bags and each other before her phone rang. But she knew immediately that their little escape was over.

She groaned and reached for her purse. She had to stretch for it, and as she did, she felt Kyle's hand skim down her side and his mouth on her nipple.

Heat pulsed through her and just like that, she was ready for him again. Good Lord, she'd never considered herself insatiable.

"I have to answer," she told him, arching closer to his mouth.

He licked and sucked. "You sure?"

"God, I don't want to. It's probably for you."

He paused, and then huffed out a breath. "Damn. You're probably right."

He was the doctor in a small town. He was the go-to guy. She knew that, and if she had even the vaguest thought of staying and being with him, she knew she'd have to share him. He'd be leaving her—naked and needy—from time to time. Period.

And—holy crap—it was already noon. They'd been up on and off through the night, but she'd had no idea they'd slept so late.

She pushed herself into sitting and immediately winced as her neck reminded her that she'd abused it. She didn't have her special pillow. Any of the three of them. She hadn't stretched before going to bed. She hadn't meditated. In fact, she'd slept on a hard floor with her body up against an almost-as-hard man. And there had been thrusting. And even a little pounding.

Even as heat infused her, she lifted a hand to her neck,

rubbing as she put her phone to her ear to listen to the voice message.

"You okay?"

She looked over to find Kyle watching her massage her neck with a concerned frown.

She shrugged. "I, um…usually use a special pillow." That sounded stupid even to her own ears.

"Why didn't you say so? We could have picked it up."

She couldn't deny that made her heart melt a little. "That kind of takes away from the spontaneity," she said, not hearing the words the person leaving the message was saying in her ear. She so wanted to be able to be spontaneous with and for Kyle. He needed some of that. If she was the only one who could really get him to take time off and temporarily blow off some responsibilities, then she had to be able to be there with him.

"But I want you to feel good." He got onto his knees, completely naked, and moved behind her, putting his big hands on her shoulders.

She tried to relax. And ignore the naked part. Which was very difficult with him pressing his front to her back. She swallowed as he started rubbing.

"Who called?" he asked, his strong thumbs digging into the muscles along her spine.

She shifted slightly. "Little less pressure?" she asked.

He let up. "Sorry."

"It's good now." She didn't want him to stop, and she knew that she needed to tell him more about her pain management. She'd love to coach him through it. She'd even thought about introducing him to acupuncture. She'd taught Kade enough to help her with it during flare-ups, and Kyle would be an excellent student. He knew the anatomy and physiology. She just had to get him to buy into the whole practice in the first place. She sighed and replayed the voice message. "It's Derek," she reported a second later. "Oh…crap."

"What it is?" Kyle immediately stopped rubbing.

"Um, Butch and—"

"Aw, dammit! Fishing." Kyle was suddenly scrambling for his clothes.

Yeah, the fishing trip that Kyle was going on so that Butch would go and feel safe.

"I can't believe I blew that off!" He pulled on his boxers, jeans and shirt, and Hannah felt a moment of sadness at losing the view. "I've got to go," he said, tossing her clothes to her.

"Oh, right." She pulled her clothes on as well, as Kyle began gathering up their bedding. "Crap, I'll just leave this for now. Your parents won't miss them?" he asked.

"No, I'm sure it's fine."

"Okay, great." He grabbed her hand and tugged her to her feet. Kyle turned his phone on as she slipped into her shoes. "Crap," he muttered again, looking through his missed calls and texts.

"I told Derek how to get ahold of you," Hannah said. He looked upset.

"Well, Butch didn't know. He probably didn't go to Derek until he was worried about me."

Okay, now she felt bad too. Obviously teaching Kyle about acupuncture was going to have to wait. A few things were going to have to wait.

"You ready?" Kyle asked, glancing up. "I need to go find Butch and make it up to him. I can't believe I forgot about fishing."

"Yeah, I'm ready."

He took her hand as they headed out to the truck, but he was clearly distracted as he ran his thumb over his screen, scrolling through his texts. He drove her to Alice's and pulled up in front. He shifted into park. "You okay if I don't walk you up to the door?"

"Um, yeah." She reached for the handle.

Then, just as she pushed the door open, Kyle grabbed

her wrist. "Hey."

She looked back. "Yeah?"

"Last night was amazing." He leaned over and kissed her. "And I know *exactly* how I blew Butch off."

She gave him a smile. "I'm sorry."

"Don't be. I'll tell Butch where I was instead of with him and he'll be thrilled."

"What? Kyle—"

He leaned in and kissed her again. "Kidding. Well, kind of. I might *hint* at what I was doing. But no details."

"I don't know…"

"I have to get him to forgive me," Kyle said with a grin. "A hot, naked girl might be the only hope I have."

Hannah laughed and couldn't resist kissing him once more. "Yeah, okay."

"I'll talk to you later."

She slid out of the truck but just before she closed the door, she said, "Last night really was amazing."

"There's more where that came from."

She gave him a wink and slammed the truck door before she could say something like "sign me up for forever".

Chapter Twelve

Kyle couldn't believe that he hadn't seen Hannah since he'd dropped her at Alice's Saturday afternoon. They'd exchanged a few texts and he'd talked to her on the phone Saturday night, but after he'd convinced Butch to head to the river with him—predictably winning the older man over with a few innuendos about what had made Kyle lose track of time—he'd been called to the hospital in York because nine-year-old Jake Harper had been taken in for an emergency appendectomy, and Kyle needed to check on him.

He'd wanted Hannah to come to his room at Ty's when he got back, but she'd told him her neck was still bothering her and had turned into a bad headache, and that she and Alice were settled in with a movie. He would have felt comfortable going over and joining them, but he realized that Hannah needed time with her family too. He offered to write her a prescription for something, but she said she had what she needed. So he'd headed to Ty's alone. Which was fine. Kind of. He was beat. The girl had kept him up most of the night.

He'd gone to bed with hot memories of the night with Hannah playing on a reel like an erotic movie.

He'd headed to her dad's place on Sunday, unable to keep from washing the windows as promised, but he hadn't run into her there, and he hadn't even finished the job before he'd been called to put some stitches into Cody Bracken's forehead. Once Cody was bandaged up, Del Cotton had called to ask if Kyle would stop by and check on his wife's complaints of lung congestion.

And for the first time in all the time he'd been the physician in his beloved hometown, Kyle wanted everyone to just leave him alone.

He wanted to be with Hannah. And not do a damned thing except kiss her from head to toe.

So when Derek reminded him that Kyle had promised to help Derek remove a tree stump from Harold Kitchner's front yard, Kyle almost lost his cool.

"What the hell is wrong with you?" Derek asked as he tossed pieces of wood into the back of his truck.

"Nothing. Let's just get this done."

"I thought after you got laid, you'd be all mellow and chill," Derek said.

Kyle pushed the plastic goggles he was wearing to the top of his head. "How do you know I got laid?"

"Um, you and Hannah disappeared together overnight and I was only allowed to call *her* cell and no one else seemed to know where you were? If you didn't get laid, you're really doing something wrong."

"Maybe we talked all night."

Derek laughed. "Yep, doing something wrong."

"Talking is good."

"Yep. So is kissing and fucking. As long as you're doing some of all of those, you're okay."

Derek was his best friend, and knew everything there was to know about Kyle and Hannah. Well, almost everything. He didn't know about Hannah's neck. Or even her accident. Kyle had never shared that with his friend. Again, Hannah had told him she was fine and, in part because he wanted to believe her and in part because he *needed* to believe her, since he'd been up to his eyeballs in his residency and hadn't had time for anything else, he'd taken her at her word.

Kyle suddenly stopped with a huge chunk of wood in one hand and a chainsaw in the other. He'd needed to believe she was okay because he'd been up to his eyeballs in other responsibilities. And he'd been so used to her *being* okay. Being strong. Being at his side.

275

He hadn't questioned if she was really okay because he didn't have time for it if the answer was no.

"You okay?" Derek asked, realizing suddenly that Kyle had stopped moving.

"I just…Hannah and I…" He looked up at his friend. "I'm in love with her."

Derek tossed the piece of wood he was holding into the truck and clapped his gloved hands together. "Yeah, man, I know."

"And I've let her down."

Derek frowned. "How?"

"I didn't go after her."

"You couldn't have."

"I should have anyway."

Derek turned toward him fully. He took a deep breath. "Yeah, you should have."

Kyle stared at him. "What?"

Derek shrugged. "She was your girl. You wanted her forever. You should have gone to Seattle."

"I was in residency. I couldn't just drop everything and leave."

"You would have been written up or something, yeah, but they wouldn't have kicked you out. You would have had to grovel or work extra shifts or something, but hell, Kyle, you work extra shifts anyway. It's like you're afraid if you sleep too long or go more than fifty miles away from this place, that it's all going to fall apart and everyone's going to get sick and die and it'll be all your fault."

Kyle swallowed. "People *could* get sick and die without me."

Derek shook his head. "Man, they're going to get sick and die anyway. That's how life goes. I mean, what you do matters, of course. And you make all the sick and dying stuff better here. But shit man, it's not like it's your *fault* when it happens."

"It could be my fault," Kyle said. "If someone gets sick

and I'm not here, they could die."

Derek shook his head. "Sometimes I think you should have become an accountant or something. Then you could have everything lined up nice and neat all the time and the answers would always turn out the way you expect and you wouldn't have to feel so fucking *responsible* for everyone. Only if they get thrown in jail for tax fraud or something then."

Kyle scowled at him. "We were talking about Hannah." Because he'd never admit that there were definitely some appealing things about the idea of being an accountant. Two plus two always equaled four. And accountants didn't get pulled out of bed at three a.m. And accountants didn't have to watch the faces of people they cared about when they said the word *cancer*. And…all those spreadsheets.

But accountants also didn't get to deliver babies and see people walk again after surgery and get to watch the faces of people they cared about when they said *the cancer's gone*.

"Yes, Hannah. Well, you fucked that up," Derek said bluntly.

"She wanted to stay in Seattle."

"So you should have gone to Seattle."

"To stay? Forever?" Kyle demanded, even as his heart thumped in his chest.

"If necessary," Derek nodded. "There are sick and dying people there too."

"But not *my* people."

"People who could have become your people."

Kyle let out a breath. "Why didn't you ever say this before?"

"Because I'm your best friend and I love having you here and this town needs you and you need this town."

"But you think I should have gone after Hannah."

He nodded. "Because I think you need her more."

Kyle sighed. "You never hold back from telling me

when I'm making a mistake. Why didn't you tell me to pull my head out of my ass?"

"Honestly?" Derek asked. "Because I really thought she was going to come home too. I couldn't imagine her not needing you."

Kyle felt his heart squeeze hard. But she *had* needed him. She just hadn't told him. Because they hadn't told each other that stuff. They hadn't needed each other. Everyone else needed *them*.

"Fuck." He threw the piece of wood. "I have to go over there."

Derek sighed. "Knew I should have told you all of that *after* the stump was out."

Kyle started to reply, but suddenly both of their phones beeped. They pulled them out simultaneously and read the messages that had come in.

"Dammit."

"Fuck."

They dropped their tools and jumped into the truck. Derek headed for the fire station. Kyle would ride along in the ambulance.

Not that there was ever a good time for a car accident out on the highway, but he was going to have to put off seeing Hannah *again*.

Son of a bitch.

After working at the scene of the accident, accompanying the two teenage boys Kyle had known all their lives to the hospital, consulting with the families, and waiting for news from the surgeon who was operating to stop the internal bleeding in one of the boys, Kyle felt like he'd put days in instead of just hours.

He'd texted Hannah a couple of times, telling her what was going on and that he'd wanted to see her, but he didn't know when he'd be back to Sapphire Falls.

She'd assured him it was fine and that she and Alice were going to bed early because Alice had to be at the hospital at six a.m. the next morning for her hip surgery.

Alice's hip surgery.

Kyle shoved a hand through his hair as he read Hannah's last message on his way to the bathroom for a much-needed shower. Damn. It wasn't that he'd forgotten, but in the flurry of the day, he hadn't been thinking about it. He'd intended to see Alice tonight and reassure her about any last-minute jitters. But it was now ten p.m. and Alice should be fast asleep.

He'd just have to see them in the morning at the hospital. Because, of course, he'd be there prior to, during, and following the surgery. It was going to go fine. He knew that. But he wanted to be there for Alice. And now for Hannah. It just felt like sitting and holding her hand during the waiting period was the right thing to do.

He hadn't always been there for her. He was still a little stunned—probably stupidly—by that realization, but it was true. He'd always counted on Hannah to be the other half of their very solid whole. She'd been part of the foundation for their families and the other people who had gotten used to counting on them. It was strange—and that really *was* stupid—to think of her as one of the people who might need him.

But he wanted her to need him. And he wanted to need her. This was what they were going to have to figure out to be together, but he knew they could do it. Just like she'd asked for his help with scrubbing Alice's cabinets and then showed him how to work on the knots in her neck and shoulders, she could show him what else she needed and how he could help. And he could do the same. Because he needed to be falling asleep with her in his arms after a day like today. He hadn't seen her, hadn't been around, but he needed to hold her at the end of a day of them both taking care of other people.

Kyle showered and fell into bed, hardly able to keep his eyes open.

But his last thought before he drifted off was that he was going to see her tomorrow, and as soon as it was even slightly appropriate, he was going to ask her to stay in Sapphire Falls. With him.

Kyle got to the hospital at five. He wanted to check on the two boys from the car accident and get his other rounds done before Alice came in. The boys were both stable and awake when Kyle got to their room, and he was able to take a deep breath, knowing they'd both be fine.

By the time he got to the pre-op area, he was feeling good. It had been a big weekend, but Butch had gotten to fish, the rest of Sapphire Falls had been tended to, the tree stump was mostly out, the McIntires' windows were mostly clean, and…he'd fallen in love.

It was interesting to think that he'd fallen in love with Hannah, but that was exactly what had happened. Maybe he'd fallen in love *again*, but this felt different than before. He'd loved her, but he wasn't sure he'd been *in* love with her.

There was no question now.

When he stepped around the curtain to the area where Alice was supposed to be, he felt his smile die almost immediately.

Alice was there. She was ready to go. But sitting in the chair beside her bed was Ben. Not Hannah.

"Hi, guys," Kyle greeted with a forced smile. Maybe Hannah was just getting coffee in the cafeteria.

But he knew in his gut that wasn't it. Ben wasn't supposed to be here. He'd only be here if Hannah wasn't.

"Hi, Kyle." Alice gave him an almost relieved smile. "I'm glad to see you."

"I'm so sorry I couldn't stop over last night," he told her, sitting down on the edge of her bed and taking her hand. "There was a car accident."

"I heard," she said. "Trevor Graves and Zach Turner. Are they okay?"

Of course she'd heard. He nodded. "Yep, they'll both be fine. It was a little scary there for a bit."

"Zach's grandmother was beside herself," Alice said with a nod. "I'm so glad they're alright."

"They are. Now how about you? I wanted to talk everything through one more time to be sure you're ready," he said.

"I'm fine," she told him with a wave. "You're here now. I'm okay."

"Where's Hannah?" he finally asked.

Alice frowned. "She's not feeling well. She'd been dealing with pain and headaches since Saturday, and she was apparently up all night with a horrible migraine. She was throwing up and everything."

Kyle felt his own frown. "Really? She didn't tell me." Her neck was still bothering her? And how could he not feel responsible since he was the reason she'd slept on the floor without her regular pillow? And there had been...some pounding. He'd tried to be gentle, but when you were buried in a hot woman you were in love with and she said, "Harder, oh my God, harder", you went harder.

He cleared his throat and focused on that hot woman's very sweet grandmother.

"I told her she should call you and ask you what to do, but she said it happens a lot and she didn't want to bother you since there isn't really anything you can do," Alice said.

Kyle worked not to overreact to that. But that was, quite simply, bullshit. "I'll check on her later," he told Alice.

"But you'll be here during my surgery, right?" she asked, squeezing his hand.

"Of course." He wanted to drive straight to Hannah and demand she let him help her. But Alice needed him here.

Then he thought about that. Why did Alice need him here? He wasn't doing the surgery. He was here to give her a pre-op pep talk and he'd be by to see her afterward. He'd be there every day in Sapphire Falls to help with whatever she needed. But during the surgery? There wasn't a reason he needed to feel responsible for being here.

And Hannah needed him.

"You know what?" he said to Alice, sandwiching her hand between his. "On second thought, I think I'll head over to check on Hannah once you're back in the OR."

Alice's eyes got wide. "You won't be here?"

"You'll be in excellent hands," he told her. "And you know that. And Ben is here for you." He glanced at Hannah's dad and got a nod and a smile. And for a split second he wondered if there were people in his life who hadn't done more, simply because he hadn't let them. He was always the one to jump in first and handle everything, not giving anyone else a chance.

Well, this was Ben's chance.

"I'll be back to see you later, but it sounds to me like Hannah might need me a little more right now," Kyle said, stretching to his feet.

"Oh, well, Kade's with her," Alice said.

Kyle fought his scowl. Michael Fucking Kade. Great. "Well, I need to see her," he said, honestly. He glanced at Ben. "You let me know if you need me to bring anything over when I come back," he said.

"No problem. I'll be here. I'll let you know how things are going," Ben said.

Kyle nodded and started for the door.

"Hey, Kyle?" Ben called out.

He turned back. "Yeah?"

"I've got this. You take care of my girl, okay?"

"I intend to, Ben. I fully intend to."

When the knock sounded on the door to Kade's room at Ty's place, Hannah knew exactly who it was.

Dammit.

She was facedown on Kade's bed, topless, and had needles sticking out of her neck and shoulders.

Kyle was going to love this.

"Are we pretending we're not here?" Kade asked. They were only partway through the treatment.

Hannah sighed. "He must know that we are. Grandma probably told him."

"I thought you said he'd be with her the rest of the day."

"I thought he would be." Kyle had left her grandmother's side to come see Hannah? That was...unexpected.

The knock sounded again, louder this time, and was accompanied by, "Dammit, Hannah, let me in."

She couldn't turn her head to look at Kade. She couldn't turn her head to do anything. Her neck had been locked up since Saturday night, and her head and back had been pounding since. She'd gotten sick last night, and her right arm was tingling. Frankly, she was a damned mess.

She did not want Kyle to see her like this. But it was time. This was part of her reality, and with the way things had shifted between them, he needed to know about this before he said things like "there's more where that came from" or "you're the only one I want here."

Being in that house had changed things for her. Having her in that house had changed things for him. And they had some stuff to figure out.

"Let him in," she told Kade.

"Okay." He didn't sound sure, but he stood from where he'd been kneeling with one knee on the mattress beside her.

She heard the door open and Kyle say, "What the hell is going on?"

"Come on in. Nice to see you too," Kade said dryly.
"Hannah?" Then a second later, she heard, "Holy shit."
"I'm fine," she said from the bed. She was lying on her
stomach with her face in a circular pillow designed to keep
the neck straight. She hated that she couldn't see him. Then
she thought maybe that was best.

"Okay, first off, you need to fucking quit telling me
you're fine," he said from right next to her. "I'm sick of
that. You have to tell me the truth."

She took a deep breath. He was right. "Then I'm
miserable. I can't sleep and I can't help my grandmother. I
can't even be with her today at the hospital. I'm pretty
much useless to everyone. I can't spend a hot, spontaneous
night on the floor with you without paying for it. It all
sucks. Is that what you want to hear?"

He was quiet for a moment. "Yeah. I guess that's what I
want to hear," he finally said.

She felt the tears welling up. She'd been in pain for a
day and a half now. Kade had come over and done some
work on her last night, which had helped, but then she'd
woken up sick to her stomach.

It had been over a year since she'd been so close to
asking for pain pills, but knowing that her grandmother
needed her, and that Kyle was right there in town and
would do anything to help her, had been the strongest
temptation she could remember. Kade had come over to do
some acupuncture and massage, but he'd really been there
to keep her from seeing Kyle. She'd been avoiding him, not
because she didn't want him to see her like this—though
she didn't, really—but because she was too afraid she'd
beg for drugs.

"I'm sorry," she finally said. "I'm sorry I let Grandma
down. I'm sorry Dad had to go instead."

"Hannah," Kyle's voice sounded strained, "your dad
isn't upset about being there. And your grandma is fine.
She's right where she needs to be, doing what she needs to

be doing. You don't have to be the one that took her."

She bit her lip on her first response to that, but then finally said, "You always think *you* have to be the one doing everything for everyone."

She heard the long breath he took in. "Yeah, I know I do."

"I was always that person too."

"Yeah, I know." There was a long silence. Then Kyle said, "Will you *please* let me give you something? Let me help you?" She felt him move closer to the bed. "This is killing me to know you're hurting and to see you like this."

Exactly. She knew that seeing her like this and not being able to do anything would be torture for him. "The needles are bothering you?" she asked.

"Um, yeah." He took another shaky breath. "They really fucking are. Please let me do something. Something *else*."

Hannah swallowed hard. This was the moment of truth. "All you can do is be here with me," she said. That was the biggest hurdle between them. The miles, the time, everything else was a nonissue if he could accept that there was nothing he could really do but be there for her and try to understand. She lifted one arm, reaching her hand out. "Will you watch the rest of the treatment?"

There was a long moment where she wasn't sure he would take her hand. But finally, she felt his big palm against hers.

"Yeah, I can try."

"You don't have a needle phobia, do you, Doc?" Kade asked.

"I didn't think so," Kyle said. "Turns out maybe I'm not as tough as I thought."

"Well, no worries," Kade told him. "Hannah here is the toughest girl I know."

Hannah felt her heart squeeze. Kade was a really good friend. "These don't hurt," she told Kyle. "They might look weird, but it doesn't hurt. And it does help."

He didn't reply.

She felt Kade move in on her other side. He started again, feeling for the right spot and then inserting the very fine needle. She also felt Kyle squeeze her hand. Hard. She squeezed back. "Relax, okay? It's good."

"I honest-to-God think I could probably watch this happen to anyone else, Hannah."

That was sweet. And a huge problem. "I was hoping to teach you some of this."

She felt his grip tighten again. "I don't know, babe." He was clearly trying to sound nonchalant. "I stick needles into people for lots of reasons—immunizations, cortisone, to drain things. But, holy shit, this is hard to watch."

Kade hit a sore spot as he was feeling with his fingers just then, and she gasped and tightened her grip on Kyle.

"Sorry, hon," Kade said softly, easing the pressure.

"Jesus." Kyle let go of her hand, and she pictured him shoving it through his hair. "Hannah, baby, please let me give you something. It's so much easier. I respect you wanting to do this naturally, but sometimes you need some extra help."

Kade inserted the last needle. "I'm going to let you guys talk."

Hannah sighed. Yeah, okay. It wasn't like she was going to get up and run after him anyway.

"Talk?" Kyle asked, as the door shut behind Kade. "Is something else going on?"

"I wish I could look at you," she said. But this was probably better. "I have something I have to tell you."

"Okay."

She could hear the tension in his voice.

"Kyle, I know…this is hard for you. I know that you want to help, but…this is what works for me."

"I get it. Or at least, I'm trying to get it," he told her. "It's just a little crazy, right? I know exactly what to prescribe. I hate that you've been miserable for two days. I hate that I had something to do with it. At least let me do what I can do."

"There's nothing you can do," she said bluntly.

"Come on, Hannah. Have you ever tried—"

"I'm an addict," she broke in. It was time to have this over. "I got hooked on pain pills right after my accident. I was trying so hard to come back from it, and get back to school and work. I was trying so hard to stay on track for you, and everything here, and they were the only thing that kept me going. And I probably would have stayed on them if it wasn't for a home health treatment I did one day. I was at this lady's house and I was helping her to bed and I noticed her pain pills on her bedside table and…had to actually fight with myself for several minutes to keep from taking some of them after she fell asleep." That had been the low point. The point where she'd realized that she'd lost herself and that she had to do something fast or she'd never find her way back.

Kyle was completely quiet. He was no longer touching her so she couldn't even read his emotions that way. She went on.

"I was this close to stealing from a patient, Kyle. And, thank God, that was a line I wasn't ready to cross. I went to a support group meeting that night instead. And I met Kade, and we helped each other through getting clean. I've been off of everything, fully, for almost two years now. But…I can't use them anymore. So I have to rely on alternative medicine. And ninety percent of the time it's enough. There are just times when things flare up and I just have to get through."

He was still quiet, but she heard him drag in a deep breath.

"There really is nothing you can do," she went on softly. "Except learn some of this, maybe. Or you don't have to. I can find someone else. But I just need you to understand that there will, definitely, be times when I can't be there for my family like I used to be, and this whole thing, this pain thing, is a part of me now. And you can't fix it."

Finally, he spoke. "Jesus, Hannah."

Yeah, well, that was one way to summarize it.

"You were addicted to narcotics?"

"Yeah." She tried really hard not to try to read his tone. Was he disappointed? Disgusted? Angry? Sad? Because she felt all of those things when she thought about her addiction.

"And you didn't tell me that either?"

"No." She felt the tension building in her neck and realized that they were going to have to start over with the treatment. "And I should have," she admitted. "I know that I made all of these decisions for both of us, without even giving you all of the information or a chance to decide for yourself what you wanted to do. And I wish I could say that I would do it differently if I had to do it over again. But I'm not sure I would." She paused. "Believe it or not, I stayed away because I loved you. Because I wanted you to have the life you'd always wanted to have. Even if it was with someone else," she added quietly.

"Hannah—" His voice sounded pained.

"But I told you now," she said quickly. "I didn't think you needed to know everything then. I thought that was easier. But now maybe there's a reason why you need to know what my life looks like, and will keep looking like."

He was quiet again for several seconds. Then he said, "Is there a reason I need to know what your life looks like and will keep looking like?"

"I guess that depends on your reaction to all of this," she said honestly.

He blew out a long breath. "I don't want you to find someone else to do this stuff," he said. "I fucking hate the idea that someone else can do something for you that I can't."

She felt a wave of relief spill over her. "Kyle, that means—"

"But yeah, I'm not good at not fixing things. And I have so many people that need me all the fucking time." He sighed. "I would want to be there for you. But then there are always all of these things…people. I've been trying to get to you for two days as it is."

She swallowed back the tears. "I know. I would be one more thing to take care of. I wouldn't be much help with all of the things you do. The things you love doing."

"I didn't mean it like that."

"But it's true."

They were both quiet. Then she said, "I think in the past, we made the mistake of making our relationship about everyone and everything else. But when I think about doing it differently, I wonder if we would have been together if not for all of those projects and things we had in common."

He didn't say anything.

"We didn't really talk. We didn't really do anything that didn't involve our families or some assignment of some kind."

He still didn't reply.

"And now," she continued, "I'm…a mess. And you have plenty of other messes in your life. You need a partner. You need someone who can get out there and do all of those amazing things right by your side." She paused and had to swallow against the tightness in her throat before she could continue. "And that can't be me."

"Hannah—" His phone started ringing just then. He blew out a frustrated breath. "I need to—"

"I know."

"Ames," he said a moment later. "Yes." Pause. "No, I'm in Sapphire Falls." Another pause. And a sigh. "Yes, I'll be right there." There was a beat, and he said, "David Butler collapsed at the diner. He's conscious now but I need to go take a look."

"Of course."

"Hannah, I—"

"Go, Kyle." She swallowed. "Go help the people you can. There's nothing you can do here."

"Right."

The next thing she heard was the door opening, the sound of Kyle and Kade exchanging a few words, and then the door shutting again.

"You okay?" Kade asked a moment later.

"Nope," she said honestly.

"I can't believe you're not coming with me," Hannah told Kade later that night. After her neck had released. And she'd cried. And she'd gone to visit her grandmother. And she'd realized that she had to go back to Seattle. The longer she stayed, the harder it would be to leave. Just like Kyle had wanted. And there was no reason for her to stay. Everything was fine here. No one really needed her. Which worked out well, considering she was pretty much no good to anyone.

"Hey, I've got a book club meeting next week and I'm set up to talk to Officer Hansen about police procedures in Sapphire Falls tomorrow. And your grandmother and Ruby expect me at poker next week too. And I'm rolling on this book. I can't mess with what's working."

Hannah couldn't believe it. She was going back to Seattle and Kade was staying in Sapphire Falls. "Fine. Whatever. Good luck writing a book without me around."

Which should have been funny. Kade was the one who thought he couldn't write without her. But nothing was funny right now.

"Don't be mad. I'll be back in a couple of weeks."

"It's fine." She was feeling better. Her grandma was out

of surgery. Her dad seemed almost happy to be there with his mom. The acupuncture treatment had helped. And Hannah had realized something very important—she simply couldn't be one more thing that Kyle had to worry about, take care of, and not quite fix.

As she'd told him when she'd first confessed about her neck, with other patients, he was able to go home at the end of the day and get away from it all. With her—he'd be living with the frustration of not being able to fix something that affected someone he cared about day in and day out.

She zipped her suitcase. "So, I'm taking the rental. You can get another car?"

"I'm not worried," he told her.

That was vague. But whatever. She needed to get out of this town.

"Call me when you get home," Kade told her.

She nodded, unable to speak suddenly. She'd call him when she got to Seattle. She was actually *leaving* home right now.

Crap.

Blinking against the tears, she pulled the bag off the bed. As she passed him, Kade pulled her in for a quick hug. "You don't have to leave."

"I don't want to be one more thing for Kyle to worry about."

Kade pulled back, but he kept his hand on her shoulder. "I'm only going to say all of this one time. This town is...special. And, while he may have an inflated ego and be a workaholic and take on more than he needs to, Kyle Ames is a good guy who I think really loves you, and who can handle what you throw at him. You surprised him with some stuff today. Give him a chance to process it. And then, if he can't poke you with acupuncture needles—which is actually hilarious, by the way—I'll just keep doing it."

She frowned. "Yeah. I know you will."

"But you'll have to stay here for that to happen."

"Here?" She looked at him. "What are you talking about?"

"I'm staying."

"For two more weeks."

"I'm coming to Seattle in two weeks. For a few days. But I'm coming back here."

She blinked up at him. "You have to be kidding me."

He shrugged. "I like it here. This book is going great. And I have an idea for a sequel."

Hannah rubbed her forehead. Kade was staying in Sapphire Falls? *Really?*

But yeah, probably. If the book turned out well, she could see him wanting to stay.

She was suddenly jealous of her best friend. He *could* just stay. Just like that. There was no reason for him not to. Nothing specific to go back to Seattle for. He could work here. He could live here.

And so could she.

Except for the tiny issue of being a burden to the man she loved.

"Kyle will think I'm staying because of him."

"Good. Because you *should* be staying because of him," Kade said. "Jesus, you think you should stay because of me? Girl, you need to get your own life. I can't be everything to you all the time."

That actually made her crack a smile. "I don't want to be a problem."

"So don't be a problem." Kade shrugged.

She rolled her eyes. "Thanks. Very helpful. I'll just get over everything."

"Good."

"Kade!"

"You need to get over this idea that you can't need anyone for anything here," Kade told her, unfazed. "I don't get that. I've been here for two weeks and everyone in this town gets to need other people for stuff. Except you. Why is that?"

"That's not true," she told him. "I'm not the only one."

"Well, you and Kyle, right?"

She sighed. "Yeah."

"And what would you do if he needed you for something?"

"I'd do whatever I could to help him."

"Then you can't leave." Kade lifted a hand to the side of her face. "He needs you, kiddo."

God, she really didn't want to leave.

"And one more thing," Kade said. "I really think that your grandmother, mom, dad, best friend," he said, pointing at himself, "and probably nearly a hundred other people here would be offended to think that you can't need us."

She couldn't help it. There was hope bubbling up in her chest. Dammit. She took a deep breath. "You really think he loves me?"

"I think he loves you more now than ever," Kade said. "You know each other now. You're older and wiser and all of that shit. So yeah, I think he loves you and, if he can come to terms with the idea that not everything goes according to plan, then I think *this* is the real thing."

She felt tears pricking her eyelids. *The real thing.* God, that sounded good. And Kade was right. This was different than what they'd had before. This was...more. They'd both grown up in a nearly perfect town with everything always falling into place for them. Now they'd both had some things go wrong—okay, that was an understatement—and they'd gotten through it. They'd had to talk things out. Confess their flaws. Face that they'd both been wrong about some things. They knew each other better now. And they knew themselves better.

The only thing left to find out was if Kyle could, in fact,

deal with the idea that things would not always go according to his plan—and if he could be okay with that.

"Okay," she finally said. "I won't leave. Yet. But if you're wrong, you have to swear to me that you're not going to use the name Aquamarine Ridge."

"Oh, sure, no worries," Kade said. "I've already changed it."

"You have?"

"Aquamarine Cove is much better."

She blinked at him. "Cove? In Nebraska?"

"Yeah, kind of like a town named something falls...where there is no waterfall at all."

Okay, he might have a point.

She let herself think about Kyle—and staying and needing him—for the first time since he'd left Kade's room earlier. She'd put it out of her head, convinced it could never happen. But now... She looked at the clock. It was after nine. He'd been gone all day. No doubt something had come up after he'd checked on David at the diner. And at some point, he'd been back to see Alice, but he hadn't been there when Hannah had. She'd been relieved and disappointed at the same time.

She knew that he'd been working all day. Helping people. Making them feel better, in a variety of ways.

But when he was done, finally at the end of the day, done with everything, then what? Who was there for *him*? Who did he talk to, who rubbed *his* neck?

She pulled her phone out and dialed Derek's number. She could call Kyle, but she needed to see him in person, and she thought maybe it would be best if she showed up without announcing it.

"Hey, Hannah."

"Hi. Do you know where Kyle is?"

"Um..."

"What?" She frowned.

"He's not with you yet?"

"Yet? I haven't seen him."

"Are you in Seattle?"

Her heart thumped. "No. I'm still in Sapphire Falls." She frowned. "Why?"

"He's on his way to the airport."

"The airport? Why?"

"He was sure you were leaving."

Hannah processed that. Kyle had assumed she'd leave. And she'd been on her way. He'd known that her first instinct was to leave.

She hated that.

"No. I'm...um, staying."

Derek blew a breath out. "That's awesome, Hannah. Seriously."

"Thanks." She was still a little nervous about it, but it felt right. "But Kyle's on his way to Seattle?"

"Well, Omaha. He can't be there yet," Derek said. "I'll try to stop him."

Hannah started for the door. "Yes, tell him to turn around. And I'll meet him halfway." She swallowed. "Which is exactly what we should have done three years ago."

Thirty minutes later, Hannah was just on the other side of York when she saw Kyle's truck heading west. She started honking and flashing her lights, quickly turning into a parking lot so she could change directions.

In the rearview mirror, she saw his brake lights, and then his truck whipping a U-turn in the middle of the next intersection. She pulled over underneath a tall light and waited. Kyle pulled up next to her a minute later. He didn't even turn the truck off as he burst out of the cab. She met him between their vehicles.

Kyle gathered her into his arms, burying his face in her neck, and just held her. She wrapped herself around him, as much of her body against his as she could get.

They stayed like that for several long, sweet minutes. Finally, Kyle pulled back with a huge, deep breath.

"You were still in Sapphire Falls?"

"You were on your way to Seattle?"

He cupped her face. "I realized there are a hell of a lot of things in this world that I can't fix or control. But there is one thing I can—being with you, wherever you are. I didn't do that last time, and I've been chasing this idea of fixing everything around me since. Now I finally realize that I've just been looking for a way to fix my heart. And the only way to do that is to be with you."

"Wow," she said softly after a moment, "that was really good."

He gave her a little grin. "Three years too late, maybe, but I'm glad I finally realized it and said it." His expression sobered. "And this... I love you, Hannah. I've always loved you.

Her eyes filled with tears. "I love you too. So much. I've never stopped."

"God, I should have come after you. I should have said to hell with my residency if it meant not coming to you."

She shook her head. "It's over now. All of that is over."

"You know, I go around thinking that I'm doing all of these amazing things for others, but you, God, you gave everything up—your hometown, your family, me, your happiness, so that *I* could have the life I wanted. The life I *thought* I wanted," he corrected. "The truth is, I've been working my ass off in part because I'm trying to fill the gaps. The lonely, empty gaps in my time and my attention and my energy and my *heart* where you're supposed to be. And I feel good about my work, but it hasn't...*worked*," he said with a small smile. "Because nothing can fill in for you."

Hannah felt a tear roll down her cheek. But she wasn't about to say anything to interrupt this amazing monologue. Kyle's thumb caught the next tear and wiped it away. "Please stay and let me try to take care of you. I'll get better at it. And there's always Hope and her shop for the stuff I'm not good at."

"And Kade," she said.

Kyle frowned. "What?"

"He's staying in Sapphire Falls too."

Kyle rolled his eyes and sighed. "Great."

She laughed softly and covered his hands with hers. "It is great. Because I've finally found the one thing you're not good at."

"Oh?"

"Sticking me with acupuncture needles."

He gave a little shudder. "Yeah. I think you might be right."

She squeezed his hands. "But you don't have to be good at that. It just so happens that I can need a lot of people. Just like they can need me. Maybe not for washing windows, but for other stuff. Like talking and laughing and learning new things."

He gave her a look that was so full of love, she felt her breath catch. "I'm sorry I wasn't there after your accident."

"I'm sorry I didn't tell you everything."

"I'm sorry that I didn't know I had a needle phobia when it comes to you."

She laughed. "I'm sorry that we're not back in Sapphire Falls right now in our house."

His expression softened. "Now see? There's something else I can fix. Right now." He wrapped his arms around her and picked her up, heading to his truck.

"We're just leaving the rental car here?" she asked.

"Is it in your name or Kade's?"

"Kade's."

"Then yeah, we're just leaving it here."

And when Hannah insisted on sleeping on the floor at their house that night, Kyle didn't protest—much. But he did insist on giving her a very thorough full body massage. Twice. And when she woke up in the morning without a single twinge of pain, she wasn't surprised at all.

Don't miss the next book in the Sapphire Falls series!
Derek and Riley's Story

After Tonight

He needs her to teach him how to be boyfriend material for a nice girl. There's only one problem—she's not a nice girl.

Sex. God.

Two words frequently used by the women of Sapphire Falls to describe bartender Derek Wright. And he's more than happy to be the local deity—until he wants to date nice girl Lucy Geller. Now his rep has come back to bite him in the ass.

So Derek enlists Riley Ames, his best friend's little sister, to help him up his good-guy game. She's known him forever; she's not afraid to tell him what he needs to hear. Better yet, she's besties with Lucy and a nice girl herself. Who better to turn him into the man Lucy wants?

There's no way Riley will let her sweet friend get snared by The Great Debaucher, as Derek is known among too many girls who lost their virginity, and hearts, to the charmer back in high school. He's not good enough—a fact she has no problem sharing with Derek.

But when he begs her to help reform him from rogue to romantic, Riley can't resist. She's been bored to tears since returning to her hometown, and this could be a fun diversion. She'll give the playboy a taste of his own love-'em-and-leave-'em medicine.

Derek's about to discover the nice Riley he used to know…has gotten a little naughty.

Find out more about

After*Tonight*

here:

http://tinyurl.com/SapphireFallsAnnouncements

And check out everything about Sapphire Falls on the Sapphire Falls website!

Meet the people, visit the places, make sure you've got all the books, and even buy merchandise!

www.SapphireFalls.net

About the Author

Erin Nicholas is the author of sexy contemporary romances. Her stories have been described as toe-curling, enchanting, steamy and fun. She loves to write about reluctant heroes, imperfect heroines and happily ever afters. She lives in the Midwest with her husband, who only wants to read the sex scenes in her books; her kids, who will never read the sex scenes in her books; and family and friends, who say they're shocked by the sex scenes in her books (yeah, right!).

You can find Erin on the Web at www.ErinNicholas.com, on Twitter (http://twitter.com/ErinNicholas) and on Facebook (https://www.facebook.com/ErinNicholasBooks)

Sign up for Erin's newsletter and never miss any news!

http://www.erinnicholas.com/newsletter.html

And join her SUPER FAN page on Facebook for insider peeks, exclusive giveaways, chats and more!

www.facebook.com/groups/ErinNicholasSuperFans

Look for these titles by Erin Nicholas

Now Available at all book retailers!

Sapphire Falls
Getting Out of Hand (book 1)
Getting Worked Up (book 2)
Getting Dirty (book 3)
Getting In the Spirit, Christmas novella
Getting In the Mood, Valentine's Day novella
Getting It All (book 4)
Getting Lucky (book 5)
Getting to the Church On Time, wedding novella
Getting His Hopes Up (a Hope Falls Kindle World novella)
Getting Wound Up (crossover novel with Jennifer Bernard)
Getting His Way (book 7)

The Bradfords
Just Right (book 1)
Just Like That (book 2)
Just My Type (book 3)
Just the Way I Like It (short story, 3.5)
Just for Fun (book 4)
Just a Kiss (book 5)
Just What I Need: The Epilogue (novella, book 6)

Counting On Love
Just Count on Me (prequel)
She's the One
It Takes Two
Best of Three
Going for Four
Up by Five

Anything & Everything
Anything You Want
Everything You've Got

The Billionaire Bargains
No Matter What
What Matters Most
All That Matters

Single titles
Hotblooded

Promise Harbor Wedding
Hitched
(book 4 in the series)

Boys of Fall
Out of Bounds
Illegal Motion
Full Coverage

Taking Chances
Twisted Up
Tangled Up
Turned Up

Opposites Attract
Completely Yours
Forever Mine
Totally His

Enjoy this excerpt from

Getting
Out of
Hand

Sapphire Falls

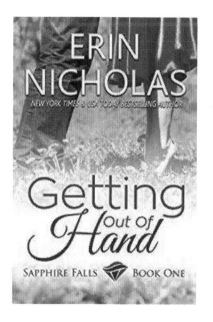

Genius scientist Mason Riley can cure world hunger, impress the media and piss off the Vice President of the United States all before breakfast. But he's not sure he can get through his high school class reunion.

Then he meets the new girl in town.

Adrianne Scott loves Sapphire Falls. The sleepy little town has been the perfect place to escape her fast-paced, high stress lifestyle. Her only plans now include opening her candy shop and living a quiet, drama-free life.

Until Mason Riley bids four hundred dollars just to dance with her.

Mason sure doesn't look—or kiss—like a genius scientist geek. In fact, he makes Adrianne's heart pound like nothing she's ever experienced. Passion like this with a guy who travels the world and parties at the White House should probably be a red flag for a girl who wants a simple boring life.

Good thing no one falls in love in a weekend.

Excerpt

"'Kay all, Adrianne's next."

A hand shot up in front before Jack even asked for a bid.

Jack chuckled and started the action at thirty dollars. It quickly climbed to two dances and fifty dollars.

Adrianne. Mason had no idea who she was, but it was obvious she was damned popular. She was no Hailey Conner, and in Sapphire Falls she never would be, but at least the guys around here hadn't missed the silkiness of the blond waves that fell to her shoulder blades, or the sweetness of her smile, or the perfect curve of her ass—

Mason straightened. What the hell was that? His type was about four years younger than Adrianne, twenty pounds lighter and *not* from Sapphire Falls.

"What's her story?" he asked Drew.

"Adrianne Scott," Drew said with an appreciative sigh. "She's new."

"Yeah. I noticed."

"Been here a couple of years. She's friends with Hailey. Everyone wants her."

He'd noticed that too. And it bugged him.

"She's not dating anyone?"

Drew chuckled and shook his head. "Nope. Not for lack of trying. She never dates. The first guy to kiss her gets a hundred bucks."

Mason raised an eyebrow. He didn't necessarily approve of guys kissing a woman to win money, but then again, he was quite sure that no man would want to kiss Adrianne *just* for money.

"Everyone wants her."

The guys in Sapphire Falls might have more taste than he'd given them credit for.

He drained the beer he didn't want and disliked immensely and decided to place a food order to go. This was all of no interest to him.

"Okay, sixty-five dollars and three dances with Miss Adrianne Scott. Going once—"

Then she laughed at something the woman next to her said.

And Mason was in trouble.

Well, hell.

"Three hundred dollars," he called out.

Every single pair of eyes in the room turned to look at Mason at the same time.

He'd never been the center of attention without a microphone in front of him and a conference logo behind him before. Certainly never in Sapphire Falls.

He stepped forward. He'd opened his big mouth, couldn't really go back now. He should probably be more surprised that he'd bid like that, but he wasn't. He was a genius after all, and while his brain and mouth almost never disconnected, paying a few measly bucks for a chance to dance all night with Adrianne Scott and hear that laugh again was a genius move.

"Did you say three *hundred*?" Jack demanded, pointing a wooden gavel at him as if challenging him to take it back.

"Yes, sir," Mason replied, looking at Adrianne when he added, "For the rest of the dances tonight."

Adrianne's cheeks were pink and her eyes wide. She wore no makeup to enhance the features that were completely captivating him. Her hair was loose and she wore a simple white cotton tank under a denim shirt with blue jeans. Simple, unadorned, and yet he had never been more drawn to a woman.

Jack looked around the room. Obviously, it was unprecedented for a man to monopolize a woman for the entire evening.

"But it's only—" Jack started.

"Four hundred," Mason answered, still watching Adrianne.

"I don't—"

"Maybe we should let the lady decide," Mason interrupted, walking toward Adrianne.

"I can't," she said, shaking her head as he advanced. She was breathing a little fast and she darted her tongue out and wet her bottom lip.

He took another step toward her. "Then what are you worth?"

She swallowed and glanced around. "There's only three dances left," she said. "I can't let you pay three hundred dollars for that."

"I offered four," he reminded her, moving in closer still.

She smiled and he couldn't stop staring at her mouth.

"I meant that even three was too much."

He was directly in front of her now, and only those within about ten feet of them could hear the conversation. "I didn't tell you what I expected those dances to be like for four hundred dollars."

Adrianne was having a hard time breathing. A man hadn't done that to her in a really long time. She liked it and hated it at the same time. She pressed a hand over her heart, which was, not surprisingly, pounding. She took another deep breath. It might be safer to say no. But she made the mistake of looking up into his eyes and knew instantly that she was not going to say no to this man. No matter what he asked of her.

He was something. He wore khakis to everyone else's jeans and a blue button-up shirt instead of a T-shirt. And he moved with purpose and confidence in front of this crowd even though he wasn't one of them. He was tall, his smile was sexy, his voice was sexy—

"How about you loan me that other hundred and I'll bid on you next hour?" Adrianne asked.

He cocked an eyebrow, having noticed her eyes on his mouth. "I'm worth two hundred less than you are?"

She shrugged. "There are ways of finding that out, I suppose," she said without thinking.

Dammit. She was flirting. She didn't do that. Not with guys in Sapphire Falls, for sure. She hadn't flirted in almost two years with anyone.

He gave her a lazy smile that clearly said he was willing to prove anything she asked and Adrianne felt her stomach flip.

She felt his gaze follow every move as she shrugged out of the denim shirt she'd worn unbuttoned over the spaghetti-strapped white tank and tied it around her waist.

"He wins," Adrianne told Jack over her shoulder. "Make it a slow one."

She took the man's hand and led him to the edge of the dance floor while they waited for the other women to be matched with dance partners.

"Is this dance auction a new invention? Because it's an effective fund-raising technique."

"Yeah, it's been part of the festival for the past couple of years. At least it's better than a kissing booth, which was also suggested," Adrianne said, smiling up at him.

He gave her a small smile in return, but his eyes were focused on her lips. Her heart tripped and she pressed her hand against her chest.

"How is dancing better than kissing?" he asked.

His voice sounded a little husky. Which was dumb, because she didn't know him well enough to really know what his voice usually sounded like.

"Um." She rubbed the pads of her first three fingers in a circle on her chest, willing her heart to slow. With a deep breath, she dropped her hand. "A dance lasts longer than a kiss, for one thing."

He leaned in closer, his eyes on hers now. "I think maybe you've been kissing the wrong guys."

18721638R00185

Printed in Poland
by Amazon Fulfillment
Poland Sp. z o.o., Wrocław